Praise for Jessica Wakefield

"*It Shouldn't Be You* had me hooked from the very first page. That irresistible *just one more chapter* pull kept me turning pages late into the night. Deeply emotional and beautifully written, this story is both heart-wrenching and hope-filled. I highly recommend this read! Five heartwarming stars!'
~ Jessica Ashley, award-winning Christian Suspense author

"I loved this sweet romance (*Right in Front of You*). Perfect for sports fans, small town enthusiasts, and anyone who adores a redemption story."
~ Andrea Christenson, author of *How Sweet It Is*

"In *Right in Front of You*, Jessica Wakefield has crafted a rich, sweet story that will lure you in and warm your heart. Readers will be rooting for Rachel and Hayden from page one."
~ Rachel D. Russell, award-winning author of *Still the One*

"Outstanding! The charming cast of characters pulled me and kept me rooting for them until the happily ever after. Emotional, deep characters and quaint setting were the perfect ingredients for a five-star read."
~ Mandy Boerma, author of *You'llBe Mine*

"This romance is so satisfying. The wonderful cast of characters, fun small town vibes, and authentic Christian content all work together to deliver a story that is relatable and endearing. Jessica has scored a touchdown with *Right in Front of You*."

JESSICA WAKEFIELD

~Liwen Y. Ho, author of *Second Chance with the Hero: A Christian Medic Christmas Romance*

"Jessica Wakefield offers a trio of delightful and embracing holiday stories that bring the enticement of Christmas romance to life...and who doesn't love beautifully written holiday romances? A must read!"
~ Ruth Logan Herne, award-winning and USA Today bestselling author

"Jessica has crafted a wonderful collection of holiday-themed stories, perfect to read while snuggling up with a cup of hot chocolate. Enjoy some new Christmas cheer, along with some swoon-worthy kisses, and savor the romance within *The Christmas Box.*"
~ Carolyn Miller, author of the *Muskoka Shores* and *Original Six* romance series

"If you like your Christmas romance sweet and heartwarming—sprinkled with a dash of magic—then check out *The Christmas Box.* This novella collection features love stories based on three of our favorite tropes: best friends to more, stuck in a snowstorm, and fake dating. If you're a fan of Hallmark and *Falling Inn Love*, this collection is for you!"
~ Jessica Kate, author of *Love and Other Mistakes*

Also By Jessica Wakefiled

The Christmas Box
Right in Front of You

It Shouldn't Be You

Jessica Wakefield

Love & Daisies Press

Chapter One

Declan Collins was in trouble again, evident by the sound of Julie, his boss, tapping her pen against the table, a steady rhythm that matched his pulse. This had been the longest year of his life. Thanksgiving had been and gone. His sister, Nicky, brought Mom back to their condo, where they celebrated the holiday in the same quiet way they did every year. Then Mom went back to her new home. Declan didn't want to think about that. Didn't really want to think about this meeting, either, or the words spilling from Julie's mouth.

"I'm sick for one day and someone posts your article." She tapped harder, the sound echoing in the spacious room. "This is *The Alexandria Gazette*—our newspaper and online presence stand for something in the community."

"It was a spoof piece, a bit of fluff, and besides, I didn't name anyone specific." Declan kept his voice light, needing to remove the irritation from Julie's face. He wanted his op-ed privileges back.

Julie frowned. Her short, blonde hair and heavily made-up face almost hid the fact that she was nearing fifty. What gave it away was the wary, suspicious expression that told the world she was a veteran of the newspaper industry. "Things like this can't happen anymore."

Declan ground his teeth. "I'm good at what I do."

"You are, and I want to give your op-eds back to you, but things like this" —she turned her open laptop toward him and arched an eyebrow, tapping the screen at the words *What's So Wrong with Emily Gilmore?*— "is what got you demoted. You kept pushing too hard on the Hamilton Group and handing articles in late. You gave me no choice but to rein you in. No more of this." She waved her hand. "Am I clear?"

"You're right, the article is unacceptable." He met her gaze and saw her shoulders sag. "I stand by my opinion on the Hamilton Group and their takeover of the Community Center. It shouldn't be happening."

Julie sighed—the long-suffering kind that parents emitted when they were ready to throttle their kids. "I know, and you did your best...but it is closing." She pushed today's paper across the table.

The write-up, including more information about the new apartment complex, covered the front page. He inhaled hard and clamped his jaw down. He hated it, but what more could he do? He'd used his ability with words to rally the community to fight for the Community Center to stay open. "I didn't mean to cause controversy for the paper. It's just...this place is important to a lot of people." Including him. Not that Julie could ever know how that Community Center had been a refuge for him, his sister and mother, back when he was an angry fifteen year old uprooted from California and dumped in Alexandria, Virginia, complete with a new last name in an effort to distance themselves from his jailbird dad.

"I'm all for hard-hitting journalism and holding people to account," Julie said. "But the Hamilton Group has not broken any laws or mishandled any money."

"I know." Declan massaged his tight jaw. If only they'd done something shady. But no, Jonathan Hamilton and his company played hard, but within the rules.

"Whether you like it or not, by New Year, this development project will start and—"

"Be turned into some bland apartment complex."

"Yes." Julie looked at him.

"And those who will need it, won't have it."

"That can't be helped. It's part of life." Julie glanced down at something on the desk. "I want you to have your op-ed back, so you need to give me another set of articles and then, it's new year, new Declan."

"Alright," he said through his still clenched jaw. "What else do I have to do?"

Julie gave a slight nod. "I realize you're going to hate this, but I have one more set of articles I need from you."

Her forced enthusiasm made him sit up. "Let me have it then."

She watched him a minute, lips pursed. The pause caused his gut to churn even more. Not good if she was stalling. "The Mount Vernon Ladies' Association is having its usual Christmas events."

Declan groaned and quickly covered it with a cough.

She shot him a warning look. "Cover and review them." She slid a piece of paper across the table. "Also, there's the annual Children's Benefit I want you at."

Declan leaned forward, studying the list: fireworks, Aladdin the Christmas Camel, and chocolate making. He suppressed a sigh and nodded.

Julie continued. "This is your last set of assignments before you can go back to your regular commentaries."

"I can do this." He pulled the paper off the table and tucked it into his folder.

Julie pressed her lips together. "Good." A beat of silence ticked between them.

Declan's whole body tensed. "There's more, isn't there?"

"Paul called me this morning. His wife went into early labor and he's on paternity leave as of now."

"You need to me to cover some of his stories?" His shoulders ached as he waited her out.

Julie nodded. "There's a party being thrown on the Saturday before Christmas at Mount Vernon. It's very prestigious. Lots of movers and shakers will be there."

He shrugged. That kind of thing drove him nuts, but he could handle it. "What's the catch?"

She moistened her lips.

How bad could it be?

"The party is being thrown by Jonathan and Vivien Hamilton."

"No." Declan sat forward, heat flushing through him. He flexed his fingers, digging them into his knees. "You expect me to review a party being thrown by the people who are tearing down the Community Center?"

Julie gave him an even stare. "Yes, I do." Her voice was a steel rod.

"What if I won't do it?" He folded his arms over his chest.

Julie's glare softened. "Don't risk your op-eds over this. I know it's awful that it's closing, but it happens all the time. Why does this matter so much to you?"

He looked elsewhere, anywhere but at Julie, and silently counted to twenty before returning her gaze. "I realize Old Town and its surrounds is an affluent area. But not everyone here has money. Being in need crosses social and racial lines. It can affect anyone at any time." He knew that all too well.

She nodded at his passionate response. "I understand your point, but there's nothing we can do about it. You have to move past this. Do the review. Prove to me you can put this behind you. You're not reviewing the Hamiltons—just the party. Remember that. And if that can't convince you, we're officially short-staffed and I need you."

She stared him down, and he finally relented with a nod.

"You'll be meeting the event planner, Addey Bennet, at Mount Vernon by the piazza this morning. She'll walk you through everything you'll need on the night of the Christmas gala—tickets, dress code, itinerary. You should only require this one meeting with her beforehand." Julie stood. "Four weeks, Declan, then you have your op-eds back." She gave him a big, encouraging smile, but it shrunk and dried up like a leaf in autumn. "It's been a difficult time for you this last year or two, especially on a personal front. Don't think we don't get that."

She continued in that soft, sad voice that whispered "poor Declan". "I hope things with your mom improve..." She trailed off, and like everyone else, averted her eyes and tried to not talk about the subject directly.

"She's sick, Julie, not dying." The word formed a lump in his throat because it wasn't true. Death was reaching its skeletal hands toward her and taking a little piece of her every day.

"We want you to know we care." She finally returned her gaze to his.

"Thanks."

He left, climbed into his car, and drove to the Old Town Community Center. He needed to see it for himself. Today's newspaper sat beside him on the seat, bearing the picture of the Community Center and the sign now placed out front, detailing its demise.

Declan got out of the car, the chilly wind rushing over him. He thrust his hands into his pockets and glared at the sign.

THE GARDEN GROVE APARTMENT BUILDING

COMING IN THE NEW YEAR

THE HAMILTON GROUP

Accompanying the sign was a glossy picture of a CGI mock-up of the future building, a six-story Georgian-style apartment complex with gardens and people boasting big smiles while sitting on the rooftop deck. It was a picture of progress and happiness. Bitterness lodged in Declan's chest. What might have happened to his family if they hadn't had this place?

The Community Center was a large, three-story red brick Federal-style building that had a black front door and windows with black shutters. It matched its historical surroundings perfectly. Inside, it was no longer the stately home it once was. It had been converted into an area where people could meet for coffee, a recreation spot for teens, and a kitchen that cooked and served meals to those in need three times a week. The second floor was made up of small offices housing legal aid, a doctor's office, and a counselling office. On the top level, it offered several rooms for emergency accommodation. Better yet, it was only a short walk to King Street—Old Town's main street.

It rankled him that something as simple as local history had been the ultimate undoing in his bid to save the Center. The building might look the part in terms of its architecture, but there was nothing historical about the house. The Historical Society couldn't list it as a building to be preserved, as it was only forty years old. He leaned against the black wrought-iron fence, wishing things were different.

The gate creaked and a shadow fell across the footpath. "Wondering when you'd come by." Eli's voice cut through the wind.

Declan looked up to see his friend, the director of the Center, heading towards him. The wind caught his longish hair, once a glossy black, now a stately white. He looked every inch his sixty-four years.

Eli handed him a cup of steaming coffee. "Black as charcoal, the way you like it."

Declan took it. The steam rising from the mug was stolen by the icy breeze. "I have to write a Christmas party review."

Eli took a long sip of his drink before replying, "You've done that kind of thing before."

"There's a catch." Declan swallowed, not wanting to say the words out loud, but with Eli, he never held things back. "In order to get my career back, I have to review a party that Jonathan and Vivien Hamilton are throwing."

Eli faced him fully, surprise in his eyes. "I didn't see that coming."

Declan grimaced and his chest tightened. "I have to prove how professional I can be."

Eli chuckled. "Julie has you between a rock and a hard place."

"Tell me about it."

"How much do you want your op-eds back?" Eli peered at him, steam rising from the mug.

"You know the answer to that, it's been the longest year of my life. All I've been doing is society reviews, museum exhibit openings, et cetera." Declan rolled his eyes. "It's well past time I was back writing about things that matter."

The silence between them lengthened, and Declan shifted against the fence and glared at the ugly sign. "This is wrong."

"You're preaching to the choir, boy."

"If Julie hadn't shut me down, I could have done more."

"Don't do it, Dec." Eli sipped his drink as he watched the passing traffic.

"Do what?"

"Try to make what happened your fault."

"But it was working." He gripped his mug tighter.

"Drink your coffee." Eli nodded at the cup. "It'll turn cold real quick out here."

Declan complied. "They're not even going to replace the services—it's as if they never existed. All for the sake of the mighty dollar and lining some rich guy's pocket."

"And the city loses out." Eli finished what Declan was thinking.

Declan glanced at Eli. Eli Greaves had been the first person Declan had connected with when he was an enraged teen arriving in Alexandria. He was the first person to see him for what he was—a hurting boy who needed love and attention. Declan had come to the Center every day after school with his sister Nicky to wait until their mother finished work. Eli was the only person outside the family who knew the truth about them, Declan's dad—all of it.

"Hasn't life taught you yet that there's always something new around the corner?"

Declan drained his coffee. He shifted his gaze towards Heritage Oaks Residence Home that was literally around the corner. Even though he couldn't see it, he knew it was there. It was a place he hated, and one he never thought he'd need to step inside. Certainly not at the age of thirty. His stomach quivered at the thought of going inside.

"How's she doing?" Eli asked softly.

Eli was more a father to Declan than his own had ever been. The man's wrinkles grew deeper around the corners of his mouth and eyes as he too looked towards the nursing home neither of them could see. Declan tried to find the words to reply, but they caught in his throat. Everything was wrong about this situation. He took several seconds to settle himself before answering. "Why don't you tell me?"

Eli was quiet for long seconds, then finally he spoke. "You're going to have to go back in there at some point. You can't avoid her forever."

"I haven't been inside since she moved in three weeks ago. I just can't seem to make it..." The words stuck. A hard knot lodged in his throat. What kind of son couldn't visit his own mother?

"She'd love a visit from you." The wind almost stole Eli's words.

"Thanks Eli, but I've got to go." He handed his mug to Eli and checked his watch. "I've got an appointment at George and Martha's.

The event planner is meeting me about the party." Declan tried but couldn't keep the contempt from his voice.

Eli smirked. "You behave yourself."

"I always do," he called as he walked off. Julie wanted professionalism, that didn't mean he had to be happy about it.

Chapter Two

Addey Bennet shivered in the cold late November morning as she typed in the security code on the panel beside the wide glass doors of Heritage Oaks Residence Home and drew a deep breath. To others, the world behind those doors was a scary unknown, and today, standing under a bleak gray sky, she could sort of see why. But the moment the buzzer sounded, and she stepped into the air-conditioned hallway, her stress rolled off her shoulders. It wasn't much but being paid to work here one day a week allowed her to find joy and life, even where others found disease and decay. In a way, it was her refuge from her busy, stressful life of event management.

The scent of thick carpet and lavender air freshener, although not great, was familiar. She smiled at the Christmas tree that sat by the window, twinkling. With only four weeks until Christmas, life was always busy. Waving to the girls at reception, Addey made her way down the carpeted hallway for a quick chat with her best friend and finance officer, Carmel Troyer. Carmel texted Addey last night, asking her to pop by on her way to work.

Halfway down the hallway, Addey drew to a stop. Her mother, Vivien Hamilton, stood in the corridor looking at the photos that lined the wall. "Mom? What are you doing here?"

Vivien jerked, then met Addey's gaze. They didn't look much alike, save for their deep auburn hair. Her eyes were clear blue, Addey's were sea green, and Addey was taller, like her dad.

"Your father had a meeting nearby, and I thought I would come in and look around while I wait for him to finish." The clipped tone and the lifted chin held Addey in place.

She gripped her hand tighter on the strap of her purse. "I never knew you visited here." Addey spoke each word with care.

"I don't normally." Mom didn't move. She just stood there, back ramrod straight, her eyes darting glances around the hallway.

Addey sucked the tension in and crossed the space between them. Well, the physical one. The emotional distance had been there since she was a little girl and couldn't be bridged so easily. She was five years old when she'd moved in with her mother's mother, Deborah Bennet, and eighteen when she took her last name, and it had changed her life. For the better.

Addey surveyed the photos on the wall. Many of them had Granny in them. After all, she had helped found the Heritage Oaks Residence Home. Addey touched a frame, holding a memory of her and Granny helping with the annual Christmas luncheon. She'd been ten when the photo was taken. "Granny would always put on a series of events at Christmas. She let me sing carols." Addey tried to smile. "I wasn't very good."

Vivien's mouth formed a tight line. "I wouldn't know anything about that."

Inside, Addey wilted, but outside, she merely nodded. "I have a meeting to get to. I'll see you Sunday for brunch, as usual?"

"Of course." Their gazes met briefly, and the distance between them stretched even farther.

"I'll walk you out." Despite the strained relationship, Addey kept trying. Maybe one day she would stop, but seeing those photos only reminded her that Granny wouldn't want her to do that.

They walked in silence out to the parking lot, where Addey's father, Jonathan Hamilton, got out of his brand-new silver Mercedes. "Ah, Vivien darling, there you are." His sharp green eyes took in the scene. "This isn't your day to be here, Adelaide."

Ah. "Morning, Dad."

"Uh-huh." He stood with the car door open, as if he couldn't wait to leave. "I've been up at the Community Center—but it won't be that for long. The sign for the condos went up yesterday." Dad might as well have rubbed his hands together and jumped up and down with glee at the triumph in his voice.

Addey nodded faintly. Everyone in Old Town knew about the fight waged by journalist Declan Collins to keep the Center from being redeveloped. As usual, Dad had won.

"See you both on Sunday," she called as Mom slipped into the car.

"Bye, darling." Mom's hand did that Queen Elizabeth wave—tiny and reserved. "Oh." Her lips turned up, as if she was trying to smile, but it looked more like an unpleasant smell had settled under her nose. "I thought you'd want to come to the Children's Benefit with me?"

Addey tensed. "Um, thanks for the offer, but that's not my thing."

Mom's face darkened. "It's a party, darling." There was an edge in her voice that usually led to either an argument or the silent treatment. Addey didn't know which she preferred.

Addey shifted under the scrutiny of her parents. *And there would be lots of eligible doctors to introduce me to. No thanks.* "Yes, but I *plan* those. I don't really want to attend one in my spare time."

"Not even for the children?" The softening of Mom's tone and the way her hand lost its death grip on the door caused Addey's heart to squeeze. Was this the way to find a relationship with her mother? Go to parties she hated? Be set up on dates with men she had no interest in? But then again, she hadn't mentioned anything about dates. Maybe coming here was her way of reaching out to her only daughter...the daughter she'd left for someone else to raise.

"I'll think about it," Addey said. "But Mom, please let me be clear on something—"

"I know," Mom interrupted, huffing. "I'm not allowed," she rolled her eyes, "to set you up."

Addey nodded firmly. "Thank you. I really appreciate you letting me decide my own love life."

"It would be nice if you had one," Mom murmured.

Addey's whole body tensed, and she averted her gaze to the dark sky. Why did everything have to be so hard with them?

Mom continued. "Can you bring the final menu options for the Christmas party at brunch on Sunday, so we can go over them?"

Addey shifted on her feet. "Sure."

Dad, his hand resting on the roof of the car, gave a curt nod. His gaze bored into hers. His gray power suit emphasized his broad, rigid shoulders and his short salt and pepper hair gave him the air of always being in control. Which he was.

He dipped his chin. "Now, remember, I want this night to be perfect. I don't need any more hassles with the press."

Did he think she *wanted* hassle?

"That Collins journalist made things very difficult. I want to debut the presentation for the new building on the big night, show everyone that the Hamilton Group is strong."

"I understand."

He nodded curtly. "And the future of your business is riding on this."

As if she didn't know that, either. "Everything will be great. Trust me." Addey plastered on her most assuring grin, the one she gave all her clients, and waved them off. As soon as they left the lot, her shoulders sagged, and she exhaled.

Footsteps sounded behind her. Carmel came over and pulled her into a side hug. "The girls at reception said you were waylaid. Come inside and have a coffee. You must need it."

Inside Carmel's office Addey dropped her bag on the floor and relaxed into the soft pale green sofa that occupied one side of the room. She pulled the rainbow crochet blanket draped across the back of the sofa onto her lap.

"You can have it back," Carmel said.

Addey shook her head. "Nonsense. It's yours—I gave it to you."

Carmel pulled her black hair into a tight, high ponytail and then poured two cups from the coffee machine that rested on a side table. Her friend had been instrumental in helping Addey get her role as activities planner—just like her grandmother had been. There were others who volunteered and carried out the program Addey designed.

"It was a shock seeing Mom here." In fact, it was a shock seeing her mother anywhere outside of their carefully-controlled, once-a-week brunches. It'd been that way for the last three years.

Carmel handed Addey a mug of coffee. She pushed her swivel chair around the front of her desk and sat, cradling her own cup. "She comes in sometimes. To see the photos."

Addey sipped her drink. "Seriously? That's so weird. Mom hates this place."

Carmel tapped the top of her mug. "Maybe not. It might be the only way she feels close to her mom...and to you."

Addey let out a short, humorless laugh. "My family doesn't do affection like most families."

"I know." Carmel's gentle voice touched Addey. It was nice to know someone didn't judge her for how she dealt with her parents.

"I think she wants to set me up with some doctor. She invited me to the Children's Benefit for the hospital." Addey scrunched up her nose. "I hate being set up. Did you know she once asked me to meet her somewhere and when I arrived, she wasn't there? In her place was the son of one of her friends."

"No!" Carmel's eyes widened.

"He was as embarrassed as me."

"Was he at least cute?" Carmel asked.

Addey laughed. "Not cute enough to withstand twenty very awkward minutes before we both made a hasty retreat."

"I don't know how you do it." Carmel's voice softened.

"Sometimes I don't know either." Addey shrugged, needing to switch the topic. "When we last spoke, you said something about your dad? Is everything okay?"

Carmel exhaled. "I went back for Thanksgiving, and he was fine, but last night he had a heart episode."

"Oh no! Why didn't you call me?"

"It was late. No point in both of us losing sleep." Carmel shrugged. "The doctor said he's fine, but they're monitoring him. Mom keeps calling and updating me. I'm expected to let my sisters know everything." The last word dragged out, but if not for the love in her eyes, one might assume Carmel was making fun of her mom. Carmel's mom was from the Philippines and expected Carmel, as the eldest, to be in charge.

"I'll be praying." That was something Addey could do—pray for others.

"Thanks." Carmel drained her coffee. Plunking the cup down, she zeroed in on Addey. "It's my turn to change the topic."

Addey settled against the cushions, her curiosity piqued.

Carmel pursed her lips. "How are you finding things here? Still enjoying it?"

"I love it here, why?"

"The parent company is talking about adding a full-time events coordinator for the three facilities they own."

"Oh, but that's not for sure?" A sliver of dread wormed its way into Addey's heart. Did that mean they would no longer need her? What would she do without this place?

"Don't look so alarmed. I just wanted to let you know what might be happening." Carmel sent her a reassuring smile. "You're so good with the residents. You make people feel special and you give them hope. Addey, you bring life with you every time you walk through these doors."

No one had ever described what she did as life-giving. Addey was a party planner and, while successful, many people viewed that as frivolous. Over a year ago, her business had become successful enough that, with her assistant on board, she could devote a day a week here.

"But someone else could bring life with them, too." *I won't be needed anymore.* Addey swallowed, surprised by the tears that threatened to fall. What was wrong with her?

Her thoughts turned to Granny. She knew her grandmother would be proud of Addey and what she'd built. But her granny was the only one in the family who would be. The all-too-familiar lump of grief lodged in Addey's chest, and weight pressed down on her. She drew several slow, deep breaths and waited for the moment to pass, as it always did. The sadness, however, lingered like a fog over the Potomac River on a cold winter's day.

"Don't think like that," Carmel said. "It's just an idea. Nothing is for sure yet."

"My parents would love it if I stopped coming here." It would make them hassle her less, which would be nice. "They view what I do here as time away from my career and, thus, it's a waste of my potential." Addey couldn't give up this place, it was part of her and Granny.

Carmel raised her eyebrows. "Wow. I wish they didn't make things so hard for you."

When Addey changed her surname at eighteen from Hamilton to Bennet, few people outside of family and close friends even knew she was their daughter. Carmel was one of those few. Her friend kept the information to herself, which suited Addey just fine. Life was easier when people didn't know she was a Hamilton.

"The money I used to fund my business was a shared inheritance from Granny to my mom and me. We both decided that, as long as I helped them out with their parties, Mom would use her share to back my business." Addey's words tumbled out. "It was an easy decision at the time. Granny would have liked us working together." She paused. "Plus, they love what the Baker/Gibson Group is offering me."

Carmel twitched an eyebrow. "And who are they?"

"I've had to keep it under wraps, but I can tell you." Addey wiggled herself into a more comfortable position. "Baker/Gibson is a company that specializes in buying small businesses, like mine, and turning them into a bigger version of themselves."

"Addey, that's amazing!" Carmel's face lit up.

"Thanks." Addey smiled. "It's a big deal. The final number on the sale of the business will depend on how successfully this upcoming Christmas party goes. The local journalists will do write-ups. I expect even some of the bigger papers will have a presence." The weight of expectation settled on Addey and the little ball of stress wound tighter. "My parents—Dad, really, is pushing hard for my success. Whether I like it or not."

"This is huge! Do you go with the company if they buy it?"

Addey nodded. "That's the idea, but nothing is final right now."

"Then I'll keep you in my prayers." Carmel tipped her head to one side. "This seem odd, but I've always wanted to ask you something?"

"Sure."

Carmel ran her fingers along the top of her mug. "How did they take it when you changed your last name?"

Addey offered a half-smile. "They gave me the silent treatment for a year, but then Dad decided that it was better to be in contact with me. Plus, I suspect Granny might have helped smooth things over."

"They didn't blame her?" Carmel arched an eyebrow.

"They did, but I copped most of the silent treatment. To be honest, it was the most peaceful year of my life." Her laugh faded.

"Wow, that's, um..."

"Don't worry, that was a long time ago. We're in a better place now." Granny's passing three years ago had made things simpler...and more complicated at the same time.

Addey stood and put the cup on the desk, eager to leave the thoughts about family. She hugged Carmel.

"I have a Christmas party to plan. Perfection is expected." Addey checked her watch. "Speaking of the party, I have to meet a journalist from *The Alexandria Gazette* at Mount Vernon."

"Who?" Carmel said. "Not Declan Collins?"

"That would be my worst nightmare. Can you imagine? He would write an awful review and ruin my business at the same time." Addey shuddered. "Thankfully, that's not going to happen. It's Paul Klein. He's supposed to meet me at the piazza."

"I'd rather deal with financial issues here than journalists." Carmel closed a file that was open on her desk. "Remember, you can handle one of their parties. And don't stress about the Baker/Gibson Group, just throw the most amazing event ever. That kind of thing is easy for you."

"I'm sure it'll be fine. What could go wrong?"

Both women erupted in laughter.

"Who am I kidding? Anything that can go wrong, will." Addey opened the door.

"But nothing major will happen." Carmel's phone rang. "Oh, still on for cooking class Monday night?"

"You can't keep me away." Addey waved.

Worry chased at Addey's heels. What if she had to give this place up? She shook the thought away. Like Carmel said, it was just talk. But her friend wouldn't have mentioned it if it wasn't a true possibility.

Addey paused at the door and took a settling breath. Her focus right now had to be the Christmas party. The future of her business and any hope of a better relationship with her parents all hung on the next four weeks.

Chapter Three

Declan didn't want to be there, but that didn't stop him from striding onto the lavish grounds of Mount Vernon, the iconic home of George Washington, twenty minutes early for his meeting. He knew he should feel patriotic, but he couldn't muster up anything more than bitterness and smoldering indignation. This historical home had nothing to do with his family's troubles. That was a long time ago, back in Los Angeles, but just being here drove him crazy. Perhaps it was what this home represented that ate away at him—wealth preserved for everyone to gawk at.

As he followed the red brick path lined with shrubs and trees, pedestrians strolled around him, some stopping to look at the foliage or sit on the artfully-placed benches lining the path. The whole place reminded him of an English estate. He kept walking, moving faster around the next bend. Then he stopped.

In front of him was a well-manicured lawn with gravel pathways framing the edges. At the end of the lawn sat Mount Vernon, home of the country's first president. The red roofed two-and-a-half story mansion with its dove-topped cupola was flanked on either side by two single-story buildings, creating a cozy feeling for such a large space. Without warning, his previously simmering fury welled, and all he could do was stand there, unmoving, staring at the fancy building. If he'd seen one, he'd seen them all.

Images of his mother stoically carrying on with life when their world had fallen apart played across his mind. How many times had she visited this place? Countless. She said it was her happy place. But how happy could it have been when she always came back sadder, and all it did was drive Declan's anger deeper?

The longer he stood there, the more frustrated he got. He shouldn't be here waiting to talk to a woman who was probably just like the Hamiltons. He turned, ready to flee, when he collided with someone coming around the corner. A flash of green caught his eye before the person hit the ground. Declan wobbled, flung his arms wide to steady himself and to keep from landing on top of her.

"I'm sorry, I didn't see you." He offered his hand. "Are you hurt?"

She took his hand, and he pulled her up. "I'm okay. I wasn't looking either." She brushed the dirt off her hands and jeans, and as she readjusted her sea-green beanie, he couldn't help but notice it matched her eyes.

She swiped more dirt off her arms. "What?"

He shook himself, readjusted his sunglasses. He didn't normally stare at women, but he couldn't help it. Her dark red hair that tumbled down her shoulders, her pretty mouth, and cute nose held him in place. The churning in his gut went from overpowering to a different kind, a quicker, lighter tumble that he hadn't experienced in ages—too long, if he were honest.

"Sorry," he said again. How many times had he said that already? "I didn't expect the view of the building."

A smile touched her lips.

"Yes." She turned toward the view that had caused the collision. "It can do that to you. And it's not even the best view, but it's pretty amazing. First time here?" She gave him a questioning glance.

"Sort of. I came as a teenager, but I wasn't paying much attention back then. School field trips..." He trailed off.

"I hear you." She started walking towards the main building. "If you promise not to barrel me over again, I can show you the best view!" she called over her shoulder. Compelled by curiosity and—dare he think it—attraction, he followed her, catching up in five easy strides.

"It's pretty quiet today." She checked the watch on her wrist. "But it's still early." She waved her hand to the grassed section closest to the house. "This is Mansion Circle."

"Are you a tour guide or something?" He gave her a sideways look. Their feet crunched on the gravel.

She shook her head. "My maternal grandmother came here often and that meant I did as well."

Declan didn't know what to say. The look on her face was sad, her voice soft.

"I hope she's well," he finally added lamely.

"She passed away three years ago." Her voice grew rough.

"I'm sorry." He ducked his head, heat crawling up his neck. "I've been saying that a lot since I met you."

She shrugged away his comment. "You didn't know." They rounded a corner, and her smile grew. "Now *this* is the best view."

He hadn't been paying attention to where she was leading him. He stopped, surprised by the view—and the woman beside him.

"This is the piazza, the east side of the house." That fond look appeared again.

He took in the scene spread out before him. Now, this was worth it. He didn't care if it was George Washington's home. All he cared about was the mighty Potomac River stretching far down below at the bottom of the hill. He could easily imagine the former president and his many guests enjoying this same view and feeling the cool air on a summer's night waft over them. The rich green lawn beckoned him to walk to the river's edge, though it was a good mile away.

"This is amazing," he said. He really hadn't been paying attention on the school field trip. Angry kids didn't focus on things like that.

"Yes, it is." She turned back and assessed him.

He met her gaze. "What?"

"Forgive me, but you seem familiar. I feel like I've seen your picture somewhere." She cocked her head to one side.

He removed his sunglasses and tucked them into the pocket of his coat. "I'm Declan Collins, journalist with *The Alexandria Gazette*."

Her breath hitched. "I'm meant to meet Paul Klein about the party. Where is he?"

Ah, so this was who he was meeting. "Paul is away on personal leave. Sudden family thing." Declan eyed Addey, who had gone a shade of white that was concerning. "My boss sent me in his place." His shoulders tensed. "You must be Addey Bennet." Why did he get the feeling Addey was as happy about his presence here as he was?

Her former confidence slipped off her shoulders like an unwanted cloak. "Yes, that's right. I'm the event organizer for the party."

***

Declan Collins! How could this happen? Addey looked anywhere but at the man beside her. She was going to be sick. The panic wound tight inside, threatening to send her running. Instead, Addey stayed put and plastered a smile on her face, hoping Declan wouldn't notice how rattled she was.

"Is something wrong?" The irony of that sentence almost made her smile—almost.

Her stomach threatened to revolt.

Addey's fake grin grew bigger and brighter, and she forced a natural tone into her voice. "Sorry, I was taken aback. You're the columnist who wants to save the Community Center."

"I'm the columnist who *didn't* save the Community Center." There was bitterness in his words. Unmissable. Like his presence. The man was inescapable.

His dark brown eyes were shuttered, and she couldn't read anything in them. His jaw was firm and set in a frown, his dark brown hair cropped short. He looked to be a couple of years older than her twenty-eight years. His arms were crossed at his chest, his stance wide. Everything about him was contained, assured. Even his tone.

"You know who is going to be at this holiday party, don't you?" Addey ventured the words, grateful more than ever that she didn't share her parents' last name anymore. She buried her hands deep into her pockets.

He nodded, his frown deepening.

"Is there a problem?" He finally spoke, directing those dark eyes straight to her, and she sucked in a breath, unable to look away from the storm brewing in them.

She shook her head, scrambling to find the words to bring calm to his expression and keep her identity a secret. "I understand from what I've read in the papers that...you know...being in the same room as the Hamiltons," she stumbled over the word, "might be, ah, difficult for all parties involved."

She didn't know Declan Collins, except by the things he wrote about the Hamilton Group—and by extension, her father—but he didn't come across as the easy-going type. Her father—oh, she didn't want to think about what might happen if they met in *any* setting, let alone at the party where they were launching the very thing this man had fought to stop. There was no way to fix this problem. Not right now.

Maybe Declan wouldn't be noticed there? No, who was she kidding? Dad would see him immediately. Her palms grew sweaty inside her pockets.

"It'll be fine," he said, and it pulled her back from her tumbling thoughts. "So where is this shindig going to be held exactly?" He looked around at their surroundings.

Addey half-relaxed for the first time since she collided with him. *Focus on the task at hand.* Pivoting slightly, she pointed to the grass section down the hill on the way to the river. "Right there, we'll have marquees set up and, of course, heaters to keep the cold at bay. There'll be music, dancing, and gourmet food. A Christmas party to make George Washington himself proud."

"That's going a bit far, isn't it?" He quirked an eyebrow. There was a twinkle in his eyes, though the rest of his face remained like granite.

"Maybe, but it'll be a fun way to celebrate the season. Anything else you need?" She kept her voice light, but her head was starting to hurt from restraining her panic.

"Shall we walk? It's too cold to keep standing here." He motioned forward, and Addey fell into step beside him but kept her hands in her pockets and a safe distance between them.

"It's a simple article, just a review of the party, and some history about this place." He shrugged, almost like it wasn't important to him. Hope surged through her. Maybe his indifference could serve her needs. If he didn't care, then it would make things easier for her. He continued talking. "It would be good for me to shadow you on the night of the party. It would help add to the article."

Addey sent him a suspicious glance, to which he cracked a smile at. She liked the way it changed his face from a hard and shadowed rock to a glimpse of sunlight on a dreary day. Giving him a grin of her own, their gazes held. Addey's heart rate picked up and she broke the connection, looking anywhere but at him.

"Don't worry." Amusement coated his voice, but she didn't dare glance at him again. "I promise, I won't get in the way and it won't be all night. It'll help me give the article more depth."

Addey pulled her beanie further down her forehead. She was done having this conversation, and getting away from Declan had become top priority, before anything more went wrong.

"I'm fine with all that," she lied. "I'll email your ticket and anything else you need to know beforehand."

He nodded. "Sounds fair."

They stopped near Mansion Circle, almost on the spot where they'd collided.

"We could have done this over the phone," she commented. "Sorry to take up your time."

He shrugged. "My boss wanted me here, so I came."

They fell into an awkward silence. Addey was about to speak when Declan spoke first.

"I guess I'll see you in four weeks." He held out his hand. "It was a pleasure meeting you, Addey. Next time I promise not to knock you over."

His smile was full this time and Addey couldn't help but stare at the transformation. It was like a cloudless, sunny day at the beach. The kind of day that you could get lost in.

"Yes, see you in four weeks," she replied. Did she sound breathless? She needed to get out of there.

Taking his hand, she shook it and dropped it quickly. Walking away, the reminder from Dad kept echoing through her mind: Nothing must go wrong with this event.

Of all the things that could have gone wrong, Declan Collins had been the furthest thing from her mind.

Now he was the only thing on her mind.

Chapter Four

Addey arrived at the Elegant Events office in the Old Town of Alexandria, still trying to wrap her mind around what had just happened. How could Declan Collins be the one reviewing the party? Wasn't it a conflict of interest? She stopped and waved at Nina, her administration assistant and front desk operator. The enticing scent of cupcakes sent her mouth watering as she passed the small conference room that was just off to the side of the front reception desk. Nina was on the phone. Nina mouthed a hello and made a face indicating the person on the other end of the line was difficult. Addey smiled, grateful for her competent staff. Nina was professional to the core, but they'd all had their fair share of clients who tested the limits of professionalism.

Like meeting Declan.

Addey dropped her purse on her desk and collapsed onto her chair. She rested her head in her hands, unable to see how this situation wasn't going to implode. Maybe not right now, but it would. She couldn't stay hidden forever. Declan was a smart guy. He wouldn't have to dig too deep to figure out who she was.

"Addey, we've got a client coming in for a meeting in ten…Oh my, what happened?"

Addey looked up at Holly Westmoore, her assistant and, really, the woman who drove the business more and more every day. Holly stood in the doorway, looking tired and a little pale, her blonde hair pulled back in a neat ponytail, her black-framed glasses askew on her face, tablet in one hand, cupcake in the other.

"You look like you've gone three rounds with your parents." Holly's crack at her relationship with her parents usually brought a smile. Instead, Addey stared at her, eyes wide.

Holly walked into the neatly decorated office and sat on the chair that sat opposite the white desk. "Spill."

"Do you remember that reporter who spent nearly a year fighting the demolition of the Community Center? The one who made sure everyone knew he thought Dad was a selfish, greedy, soulless leech who cared for nothing but lining his own pockets?"

"Well, I don't think he used those exact words, but yes. And might I venture, you hold a similar opinion…" Holly gasped. "Sorry Addey, I didn't mean you agree with the selfish, soulless greedy leech part, but the part about knocking down the Center—"

A small chuckle escaped. "I know what you meant."

"So, what about this reporter? I thought he'd gone quiet on that issue?" Holly said.

"He has."

"What's the problem, then?"

Addey forced the words from her mouth. "He's been assigned to review the Christmas party my parents are throwing to launch the new building…"

Holly deposited the cupcake on the desk. "You need this more than me."

Addey took the cupcake and took a big bite. Cinnamon and coffee flavored. Not the best, but still good.

Holly's expression grew serious. She put the tablet on the table. "I take it he doesn't know who you are?"

Addey leaned back and closed her eyes. "Not yet but he will at some point."

"Why would he?"

Addey opened one eye and assessed her friend and colleague. "It doesn't take Sherlock Holmes to figure out who I am. He's going to think I'm exactly like my father and give the party a bad review—which is detrimental for my business."

Holly cocked her head, screwed up her face and twisted her lips at the corner—her thinking face. "We can do this, Addey."

"Seriously?"

Holly nodded, a smile beginning to emerge. "You're Addey Bennet. I knew nothing different until your mom came in during my first week and made it clear who she was and insisted on seeing you."

Addey nodded, then took another bite of the cupcake. "I remember that. You were so confused."

"The point is, I wouldn't have known if I'd never crossed her path. You are Addey Bennet."

Addey tapped the desk, trying to see a way through this mess. "But Holly, the Baker/Gibson Group expects an impressive night. We have to deliver. I met this guy today. He'll happily ruin this event. My parents don't want that and my business could be ruined if he does that. Everything you and I have worked for could be gone."

Holly sat forward. "Can you get your parents to drop the new building presentation from the party agenda?"

Things had been settled between her and her parents for a while now, rocking the boat would make it worse. Did she want to upend the fragile peace they had?

Addey took another bite of the cupcake. The sugar hit only increased her headache.

Holly pressed the tip of her pencil on her lip. "What if they hold a smaller party on New Year's, and do the presentation then? You know, new year, new building?"

Addey thought about it. It might work if she could get her parents on her side without telling them why. At Sunday brunch she'd broach the topic.

Holly picked up her tablet and rubbed her eyes. "So, we have a plan, then? You get your parents to think Christmas and Christmas only, and keep Declan as far away from you as you can. Really, he doesn't need to see you until the night of the party."

"You're still tired." Addey pushed the cupcake away. "You've been under the weather for weeks now."

The tablet pinged and Holly glanced at it. "Our client's here." She stood. At the door, she paused. "I'm just fighting off a virus. You know how it is? I'd better meet our client."

Maybe Holly was right, and she was fighting off a virus. But doubts lingered. But right now, the client needed their attention. This was the woman who wanted to throw a lavish birthday party for her two Maltese dogs. There were days Addey truly wondered about people's priorities.

Addey stood and pocketed her phone, then grabbed her own device. *Focus on the new client and let the worries of tomorrow worry about themselves.* Even as she thought her positive mantra, which wasn't exactly a prayer, doubts chased the words away. This should have been easy. Throw a party. Now it was so much more than that. Her business was at stake, and her relationship with her parents, too. No matter which way she looked at it, the situation was untenable.

Still, Declan's smile lingered in her mind. What would it take to get him to laugh? *No!* These thoughts had no place in her life—not now or ever.

Determined to get a grip, Addey sailed into the conference room, a smile at the ready when her eyes landed on two Maltese dogs sitting on chairs at the table, dressed in pink ribbons with bonnets on their heads. She fought the urge to roll her eyes.

This day was getting harder by the hour.

***

Declan slapped the puck toward the net. It sailed in. He grabbed another from the bucket and repeated the move—only harder this time.

"Easy does it there." His best friend Camden stood a short distance away, his own stick in his hand. "What's riding you?"

Declan slammed another puck, and it shot across the ice. "Nothing, I'm just eager for our game next week." The cold air felt good. It invigorated him, feeling his cheeks go red from the cold, having to move to keep warm. Playing with his friends every week was the outlet he needed, especially when his world had been upended.

He repeated the action, then moved away so Camden could have his turn. Camden chased the puck around the net before flicking it towards the goal. It slid past. Declan charged after it, breathing hard, as he worked the puck around the rink, pouring all his frustration into the disk. Finally, he flicked it towards the net and watched with satisfaction when it found the corner of the goal.

He raised his eyebrows at Camden and shot his stick high in the air, sucking in breaths.

Camden laughed. "Show off."

"We both know you can beat me for speed." Declan skated over to the bucket and shot some more into the net. "But I'm a better shot than you."

"No arguments from me there." The two men took turns shooting the puck. "Still haven't said what's riding you."

Declan shrugged. Ever since he'd been told he had to review the Hamiltons' party and then met Addey, his world had tilted. Addey Bennet swirled through his mind since they'd met. He thought about ways he might get to see her again, but nothing came to mind. He didn't want it to either, not seriously. It was enough to have to attend the event thrown by the Hamiltons, he didn't need to spend any more time with the woman charged with throwing the party. Not that it was her fault. She just got lumped in with difficult clients who paid very well.

"Earth to Dec..." Camden waved his stick in front of Declan.

Declan shook his head and got his head back into the game. "It's work stuff."

Camden skated around the area they occupied while he waited for Declan to keep talking. Declan took another slap at a puck. He missed. "My last assignment before I can return to my op-eds is reviewing a Christmas party thrown by the Hamiltons."

Camden's laughter filled the air.

"I'm glad someone sees the humor in all this," he said dryly.

"Julie is really making you earn that column back." He kept laughing before pulling himself back together. "So, what are you going to do?"

"It's just a party. This will be like all the other society events I've had to do this year."

Even as he spoke the words, his chest tightened. Images of the new sign at the Community Center flashed through his mind. He tightened his grip on the stick and slapped another shot. The stick scraped across the ice, and the puck missed the goal, skittering out of control until it came to a slow stop.

His buddy eyed him. "You sure you can do that? The Community Center means a lot to you."

Camden knew him well. They'd been friends since college, but Camden didn't know everything about Declan's past, just that his parents divorced and that he didn't see his dad.

"I'll be nothing but professional. I've already met the event organizer, who's given me the basic rundown so I'm on the right track already." He tried sounding casual but Camden shook his head, clearly not buying it.

"I know you're professional, but don't let this situation get away from you. I see it there." He pointed at Declan. "Right there in your eyes how much you hate doing this."

"It'll be fine. No matter what happens, I'll do what's needed to make this a success." He picked up the bucket, and they began chasing down stray pucks. "Let's call it a night."

Camden's words carried more weight than Declan let on. His friend was right—Declan was angry, and he didn't know what to do with it. Deep down, he was afraid this anger would never go away.

But maybe more than that...he didn't know if he would ever be ready to live without it.

Chapter Five

Thursday was Addey's regular day at Heritage Oaks. A sense of calm settled over her. The rightness of what she was doing. But that rightness tilted. Would someone else be walking these halls soon? Would they know that Maude's grumpy exterior hid a beautiful soul? Or that Saul liked to eat at exactly six o'clock on the dot every evening? For the past year she'd had the best of both worlds. A business thriving in an industry she loved and a side gig helping some of the most vulnerable people in society. But she couldn't shake the disquiet rattling her soul.

Waving at the nurses walking to and from different sections of the home, she came to the end of the long hallway and went through the middle of three doors. The first led to a small outdoor garden area, the third led to a large multi-purpose room, often used for the dancing classes she held for the more able-bodied residents.

The middle door was the main dining and lounge room. The room was painted a creamy green color. Addey hated it and would love to change it to something more inviting, maybe a soft peach or a calm blue. She'd have to get funding and permission first. *No, that will be someone else's job.*

Rectangular tables set to seat six people were scattered around the large square room. Off to the side was a sliding door, which led to the outdoor garden. On the other side, directly opposite the tables, were two large sets of wooden paneled doors connecting the dining area to the multi-purpose room next door. It was rare that these rooms were opened to share the same space. Two large picture windows on one side brought in much needed sunlight.

"Miss Addey!" Vera Simpkins called from her recliner. Vera, with her white curly hair, laughing eyes and high cheekbones, was always ready to encourage others. Addey walked over and gave the woman a long hug. She felt smaller today than last week—bonier, perhaps. Addey's heart thumped deeply in her chest, and she held back her rising emotions. Vera didn't need Addey blubbering all over her.

"How are you today, Mrs. Simpkins?" She pulled up a chair.

Vera gave her a cheerful but tired smile. "We got a new resident."

Addey nodded, thinking that someone must have passed away. She looked around the room, trying to see who was missing.

"Oh, it's not a death this time," Vera said, obviously catching onto Addey's train of thought. "Although it usually is." She frowned. "No, Stanley's family is moving to Florida, and they don't want to leave him here without them close by."

"I'm so pleased for him."

"Oh, he's excited. He's always wanted to live near the ocean. They've got a trip planned for Disney World, too. You should have seen him, Miss Addey. He's been grinning and chatting away like a bird on a spring morning."

"I'm sorry I missed him."

"Well, I hope the new person fits in well, that's all," a raspy voice piped up from nearby. Addey turned, knowing who it was instantly. Maude Hallet was the most outspoken resident, and she let everyone know her thoughts on things ranging from the quality of the food, to the temperature of the room, all the way to who was sitting in someone else's spot. Heaven forbid, if anyone sat in her chair. Despite all that, Addey enjoyed her company and wasn't ruffled by her critical ways.

"Morning, Maude." Addey gave her a wave. Maude frowned and Addey let it slide.

"I was thinking about a Frank Sinatra Day sometime in the next two weeks?" She spoke louder, knowing she would have to talk to each table, but this would gauge enough interest. Several heads turned and looked at her.

"I suppose he'll do," Maude grunted from her seat.

Other voices chimed in, adding their agreement to the plan.

Just then, nurse Fiona entered the room, holding the arm of a woman Addey had never seen before. Addey couldn't take her eyes off her. Young, far too young to be here—the woman had to be in her early sixties—with a pleasant and graceful air about her.

Her graying blonde hair was cut in a soft chin-length bob. The newcomer looked around the room with apprehension in her eyes. Addey was immediately drawn to her, but she couldn't explain it. Rising, she walked over.

"Hi, Fiona," Addey spoke softly.

"Hey, glad you're here Addey," Fiona said as she directed the woman to one of the many recliners positioned around the room. All of them faced the large flat screen TV where the HGTV channel was playing on low.

"Come on, let's get you comfortable." Fiona assisted the woman. The newcomer was tall and carried an air of refined elegance to her. She walked well, with minimal assistance, to the recliner.

"Susannah, this is Addey. Addey helps with activities around here. You'll see her from time to time." Fiona's voice was clear and strong. Fiona, like all the nurses, was deeply devoted to her patients but firm in her manner. "This is Susannah's first time venturing out of her room."

Susannah gave Addey an appraising stare. "Nice to meet you, young lady. You remind me of someone, but that life has long since gone." Her voice faded, her brown eyes deep pools of sadness. It poured out of her onto Addey, and Addey wanted to run from it yet gather this lovely woman in her arms at the same time.

"That's Stan's chair."

"Maude, don't be mean. Stan's no longer here, you remember?" Fiona straightened and gave Maude a long look, but a small smile twitched at the corners of her mouth.

"I'm not stupid, you know. Of course I know he's gone, but it's still his chair." Maude lifted her cane off the ground and shook it.

"I'll move if you like." Susannah smoothly rose, albeit slowly. "Would you like some company?" she asked Maude.

Maude's mouth pinched into a thin line. Nearby Vera tried to suppress a laughter but only succeeded in snorting.

"I've been told my memory is fading." Susannah had a twinkle in her eye as she walked towards the grumpy woman. "So, we might as well be friends now in case I forget you later."

"You can do what you like," Maude muttered.

Susannah smiled. The apprehension Addey had seen before seemed to melt away as she took the spot next to Maude. The younger woman engaged the older one in quiet conversation while pulling out a faded pack of cards from her black cardigan pocket. "Do you play Go Fish?"

Maude nodded, still frowning.

"Good, I'm rusty with the rules, so can you help me?"

Addey marveled at the scene before her and Fiona sidled up next to her. "Come on, I'll fill you in."

"She looks so young and healthy to be here," Addey said as they arrived at the nurses' station.

Fiona nodded. "She is, except she has early onset Alzheimer's. It's gotten to the point that her two kids can't look after her without one of them having to be there twenty-four seven. They both need to work to afford this place."

"That must be so hard for them." Addey wanted to cry. As much as she hated people having to live in these homes, she knew that in some cases there was no other option.

"They've been struggling with it, and I know they're feeling pretty lousy about the whole thing."

"She's okay right now, though?" Addey nodded towards the dining room.

Fiona nodded. "Yes, but there are days when she's lucid and it's as if nothing's wrong, then there are days when she can't remember where she is or who her kids are, like so many with this awful disease."

Situations like this broke her heart. "Do her two kids come often?"

Fiona nodded. "Her daughter comes every day after work. She gets a visit from Eli from the Community Center every day. Her son has been here once—the day they moved her in."

"It's too hard for him?" Addey ached for the family. Too young to be here, but with no other options. "Does she ask for him?"

Fiona shook her head. "No, I think she understands and doesn't want to push him."

"He needs to make the effort." Addey gripped the counter.

"I know, but you understand, too, how hard this is for families. They need time and space to get their head around this new world they're in."

Addey frowned. "Still, they need to put their parents first."

"That's what they're trying to do by bringing them here." Fiona gave her a pointed look.

"That's not always the case."

Fiona picked up her pen and began filling in some notes on a form. "I know," she said quietly. She looked up from her paperwork. "But with this case, this family, this is the best they can do."

A deep sadness settled on Addey's shoulders as she left the home at the end of the day. She'd spent the morning with the residents just talking to them, connecting with them, before they put a classic Cary Grant movie on. It wasn't fair that she got to leave here and so many of them never did.

She hated this existence, but she knew it was necessary as well.

Driving away, her thoughts flicked back to Susannah. It was people like her that made Addey want to bring joy to their lives. To the whole family, if she could. They deserved to have the best life in these final years when a nursing home was the only option they had left.

Chapter Six

Addey put her phone down and strode from her office and stuck her head in Holly's open door. "Holly, I've got news—what's wrong? Are you okay?" She rushed in as her coworker slowly raised her head from her desk.

"Oh, I'm sorry! I just put my head down for a few minutes." Holly tried to gather her things, but she couldn't seem to move fast enough, fumbling papers.

"Just stop." Addey stilled Holly's hands and found them trembling. "I'll get you some water. Sit there and don't move." She returned with a glass of cold water and painkillers. She put them on the desk. "Take this."

"Really, Addey, I'm fine. I have to run the Bradley Launch Party tonight." Holly's voice was shaky and her makeup couldn't hide the dark smudges under her eyes.

"You must be coming down with something. Get yourself to the doctor." Addey crossed her arms and thought through what she needed to do. "And you are going home now and taking the whole weekend off." Holly protested, but Addey cut her off. "No, I'll run the launch party tonight, and I'll take the family reunion tomorrow night as well. Give me everything you have and go home."

Holly rubbed her head and closed her eyes. "But what about tonight? The Franklin party? You can't be at two places at once."

"That's what I was going to tell you." Addey sat in the chair across from Holly. "The Franklins just called. Their grandfather had a heart attack, so they have to postpone."

"Oh, no!" Holly looked up. Her face was still too pale for Addey's liking. "But we'll lose money...I'm sorry. How thoughtless of me. I hope he's okay."

"That's what deposits are for. Also, they postponed, not canceled." She smiled, trying to reassure Holly. "They intend to go ahead with the party, they just want to wait until he's better. After all, the party is in honor of his retirement."

"We should pray for him." Holly sat up straighter, but it didn't fool Addey.

"I think we should add you to that prayer list." Addey let the feeling of disquiet pass her by. Praying for others, she could do. How could she not, when she saw the hurt and dying at Heritage Oaks each week? But she never stopped to pray for anything for herself. It felt selfish.

"I'll be fine by tomorrow. I can do my job." Holly stuck her chin out and Addey nearly smiled.

"I know. You're very, very good at this job, but I also know how busy it can be. Sometimes you've got to take a break and accept a little help. I'm taking some of your load. Go home and rest up."

Holly stared at her for several seconds before finally nodding. Her shoulders sagged and Addey knew she'd done the right thing. "I'll see you Monday."

Addey turned to leave, but Holly called her back. "I found something you should see."

She joined Holly at the desk as Holly pulled up an article on the laptop. It was an article titled: *What's So Wrong with Emily Gilmore?*

"What's this?"

Holly pointed to the name under the article: Declan Collins.

Addey's eyes narrowed as she read.

I've seen the show Gilmore Girls, *I couldn't escape it. My sister loves it and that meant I endured more episodes than I'd like to admit. Now, the show has some positive attributes: It's funny, witty, and makes a good social commentary on class divisions. That's where the good stops. I'm not critiquing the show, but I want to introduce the idea of Emily Gilmore.*

Emily Gilmore is a career wife. She takes care of the home front with precision and with an iron fist. She assists her husband's career by being a professional party thrower of the highest standard, and presides over boards, committees, and auctions that only other people in her sphere are involved in. In short, Emily Gilmore wields power and control in a world the average American doesn't get to see or experience.

While she is only a fictional character, there are many, many real-life Emily Gilmores in this world. Like the matriarch of the Gilmore Clan, these women are married to wealthy men, they, too, run their homes in complete order, sit on boards that essentially do nothing overall for society at large, and ensure their children are the best dressed, in the best schools, and take the best extracurricular activities.

In this world, the rules are strict and breaking them is the unforgivable sin. Ostracization is the punishment for stepping outside the rules that govern this society. Lost the wealth? Piled on the weight? These will get you a quick exit from the sphere in which you once existed. Make no mistake, they do not let you back in. There is no grace in this world. Only malicious silence, aided by husbands more interested in making money than using it to help others. Afterall, there is no world outside their crystal sphere. Well, not one worth putting a toe into—

Addey stopped reading. "Is this a social commentary or a spoof article?"

"No idea," Holly replied.

"Well, whatever it is, it's very clear that he hates the world my family comes from." How could someone be so prejudiced against one group of people? "What happened to the man who used to write about issues of injustice?"

"Well, he did think the Community Center closing down was an injustice." Holly offered quietly.

"I guess." Addey's shoulder's sagged as she leaned harder on the desk. "But why did this get published?" She pointed at the screen and ran a hand over her face, remembering him at Mount Vernon when they met, granite-like in his demeanor. Obviously, he was as hard in his views as well.

"It's free speech, and he didn't name anyone specifically so he can say what he likes." Holly gave Addey a sympathetic look. "Lucky you hardly have to talk to him."

"Lucky," Addey murmured. "Can you send this to me?"

"Sure," Holly said. "I'll email it before I go."

Addey walked back to her office and shut the door. She slumped into her chair with a heavy sigh. Holly should see a doctor—something was obviously wrong—but that wasn't Addey's call. Working this weekend was something she needed to get her head around. She was tired just thinking about it all. And now seeing Declan's article! It made her furious, but she couldn't deny there was truth in his words. She'd seen it happen to Granny and even Grandmother, Dad's mom, had mentioned being "cut" for a time.

She massaged her temples, questions swirling through her brain. How did Declan know anything about that world? Who was he talking to? And she was definitely snuffing out the stupid flicker of attraction now that she knew his true colors.

Her tablet pinged with Holly's email with the article and all her notes and references for the Bradley Party that night. Addey smiled ruefully. There was nothing like helping a family through a family reunion when her own family was such a mess. *Oh well.* She shuffled through Holly's notes, but one thought kept invading. *He's going to hate that I'm their daughter.* Yes, he was, but there was nothing she could do to change that.

Putting the tablet down, Addey leaned back and exhaled. Telling Declan Collins who her family was just got a whole lot harder.

***

Declan needed cupcakes. His mother loved caramel and vanilla, and he was on a mission. Miss Cupcake was the café that sold the best cupcakes in Alexandria, and it was in Old Town. The tree-lined, cobblestone red brick sidewalk that framed the historic district of Alexandria was something he had taken a long time to love after moving here. Walking around here was like stepping back in time compared to Los Angeles.

Saturday arrived cold and clear. No breeze wafted off the Potomac. He really didn't want to go to Heritage Oaks today, but he couldn't ignore his mother any longer. What made it worse was how understanding she would be. Cupcakes would be his armor. He pushed the door open, and the tantalizing smell of warm, baked cupcakes and freshly-brewed coffee drew him deeper inside. Stepping up to the display case, his mouth watered at the variety of cupcakes on offer. Caramel, vanilla, cookies and cream, choc mint, red velvet, lemon meringue, rainbow, mocha, apple cinnamon, and other flavors lined the holly-stenciled display cases.

The coffee grinder hummed away. The shop was otherwise quiet, with only two other customers. Christmas music piped low from the speakers, a subtle reminder that the next season of merriment was almost upon them. He was about to place his order when the door opened, admitting another patron. A flash of blue caught his eye. He turned and came face to face with Addey Bennet.

His pulse immediately picked up at the sight of her. Dressed in black jeans and a light blue sweater, she looked fresh and lovely. He smiled. "Addey."

Her eyes widened, and his smile faded when she didn't smile back. "Hi, Declan." Her voice was polite but cool. Her lips turned up in a smile that didn't meet her eyes. "I'm getting coffee and cupcakes..." She glanced at the display of cupcakes. "Obviously." She avoided his gaze.

"Same." He shifted between his feet.

He placed his order and made room for Addey. Addey stepped up to the counter, doing the same thing. An awkward silence, filled with Christmas music, stretched between them. Declan tapped his foot on the floor, glancing at the staff, needing his coffee.

When his name was called, he exhaled and took his coffee to a table at the back. Snagging a newspaper from the empty one next to him, Declan flipped through it, trying to focus on the articles, but he was acutely aware of Addey's presence. He liked Addey—what he knew and saw of her anyway. And he didn't quite know what to do about that. Judging by her reactions to him, maybe she didn't like him back. Declan didn't put too much stock in what people thought of him, but it was different with Addey. *She* was different.

The waitress, Lilly, appeared, a cupcake balanced on a plate in her hand. She placed the plate on his table.

"Thanks." He nodded at Lilly. He caught Addey's eye as she turned to find a table. Their gazes collided before he looked away. The place was too quiet this morning.

"So, I saw online that the Community Center is really going to close," Lilly ventured.

Declan nodded, holding back the frown that was ever too present when it came to that place. "There's nothing that can be done to save it."

"That's too bad," she replied, a dull note to her voice. Declan didn't know why a young college student should care about the Community Center, but he was glad she did. It gave him hope. He watched Addey take a seat at the table only two spots away. How could he not? She drew all the attention. She was fidgeting with her phone. He guessed she wasn't working but maybe listening to him and Lilly. That wouldn't be hard, considering how quiet it was. And he kind of liked that she was probably eavesdropping.

"Addey?" He called. "What do you think of the Community Center closing?" He wanted to know her thoughts. Whether she liked him or not.

The phone jerked in her hand and her head shot up, her eyes meeting his. She looked like a deer caught in headlights.

Her mouth opened, but no words came out. Declan leaned forward. She had thoughts and was struggling to share them. Addey was intriguing. She appeared to be two different people, confident and assured, or on the verge of a panic attack. He found himself drawn to both sides of her.

"I wish we could keep it." Her soft and hitched reply captured him. She licked her lips and glanced between Lilly and Declan.

Declan rested his elbows on the table, unable to look away from her. "Would you like to continue this conversation at my table?"

"I'll bring your order out in a minute." Lilly left them alone.

Declan and Addey stared at each other for several long, drawn-out seconds.

Finally, she stood and walked over. "I guess I can do that."

Chapter Seven

What am I doing? Addey's heart thumped as she crossed the shop and slowly lowered herself to sit opposite Declan. Why did the person who hated her family have to look so good? Window shopping on a rare free Saturday morning only reminded her she was hungry and hadn't had breakfast yet. Heading to the cupcake store was supposed to be simple. But there was nothing simple about Declan Collins. His clothes were freshly pressed, and he was grinning wide the moment he saw her—and she nearly let the door swing shut in her face. It reminded her of the time she walked into the glass door outside her church at fifteen, too busy staring at Eric Mayer to watch where she was going. Like Eric back then, Declan had now caught her off guard.

Both times she'd come face to face with this Declan Collins, he'd upended her day.

That smile—she could stare at it all day. But then the article, and her parents, flashed through her mind, and she knew she'd better pack away any attraction she felt toward him.

His presence, the way he invaded this space between them, it was like she couldn't escape from his orbit.

"So, you're in favor of keeping the Community Center?" He didn't waste any time as he took a bite of his cupcake. His large frame dwarfed the small table, and he had to sit with his legs out to the side.

"Yes, but many people are." She shrugged.

"I know." He quirked one eyebrow. "But what's your story? Why do *you* want to save the Center?"

Too many questions and, under his probing gaze, she could tell he didn't miss much. She was very grateful right now that she didn't really resemble either of her parents physically and that her mother didn't love being in front of cameras. Mom was a behind-the-scenes, in-charge woman. Lilly came and put Addey's order down on their table and gave them both quick smiles before dashing off.

Addey took a drink of her coffee before searching for a safe answer to Declan's question. "It's a place that provides essential services to the community, so it should be saved. People need it. It's that simple. Don't quote me on that though."

His face darkened. "I might have a year ago, but I'm not covering the Community Center anymore."

"Why is that?" She leaned forward.

"My editor felt my skills would be used better in other areas." The words landed like he rehearsed them.

Addey grabbed her phone and pulled up Holly's email. "Like on writing articles about Emily Gilmore?" She held up the phone.

Declan reached for the phone, his hand brushing her wrist. Addey stilled at the warmth of his fingers on her skin. *My parents hate him. And he hates my world...and my parents.*

Addey put the phone on the table and rubbed the spot where he touched her. Their gazes connected.

Addey looked away. *Was it hot in here?* She pointed at his plate, needing to *not* talk about the Community Center or his article. "Surprise flavor?"

He frowned at the topic change but apparently chose to let it go. He glanced down at his plate. "Vanilla."

"Really?"

Declan sat back, assessing her with his intense brown eyes. He raised one eyebrow. "Why are you so shocked?"

"I don't know." She stirred her drink and looked out the window. "It's such a safe choice. I figured you for something more daring." Vanilla was such a plain flavor for a man who was anything but.

"I like that I surprise you." He took another bite of his cupcake.

Addey looked at her own cupcake, feeling her cheeks warm.

"And what flavor are you eating?" He eyed her plate.

"You couldn't handle it." Addey grinned. "Apple and cinnamon would knock you off your feet."

Declan laughed. The sound was enticing, and it almost made her forget why she needed to cool her attraction to him. Yet, flirting with him was as natural as breathing. When was the last time she flirted with someone? Addey had no idea. She was so busy working and avoiding the men Mom set her up with that the idea of dating someone of her own choice was chucked in the too-hard basket.

"Tell me, what does an event planner such as yourself do on weekends?" He changed the topic with an ease that didn't match the man she'd met or the man who wrote the article she read yesterday.

She shrugged. "Tonight, I'm running a family reunion at one of the restaurants nearby."

"Family reunion, huh? That should be interesting." A frown touched his forehead before it disappeared. "I'll bet there'll be fireworks."

"There might be some truth to that. I've certainly seen fireworks happen at parties," she conceded. "However, I don't expect it at this party."

"Why not?" he asked.

"This family is different. They want it simple and low-key, just a place for the family to eat, share stories, and dance. It's lovely really."

He looked skeptical. "How many families do you know that are Brady Bunch perfect?"

She took a sip of her drink. "Not many." Goodness knows her family was nothing to model off. "But every once and while, people surprise you."

He watched her for a long moment. "They sure do."

She checked her phone and saw the email from Holly with the article he wrote attached. The questions burned and she found her courage.

"So..." she hesitated. "Why did you write that Emily Gilmore article?"

She grabbed her phone, the article still on the screen, and pushed it across the table and watched him take it in.

His smile widened. He pushed the phone back towards her. "It wasn't supposed to get published." He settled back in his seat. "I wrote it as a spoof, a fluff piece. My colleague saw the title over my shoulder and he wanted to read it." His eyebrows made a quick arc, a smile half tugging at one corner of his mouth. "Next thing I know, it's online and making the rounds." He half shrugged, as if to say, what can you do?

"You don't really think these things, do you?" Addey held her breath, her cupcake forgotten.

"Would you think less of me if I said yes?" He trained his intense gaze on her.

Addey sat back and dropped her shoulders. "I don't know...I'm trying to understand."

He grew serious. "You know why the Community Center is being knocked down?"

She stopped and stared, trying to gather herself. She reached for her napkin and pressed it into her fist. This was very dangerous ground she was on. "Because developers bought the building." She made effort to keep her voice even.

"I can't fight that kind of money. No one can." He pushed his plate away, his face closing off.

"You don't like the wealthy, upper-class, whatever you want to call it, do you?" Addey asked.

He scoffed. "What's to like?"

Another reason to put her attraction to him in a box and never open it again.

Addey scrunched the napkin until her fingers hurt. "How can you say that about a world you know nothing about?"

"And you do?" He nailed her with such an intense stare that she couldn't look away.

"I don't try to hate people I'm not familiar with." She pushed her phone towards him, the article still on the screen. "This makes me think that you might have some issues with a certain social group in our community. Aren't you required to be unbiased?" Maybe if she pressed him on this, it would make her dislike him. And then she would be forced to stop being attracted to him.

He pushed the phone away. "You've obviously never met anyone in your life then?"

"Excuse me?"

"No one is unbiased, but my job is to keep my bias from sneaking its way into my work."

"I think you failed." Big time.

He seemed to consider her words, his fingers drumming the table. "Maybe." He nodded towards her phone. "I stand by what I say, and maybe I got a bit carried away. But it doesn't change the fact that those in powerful positions use their influence and their money to achieve their ends with no consideration for the lives of others." His voice grew strong and his eyes bright.

Addey gripped the napkin tighter. "You can't put that on one group of people. Everyone is out to help themselves."

"I don't deny that, but tell me..." He leaned forward, his voice deep. "One rich man's decision has the power to affect many, but the decision of an average Joe has the power to affect just himself. Who has the responsibility to use their wealth and influence to help the community as a whole?"

"'To whom much is given, much is expected?'" She met his gaze, the words ringing true inside her.

"Got it in one," he whispered back. Addey couldn't tear her eyes away from him. It was like she was tumbling around in a clothes dryer and couldn't get out. Lilly appeared by the table, breaking the moment. Addey rolled her shoulders, trying to release the built-up tension.

"Can I get you anything else, guys?" She was looking between them, curiosity and uncertainty lacing her words. She had a box of cupcakes with her.

"I'm fine, thank you." Declan gestured to Addey.

Addey waved her hand. "I'm good, too, thanks."

"Okay, here are the vanilla and caramel cupcakes you ordered to go." She placed the box on the table beside Declan.

"Thanks," he replied.

Lilly left and Addey blurted out the question that had been hovering on her lips before they were interrupted.

"But you can't expect people to do that. Don't they have a right to use their wealth as they see fit?" She shifted, uncomfortable with the whole situation.

"That's why I'll always fight for the right of the little guys—the ones that need a voice. I can deliver that." He drained his coffee and wiped his mouth on the napkin.

"You're a passionate man, Mr. Collins." She eyed him. He stood.

He pulled out his wallet and dropped some bills onto the table and put his cup over the money. "Addey, I do what needs to be done." He moved to go but stopped as he passed her. "See you at George and Martha's in four weeks."

He took the box of cupcakes and left. Addey knew two things for certain. She had to get her parents to ditch the announcement at the party...

...and figure out how to keep the attraction she'd been boxing up safely in check.

Chapter Eight

Addey was heading into enemy territory again. Sunday brunch shouldn't be that painful, but it was. She walked through the black front doors of her parents' palatial, riverfront home, armed with two large cups of coffee and a newspaper under one arm.

"Have you seen this?" Mom accosted her at the doorway and thrust a tablet at her.

Addey brushed her away. "Mom, give me a sec to put this stuff down."

"Vivien, give the girl some space." The voice of Grandmother Hamilton stopped Addey in her tracks. She looked up to find Charlotte Hamilton—her father's mother—sitting in the white, square leather armchair closest to the French doors. *Coiffed* was always the word that came to mind when Addey saw her. With tailored clothes, her ash blond hair cut short to her chin, and long, bony fingers, she might just be the fiercest woman Addey ever met.

"Grandmother, nice to see you." She set the cups on the coffee table and tossed the newspaper beside them. Dad still liked to read a real newspaper, while Mom had been using a tablet for ages.

Addey flopped onto the sofa and bounced a little. Why couldn't her mother buy comfortable furniture? Everything was square or hard. Nothing squashy, nothing you could sink and relax into.

"Are you well?" Addey asked, giving Grandmother her full attention.

"I am, yes, thank you for asking. I've been busy up at Mount Vernon. You know how Christmas is there." She spoke with an easy command, her elbows resting on the edges of the armchair, but her pale blue eyes told Addey she knew more than she was letting on. Grandmother always knew more than she was letting on.

Addey let Grandmother's words, and the unspoken ones, sink in. While she wasn't close to her grandmother, a sort of unspoken friendship existed between them. Grandmother had a will of iron, but she managed to couple it with the ability to stay out of people's business. It was a quality Addey admired.

"I was at Mount Vernon the other day, sorting out a few things for the party," Addey said, taking a sip of her drink. She gestured with her cup toward the newly-decorated French doors that opened onto the expansive deck overlooking the river. "That's really pretty stenciling, Mom."

Her mother gave her what was meant to be a warm smile, though Addey felt none of it. "Thank you. I had the corners frosted with holly to lend some spirit to the room."

There was already plenty of spirit in the room—just not the kind that came from window treatments.

"Yes, some of the ladies saw you there and let me know." Grandmother had been high up in the Mount Vernon Ladies' Association several years ago. The group owned, operated, and maintained the house and its grounds year round.

"How often are you at Mount Vernon, Charlotte?" Mom piped up from her spot diagonally opposite Grandmother.

She sipped her tea. "Not as much as I used to be. Sometimes we get so caught up in things, we can't see the forest for the trees."

"That's very deep for a Sunday morning." Addey eyed her warily.

"Yes, what are you getting at?" Mom added, as she, too, sipped her tea.

Grandmother gave a wave of her hand. "I suppose it is. I simply meant that it took more of my time, that I didn't do anything else."

"So then, you're glad to be less involved?" Addey ventured, filling in the blanks.

Grandmother smiled, her teeth straight and dentist white. "Yes, I think that sums it up nicely, Adelaide."

"The article, have you seen it yet?" Mom piped up, reigniting the topic she'd started on when Addey arrived.

Addey crossed her ankles and shifted, trying to get more comfortable. "I haven't looked at the news yet this morning."

Mom pushed it onto her lap, open to an article with a very familiar title: *What's So Wrong with Emily Gilmore?* Her heart sank. *Why did Mom have to see this?* Addey rubbed her forehead. Anything would be better than sitting here under the microscope of Mom and Grandmother. Clearly Declan's article had been picked up by the bigger Washington D.C. paper and was making the rounds online.

"Read it and tell me this man isn't on a mission to take our family down." Mom started wringing the corner of her white day jacket.

"I read it this morning, Vivien. It says nothing about this family, or any family for that matter," Grandmother said.

Addey pretended to read the article. She put the device down and gave her mother a sympathetic look. But all she could see was Declan in the café yesterday, expounding on his very biased views of the class she belonged to. Her stomach cramped and she worked hard to remain calm. Her parents needed to drop the building announcement from the party.

"I agree with Grandmother. He's not talking about our family. He's just making a general comment, I think. Albeit a very bad comment."

Mom actually smiled at Addey's words.

Dad came in and stopped when he saw them all, his eyes widening in surprise. "What, no arguing? It must your influence, Mother." He strode over and dropped a kiss on Grandmother's cheek.

"Hand me that other coffee, Adelaide." Dad sat down beside Mom and reached for the cup, which Addey handed over, along with the newspaper.

"What were we discussing so cordially before?" Dad settled back on the couch, one leg propped on the other.

"Declan Collins's rather unpleasant article. It takes jabs at our social world." Grandmother sounded very unconcerned.

"Of course, it does," Dad boomed. "Would you expect anything less from the man?"

"Can we talk about something else, please?" Mom huffed. She turned to Addey. "What have you been doing this weekend?"

Addey's mind reeled back to yesterday's chance meeting with Declan at the café. She could clearly see him in her mind's eyes. His dark eyes alight with passion as he talked about the rights of the people, she could hear the strong voice calling her to sit with him, and mostly she remembered the heart-stopping smile he delivered at her arrival to the shop. Oh yeah, she wasn't telling them a thing about her weekend.

"You're blushing, darling." Mom's gaze was like a laser.

"It's hot in here, that's all." To prove her point, she removed her denim jacket and put it on the sofa. She took another drink of her coffee and eyed the clock. Still an hour to go.

Dad peered at her over the newspaper. Grandmother lost her disinterested look, leaning forward in her seat, curiosity blazing.

Mom smiled gleefully. "So, who is the man who has inspired your flushed cheeks?"

Addey spat her coffee out and it sprayed across the coffee table. "Mom!"

"Adelaide, really…" Mom chided as she stood up and called for someone to clean it up.

"I'm not the one making wild assumptions." Addey tried to wipe the liquid up with a tissue she found in her purse. Within moments a maid came in with a rag.

"So, there is someone." Mom clasped her hands together. "Who is he?" She leaned forward, eyes bright, her smile eager.

Addey had to stop this before it got out of control. Jumping up, she went over to the table that was placed against the wall, wrinkling her nose at the small plates filled with smaller portions of food. For some strange reason, Mom always had them eat their food in the front sitting room when Addey came over. It was just another sign that Addey wasn't worth the extra effort of using the actual dining room.

Taking a piece of the cheese and dill vol-au-vent, she hid a grimace and swallowed, using the moment to stall and attempt to push all thoughts of Declan from her mind. "There is no one, okay? My weekend was filled with running a family reunion yesterday, and now being here today, that's it."

Grandmother sat back in her chair, her expression neutral, but Addey could feel her stare. She reached for minuscule apple, rhubarb, and raspberry tart. The sweet mixed with tart flavor exploded in her mouth. Okay, so maybe brunch was worth it to eat this again.

"A family reunion? They're always so unpredictable." Mom stayed on topic, but Addey could plainly see by the brightness in her eyes that she wanted to know more about the handsome man Addey had apparently been seeing.

"Well, that's true, but this one was lovely. Everyone was happy to catch up and if there were any simmering issues, they didn't boil over that night." Addey replied, enjoying not bickering with either of her parents for once.

"So, everything is on track for the Christmas party?" Mom stirred her cup of tea.

"Yes. Your emails last week really helped clarify the guest list, the menu, and the music. The RSVP date is next week, and I've already heard back from several guests. Everything is running smoothly." She gave them her confident client smile.

Mom looked pleased. "Good. I want this to be a party to remember."

Addey refrained from reaching for another tart. It was a perfect opening. "Speaking of the party, can I run an idea by you both?"

Mom and Dad stopped what they were doing and looked at each other, before regarding her wearily. Even Grandmother leaned forward just a touch while she sipped her tea.

"Don't look so suspicious, this is just something I've been thinking about since last week." Addey injected confidence into her voice. She was going to have to work hard to sell them on this.

"We're listening," Dad said evenly, though his arms were already crossed over his chest, and Mom's expression seemed tight. Braced, probably.

Addey drew a breath. "About the building launch...can I ask why you want to do it at the Christmas party?"

Dad's face darkened. "What does that matter?"

"I'm just wanting to put the best spin on this, and maybe, with such bad press over the past year, it might be better to make the official launch at New Year's. You know—new year, new building—"

"We decided it would be done at the party, and our friends are expecting the announcement," Mom interrupted.

"I thought you said you'd support this development—regardless of your feelings." Dad's voice was low and hard.

Addey held up her hand, scrambling to stop this from going further south. "I am, Dad. I was just making a suggestion. I want the best for you both." She gentled her tone and threw out an encouraging smile.

Dad's face softened. "I appreciate what you're wanting to do, but our answer is no. We will launch at the Christmas party." He stood up and checked his watch.

Addey's heart sank at the finality of his words—there was no way out of this.

"Well, I think we've talked enough for one morning," Dad announced.

Addey took the cue, relief whooshing through her at being able to leave. She grabbed her things. Dad nodded at her and Mom gave her a stiff hug.

"Don't think I don't know you've met someone." Mom air-kissed Addey on the cheek, her hands firm on Addey's shoulders. Mom whispered, pulling back from Addey and giving her a knowing look. Addey's cheeks warmed again, which brought a triumphant smile from her mother.

They would hate her, just like Declan would, when this all came out. She fought the urge to run and, instead, walked confidently from the house.

She was almost to the car when Grandmother's voice stopped her. The older woman was purposeful in her stride, giving off an air of command that she never relinquished.

"Your poker face has improved over the years." Grandmother gave Addey an approving smile.

"Thanks...I think." Addey fiddled with the strap of her purse.

"But I can still see straight through you. I know who the reporter is."

Figures. The big question was, what would Grandmother do about it?

Grandmother continued. "Your parents don't seem to care who shows up to review the party, which is good for you."

"How do you know who the reporter is?" She didn't know why she bothered asking the question. She knew the answer the minute Grandmother replied.

"When you were at Mount Vernon the other day. Some of the ladies spotted you talking with a rather handsome man."

"That could have been anyone..." Addey readjusted her purse strap.

Grandmother stared her down. "But it wasn't, was it?"

Addey shook her head. "Are you going to tell them?" Panic curled in her belly.

"Darling, if I was going to say anything, I would have said it already." Grandmother's lips tipped into a playful smile.

"You think this is funny, don't you?" Addey cocked her head to one side and rested one hand on her hip.

"Well, *funny* isn't the word I would go for. More *amusing.*" Her smile disappeared. "I make it a point not to get involved in my son's life. That goes for Vivien and you."

"So...that means what?"

"It means, I'm going to enjoy watching these events unfold. But a word of advice, my dear..."

So much for not interfering. "What's that?"

Grandmother laid a hand on her arm. "I think you should tell him who you are."

Addey stepped back. "I was going to, but that article..."

"Oh, that's nothing." She raised an eyebrow. "The issue is, he's going to find out one way or another, and it's better coming from you…"

"He'll hate me and give the party a bad review. My business sale won't go through if the party gets eviscerated. You know Mom and Dad want this event to go off without a hitch, and Declan is not just a *hitch*." Addey struggled for a breath. "He's an iceberg and my parents are the *Titanic*," she hissed, afraid that even saying his name here would bring them running.

"But it's not your fault that Declan was given the job—"

"They'll still blame me," Addey said, bitterness laced every word.

"He's already going to struggle to write a good review, so don't worry about that." Grandmother gave a small chuckle. "What does it matter if he hates you?"

"My business is at stake here." Addey closed her eyes. "No matter what I do, they're going to hate me."

"Who?" Grandmother spoke. Addey opened her eyes and saw the frown on her face.

Addey remained silent.

"You mean your parents?"

"Well, they don't love me." Addey covered her mouth. "Sorry. I didn't mean that."

"Of course you did, or you wouldn't have said it." Grandmother's gaze was like lasers.

Addey winced.

"I may not get involved in my son's life but that doesn't always mean I agree with everything he does." Grandmother let out a barely audible sigh. "Now, I still think you need to tell this reporter who you are. It's only fair."

Addey nodded faintly. Did Grandmother not approve of the way her parents dumped her on Granny? For a moment, she allowed hope to blossom in her heart.

"Tell him, Adelaide." Grandmother repeated, before following Mom and dropping an air-kiss on Addey's cheek.

"I'll set up a meeting with him." Even as she said the words, her stomach churned.

"Good girl. Now let me know when you are next coming to Mount Vernon, and I'll arrange to meet you." She left Addey standing in the stone driveway with the towering dogwood trees.

Grandmother was right. Addey had no choice.

Declan needed to know who she was.

***

"Mommy, look, it's the camel!"

"Anabel, slow down!" The mom called after her excited daughter.

Declan followed the mother of the little girl at a much slower pace. He wasn't in the mood for watching a camel but he was here dutifully fulfilling his last set of assignments. He sighed and clenched his jaw.

The wooden slatted fence was surrounded by young kids and parents, all taking photos of Aladdin the Christmas Camel. A yearly feature at Mount Vernon, drawing crowds every year.

"Mr. Collins!" a voice called out.

Declan headed towards Sarah, the college-aged guide with blonde braids who was showing him around.

"So, tell me why there's a camel here at Mount Vernon?" Declan pulled out his phone and pressed record. "You mind?" he asked Sarah as he nodded to the recording.

"Not at all," she smiled. "In 1787, George Washington had a camel brought in to entertain his guests—"

"Any guests in particular?" Declan interjected.

"No, since it was Christmas time, it was mainly just family around, so pretty quiet. We don't know exactly why he did it, just that he did." Sarah's eyes were bright, and her voice bubbled with enthusiasm.

"You like working here?"

"Oh, yes. I studied history at college, particularly the Revolution, and working here is just a bonus."

Declan nodded as he watched the camel wander around the yard, eating. "The camel seems okay with the crowds," he noted.

"Oh, yes, he's very calm. We have a hard time getting the kids to not touch him, though. Washington was also known to pay for other exotic animals to visit the grounds." Sarah seemed happy to talk and add information and Declan wasn't going to stop her. He had to admit that this was more interesting than he thought it would be.

"What other animals?" Now he was genuinely curious.

"Elephants, tigers, sea lions..." As she rattled off the names, Declan seriously wondered how the man had managed that. He was impressed.

"It must have been strange for folks back then to see something like a camel," he commented. The smell of hay in the air was strong but not overpowering. It added to the farm-like feel.

Sarah nodded, enthusiasm bubbling from her. "Oh, it was. I mean you had to pay for the privilege, of course, but back then it was the only way to see things outside of the limited world they knew."

Ha. Paying for the privilege. That's how the world worked. He nodded at Sarah, even as his thoughts ran back to Addey and the cupcakes he hadn't taken to his mother. He hadn't gone to visit after all, feeling too worked up, and he didn't want to worry Mom any more than she already was. That's what he told himself anyway. Truth was, Addey had gotten under his skin, and he didn't know how to get her out.

Anabel, the same little girl he saw before, ran past, her pigtails flying in the cold air, her mother slowly jogging behind her.

Addey was certainly interesting, but something was...off with her. He knew it from the moment he met her. She didn't like to talk about herself, but then again, he wasn't keen on talking about his personal life. In fact, he avoided it as much as possible, so maybe he should cut her some slack there. At least he wouldn't see her again until the party.

An idea surfaced into this mind. "Sarah, what do you know about the Christmas dinner being held here in December?" Might as well do some leg work now. Find out what he could about Addey without asking her directly.

Sarah grew thoughtful. "Well, it's a really fancy Christmas celebration, lots of the 'who's who' in society will to be there. It's Addey's Bennet's brainchild. She does fabulous events."

"Know anything more?" he prompted, needing more information.

She shrugged. "No, sorry. It's the first of its kind this close to Christmas, if that helps."

When Anabel ran up asking questions about Aladdin, Sarah bent down to talk to her. Declan pressed stop on his phone and signaled to Sarah he was done.

"I'll be in contact if I need any more information," he said. Sarah glanced up and nodded with a smile before returning her attention to the little girl.

Declan's thoughts whirled while he made his way to the parking lot. The Hamiltons were powerful people, and Addey was an event planner, so it was natural they would ask someone like her to pull this thing off. Still, something nagged at him, and he couldn't let it go.

And speaking of not letting things go—the guilt that he hadn't visited Mom in a while tugged once again. He had to make it happen. But seeing her there was a stark reminder in all the ways he'd failed her.

Chapter Nine

Addey stirred the eggs in the pot and frowned. "I thought scrambled eggs were supposed to be easy?"

Carmel leaned over and peered at Addey's cooking. "Um, I think you let it sit for too long. You have to keep stirring it."

Monday night cooking class was a new tradition the two of them started back at the beginning of September. A way to try something new. Neither of them were great at cooking when they first attended the class. But judging by Carmel's fluffy, bright yellow scrambled eggs, she was quickly becoming a master.

The instructor, Frances, a local chef, walked up and tapped Addey's pot, then looked between her and Carmel. Addey could have sworn the older woman suppressed a sigh.

"Remember, the next two weeks are going to be intensive Christmas-themed cookie making. Make sure your partner is with you so you can get through it all."

As if Addey didn't need any more reminders of how bad a cook she was. "Keep stirring and take it off before it becomes like rubber, dear." The last word seemed to be squeezed between Frances's teeth.

"Too late." Addey poked at her wobbly eggs as Frances walked away. "At least they're a nice yellow."

"You can share mine." Carmel carefully tipped her eggs onto her plate and arranged them next to the salad and Turkish bread.

Addey tried to be careful with her eggs, but they didn't leave the pan. She scraped them out, cringing with every drag of the wooden spoon. The eggs ended up in a gelatinous clump next to her bread. "I can't eat this."

Carmel put her hand over her mouth, her eyes bright, her shoulders shaking.

Addey pointed her spoon at her friend. "You're enjoying this."

A clump of egg fell from the spoon and plopped onto the plate.

They burst out laughing.

They sat down at the table in the kitchen bays of The Quiet Chef—the name of the school they attended. The class was located in Belle View in an old brick two-story building that was previously a clothing store. "You know, Frances isn't *quiet*. It's such a weird name for the business."

Carmel cut her Turkish bread in half and put some on Addey's plate. Next went the eggs. "Maybe she didn't start it. Maybe it's not her business."

Addey tucked into the food. "This is so good. Ever think about changing careers?"

Carmel rolled her eyes. "It's scrambled eggs, Addey. You'll get better. Practice is all you need."

"Thanks." Addey bit into Carmel's light and fluffy scrambled eggs. She closed her eyes. "This is so good."

Carmel grinned, taking her own bite. "It's pretty good." She eyed her over a mouthful of salad.

Addey sensed the mood change. "What?"

Carmel paused, fork halfway to her plate. "Have you made a decision about telling Declan who you are?"

Addey cut her bread. "No, but I need to do something, and soon."

Carmel put her fork down. "I'd say that's a good idea."

Addey shifted in her seat. If she told him, her career would be over, and her parents would hate her—again. Holly and Nina would be out of a job, and the pay from Heritage Oaks wouldn't keep the lights on in her townhouse.

"You're thinking of all the worst-case scenarios, aren't you?"

"I'll lose everything if he finds out," Addey whispered.

Carmel frowned. "You're being a defeatist. You can't help who your parents are any more than he can. He's been hired to review a Christmas party."

Addey took a quick breath. "It's actually a surprise launch of the new apartment building replacing the Community Center." Addey didn't look away as she spoke.

Carmel's mouth dropped open. "You really need to tell him. It's a conflict of interest for him. He would need to remove himself from the review."

"I tried to get my parents to change it to just a Christmas party, but they said no." The hollow feeling in her gut expanded.

"Just tell him. It's never as bad as you think it's going to be." Carmel's no-nonsense words cut through her whirling thoughts.

She took a breath and nodded. "You're right. I mean, if I could change my last name at eighteen, I can tell Declan Collins who I am."

Carmel grinned. "That's the spirit. I'll be praying for you."

Addey only nodded. It was nice to know someone was praying for her, as she didn't do it for herself. "I'll send him a message in the morning."

***

"Need any help this morning?" Declan asked Eli as he climbed out of his car. He blew on his hands to warm them. The air was cold and the sky was cloudy. Declan tried to ignore the sign out the front of the Community Center but he couldn't. It was a stark reminder of his failure. So, he focused on Eli instead.

"Nope, I just got back, actually." Eli opened the back of the van and started pulling out crates of food.

Declan raised his eyebrows. "We usually don't leave until six-thirty."

"They didn't have much today, just the two crates."

The Community Center picked up food from a nearby bakery that donated leftovers to the Center. Some weeks it was more like a feast and others, like today, more like famine.

He grabbed a large crate and walked behind Eli into the Community Center. The kitchen was quiet this morning. May and Georgia, the ladies who ran the kitchen, were not in yet. He and Eli put the crates down and walked back outside.

"I thought I'd visit Mom this morning after I grab breakfast," Declan said as they stood by their cars.

"She'll be pleased to see you." Eli nodded. "About time you visited."

Declan kicked the ground with his shoes. "I chickened out last week." The run-in with Addey had rattled him. But he knew it was more than that. He used the conversation with Addey as an excuse to avoid going to Heritage Oaks. He hated that his mom was there and he hated that he couldn't look after her in her own home.

He'd failed her.

"Then it's good you're going today." Eli zipped up his black jacket.

"Thanks, Eli."

"For what?"

Declan drove his hands into his jacket pockets and bunched them into fists. "For not making a big deal about it."

Eli slapped him on the shoulder. "Dec, I learned long ago that you'll do what you want when you're ready and not a minute sooner."

"Take it easy, old man," Declan teased. His phone buzzed, and he pulled it out of his pocket to see a message from a number not in his contacts. Curious, he opened the text.

Morning Declan, Addey Bennet here. Can we arrange a meeting for today? It's important. Thanks.

The intrigue that lit inside him couldn't be snuffed out. He was going to see her again. This time would be different. He would apologize for being an idiot on Saturday.

"I'll talk to you later." Eli interrupted his thoughts.

Declan jerked his head up. "Sure thing."

Declan stood there, the apartment sign seemingly glaring at him. He looked at the sign and pressed down the bitterness that never went away. His hand hovered over the message he typed out. At the last second, he erased it and pressed the number instead. He waited, holding his breath while the phone rang.

***

Addey's hand jerked when her phone rang. She stared at the number and knew it was Declan, even though she hadn't saved his number in her phone yet.

He's calling. Her palms grew sweaty at the thought of talking to him, of telling him who she was. Taking a calming breath, she grabbed the phone before it stopped ringing.

"Hello?" she said in her most professional voice.

"Addey? It's Declan Collins. I received a message from you just now." He sounded as professional as she did.

Did he know he had a great phone voice? Solid, clear, and just deep enough to be sexy. How could he be both irritating and alluring at the same time? Addey's cheeks flamed and she ran a hand over her face. "Um, yes. I hope it wasn't too early. I like to get on jump on the day." *You're babbling.*

Declan chuckled and she could picture his smile, the one he gave her at the café on Saturday. "No, it's fine. I'm a morning person too. You wanted to arrange a time to meet?"

"Yes." Addey chewed her lip. "Today, if possible."

"Okay, well, I'm full up today. But if you're free tomorrow evening I can meet you after my hockey game. There's a café nearby. We can talk then." His words came out in a rush. Was he nervous? Did that mean he was he interested in her? She was so out of practice. Addey rested her head on the desk. What would he think if he could see her now? That didn't matter. Addey shook the thought away. Even if he was on same crazy planet, attracted to her, the minute he found out who he was, he would run in the opposite direction.

"Yes, that's fine," Addey replied, still keeping her voice clear and upbeat.

"Eight good?" He coughed. "At the café on the corner, across from the ice stadium?" He sounded more in control now.

"Yes, that's great. See you tomorrow."

She hung up and just sat there staring at her phone, breathing hard. This was going to be a disaster. All of it—her attraction to him. Maybe his to her? And the cherry on top, the fact that he hated her family. She felt like she was in a bad rom-com, and she couldn't get out.

Chapter Ten

Declan's heart pounded as he approached his mother's room, a bouquet of daffodils in one hand and a fresh box of caramel and vanilla cupcakes in the other. He couldn't believe he'd waited almost a whole extra week to see his mom. The guilt ate away at him.

He hated the smell of this place—cafeteria food mixed with the smell of aging. It seemed like death lurked in the hallways, waiting to steal those living inside, slowly, day by day, until there was nothing left but an empty shell. Then they were carted away, and others took their place. There was no dignity in this life.

Pausing outside his mother's room, he took several deep breaths in an effort to steady himself. He had no idea what might be in store for him when he stepped through the doors. He took one final fortifying breath and knocked quietly before entering. Mom was sitting in her recliner by the open French doors that led out to the garden. She was crocheting and tapping her foot to the sound of Frank Sinatra crooning softly from the little speaker they'd brought her that sat on the table beside the recliner.

"Hi Mom," he said, his steps tentative as he crossed the room. She turned, a smile spread across her face, her eyes wide and bright as he got closer. His heart lurched and guilt flooded through him. He should have come sooner, how could he leave her here for four weeks and not visit? What kind of son lived so close and couldn't man up enough to visit his sick mother?

"Declan, come here, my boy." She reached for him, starting to stand but Declan picked up his pace and reached her first.

"Sit down, Mom." He tried to gently push her back into the chair but she shook her head firmly. She hugged him and Declan stood there for long minutes hugging her back. She wasn't frail, but she was far too young to be in such a place. He and Nicky had been left with no other option.

She pulled away enough so she could see him clearly, her gaze earnest. "You look…" she paused as if trying to find the words, her face scrunched in concentration. He waited her out. "You look tired. You've been…working…busy…" The words came out slower, like she was trying hard to find the right ones. Something that happened more and more. "I can't find the right words." Her shoulders sank and her eyes darkened. "I can't find the right words," she repeated.

He gently led her back and helped her sit. "You're doing just fine, Mom."

He looked around and pulled up a plastic chair beside her. "I brought you something." He held out the flowers and the cupcakes.

Her eyes lit up when she saw them. "Oh, flowers, thank you! Are those cupcakes? What taste are they?" She opened the box and inspected them. Mispronouncing and replacing words were both common for her now.

"Caramel and vanilla."

She put them aside on the little table.

He rested his elbows on his knees. "I'm sorry I didn't come sooner."

She held up the bright pink wool of half-finished work. "It's okay. It's hard. For all of us." Her smile was weak, and Declan hated himself all over again.

"What are you crocheting?"

"I'm making a blanket for..." She sighed as she tried to get the right words. She reached for a little notebook that she kept with names of people and important dates and flicked through it. "Maude...she's in room fourteen." She smiled triumphantly. "She's one of the older residents. I thought she might like it."

"Always thinking of others." He gave her hand a squeeze.

"I can still remember how to do this at least." She moved quickly with the wool, and it gave him hope. The doctor said being creative was one of the ways to slow the disease's progress. Early onset Alzheimer's. He hated saying it, so he tried not to. He was still amazed at how she could struggle with words and memories for what seemed like ages and then, for a while, it would seem like there was nothing wrong.

"Tell me, are you still on that crusade about the Community Center?"

Declan flinched and saw her watching him with those knowing eyes.

"I haven't been working on that for months," he supplied, threads of dread creeping around his chest as he waited to see if she would remember.

She nodded. "I know they forced you off that, but you never give up, Declan. You're like a dog with a bone."

He breathed a sigh of relief even as he hated her words. She was too smart for her own good most of the time. She smiled slyly at him. "Don't sulk, you know I'm right and I wouldn't have you any other way." She reached over and patted his cheek.

Her smile faded and she turned serious. "You know, I'm not dying any time soon."

"I know." He managed the words out around the lump that formed in his throat.

"My diagnosis is not the end, Declan, and it's scary for me as well, but I want to live the best life I can while I'm alive."

"Don't, Mom. We're not talking about this." His voice was strangled.

"Have you told your father?" The words were like a bomb going off inside him. He sucked in a breath and tried to remain calm. If he got upset, it would make her upset, and then a downward spiral would hit them all.

"No, and I'm not going to."

She watched him for a long time. "You'll have to forgive him one day."

"Well, that's not today." He bit out the words, his fists clenching . He would die before he let his father know about Mom's diagnosis. Edward Sheridan was in jail where he belonged.

"I want him to know before I die that I forgive him," she said simply. He couldn't look at her, but he knew that voice. It was the voice that had him running when he was little whenever she caught him doing something wrong.

"What do you have on the schedule today?" Declan reached for the flowers and took them out of the paper. He stood and found a vase on top of the slim wardrobe.

"The girl who runs the social things is having a Frank Sinatra Day next week. Can you come?" Mom's foot kept tapping, but he noticed she had the notebook back in her hand. He could see words—*Frank Sinatra, Thursday Next Week*— were heavily underlined.

Declan ducked into the attached bathroom and filled the vase with water. He set it on the table with the flowers nestled in. "I wouldn't miss it for the world."

"Will you save me a dance?" Mom's hand trembled as she put the notebook down.

Declan nodded. "Yes, Mom, I'll save you a dance." He didn't know if Mom could feel the life leeching out of the room. Maybe it was just him. To change the mood, he pulled the cupcakes over. "Want to share one with me?" He pulled one out, cut it in half and put it on a little plate on the table.

Mom took a dainty bite. "We used to do this, didn't we?"

"We sure did." Declan polished his half off in one single bite. He was instantly reminded of Addey at Miss Cupcake. He was seeing her tonight. A curl of hope rose in his chest. Shaking himself, he pulled himself back into the present. "You remember the dining table overlooking the park across the street? We would sit there and eat our cupcake on Saturday afternoons—"

Mom's brows pulled together. "What are you talking about, Edward? Our kitchen overlooked the pool. How can you forget such a thing?" Mom put down the cupcake and narrowed her eyes. "Where have you been lately? I've had people coming to the door asking for you for days. Edward, tell me what's going on?"

Declan counted to twenty, fighting off the sinking feeling that threatened to overwhelm him. Once he got to twenty, he looked back at his mother.

"I've been busy, Susannah. You know I've got everything in hand." Declan spoke calmly, but every word was torture to get out. Being mistaken for his father was worse than Mom forgetting him.

"I trust you, Edward. Just talk to me more often, would you?" She had resumed her crocheting, the cupcake now forgotten.

Declan closed his eyes and managed a nod. "I'd better get back to work." He heaved himself off the chair, tucked it back in its place. "I'll be back tomorrow to see you. Nicky will be by Friday or Saturday."

"Nicky is in school," Mom shot back.

"Of course, she is." Declan tried to give her a goodbye hug, but she was busy crocheting. "See you later."

She didn't reply as he left the room. The trail of regret and failure felt like a chain dragging behind him, pulling him down.

***

Addey sat in the parking lot of the ice stadium, trying to breathe steadily, fingers drumming on the steering wheel. She was early. Should she wait at the mall, or was it better to wait here? Frankly, the thought of sitting in a café with him when she dropped her bomb didn't sound appealing. Maybe it was better to do it here, standing in the parking lot. A bit like ripping off a band-aid.

Her phone rang and she saw it was her mom. Addey stared at the lit screen and debated if it was worth answering. Probably not right before meeting Declan. She massaged her temple. The headache that had started the minute she'd messaged Declan yesterday had only intensified as the day wore on. Last night she'd popped some Advil to ease the pain and to get some sleep. Talking to Mom would only bring it right back. But then if she didn't answer, it would be harder tomorrow.

Suppressing a sigh, Addey picked up the phone. "Hi, Mom."

"Adelaide, I haven't heard from you about the Children's Benefit. I need to know."

Addey groaned. "I forgot, Mom, I'm sorry. It's been a busy few days."

"I'm sure it has." Mom's clipped words pressed against Addey, making her squirm.

She watched the ice rink and tried to imagine Declan skating, hockey stick in hand and the image more than intrigued her. She found herself wanting to see it. Which was insane. She barely knew this man. All she had to do was think about his Emily Gilmore article and that doused any notions she had about him. He hated her family and anyone in that circle.

"Adelaide, are you listening?" Mom's sharp tone yanked her back into the conversation.

"Yes, of course." She touched the steering wheel, needing to feel something under her fingertips. "I can't make the Benefit. Thanks for inviting me, though."

There was silence on the other end of the line.

Addey's heart sank.

"Well then," Mom snipped. "I thought we were making headway. I thought we were working together with my mother's inheritance—" The words were like a steel knife. Mom kept talking, harsh words buried under a deadly calm tone. "That money was meant to bring us closer, but you've only seen it as a way to start your business, and then you'll move on and forget us, like you've always done." Mom's voice cracked at the end.

"That's not true, Mom. None of that is." Addey wanted to cry, but she held it back. "How can you say that? Granny never wanted that money to come between us. She always wanted us closer."

"Oh yes, then changing your name from Hamilton to Bennet was a sign of how close we are." There was venom in every word. Addey flinched.

"You guys let me live with Granny. You didn't say no. I was five." Addey whispered, her voice hoarse.

"We didn't expect you to stay away forever."

"I see you every week, Mom." Addey didn't know how to have a conversation with her mother. She didn't know which way was up when it came to this relationship. Why had Granny asked to have her and, she wondered for the millionth time, why did they let her go?

"I'm not having this conversation." Mom's stiff voice cut through Addey. "Have a good evening."

The silence was deafening. Addey pressed end on her phone and let it drop into the console. It bounced and clattered to the floor. There would be repercussions for this later. Why did everything have to have so many consequences? Why couldn't her "no" just be accepted? Why did she constantly have to be someone she didn't want to be?

"No matter what I do, no one is happy." Her choked voice echoed around the car. A tear rolled down her cheek and Addey swiped it away. *God, thank you for Granny.* She checked her face in the visor mirror and found it pale, but it was cold outside. Maybe Declan wouldn't notice. She pinched her cheeks and applied some lip gloss.

She climbed out of the car and squared her shoulders. Time to rip off the band-aid.

Chapter Eleven

Declan skated to a stop, breathing hard, sweat dripping off him. His team had lost, but the game had been a good, hard battle.

"Better luck next week," Camden puffed as they exited the rink.

Declan peeled off his shoulder pads, dumped his helmet and removed his skates, then checked his watch. It was almost eight. He had enough time to grab a quick shower in the lockers before he met Addey.

"Somewhere to be?" Camden quirked an eyebrow as he pulled his skates off.

"Work thing." Declan kept his face down as he stored his skates in his sports bag.

"This late? That's odd." Camden's curiosity was evident in his voice.

"Don't you have a senator to guard?"

"If you call driving him to and from his house guarding," Camden snorted. He eased himself out of his skates. "But don't think I didn't notice the topic change. You've been distracted all night."

Declan ignored him.

"I'll see you at the next game," Camden said.

"See you." Delcan waved, heading to the lockers.

Ten minutes and a hot shower later, he shouldered through the rink doors, the blast of cool air welcoming after the steamy locker room.

Declan adjusted the bag on his shoulder, hockey stick in his other hand. Casting a glance at the mall across from the rink, he upped his speed and went to drop his equipment at his SUV. He got no more than three steps when he saw her.

Addey was leaning against her car in the parking lot. He slowed his steps and smiled. She returned the smile, but even from here, he could tell it was fake. He slowed his steps, his gut tightening. As he got closer, he could clearly see her tight lips and pale face, and even still, with her hair swept down her shoulders, she was gorgeous.

"Hey." He spoke softly, almost afraid of what she had to say.

She tried to smile, but it didn't meet her eyes. "Thanks for meeting with me."

"It sounded important." Declan rested his stick against her car—a deep blue sedan. "Do you still want to grab a coffee?" The fact that she met him here, rather than at the café had him worried.

"I got here early and sitting here was easier..." She trailed off and went a shade paler.

"Addey, is everything okay?" Declan took a step closer. "I know we don't know each other well and," he aimed a smile, wanting to ease the troubles off her shoulders, "I don't make the best first impression, or in our case, second impression."

This won him a faint smile and he cheered inside.

"But whatever it is, it can't be that bad. This have something to do with the party?"

Addey met his gaze, her eyes bright with emotion. "Yes and no. Maybe."

"Then let me put my stuff away and we'll have coffee, okay?" He picked up his stick, watching for her reply. She nodded and this time the smile reached her eyes.

When he came back, she had a bit more color, and her frown had softened. "Shall we?" He took the lead, Addey matching him stride for stride, and he was reminded of how tall she was.

They found the little café tucked away in the corner of the mall. Addey led them to a seat in the far corner, and Declan tried not to admire how well her jeans and boots fit her. He was unsuccessful, but as he slipped into his seat, he put his professional demeanor on. This was not a date. A flicker of disappointment raced through him, but he didn't let it linger. Life was nothing but people letting you down, so Declan tried not to dwell on things too much.

Except the Community Center. That was the one thing he clung to like a burr on a saddle, and even with all his efforts, it had still failed. See, this is why he hated committing, because no matter how hard he worked, nothing was ever guaranteed. Look at his mom, dying in a nursing home...

"Now you look like you've got a fierce fight going on inside." Addey's words, tempered by a smile, pulled him up.

Declan relaxed his shoulders. "Sorry. My thoughts get away from me sometimes."

"Unpleasant thoughts?" Addey sat back, the light in the café turner her hair a deeper shade of auburn, her sea-green eyes deeper. She was stunning and Declan was sure she didn't know it.

"No unpleasant thoughts right now." His voice sounded scratchy.

She met his gaze and held it for several long seconds. When she looked away, he saw her cheeks flush. So, the attraction he felt was mutual, but why then did she look like she'd been given a terminal diagnosis or something? "I'll get us drinks. My treat. What would you like?"

"I'll pay my share." She started to stand, but Declan beat her to it.

"Let's let the newspaper pay for this, then, since this is a work meeting."

Addey chewed her bottom lip and finally nodded. "Okay. I'll have a hot chocolate, thank you."

"Coming right up." He hurried to the counter and placed their order to the harried-looking barista, stepping out of the way of the customer behind him. He rocked on his heels, using all the self-control he could muster to not peer over his shoulder and watch Addey as he waited. What was so important that they needed this meeting? The barista handed him the drinks.

Declan returned with her hot chocolate, and his black coffee, and sat down. Addey had shredded one of the napkins into little pieces.

"Thanks for this." She took a careful sip of the steaming drink. "How long have you played hockey?"

Declan sipped his own drink. She wanted to make small talk then. He'd let her lead the conversation and see where it went. Besides, he didn't want to leave her company so fast anyway.

"I played through school growing up, found a team here. It's a good way to burn off work stress." He shrugged, watching her.

"Where did you grow up? Your bio in the newspaper doesn't say." She was now taking the shredded napkin and scrunching the pieces in her fingers.

"California." Declan's shoulders tensed. A default whenever anything from his past life came up.

Light diffused across Addey's face. "California boy, huh? Do you surf?"

Declan tried to smile despite the weight pressing in. "I never learned." He hoped she didn't want to pry more into his life, because Addey Bennet would find herself out of luck.

"Do you ever go home much?" Addey's eyes focused on him in a way that kept Declan on edge. Like she could see more than he wanted to share.

"To California?" He gripped his mug. "No. Not much family left there. No point going where you're not wanted." Now where had that come from? He mentally shook himself. This conversation needed to move on.

Addey's shoulders relaxed as she took a longer drink.

"So..." He wrapped his hands around his mug. "What do I own the pleasure of your company?" He lit his voice and relaxed into his seat.

Addey looked around the café before her gaze landed back on his. "I guess I wanted to ask about your family before I told you a story about mine."

***

Addey's heart tripped as she looked at Declan, his knuckles white on his coffee mug as he'd talked—very minimally—about his family. His last comment had filled her with both hope and sadness. Hope that he might understand the pain that family can bring, but also sadness that he knew that kind of familial hurt. And she sensed it was deep. Whatever was in his thoughts appeared on his face like words in a book. Addey found herself wanting to erase them and make him smile, the same way he did when he walked out of the stadium and saw her.

Addey had felt awful before he appeared, but the sight of him—wide shoulders, dark hair damp from a shower, bag slung over his shoulder, hockey stick in hand—had nearly taken her breath away. The man was hot and a danger to her well-planned life.

"I like stories." His quiet words prompted her back to the reason she was here. *Band-aid ripping.* Addey took a fortifying drink of her hot chocolate and met his steady gaze. Not a friendly expression, but a clear, resolute one. In her gut she knew telling him her identity was the right thing to do, and it was something a man like him would appreciate—she hoped.

"I don't know if you're going to like this particular story." She gripped her mug, her heart pounding in her ears.

"I find usually just starting helps." This time his eyes softened, and his gentle smile gave her the courage to proceed.

Addey took a deep breath. *Here goes nothing.* "I grew up with my grandmother. My parents were busy people, and it seemed better for everyone if I just lived with her."

Exhaling, she shook her shoulders and repositioned herself.

Declan sipped his coffee, his gaze never wavering.

The quiet intensity that came off him scared her a little. But she could—no, she would do this. "I did spend time with my parents through weekly dinners, and they'd sometimes come to my school events..." She took another sip, trying to push away the memories of all the times she'd looked for them in a crowd of other parents, never knowing if they'd be there. "But Granny, she was always there. Rain, hail, or shine." Addey's heart squeezed afresh at the pain of her loss which, for a few moments, felt like it was yesterday, rather than years ago.

"She sounds like the perfect person to raise you," Declan commented. He no longer touched his mug, rather, he'd leaned forward, elbows resting on the table.

"She passed away three years ago." Addey's words hitched a little, and she looked away from Declan. She swallowed and then jumped at a touch on her hand. She looked down at his hand covering hers, there for barely a second before he pulled it away.

"I'm sorry about your grandmother. That's rough."

Addey raised her head and saw a depth of emotion she didn't expect. Raw emotion simmered in his eyes, brimming over into his mouth by way of taut lips and rigid shoulders. What was his story? What drove him to hate the world she came from? Right now, Addey suspected it was more than just anger about the Community Center. Something had happened to him.

Something had wounded him.

She acknowledged with a nod. "Like I said, she was always there. She taught me how to drive, helped me fill out my college applications, she tried to teach me how to cook, and mostly she tried to keep my relationship with my parents going."

"How'd that work out?"

Addey didn't miss the thread of contempt in Declan's comment and almost smiled. He understood the situation. "I changed my last name to hers when I was eighteen."

Declan let out a restrained laugh. "You've got spunk, Addey Bennet."

She winced. "Well, actually...that's why I called you here."

"What do you mean?" He frowned.

It was now or never. She squirmed under his steady appraisal. "My birth name is actually Adelaide Hamilton."

He blinked at her. "You mean..."

She nodded, swallowing. "My parents are Jonathan and Vivien Hamilton."

Chapter Twelve

"I'm sorry—what?" Declan blinked, slow and disbelieving, as if the words hadn't landed right the first time. His voice rose, sharper than intended. A few heads turned.

He caught himself and sank back into his chair, rubbing a hand over his mouth.

"My parents—" Addey began again.

"I heard." Declan's voice dropped low, tight with effort. His eyes fixed on her, jaw tense, trying to rein in all his emotions.

It explained her reaction to him at Mount Vernon, at the café on Saturday. The article. Everything. She thought he hated the world she came from. And he did. He would not deny that or change his stance. Even if she made him want to try.

Addey looked away, her top lip working away at her bottom lip.

"I knew they had a daughter." He dropped the words into the gap between them. "But how could she be you? I mean, you're never talked about. You're not mentioned, never seen in photos."

"I know." Addey met his gaze and the pain he saw there reached in and pulled at his heart. The unwanted, discarded kid. He put his hand on his mug and then took it away, shifted in his chair. What was he supposed to do with this information?

He finally looked at her directly. "Why did you tell me this?"

Addey started shredding a brand-new napkin "I knew I couldn't keep this from you for very long." She paused, sucking in a breath. "And it was the right thing to do."

The simple words sent a calming shot through Declan, but only for a moment. Because telling him this only meant one thing. He knew how it worked, how this world worked. He began tapping his fingers on the table. Faster and harder.

Addey's face was drawn, and she'd stopped shredding the napkin. Now it was her turn to watch him. Declan turned so his body angled away from hers.

"You figured that if I found out later, I would give the party a bad review and that, in turn, gives your business a bad review?" He cocked his head. The shock was wearing off, anger invading. "Did your parents tell you to do this?" They probably did, wanted to keep their noses clean with the press.

Addey colored and her eyebrows shot up. "How can you say that after what I just told you?"

Declan shrugged, but her words had merit. The twinge in his conscience was there. From everything he'd read about her and her family, any relationship they had was clearly kept under the radar. Almost non-existent from what he saw. And if Addey was to be believed, the relationship was frosty at best. He could well imagine the Hamiltons palming her off to someone else to raise. Frankly, he was surprised it wasn't with a nanny. His own mom had not used nannies for him and Nicky. The only time they had a nanny was if she'd had to go away with Dad, and she hadn't done that often.

"I don't know what you want me to say." Declan ground his teeth, trying to sort out the anger at her parents and the compassion for her situation. But it all came out in a confusing dark ball hardening inside him.

"Nothing." Addey raised her chin. "I just wanted you to know. Treat it like nothing new has happened. We don't have to meet again until the party, but I wanted to do what was right."

"Doing what was right would be not taking the job." The words were out before he could stop them. He regretted it the moment the words were said, but it was the Hamilton Group. Everything about them he despised.

"Declan Collins." Addey leaned closer, her eyes sparking. "I don't agree with what my family is doing with the Community Center. But don't you dare suggest that planning a Christmas party is the same thing as tearing down a place that helps people."

Declan folded his arms across his chest. "I didn't mean—"

"Yes, you did, and don't try to deny it." Addey stood, roughly pushing the chair back. She pulled out some bills and dumped them onto the table. "Don't worry, I'll pay for the inconvenience of you having to have coffee with someone like me." She turned to go but stopped and glared at him. "I thought I might be wrong about you. I thought there were hidden depths to you, I thought you can't possibly be the same man I see in the newspapers. But I was wrong. You're exactly that guy."

Declan watched her stride away and he could feel the gazes of everyone in the café. He got up, ignored the glances and whispers, and walked out. Memories chased him up the cold street. Hiding in the house as reporters clamored at the front gates. Whispers and stares of the other kids at school. The outright abuse they'd received from families—abuse that was deserved in part for his father's crimes. School had stopped for a while and really it only resumed once they'd arrived in Virginia, with new last names, no money, and their dad in jail for stealing millions from hundreds of people.

But no matter how fast he walked, he could not outrun Addey's words. The arrows she'd shot were true and he hated it, because for the first time in a long, long time, someone had seen something in him, beyond the anger and the critical words. Hope bloomed in his chest, but then the image of the Hamilton Group's sign out front of the Community Center ate it away. How could the Hamiltons just leave people—people like him—in the lurch, with no help? Because, that's what the rich did. They took from the poor and kept taking, and then did everything they could to silence the voices trying to hold them accountable. Him included.

And Addey was one of them.

He stopped walking and sighed, so deep and long it almost hurt. Was she? He didn't know her well enough yet. Except, he was good at reading people. He saw clearly the hurt she carried from being dismissed by her parents. He heard it in her voice. He had enough information in front of him to know they did not have a loving relationship. It still rankled him, though.

Declan shoved his hands in his pockets and found that he had walked in no particular direction. Stuffing down a groan, he trekked back to the stadium. There was one issue he didn't want to think about, and he'd been pushing the thought aside ever since Addey had dropped her bomb. But the thought would not go away. It poked at him until he gave it space in his head.

He was attracted to the daughter of Jonathan and Vivien Hamilton.

***

Addey called Carmel as she sped through the streets of Alexandria. The beltway was quiet. The Potomac beside the road swept past in the darkness.

"What's up?" Carmel answered.

"I told Declan." Addey's words came out breathless. "I told him who I was and then I called him out for being a jerk."

"Calm down, Addey." Carmel spoke using her measured tone. Did she use that on the residents? Did it work? Because it wasn't working on her.

"I don't get angry at people. I smooth things over. I don't confront outspoken journalists and throw money on the table!"

"Did you really throw the money?" Carmel asked.

Addey slowed the car, worried she would get ticketed for driving like a maniac. "I dumped it. It's practically the same thing."

Carmel laughed.

"Why are you laughing?"

Carmel paused, and Addey could imagine her friend squinting and tugging at her ponytail. "Because I think this guy pushes your buttons, and it's been a long time since that's happened."

"What are you saying?" Addey gripped the steering wheel as she waited for Carmel's reply. And tried not to think about how good looking Declan Collins was, or the eye contact that had gone on too long at the café. Or his hand, resting ever so briefly on hers. She shook her head, desperate for the thoughts to go away. She was not attracted to Declan Collins. It was bad enough he was reviewing the Christmas party.

"Carmel?" Addey turned off towards her townhouse.

"I think you should give the guy time to calm down. It probably rattled him."

Addey frowned. "You're defending him?"

"No..." Carmel dragged out the pause. "I'm saying that Declan Collins is someone who uses his words to best effect—in both positive and negative ways."

"I haven't seen much positive from him." Addey muttered.

"He did keep the Community Center open another whole year." Carmel's pointed comment hit its mark.

"True." Addey drew out the word, wishing it wasn't true.

"But I'm glad you put him in his place," Carmel giggled. "Good for you! That must have been hard but satisfying."

"It was. I'm still shaking." The adrenaline from the encounter was slowly fading as she drove towards her townhouse. "Plus, I had words with Mom tonight before I met with Declan. Or, should I say, she had words with me." Addey bit back a sigh. That's all she did when her parents were concerned. "Mom accused me of not needing her or liking her or...I don't know anymore. I lose track of all my sins with them."

"I wish it wasn't so hard for you."

Addey could hear the compassion in every word her friend spoke. "I know. I gotta go. I'm home now."

"Okay, try and get some rest and I'll see you Thursday."

"See you." Addey pressed end on her phone and sat in the driveway of the townhouse she'd shared with Granny for twenty-three years. Situated on the corner, it occupied a bigger footprint. White brick mixed with red brick and a stately black door led to the comfortable two-bedroom home. Black shutters on the windows, a now-dead rose garden—Addey had no green thumb, that was for sure.

She climbed out of her car and shut the door, following the neat red brick path inside. There, she shut the door against both the cold and the nightmare the evening had turned into.

She dropped her bag on the floor with a thud, unzipped her boots, and kicked them off, placing them beside the door with her other shoes. Only hers, now. Even though it had been over three years, the quietness of the house without Granny was still overwhelming. And tonight, the phone call with Mom and the Declan debacle was a stark reminder of how little she actually had. No family to come home to, at least not one that wanted her, a tiny circle of friends that she didn't see as much as she could, save for Carmel, and a business that thrived, even if she didn't always love it.

But life wasn't about loving things, it was about getting through with as little fuss as possible.

In the kitchen she prepared a hot chocolate using Granny's sea-green, mermaid-handled mug. It was so out of place in the orderly kitchen where Granny's presence lingered. The pastel green KitchenAid mixer sat in the corner, mostly untouched. Addey tried to use it once or twice a year in homage to Granny, but even the weekly cooking classes weren't making much of a difference in her cooking skills.

She sank onto the couch and flicked on the TV, catching some Hallmark movie. After a few minutes, Addey turned it off. The guy getting the girl only reminded her of the other thing she didn't have—romance. How long had it been since she'd dated? Being a Hamilton, even if she wasn't one in name anymore, was always an obstacle. As soon as someone found out who her parents were, they either only wanted her for the family money, or they ran in the other direction, too intimidated to stay.

A slow smile spread across her face. At least she knew one thing, Declan would not be intimidated by her parents. Then her smile faded. Declan wanted nothing to do with her. And he shouldn't.

There was nothing there between them. All she had was the peace of knowing she had done the right thing.

But when she went to bed, the feeling of peace that should have come, never arrived.

Chapter Thirteen

Thursday seemed to be the main activity day at Heritage Oaks and it was going to be Declan's regular day to visit, on his lunch break or after work. Sometimes both, but he liked the break-up of his week by visiting Mom at the tail end of the week. Plus, getting her out of her room and mixing with the other residents would be good for her. From what Nicky had told him, she didn't leave her room much.

This afternoon he found her crocheting away, listening to Bing Crosby instead of Frank. The light was dim as the sun was almost fully set. Even though he was used to the earlier nights during winter here in Virginia, sometimes he missed the California sun and the hours it shone well past when work finished for the day. And the beaches. But no. California was somewhere he would never go back to.

"Hey, Mom." Declan brought a spray of white gerberas and red carnations with him. The woman at the florist had said something about it being a festive kind of arrangement. All Declan knew was that he wanted to make his mom smile, so he'd paid the exorbitant price without batting an eyelid.

Mom looked up from her crocheting and frowned. "Who said you could come in here?" The sharpness in her voice could cut through metal. Declan eased himself into the room.

"Mom, it's me, Declan, coming for a visit." Declan found the vase from last week empty, the flowers he brought last time, gone. Discarded, like his mother's memory. He repeated the routine from last week, filling the vase and setting the flowers on her little table, all while thinking of the best way to handle her current mood.

"My son is away at college. I don't know who you think you are." Mom's high-pitched tone tore at him.

He knelt beside her and clasped her hand, but she pulled away. "You miss Declan, don't you?" He softened his voice and tried to catch her eye, wanting to connect with her feelings and trying not to react to her agitation.

Mom shook her head, faster. The crochet needle dropped to the floor. "I want you out of here."

A nurse walked in, and Declan glanced at the name printed on her shirt. Fiona. "She's having a bad day." Declan moved back as Fiona tried to settle Mom. But Mom continued fighting her.

"Susannah, would you like to listen to some Frank Sinatra?" Fiona spoke clearly and calmly as she picked up the crochet needle and put it out of Mom's reach.

Declan should have never let her have that needle. She could hurt herself or someone else, but the doctor had said it was okay for now. Maybe it was time to have another discussion with the doctor.

"I want him gone." Mom pointed at Declan, eyeing him like he was a monster.

"I'll be outside." Declan backed out of the room, his chest tight as Mom continued to argue with Fiona. Today she hated him, tomorrow, what would it be? Better yet, in an hour, would she talk to him like nothing had happened? This disease was like a rollercoaster and he couldn't get off it. The highs and lows just kept coming and while he understood that this wasn't her fault, that she didn't mean what she said, he still struggled with dealing with the reality of this new world.

"Declan, what are you doing here?" Addey's voice was like throwing a loop-de-loop in his rollercoaster where it didn't exist before. He turned to see her standing a few feet away, her forehead wrinkled, eyes darting from the room where Fiona had finally got Mom calmed down, to him, standing there like an idiot.

"I could ask you the same thing." His words came out croaky. *What are you doing here?* His thoughts echoed her words. She was the last person he wanted to see, and he'd bet his house that she was none too pleased to see him again.

"I'm the events coordinator. I work one day a week here. Every Thursday." She spoke slowly, and this time she was trying not to look at the room he was standing near.

Declan made it easy for her. He walked away and stood near an alcove with a squishy chair, and a window looking out to the courtyard. Of course she worked here, because the way he treated Addey the other night, he deserved for her to see his life in all its brokenness. He leaned against the wall looking up at the ceiling, arms crossed over his chest and counted to twenty. He got to twelve when Addey spoke again.

"You didn't answer my question." Her voice was much closer, indicating she'd followed him. There was no anger in her words, just a question, direct and clear.

I can't hide this from her. Declan finished counting to twenty in his head, before he looked across and met her steady, expectant gaze. He opened his mouth to send her a biting remark, but at the last second, he held back. It would only confirm what she already thought about him. "My mom is a resident here."

Before anything else could be said, Fiona joined them.

"Is Mom okay?" Declan asked, his voice strained, his heart tired.

Fiona glanced at Addey, asking a silent question.

"I'll leave you two alone—" Addey began.

"No, stay," Declan countered. It would be easier this way. Less for him to explain.

With another glance between the two of them, Fiona spoke. "Your mom has been a bit agitated today. She wanted to stay in her room and she's been mostly settled—"

"Until I showed up?" Declan ran a hand through his hair.

Fiona laid a hand on his arm. "You showing up did not trigger this. She'd been unsettled today, and you know sometimes that happens. It can be a change in routine, the medications, something going on that she is struggling to articulate."

"Then I walked in and made it worse." He flicked his gaze to Addey. "It's something I'm good at, it seems."

Addey looked away. Fiona watched the two of them. Declan wanted to leave. Everything felt too close—the walls, the people, his failures. Addey now included on the ever-growing list.

"I'll come back and check on her before I leave." He pushed off from the wall just as Eli walked down the carpeted hallway.

Eli joined them. "Did I miss a party?"

Fiona and Eli nodded at each other. "Mom is having a bad day." Declan set his jaw and tried to say the words without malice. But he didn't do a good job. Eli raised his eyebrows and nodded. He cast a glance at Addey. Addey glanced at Declan. Fiona just watched it all.

Eli turned to Addey. "I don't believe we've met."

Declan stepped up. "Eli, this is Addey." Declan looked at her, but the way she worried her bottom lip, he knew she was concerned he would expose her. "Addey Bennet is the events coordinator here, and she's also the one organizing the Christmas party."

The relief in Addey's eyes as she flicked him the barest smile eased the tension in his shoulders.

Eli smiled, offered his hand. "Pleasure to meet you." He grinned at Addey before giving Declan a sideways glance, amusement twinkling in his eyes. "Don't let this guy intimidate you. I've known him since he was a scrawny fifteen year old. His bark is way worse than his bite."

Declan rolled his eyes and shook his head.

Addey laughed. "I won't let him push me around, will I?" She cocked her head towards Declan, a glint in her eyes.

"No, ma'am." Declan put on a thick southern accent, which brought a knowing head shake, and a smile she tried to hide. Despite everything, hope surged inside him. Maybe Addey hadn't written him off completely, though he deserved it. Now was not the time to apologize. He'd do that later, when he didn't have an audience.

"Why are you out here?" Eli asked.

"Mom tossed me out," Declan said, all merriment vanishing.

Eli frowned. "I'll stick my head in and see if she'll accept my company."

Declan wasn't going to stick around and watch Eli get accepted, probably even remembered. Without another word he rambled down the hall, anything to take him away from the pain of his mother's rejection.

And Addey's far too alluring presence.

***

Addey watched Declan walk away, still shocked to see him here. His mother was a resident? *Why didn't Carmel tell me?* Surely she knew who he was when they placed his mother here.

"Do you remember when you met Susannah?" Fiona asked.

"Of course—" Addey stopped and her heart ached. "No, that's too cruel."

Fiona nodded.

The woman, far too young to be here. Early onset Alzheimer's.

The son who couldn't bring himself to visit.

The adult kids who had no choice to put their mother here. Puzzle pieces of the man who made up the intimidating Declan Collins began to take shape. The wall of words, the simmering anger, the pain, all started to make sense.

Fiona, alerted to another resident who needed help, bustled away.

Addey stood there, feeling...what, she didn't know. Declan had protected her identity. For a moment, she hadn't thought he would. The man today was not the man she had coffee with two nights ago.

"Addey?"

Addey turned.

Eli walked over, his kind eyes holding a measure of pain. "Susannah didn't want company." The older man spoke with a calm assurance that was completely opposite to the obvious pain that radiated from Declan. Addey liked him. This was not a rushed man. His almost all-white hair was longish, his shoulders square. His height was not intimidating, but that didn't mean he couldn't hold his own. He had a quiet strength that just came off him like sunshine on a cloudy day. If Eli liked Declan, then maybe Addey was right. Declan had layers underneath all his anger.

"Declan was kind enough to not say anything, but I'm the director of the Community Center."

Addey gasped. Her father was putting this man out of a job. "My clients—" She paused at the absurdity of her words, but as much as she instantly liked this man, she wasn't going to tell him her secret. Declan knowing was more than enough.

"You don't have to say anything," Eli said. "I've settled the matter within myself and the Lord. I'm at peace with whatever comes. Declan has a ways to go on that road." He winked. "Besides, I'm too old to get worked up over things I can't control."

Addey smiled in spite of the worry growing inside. "How did you meet Declan?"

"At the Community Center." Eli watched her with patient, kind eyes.

What? So that meant... "So this is personal for him," Addey whispered. *Really personal.* "When was that?"

"I'll let Declan tell you. It's his story, not mine." Eli's expression was still open, but unreadable. He was protecting Declan. That made her like the older man even more. "Let's go find him."

Addey fell into step beside Eli. "He's probably causing mischief."

Eli chucked. "You're not wrong."

As they walked in silence, Addey asked the question that kept bouncing around her head. "What makes you think Declan will tell me his story?"

Eli gave her such a fatherly look of affection that Addey wanted to back away. Her own father had never looked at her like that, instead he only offered stares of disappointment, resentment, irritation, and boredom. Never this warmth. What would it be like to be loved by someone the way Eli clearly cared for Declan?

"You're not intimidated by him. That's rare. Declan has walls, good reasons for them, but it's about time someone challenged him to take them down." When Eli touched her arm, the caring gesture made her heart ache.

"You think I'm that person?" This time Addey did step away. He was wrong. Declan would let no one in. Besides, Eli didn't know who her parents were. He would change his mind when he found out.

They all did.

"You could be. I'm just happy to see someone get a look over that wall he's got up." Eli finished talking and continued down the hall.

Addey followed him inside the rec room and stopped, mouth open. Declan was playing cards with Maude and...

Maude was smiling.

Chapter Fourteen

armel joined Addey in the doorway of the rec room. "Declan appears to be a man of many layers."

"Let's go for a walk." Addey moved off to find a private place. Carmel took the lead to her office. Shutting the door behind them, Addey faced her friend.

"Declan's mom is here. You knew who he was and let me get ambushed by him."

Carmel arched one eyebrow. "That's a bit much don't you think?"

Addey huffed and sunk onto the sofa. She knew she was being petty. But right now, it was hard to care.

"It would have been unprofessional of me to say anything to you about a resident's personal situation." Carmel's clear voice rang through Addey. "Especially as they'd asked for privacy."

Any fight she had inside, deflated. "I know..." Addey drew out the word. "When I met Susannah last week, Fiona gave me the basic rundown of Susannah's condition and situation. I felt so awful for her and now to know it's Declan's mom—it just makes it worse."

Carmel sat down next to Addey. "I know."

A long beat of silence hung between them.

"He's the most confusing man I've ever met." Addey buried her head in her hands.

"I know that, too."

Addey looked up and narrowed her eyes. "Then why are you smiling?"

Carmel just kept grinning. "Just admit that you like the man and it will make everything easier."

"I can't like him. Do you have any idea what would happen if my parents found out?" Addey's voice cracked as it rose, sharp and unsteady. The sound scraped at her throat, and she flinched, as if surprised by her own unraveling. "And he's horrible. He hasn't even apologized for his behavior the other night."

"You're twenty-eight and not beholden to your parents." Carmel said. "And I didn't say you should date him, just admit you think he's a babe."

Addey glared at her friend, who got up and went to her desk. Addey sat there stewing, torn between taking Carmel's advice and ignoring it. Declan was the biggest contradiction she'd ever met and it was doing her head in. "Okay, I'm going back to the rec room. I'll pop in and see you before I go."

"You ready for the cookie baking extravaganza?" Carmel said.

"Can't wait." Addey reached for the door, but before opening it, she spoke again. "Fine, I think he's a babe." She yanked the door open and walked out to the sound of Carmel's laughter.

Back at the rec room, Addey found Declan still playing cards with Maude, but they'd now been joined by Vera and Saul. Standing there, she watched Declan smile at Maude, say something she couldn't hear and Maude respond with her own grin, but it was Maude's eyes that caught Addey's attention the most—they were sparkling.

At that moment Declan looked up and saw her. His gaze was intense—like everything else about him—and he was so much more than just a babe. He was a headache, an unapologetic, stubborn headache. Giving herself another second to get herself together and find extra reserves of patience, Addey gave him a quick smile and crossed the floor to the group.

"We're playing Casino." Declan glanced up at her as he dealt the cards with a quick hand.

"He's cheating." Maude shot Declan a beady look, but her eyes held hints of warmth.

"I'm not cheating. I play hard but within the rules. You just don't like that I'm not giving you any breaks, Miss Maude." Declan stared the woman down, but a smile lurked at the corners of his lips. Saul and Vera just laughed.

Play hard but within the rules. Now didn't that just sum him up perfectly.

"These two have been bickering since this young man sat down." Saul lifted his gray fedora and scratched his nearly bald head. "If he wasn't young enough to be Maude's grandson, I'd have thought they were married."

"Hear, hear!" Vera cheered as she and Saul laughed, their cards falling onto the table in a heap.

Maude frowned at them and Declan sat back taking in the scene. That's when Addey saw it—the man behind the harsh words. His shoulders were relaxed, his foot tapping on the floor, his eyes bright, and the slight upturn of his lips. He was enjoying himself. But he wasn't like that around her. He couldn't be, because Addey represented everything he hated about the world.

Babe or not, she was a thorn in his side just as much as he was one in hers.

"Glad you're having fun. Maude, don't let him best you." She touched Maude's arm, giving it a gentle squeeze.

"He never will, Miss Addey." Maude turned back to the others. "Are we playing or not?"

Addey made the rounds of the room, stopping to talk to everyone, nodding at Eli who was with June and Gerald in one corner watching the TV. She packed up left-out cards and helped wipe down tables, all the while trying to ignore Declan...though she couldn't help but steal glances at him. One last sneaky glance before she left found Declan staring back at her. Her stomach flipped and she grabbed a cushion and pushed it onto a chair. Wiping her hands down her skirt, she picked up her purse.

"I'll see you all next week," Addey called, retreating, but really, she was running from his presence. Outside, she drew in deep breaths, letting the cool air settle her nerves and the dim light shroud her.

"Addey, wait." Declan's voice rang out across the parking lot.

Stuffing down a strangled groan, Addey turned, schooling her features into something that she hoped resembled pleasant. Without warning, an image of her mom popped into her head and Addey cringed inwardly. Being like Vivien was something she never wanted to be.

"Yes?" She hoped she sounded less irritated than she felt.

Declan strides ate the distance between them easily. "I didn't know you worked here."

Addey nodded, waiting for him to continue.

Declan shifted on his feet. He looked at her and opened his mouth but shut it before anything came out. He frowned, his brown eyes troubled. "I'm sorry."

Addey stilled, her gaze fixed on him.

Declan ran a hand along the back of his neck. "I can't pretend to be happy about what is happening to the Community Center. I'll never be happy about that—" She could hear the edge in his voice and Addey thought back to Eli's words. "But that doesn't mean I wasn't out of line the other night. I'm sorry." His voice dropped low, his eyes catching hers, sincerity dwelling in their depths. He backed away. "Have a good night."

Addey stood unable to move, wavering between walking away or saying something in return. She chose the latter. "I'm sorry about your mom."

Declan stopped and gave a hard nod, his expression clouding, clearly not a topic he was comfortable discussing. Addey didn't blame him. She couldn't fathom seeing a parent you loved slowly succumbing to a disease that stole their mind. Declan was almost to the steps when Addey called out again.

"Thanks for not letting Eli know...about me." The words came out a little wobbly. *Why can't I just let him walk away?*

Declan nodded, still backing away. "Well, you are Addey *Bennet*, right?"

"Right," she echoed.

"I won't be such a jerk next time we see each other. Scout's honor." He held his hand up in the Scout salute and Addey couldn't help herself—she laughed.

"You were never a scout."

The smile he'd given her at the café the other day spread slowly across his face, making her heart flutter, knowing she'd put it there.

"How do you know I wasn't a boy scout? I could have been one." His confidence was both endearing and irritating—which was part of his charm. And he knew it.

Addey rolled her eyes. "In your dreams."

He chuckled, the sound music to Addey's ears. She was in trouble. So. Much. Trouble.

Just then Carmel raced out the doors, nearly colliding with Declan. She didn't say anything to him, just kept running toward Addey. Addey rushed to meet her, Declan joining them.

"What's wrong?" Addey took hold of her friend's arm.

Carmel paused, trying to catch her breath. "My mom just called. My dad had a heart attack."

***

Declan didn't know what to do as Addey pulled Carmel into a hug. He hovered, feeling stupid, but walking away would have felt even worse. So, he just stood there.

"I've got to go back home, they've taken him to the hospital, my mom is beside herself, I have to call my sisters." Carmel's words ran over each other.

"Of course. I can drive you to your place if you like?" Addey's voice was soothing. "What do you need me to do?"

"Pray." Carmel looked at both of them. Declan simply nodded. No point in letting anyone know his last conversation with God was in the car as they left California to drive to the other side of the country fifteen years ago.

"Yes, of course." Addey nodded, her voice rough.

Carmel almost made it to her car when she spun around. "I won't be able to make our cooking night. I don't know how long I'll be away. I'm sorry." She sounded genuinely upset and Declan looked across to Addey.

"Don't worry about it, it's just a cooking class—"

"But we need two people these next two weeks. She was very specific about that." Carmel's voice went up a few notches. Declan thought it must be shock, because this was not normal behavior for someone whose father had just had a heart attack.

Addey, seeming to think the same thing, waved her hand as if trying to settle her friend. "Everything will be fine. I can manage on my own."

"You can't cook scrambled eggs." The deadpan tone and expression would have been funny in a different situation.

Declan noticed Addey didn't deny it.

"I'll go with her." The words were out before he could stop them.

Both women stared at him. Addey's mouth hung open. He didn't know what had come over him either.

"Thank you, Declan." Carmel nodded.

"Will you go see your dad now?" Declan prodded.

Carmel gave a watery laugh before climbing into the car. "Yes, and thank you both. Prayers please, and I'll call you, Addey!" She peeled out of the parking lot.

Declan and Addey stood side by side, saying nothing. His thoughts churned. What had he gotten himself into?

"You don't have to come with me." Addey finally broke the silence.

"Can you really not cook scrambled eggs?" He eyed her.

She didn't reply, just returned his sideways look with one of her own. "They were completely inedible."

And they both burst out laughing because there didn't seem to be anything else to do right then. Laugh or cry, wasn't that the saying?

Chapter Fifteen

*C**all Addey.*

It was the one thing Declan had to do today. But he hadn't yet. Instead, he'd read the paper three times, went over the articles he needed to write that week, and was now cleaning out the fridge—which didn't take long because there wasn't much in there. He wrinkled his nose at several questionable jars that he wasn't going to open—from the looks of them, they were definitely growing things. They clunked into the trash, along with days-old bread and limp salad.

Pulling out the eggs, onions, peppers, and some bacon that needed cooking before it joined the others in the bin—all that was left in the fridge—his thoughts skittered to Addey. He cracked the eggs into a bowl. *Who can't cook scrambled eggs?* He chuckled. Before the move to Virginia, Declan couldn't cook anything, but having a single mom who worked, he quickly learned.

The front door burst open. His sister, Nicky, walked in struggling with several grocery bags. Declan switched off the frying pan and walked across the lounge room.

"Thanks," she huffed, dumping most of the bags in his arms. "Hmm, smells great in here. Can't believe you found something to actually cook."

He followed, barely able to see over the overflowing groceries, and put them on the bench. "Did I miss something? Are we feeding the whole building?"

"We didn't shop last week, remember?" Nicky started unloading the bags, opened the fridge and raised her eyebrows. "You cleaned out the fridge."

Declan shrugged.

"You cleaned it out and scrubbed it down." Nicky put away the food, shaking her head, but he heard laughing from behind the fridge door. "Okay, fess up, who's the girl?"

"There is no girl." *Liar.* "It just needed to be done." Declan grabbed two plates and served up the omelets. "How was church?" Nicky had started back going when Mom got sick. Declan never went with her.

"You'd know if you came," she commented without looking at him. It was the same conversation, but Declan was grateful that his baby sister never pushed beyond the one comment. He knew he'd go back when he was ready.

Problem was, he didn't think he'd ever be ready.

While Nicky was busy, he slipped out of the kitchen and pulled out his wallet, then quietly tucked several bills into her purse. It was more than his share, but he did it every week and she didn't comment.

He returned to the kitchen. Their condo wasn't big. Three teeny bedrooms, one bathroom, one decent sized lounge room with a galley kitchen off it. They'd set up a small dining table by the big windows that overlooked the park below. It wasn't a high-rise, just a simple three-story complex in a leafy, quiet part of Alexandria, a short drive from Old Town. The only reason they could afford Heritage Oaks was that they owned this place. They'd taken out a new mortgage on the condo to pay for her ongoing medical care and living costs. It was their only home since they'd arrived in Alexandria. He was forever bend to return the hug. "She forgot where she was. I heard her crying when I came up the stairs. I opened the door and the smoke came out. I pulled her out and called 911."

Declan leaned back to get a good look at her. The words rushed out in between gasps, her cheeks flushed, her eyes wide with fright. She was still wearing her hair salon uniform, her once-dark hair was piled high in a loose bun, a large pink strip of ribbon a neon sign amongst the snow-white hair.

"I'm so glad you were there and that both of you are okay." He gave her another squeeze.

"I called Eli, he's on his way."

Eli would come. Despite everything going wrong, for a brief moment, Declan felt cared for.

No one had cared when they'd left Los Angeles. Mom had changed their last name before they left to keep them out of the press, especially after Dad's sentencing. She was stoic and elegant in everything she did. She never let the hurt show, but Declan would sit outside her room at night and listen to her crying. And now it was killing him to watch her slowly fade away.

They stayed the night at Mrs. Finch's house. The kitchen was the only room to sustain significant damage. Thankfully their insurance covered it. For six months while they'd waited for the insurance money to come in and for the repairs to be completed, they'd lived in their condo while eating all their meals with Mrs. Finch. Eli had come over every day to join them for breakfast. He stayed with Mom or took her to the Community Center until Nicky got off work at three. Then Declan would take over after he came home from work. He and Nicky split the weekends between them. While all this was going on, it was decided that they needed to find Mom a place in permanent care.

grateful that Mom had squirreled away some money in the course of her marriage. He'd never asked her why she'd done that, but it occurred to him that it was about time to know. On one of her good days, he'd ask.

Nicky handed him the plate and wordlessly walked to the table. He joined her and just let her decide when she was going to talk. She was spunky, but prone to sulky moods. He learned long ago not to press her.

"So, you finally visited Mom?" She bit into her omelet.

"I went twice this week."

"Wow, making up for lost time. You're a saint." Her barb stung.

"Drop it, Nicky. I'm going regularly now, okay?"

Nicky kept eating, the silence around them brittle. Each of them had taken Mom's illness and her move to Heritage Oaks differently. Declan had run from it. Sure, he'd done what had to be done, but otherwise he'd buried himself in work and tried not to think about the fact that he couldn't care for his mother.

For Nicky, it consumed her. She stayed busy, never sitting for long, always trying to find the best way forward, the best facility, the best doctors, the newest medication. She visited every day and it was killing her. Dark circles under her eyes, premature frown lines that a twenty-seven year old shouldn't have. Even Declan could see she was tired, and that she needed a haircut. Her chestnut brown hair hung almost to her waist, a far cry from the shoulder length she'd worn for years. In fact, Declan didn't know the last time she'd gone to the salon. Not that he paid that much attention, but given their life, even he knew it was too long between visits.

"Are you going to get a haircut soon?"

Nicky raised her head, brow crinkled, as if he'd asked if she was going to go swimming naked in the Potomac. "What?"

"I was just thinking it's been a while since you got it cut. Don't you normally like it shorter than that?" He fumbled with his fork. He should have kept his mouth shut.

Nicky sat back and blinked several times. "I haven't gone to the salon since Mom got diagnosed." Her voice was unsteady, and her lip trembled.

"I'm such a jerk, Nicky. I know that was your thing with Mom."

"I saw her today." The words were quiet. "I went to pick her up for church."

His chest constricted and he held his breath, afraid to ask.

"She keeps thinking I'm Dad," Declan said as calmly as he could. The resentment that usually reared its head didn't, and instead a melancholy spread over him. This was their life now, waiting with bated breath every time they saw her, wondering if she would remember them. "How was she today?"

Nicky didn't say anything, just let her head hang low, her hair obscuring her face. Finally, she looked up and tears glistened in her eyes. "She didn't want me to leave. She kept talking about how Dad should be coming soon to take her home."

Declan stood up and hugged Nicky from where she sat. His sister's sobs filled the room. He recalled the day they knew Mom had to go into full-time care.

Declan had pulled into the parking lot to find the fire department parked outside the complex. Nicky had pulled up behind him. His heart lurched in his chest when he saw the smoke billowing from the window of their condo.

Nicky ran, screaming. "Mom! Mom!"

Declan grabbed her and pushed past the firemen until a police officer stopped him.

"That's our place. My mother's in there!" He pushed the man, but it did no good.

"I'm sorry, you can't go in there, it's not safe." Declan glared but the man wasn't budging.

"Where's our mother? Her name is Susannah Collins." Declan used his height to stand toe-to-toe with the cop.

The man's hardened expression cracked. "She's been asking for her kids, follow me."

He led them away from the building, towards an ambulance van parked at the opposite end of the parking lot. Nicky latched onto Declan's hand and he squeezed it.

"I've got some very worried people here to see you, Mrs. Collins," the officer said. The paramedics stepped aside to reveal their mom sitting on a gurney. Nicky rushed forward and grabbed her in a fierce hug. Declan sagged against the van, his legs weak.

Mom looked around, gaze landing from person to person. "What's going on, Nicky? Why are you all here? Dinner's not ready yet."

Declan's heart sank and desperation threatened to take over and drown him. He squeezed his fists open and closed several times as he stared down at the ground. His vision blurred with unshed tears. He swallowed down the lump in his throat. He would stand up and do what his family needed. He'd be strong, he'd bear this for Nicky and Mom.

He'd do what his father had failed to do.

The paramedics exchanged looks, then one of them nodded to Declan and he indicated with his head that he wanted to talk privately. Declan nodded, before leaning over and giving his mother's hand a squeeze. "You look so much like your father," she said, her voice unsteady, her hand shaking. "Nicky, stop crying. Dad will be here soon to fix everything."

He heard Nicky choke back a sob as he absorbed the sucker punch to the gut his mother had just delivered. He kept walking, head held high, shoulders back. The paramedic stopped several feet away.

"Your mom is okay. A neighbor called 911 and got her out. I don't know about the damage to your place. You'll have to talk to one of the firemen about that."

Declan nodded. It was probably Mrs. Finch who called it in. She was a good neighbor. She used to babysit him and Nicky in the first couple of years. Not that a fifteen year old and a twelve year old needed babysitting, but Mom insisted on Mrs. Finch checking on them every couple of hours while she worked, especially during school vacation. Declan had allowed it to keep Mom happy in those early miserable years.

"Your mother's not well, is she?" The uniformed man's close-cropped brown hair was sprinkled with gray, and his eyes were like old souls.

"There's nothing that can be done." It was the first time he'd spoken the words out loud. He wanted to punch something, the unfairness roared up like a lion and it waged a mighty battle inside him.

The paramedic put a hand on his shoulder and squeezed, understanding pouring out of this...stranger. Declan wanted to hit him, to lash out at someone, but he kept his cool, counting to twenty. "It's okay to be upset, it's okay to hate this."

Declan shrugged the man's hand off.

"Is it early onset?" he asked.

"Yes, we found out two years ago. We've been going along fairly well until recently, but today..."

Today needed no explanation.

Just then, Mrs. Finch came running up. She threw her arms around Declan, dragging him down with her small but bony grasp. He had to

He and Nicky shared power of attorney over their mother. It should have been harder, but when the diagnosis had first come in, Mom had planned out the next steps of her life. She was prepared for this moment whenever that came. It had taken them months to get into Heritage Oaks Residence Home. The waiting list was long, but it was worth it as it was close to their home and to Eli at the Community Center. So, between Declan, Eli, Mrs. Finch, the nurse provided by the Community Center, and Nicky, they had someone with Mom twenty-four hours a day until she moved to Heritage Oaks.

And here they were, one month into Mom's nursing home care. It was easier knowing she was well looked after, but the crushing guilt that life was simpler with Mom in care was as overwhelming as the guilt of failing to take care of her in her own home.

Nicky stopped crying and wiped her tears. Declan sat back down. Neither touched their food. "It'll get worse. One day she won't know us at all." Her voice was scratchy.

"I know." He squeezed her hand. "But let's take everything one day at a time."

She smiled but it didn't reach her eyes. "Yeah, because you're *so* good at that."

Her attempt at teasing him lifted his spirits.

"What's your plan for this week?" Nicky asked.

Declan let her change the topic. They both needed it. His thoughts went straight to Addey. He really should call her. "I think I'm going to a cooking class tomorrow night."

"You're what?" Nicky's eyes widened. "What on earth for?"

"I said I'd fill in for someone who can't go." Declan picked up the plates and took them to the kitchen.

Nicky followed him, planted her butt on the back of the sofa, and crossed her arms over her chest. "I didn't know Camden was taking cooking classes."

"He's not." Declan emptied the plates and put them in the dishwasher. "Otherwise, this week's plans are the same as they always are."

"Don't change the topic. Who's taking the class?"

Declan huffed. "Just someone I know, okay?"

Nicky shook her head. "Nope, you don't get off that easy." Her eyes lit up and a slow, knowing grin spread across her face. "You met someone. That explains the fridge cleaning."

"Drop it, okay."

"Oh, she must be special if you're getting defensive already." Nicky's grin widened. "So, have you called her?"

"What for?" Declan stepped around his nosy sister. To say Addey was special wasn't true, not yet at least. But she could be, and he wanted to find out, he wanted to see if the sparks between them could turn into something more...maybe. He didn't know, but he couldn't shake her from his mind. Besides, given everything that had happened between them, he didn't think Addey would want him at the class.

"To confirm if you're going tomorrow night." Nicky enunciated every word, using her teacher voice, the one she reserved for the kids she needed to be really patient with.

"Not yet," he bit out.

Nicky grabbed her phone from her pocket, held it up to Declan and tapped the time.

"Very funny." Declan grabbed his coat and walked outside. He rounded the little park and kept moving with no real direction. It wasn't until he reached the small set of shops near their home that he worked up the courage. He pulled out his phone, heart pounding, and called Addey.

Would she answer when she saw it was him?

Chapter Sixteen

Call Declan.

The thought, or rather, the task had been playing on Addey's mind since Thursday night but she'd yet to do it. Now was not the time either. She held her two cups of coffee and a newspaper under her arm and made the weekly trek inside her parents' house for Sunday brunch, after the early church service she went to. Carmel had sent her a quick text message this morning saying her dad was stable but still in the hospital, so there was no way she was going to make cooking class tomorrow night, not while she was in San Francisco.

Again, Declan and his engaging smile, his fierce passion, plagued her thoughts, even as she stepped into the sitting room, back to the uncomfortable sofa. No one was there. Relishing a moment alone, Addey set down her things and opened the French doors that led to the expansive deck that overlooked the Potomac.

"It's a lovely spot, isn't it?" A male voice spoke behind her.

Addey jerked, hand clutching her chest. She turned and found herself in the presence of a man she had never met before.

"Sorry to scare you, I thought you heard me come in." He was well-spoken and neat. Neat blond hair, neat black slacks, and a friendly face.

"Thick carpets." Addey pinched her face into what she hoped was a passable, pleasant expression.

He chuckled. It sounded neat as well. "Your mom invited me…"

Addey froze, trying desperately to make sure the swell of disappointment and frustration didn't show, even though it swirled inside her, like a tornado, slowly gathering speed.

"You're Addey, right?" The tilt of his head and the slow way he spoke told her he was picking up on the bad vibes.

"Yes," Addey nodded, keeping herself an easy distance from the man. "And you are?"

His shoulders dropped just a little. "I'm Justin. I work with your dad."

Of course, he did, but at least he's not a doctor. Addey went back to the couch and eased herself down, minimizing the bounce effect. "Are my parents here?"

Justin ran a hand through his hair—not a strand moved. "They're coming." He coughed. Addey wanted to sit and let him squirm, but she wasn't raised that way. Sighing inwardly, she gathered up all her social reserves, stuffed down the frustration at her mother and spoke to Justin.

"What do you do at my dad's company?" Addey sipped her coffee and tried not to look at her watch.

Seeming to sense the change, Justin lowered himself to the sofa across from her. "I'm in P.R."

Addey raised her eyebrows. "So, this last year or so has been interesting?"

Justin settled back against the sofa and gave her a rueful smile. "You could say that. I'm just glad we can finally move forward."

Addey's heart beat sped up. "You mean the closing down of the Community Center?" Addey smiled as she spoke, but Justin's microsecond frown told her enough. "Dad is expecting good publicity from the party."

Justin nodded. "He sure is." He drummed his fingers on the sofa. "Besides party planning, what else do you do?"

The way he said party planning made Addey cringe inwardly. Here was another person who thought what she did was nothing special. "I take a cooking class with a friend."

Justin nodded.

"You never told me that, Adelaide." Mom walked into the room, giving Justin a bright smile. "Sorry we're late, Justin. I hope you two were finding things to talk about." The cheeriness in her voice made Addey's stomach roil.

Justin stood and kissed Mom's hand and Addey coughed. Mom sent her a sideways glare. Addey held up her coffee cup. "Swallowed wrong."

"Cooking classes? That must be fun." Justin sat back down on the sofa, glancing between Addey and Mom.

"It is. We're doing a Christmas theme over the next two weeks. I'm looking forward to it." Despite the current situation, Addey meant what she said. As to seeing Declan, did she really want to do that again? Her heart said yes, but her head said no. "But my friend can't make it tomorrow as she's out of town, so I'll be managing on my own." *Why on earth did I add that detail?*

"I like cooking." Justin threw in. "My mum taught me to cook four meals, that way I'd always have enough for a week's worth."

"That's a good idea." Addey considered Justin, admitting to herself that he wasn't quite what she'd initially thought.

Dad walked in and grinned. "Justin. Vivien didn't tell me you'd be here."

That makes two of us.

"Justin has been my right hand this past year," Dad said, taking a seat beside Addey and picking up his drink. "He's been making sure we get back on track since the redevelopment was delayed for so long." Dad scowled. "This unveiling of the building has to be perfect."

Justin nodded, smiling. Did he actually speak his mind around Dad or was he just a "yes man"?

Addey's irritation dug a little deeper. "Justin," Addey asked, "do you think the timing for the unveiling of the new building is the best thing? I'd like your take on it, considering all the bad press that's been happening."

The frozen expressions on her parents' faces didn't seem to bother Justin. He leaned forward. "I've been thinking about that." He tossed a glance at Dad, who only managed a nod. The pressure in the room rose. Addey's throat closed up, each swallow rough and dry like sand. She was going to pay for this. Mom knew not to try to set her up and that was exactly why Justin sat across from her.

"I think it's risky. I mean, it's my job help assess how something is going to be received by the public. Public sentiment was not in favor of closing the Center." He looked at Dad, met his gaze, and plowed on. "But my ultimate goal is always in the best interests of the Hamilton Group."

Justin had more backbone than Addey thought. She was impressed. "What are you saying, then?"

"He's saying we shouldn't do the unveiling." Dad's voice was thick and rigid.

Justin hesitated, looking at all of them. "I think having another discussion on this is worthwhile."

Dad grunted.

"Then we'll leave that to you and Jonathan for a work day," Mom said, her tone light—too light—and her smile just a touch too polished. She glanced at Justin, then back at Addey with deliberate brightness. "Adelaide, Justin was just saying how much he enjoys boating on the river."

Justin's shoulders lifted in a slow shrug, his eyes catching hers with a hint of apology. His mouth twitched, not quite a smile—more like a silent wince that said, yeah...I didn't ask for this either.

"Adelaide's been taking a cooking class, Jonathan." Mom's eyes grew bright and warning bells sounded in Addey's head. She pressed deeper into the sofa, trying to distance herself from something terrible coming her way.

"Justin, since you like cooking, and she's on her own, you should join her at class tomorrow."

Addey coughed again. Justin froze, his own expression blank.

"The idea has merit," Dad piped up beside her.

This was payback for bringing up the taboo subject.

"Well, what do you think?" Mom asked, looking between Addey and Justin. Addey said nothing, just sat there and let the anger build. Why wouldn't Mom learn that messing with her private life was *not* okay?

"I think it's up to you." Justin looked at Addey, his words slow and deliberate. He was giving her an out.

Addey's phone rang, disrupting the tension in the room. Searching through her purse, she unearthed the phone and froze.

It was Declan.

Heart rate skyrocketing, Addey shielded her phone and stood. "I need to take this." She all but bolted through the French doors and ran to the furthest corner of the deck, far away from her parents.

With shaking hands, she answered the call. "Hi." Her voice sounded strangled.

"Hi yourself. Is this a bad time?" His voice would normally send a thrill down her spine, but today it was a different kind of thrill—panic piled upon panic.

Addey pressed her fingers to her forehead, willing the pressure to steady her breath. Her voice barely rose above a whisper. "I'm at my parents' house."

"Say no more." His serious and alert tone eased the mushrooming ball growing inside—a little.

"I'll call you as soon as I can," she replied, keeping her voice low. She hung up and sagged against the railing, her hands shaking. Declan called, despite the circumstances—he'd called! Stupidly, her heart leapt.

"Adelaide, Justin is leaving. Come say goodbye." Mom stood at the door, arms in the pocket of her tailored suit, and a long, penetrating stare aimed at Addey.

"He isn't staying for brunch?" Addey pocketed her phone, meeting Mom in the doorway.

"Something last minute came up." Mom's clipped tone ringed with accusation.

Addey shouldered past her mother. She was going to have it out with them. Mom knew not to do this, and she'd done it anyway.

Justin was waiting by the sitting room doors.

"Nice to meet you," Addey said.

"Thanks," he hesitated, casting a glance across the room. "Enjoy your cooking class tomorrow."

Addey kept her smile plastered on. "I will."

Justin gave one last nod and walked out.

The sudden absence of voices was deafening.

The only sounds were the ticking of the grandfather clock, located in the foyer, and Justin's footfalls echoing across the tile floor. The front door clicked shut and the silence continued.

Addey watched her parents. Dad was reading his newspaper, but he wasn't turning any pages, and Mom was shifting in her seat. The sound of Justin's car driving away hummed in the distance of the stifling, silent room. When she couldn't bear it anymore, she opened her mouth to speak, but Dad was already on his feet.

"What was the meaning of that? Asking Justin what he thought about the development." His voice boomed.

Addey backed up but crossed her arms across her chest.

"I might ask you the same thing." She looked over to her mother. "I told you to stop setting me up."

Mom brushed her skirt. "I don't know what you mean."

Addey huffed. "I'm so tired of this."

"You haven't answered my question," Dad pressed, his newspaper forgotten on the coffee table. "Why do you want us to halt the unveiling of the new apartment building so badly?"

Addey rubbed her temples. Why did everything have to be about them? Why couldn't they see the reasonableness of cutting something that didn't need to be part of a Christmas party?

"Dad, in case you've forgotten, I have a stake in this party going well. The Baker/Gibson Group wants a flawless event and I have to give that to them if I'm going to get the best price for my company." Addey's voice rose, but she tamped it down. She'd already rocked the boat enough for one day. There was no need to sink it outright.

She swallowed down the frustration and tried again, forcing calmness she didn't feel into her voice. "The bad publicity of this building can affect the sale of my business, or don't you care about that at all?" *Or me?* Addey almost added. She couldn't go there, as much as she wanted to hear the words that would make her heart soar—"we love you, want you"—she strongly suspected that if she ever outright asked, the answer would break her heart.

"You still shouldn't have brought it up." Dad glared.

"You shouldn't have invited Justin." Addey aimed her words at Mom.

Mom finally stood and moved to Dad's side. "Justin is nice and he's a good man. Likes his family—" She paused. "I thought you might hit it off."

Addey wanted to scream. "That's not the point. Mom, I've asked you to stop doing this and yet you can't help yourself."

An idea launched into Addey's brain, and it was a terrible one, but once it took root, it wouldn't leave. Addey shook her head, trying to dislodge the idea. "I have a life and I will run it myself." Images of Declan chased through her mind.

Mom almost rolled her eyes. "Well, you haven't shown much ability in running your life well, Adelaide. You have no boyfriend, you don't go out, and you spend most of your free time with dying, old people."

Addey backed up and met the wall, her chest tight. "I quit."

"Quit what?" Dad said slowly.

Addey was staring down this bad idea and knew she was going to regret it. "The party. Go find someone else to run it." *What am I doing?* This would damage the sale of her business.

"Fine, we will," Mom snipped back, her face hard. She was calling Addey's bluff and she knew it. Addey knew it.

"Vivien," Dad rounded on Mom. "You can't be serious."

Mom arched an eyebrow at Dad. "If she hates the job so much, then let her quit. We can find someone else to finish what she started."

Addey fought back tears. She had no value to them, even in a professional capacity. She was nothing to them except an obligation to fulfill. Addey's heart wrenched, but she remembered Granny. Her unconditional love. Granny had kept Addey's life stable for years. Squaring her shoulders, Addey stepped forward. She was not going to let them see how much they hurt her. Years of hurt that piled on until she might break. But she hadn't broken—not yet and not now.

"Fine, you plan your party. I'll see you later." When, she didn't know. Going to Sunday brunch was not going to happen either. Addey was tired of arguing, tired of trying to be worthy, when all she was to them was a disappointment.

She'd have to call Mark from the Baker/Gibson Group and explain the situation. Hopefully it wouldn't affect the sale of the business too much. Addey sat in her car and took a shuddering breath . What would Mark think about this new development? Would they still want to buy Elegant Events? Too many questions and no clear answers battled but there was one thing Addey knew for sure—she'd already rocked the boat so she might as well head into the storm.

As she drove out, leaving the house with too few memories behind, she called Declan on Bluetooth.

He answered on the first ring and it only strengthened her resolve. "Addey, I'm sorry about my call earlier." This time his deep, assuring voice soothed her.

It shouldn't have, but it did.

"That's okay, you didn't know." She breathed through the uptick of her pulse and the unsteadiness in her voice. "Is your offer to come with me tomorrow night still good?"

"It is, only if you want me to come." The hesitation in his voice made her smile. She, Addey Bennet, made this iron will of a man uncertain of himself.

"I'm sure." She spoke with confidence. Peering into the mirror, she could no longer see her parents' house. Addey pressed harder on the accelerator.

"Good. I'll be on my best boy scout behavior." His teasing tone brought a smile to her lips and the further away from her parents she drove, the bigger the smile got.

Oh yes, she was headed into a storm, all right.

Chapter Seventeen

"You're going to the cooking class then?" Nicky asked as she graded a pile of tests at their dining table, but she sent him a sneaky smile.

Declan adjusted his collar. "Can we drop this, please?" Declan frowned, checking his watch. He wanted to get away from his sister's not-so-subtle ribbing, but if he did, he'd be early. He and Addey agreed to meet outside a few minutes before class started.

"So, does this mystery girl have a name?" Nicky prodded.

Telling her would open a door he wasn't ready to yet. But he couldn't not answer the question. "Addey."

"Pretty name." Nicky batted her eyelashes.

"Go back to marking," Declan glared, but he tempered it with a half-smile. It was nice to see Nicky happy about something. "It's been good visiting Mom." He smoothed his collar.

"She was good today." Nicky sobered, a shadow falling across her face. "I think I'll take her out to get her hair done this week."

"That's a great idea." Declan opened the fridge for no real reason, just something to do with his hands. Mom, Addey, her parents, his column—it piled on his plate. Could he manage it all? Shutting the fridge along with the train of his thought, he grabbed his coat. "I'm out of here."

"Have a great date," Nicky called, unable to keep the amusement from her voice.

"It's not a date!" He shut the door behind him.

"If you say so!" Nicky's muffled reply through the door was far too light and airy.

This was *not* a date. It was cooking class. With Addey. His heart tripped as he drove to Belle View, found a parking spot and hoofed it through the stiff breeze to the renovated brick building. He found Addey waiting for him outside, just like they agreed. The light cast a pale glow on her and she had her hands buried deep in the pockets of her stylish black coat. She was hopping from one foot to the other. Was she nervous? Cold? Both?

"Addey," he called as he drew closer.

She turned. "Hey, Declan," she breathed out his name and smiled, but it didn't reach her eyes. "Ready?"

Declan opened the door for her, letting Addey take the lead. He was walking into her world. His aim for tonight was to see if he could make her smile. And he really wanted to make a better impression.

Addey stopped just before the entrance to the kitchen and Declan bumped into her, his hands landing on her shoulders. Turning, she was far too close. He could see the sea-green of her eyes, the flush on her cheeks, the way her red hair fell as she tilted her head. "Tell me you can cook?" Her words were raspy.

The desperate plea in her voice warmed his heart. She was worried about her cooking abilities? He put his hands back on her shoulders, gently turned her around, and spoke in her ear. "Come on, there's nothing to be afraid of." Then he propelled them both through the door.

***

"Ugh, you *can* bake. Life isn't fair." Addey narrowed her eyes as Declan pulled the tray of perfect sugar cookies out of the oven.

"It's not that hard. You just follow the recipe," Declan said, looking far too good in his black apron, sleeves rolled up to his elbows. A babe and a whiz in the kitchen—life really wasn't fair sometimes.

"That's what Carmel says." Addey looked at her tray of mismatched, half-baked cookies. "I think she should change careers."

Declan chuckled and Addey had to admit, she loved the sound of it. She tried not to watch him too much, but his presence was overwhelming in the small kitchen space they shared. When they'd walked in, everyone stopped to see the man that definitely wasn't Carmel. Addey wanted to hide. What if someone recognized him? Knew he was the journalist who her parents hated? Knew who *she* was?

Though the thoughts were absurd, they didn't abate. The stress of the moment had finally broken when Frances asked where Carmel was. Addey mumbled something about a family emergency and practically leapt over to her kitchen bay, grateful to be doing anything other than have people stare at her, at Declan...at *them*.

"Yours are good too."

Declan peered over her shoulder, but she could hear the restraint in his voice.

Addey frowned. "They're too crumbly." She tried to pick one up but it broke apart in her hand and the center was too soft. "Look." She held up a piece that showed the gooey middle.

Declan took the broken cookie, his fingers grazing hers, and Addey felt the ripple of attraction all over again.

"But that's the best bit." His gaze seared hers as he popped the cookie into his mouth.

Addey couldn't look away from him. He had a crumb on his lip. Her fingers twitched, wanting to reach out and brush it away. Instead, she kept her hand firmly on the tray.

"Yep, it's good."

"You're just being nice," Addey sighed and went back to taking her ruined cookies off the baking tray.

"And since when am I known for that?" His voice was close, and she shivered at his nearness.

Addey turned her head, his mouth was almost level with hers. She stilled, unable to move. His eyes were deep brown, coffee-colored, with a touch of amber in the center.

"Fine, but still, you're being too nice about my terrible cooking skills."

Declan reached down, his chin brushing her shoulder. Addey could have stayed all night, right there, with his manly, ice-rink scent, and his body keeping the rest of the kitchen out of sight.

"I think it's just undercooked. Put it back in the oven for another five minutes and see if it's any better."

Addey sighed as he moved away. She was both grateful for the space and missed it at the same time. Yep, she was going crazy and her parents' worst enemy was to blame. She really needed to pull herself together.

"I've been doing this for almost ten weeks and the only thing I can make really well is boiled vegetables," Addey said.

"That's a meal in itself." Declan wiped the bench down. His shoulders shook as he coughed into his elbow.

"You're a real pal." Addey plonked down onto the seat at the circular table in the bay. "How did you learn to cook so well?"

His shoulders stiffened. Addey knew she'd found a topic he didn't like. Hope nosedived when she took in his guarded expression as he joined her at the table, but then he surprised her. "My parents split up years ago, my mum had to work, my sister Nicky was twelve...someone had to cook, so I learned." He shrugged, his voice casual, but there was nothing casual about the dark shadow in his eyes.

"I'm sorry they split up, that must have been hard." Addey kept probing, not sure why, except she wanted to know this man better, know what made him smile, what made him mad—besides her family—and what he liked to do for fun. Her thoughts skittered back to her parents and their argument yesterday. The decision to pull out from the party was going to cost her, and doubts plagued her.

"It was the best thing for everyone, believe me." The dark tone wasn't lost on her, but then he smiled. Although it didn't meet his eyes, it still changed his face for the better. "Speaking of families, how was it at your parents' yesterday?"

"I quit being in charge of the party." She spoke softly, not wanting to be overheard, but with the noise of pots and pans, and the din of voices, it was unlikely.

Declan's eyes sharpened. "What happened?"

Addey played with the oven mitts. "My mom tried to set me up with a guy, which she promised she wouldn't do." She hadn't called Mark from the Baker/Gibson Group yet, choosing instead to put it off, because she was scared to call. Scared to see her business, and herself, lose this opportunity.

"Let me guess." His smile was sardonic and tone bleak. "You're not capable of choosing someone good enough for them?"

Addey didn't bother replying. The truth was right there, sitting at the table, handsome, intense, and too intriguing for Addey to walk away from. "Nope. And my mother knows she's not supposed to do that. She broke our agreement, so I quit the party."

Declan raised his eyebrows, and a slow grin spread over him. "I'm sorry I won't see you at the party. You were the only person I was looking forward to seeing."

The words, the warmth in them, heated her cheeks, and when she looked across at him, the intensity there, she found the same look that had pulled her in and refused to let her go at the café last week. And here they were.

"You're very confusing," Addey whispered.

"Is that a good thing?" Declan leaned in, his gaze holding hers.

"I haven't decided yet." Addey swallowed the rising lump in her throat, her words coming out throaty.

Declan's easy smile lit a fire in her belly. "I'll have to work on clearing up your confusion."

Addey's cheeks heated, she averted her gaze, her pulse thrumming in her ears.

Yep, the storm was building.

The timer beeped, breaking the moment. Addey jumped up, oven mitts in hand, and pulled the last baking tray out of the oven.

Declan grabbed her tray of broken ones and put them back in the oven. "We'll turn the oven down and let them slowly bake." He adjusted the dial.

Together they set about decorating the cookies, well, Declan's cookies. Addey moved her icing pen over the cooled cookies, creating the lines of the Christmas tree shape. She added lines in the middle to show the tree branches, and used red and silver edible glitter to evenly cover the inside.

"You underestimate yourself, Addey. That's amazing," Declan said.

Addey looked at him and back at cookies. "I'll admit they look better than yours."

She tried to stifle a giggle, but it didn't work. The icing pen Declan was holding looked tiny in his big hand, and his Christmas tree cookie looked like a five year old had tried to ice it.

"Baking and decorating are two completely different skills." His wounded voice and pout would have stopped her cold, if not for the sly twinkle in his eyes, which made her laugh harder.

"You're right." Frances chose that moment to descend on them. "They are two different skills and you two complement each other well."

Declan sidled up next to Addey and winked at her. "Couldn't have done it without Addey."

Addey ducked her head. "Thanks, but Declan's the star here. I think I'm his assistant, much like I am with Carmel."

Frances shook her head. "Today has been about teamwork. As it always is." She looked between them. "You two make a good team."

She walked off just as the oven timer dinged. Addey raced to grab the oven mitts and pulled her broken cookies out and put them on the bench. The centers of the cookies were no longer gooey.

"See, it's better than you thought it would be." Declan nudged her arm, his eyes crinkling at the edges. He was better than he thought he was. Did he know that? Right now, it was hard to reconcile the man here with the man who used his words like a weapon against her father.

"Thanks," Addey mumbled, looking away. "How's your mom doing?" A change in topic was needed.

"She's been good the last couple of days." His face closed off and Addey knew there was so much more to this man than he let others see. "The good days are almost as often as the bad days now."

"I like your mom," Addey said, smiling easily just thinking about the sweet lady. "She's so excited about the Frank Sinatra afternoon this week."

"I know, she keeps showing me how she underlined it in her little notebook." His warm gaze met hers. "It's good what you do there, you know."

Addey shrugged, but it was the second time she'd been complimented on the work she did there. Funny how she didn't think of it as work, but something that was giving back to the community, something that would honor Granny.

Declan sat back down, and they kept decorating, working in comfortable silence.

After several minutes, Declan spoke. "So, what so happens with all this food?"

Without thinking, she replied, "We keep a little of it, but most of it is going to the Community Center as gifts."

Watching Declan's handsome face morph from surprise to guarded, Addey held the icing pen rigid in her grip. "Oh, I'm sorry. I shouldn't have mentioned it."

He gave a tight smile that didn't reach his eyes. "No worries," he said lightly, though his voice had an edge to it. "It is what it is."

***

Addey's words were barely audible, but he sensed the pain in them all the same. He ran a hand down his face and looked at her. Round eyes, lips parted slightly, her face drawn—even when sad, she was gorgeous.

He sighed. "I just can't accept that it's going to close," he said. His chest felt tight. There it was again, the rising anger, bubbling away—always. He looked at Addey and hated the look in her eyes—fear? Anger? Worry? All of it? He started counting to twenty.

"Why do you do that?"

Her question caught him off guard, and he looked at her. "Do what?"

"Cross your arms and stare at the ceiling. You did it at the Heritage Oaks too."

Observant woman. "I'm counting to twenty."

She tilted her head. "What for?"

"I'm trying to stop myself from saying things I'll regret."

She quirked a smile, but her eyes still held uncertainty. "Your own version of anger management?"

Declan's laugh was hollow. "Something like that. Eli taught me to do it. He told me it would help me to think before I said something stupid." He shrugged his shoulders. "Doesn't always work, as you know."

Addey played with the oven mitts, similar to the way she played with the serviettes at the café after ice hockey. "I'm sorry I brought up the Community Center."

"Wasn't your fault."

"Feels like it..." She looked away, and it cramped his heart. He was trying to make a better impression on her. Finally, the anger that had surged found a fissure to escape from. The tension in his chest eased. Maybe it was the setting, the people, or simply Addey. But he was determined that tonight was going to end on a better note.

"Let's finish up and get out of here."

Addey's wary gaze caught his. He nudged her foot with his. "Let's pack up and play tourist."

"I don't know..."

Her hedging only made him more determined. "Come on, we can't let all this effort go to waste."

Eyeing him. "What do you have in mind?"

"It won't be scary. Boy Scout, remember?" He winked, trying to lighten the mood. "Lincoln Memorial at night is really cool."

Her full bellied laugh shot through him like a warm drink on a cold day. "Alright. I haven't done that in ages."

They finished decorating the rest of the cookies, put Addey's over-baked, broken ones in a container, cleaned up the kitchen, and headed out into the cold night.

"I'll drive us." Declan headed towards his car, his steps light, his heart beating faster than it had a right to. He hadn't ruined the night.

His phone rang.

It was Heritage Oaks.

***

Declan strode down the hallway so fast Addey had to jog to keep up with him. He'd accepted her offer to drive as her car was closer to where they were standing when the call came through. Addey, still clutching the cookie packet, stopped short when she heard the distressed voice of Susannah Collins. Declan plowed ahead to where a nurse was waiting for them, but Addey couldn't keep going. They didn't need her sticking her head in—not now.

"I don't want to be here. Where is my son?" Susannah's frightened voice pricked at Addey's heart. This must be killing Declan.

"I'll give you a chance to settle your mother." The nurse, a woman Addey didn't recognize nodded to Addey before she walked off.

"Mom, I'm here." The rough tone of his Declan's only added to Addey's heavy heart. "I won't leave, it's okay. Let's put Frank on."

"I don't want Frank! I want to go home!" Susannah's voice cracked, rising higher.

"I know, Mom." Addey could hear rustling around the room. "Let's look at some photos." Declan's voice continued, soft and unhurried.

"Take me away from here." The pleading broke Addey's heart, and she pressed her back hard against the wall, not sure what to do. In the end, she did the only thing she could think of—she prayed.

A dark-haired woman with tight lips and a determined stride raced past Addey. "Declan, is Mom okay?"

That had to be Nicky. Declan had called her on the way here. Addey could easily see the resemblance between the siblings. Taking a breath, Addey stepped over to the door and peered in. Susannah sat on her recliner, tears streaking down her cheeks, arms gripping the armrests so tight her fingertips were pink. Declan knelt beside his mother, trying to soothe her. Nicky hovered at the back, her mouth set in a grim line.

"Mom, it's Nicky. I'm here too." Nicky's voice was raspy.

"Nicky, Declan won't take me home." Susannah glared at Declan. Declan rubbed his temples.

"Mom, it's okay. I'll stay with you," Nicky spoke softly, but Addey saw the siblings exchange looks.

Addey had an idea, but it really wasn't her place—she planned events, not calmed anxious Alzheimer's patients. But sometimes, someone different could help. She'd seen it many times since working here. Inhaling a breath of courage, Addey cleared her throat. Three sets of eyes met hers.

"Who are you?" Nicky and Susannah said in unison.

"Addey?" Declan said, as if he'd forgotten she was here.

"I have an idea." Addey gripped the doorframe.

"I'm all ears." Declan said.

"Declan, we don't need another person here." Nicky spoke through a clenched jaw.

"I know...cards," she said weakly. "Susannah, do you remember me? I'm Addey, I help out here from time to time." She didn't enter the room but made sure she caught the older woman's eye—the poor woman was frightened and Addey wanted to cry but wouldn't. It wasn't her place to grieve this loss.

"I think so..." Her words came out slowly. "Can you take me home?"

Addey closed her eyes and swallowed back the lump forming in her throat. She opened her eyes. "No, Susannah, I can't." She glanced at Declan, who had gone pale, the pain radiating off him bleakly. "But would you like to play some cards?"

"Can we go home after that?" Susannah's voice wobbled, her hand shaking.

"Have some water, Mom." Nicky held up a cup to her mother's lips. "We'll talk to the nurse about that, but let's play cards first?"

"Alright." Susannah's eyes still darted between her kids, her words coming out slow. "Will you stay, Nicky? Declan?"

Declan nodded.

Addey walked in until she was in front of Susannah. Declan stood, gave Addey his chair and knelt on the ground.

Addey tried to say thanks, but Delcan squeezed her hand. "I'm fine."

For the next ten minutes the little group played Go Fish. The tension in the room had eased and Susannah's eyes had lost some of their fear.

Addey slowly stood, patting Susannah gently on the hand. "I'll let you rest now, but I'll come in and see you later."

Declan stood, leaning down to hug his mother. "Let me just walk Addey out, and I'll be right back. I'm going to call Eli. Nicky will stay here with you."

Nicky sent Addey a wan smile. And she mouthed "thank you" as Addey backed out of the room. It was time for her to leave. "Here." She pressed the container of cookies into Declan's hands. "You might need this." Addey tucked her hair behind her ear. "I hope she improves tonight. I assume your sister can drive you back to your car?"

"Thank you," he nodded, his soft words wiggling into her heart.

"I didn't do anything."

"You changed the mood in the room. Mom must see you as someone—safe." His mouth turned down. "Thanks for...I don't know...being you." The smile he gave her was sad. "I had a good time tonight, thanks for inviting me."

Addey swallowed, this time a tear forming. But she didn't blink, lest it fall and Declan would know how much his words impacted her. Being herself was always problematic. Mom and Dad never seemed to like her, no matter what she did or didn't do.

"From memory, you invited yourself." Addey smiled despite the situation and she was rewarded with one in return—it warmed her heart.

"Well, thanks for letting me invite myself." The rich timbre of his voice sent a shiver down her spine.

"I'd better let you get back in there." Addey backed away. "Good night, Declan." She turned and walked down the hall when he called out.

"Addey, for the record..."

She turned back to face him, raised her eyebrows.

"I'm glad your mom's match-making schemes didn't work." Their gazes caught, holding her in place, her heart beat faster. Hope, delight, and, yes, fear, infused over Addey.

"Me too," she said. "You're a surprise I didn't see coming."

Chapter Eighteen

Addey walked down King Street, huddled deep into her jacket, the chilly wind blowing her hair behind her. Christmas wreaths hung from the iconic iron lamp posts. The shops were bordered with green, twinkle light-infused garlands, while red Christmas bows hung from doors throughout the main street. In a different mood—when she hadn't just quit the party and disappointed her parents yet again—she might slowly wander and drink in the holiday spirit. On top of that, she hadn't slept much last night, worrying about Susannah, thinking about Declan.

Always thinking about Declan.

The local bagel café, where she was meeting Holly for breakfast, pulled her inside, the freshly-baked bagel and coffee aroma calling to her. Inside it was warm and toasty. People gathered at tables, talking and laughing. She spied Holly sitting in a booth, her tablet open, pen tucked into the corner of her mouth, glasses slipping down her nose.

"I need coffee." Addey sat, rubbing her hands together.

Holly grinned, pushing her glasses up the bridge of her nose. She tapped the second cup on the table. "Already got you one."

"I don't know what I'd do without you." Addey sipped her drink, savoring the warmth it spread through her body.

"Hopefully you'll never have to know." Holly grinned, but it faded, her forehead wrinkling. "Are we still not doing your parents' Christmas party?"

"Nope. Mom and Dad keep calling me, but I'm not taking their calls." Addey stood. "I'm going to order. Have you ordered yet?"

Holly shook her head, worry still tracing across her face. "What about Mark from Baker/Gibson?"

Addey sighed. "I don't know yet. He might still want it, without the party, but I'll cross that bridge when I get to it. Do you want your usual?"

"Yes, please."

"I'll be back." Addey weaved through the tables until she was at the counter. She placed their orders, asked for another two coffees, paid and waited at the receiving bay for her order. The mid-twenties girl with blonde streaked brown hair put her food on the waiting area, and Addey grabbed them and went back to where Holly sat.

"By the way" —Addey opened her wrapped blueberry and cream cheese bagel— "you're looking better this morning."

Holly unwrapped her bacon, egg and cheese bagel and took a bite. She closed her eyes and sighed happily. "You're right, I did need to rest. I'm feeling stronger. Still tired, but that's just life, right?" She lifted a shoulder, a tight smile that didn't do anything to make Addey worry less about her right-hand girl.

"Good. Take care of yourself." Addey was about to take another bite when her phone beeped. She glanced at it and put down her food.

"It's Mom." Addey went to swipe the text off her screen, but her finger stilled at the words in the message preview.

You need to call me. You have contract obligations to fulfil.

"You look pale," Holly frowned.

"Contract obligations." Addey looked up at Holly. "Mom is playing hard." This was her punishment for walking away, for calling Mom out on her behavior.

"You'd better call her." Holly's big eyes got bigger. "Your mother is scary."

Addey huffed. "Don't I know it." She stood and found an empty corner to make her call. She didn't want to have this conversation face to face. That would be too much. With a shaking finger, she pressed Mom's number.

The phone rang for several long seconds.

Addey was about to hang up when Mom answered. "Good morning." Her crisp, clipped voice did nothing to assuage Addey's worry.

"Hi, Mom." Addey paused, closed her eyes and gathered her resolve. "I got your text."

"I gathered." Mom's smug voice grated on Addey's nerves. "Before I discuss our situation" —Addey took a deep breath, a pain beginning to start at the back of one eye— "I went to the Children's Benefit. It was lovely, except that Collins journalist was there. I saw his article today. Seems he's happy to take a positive spin on our people when it comes to money for children, but otherwise, we're all beneath him."

Addey inhaled, her shoulders becoming rigid. "Did you talk to him?"

"Of course not. I won't lower myself to engage with such a man," Mom said. *In fine form today.* "And you'd do well to remember that. People like him love to create chaos, and we—you and I, your father—we're his targets."

Addey scoffed. "You make him sound like a hitman. He's a journalist, Mom. Not the devil."

Mom huffed. "You think too well of people, you always have."

Addey squeezed her eyes shut. *Naïve.* Mom didn't need to say the word aloud. "I prefer to believe the best in people. It's called grace and second chances." Something her mother never seemed to give her.

Mom huffed. "Just remember, people like *us* need to be careful of who comes into our lives."

Mom's snobbery knew no limits. Addey couldn't imagine Declan "targeting" them the way Mom was thinking. Sure, he would struggle to be unbiased, but he wasn't the man Mom thought he was. Well, at least, the man she was getting to know.

Fear settled in her gut. What would they say if they knew she had been spending time with him? Would they cut all ties? Would they blame her for something that was out of her control? Despite all the raging questions, her fears, and her mother's words, she liked the man she was seeing. But she wanted her parents to love her, too.

Was seeing Declan worth giving up an opportunity to find peace, acceptance and, dare she hope, love from the only family she had left in the world?

"Let's talk about the real reason you called." Addey veered into safer territory—Declan versus contractual obligations. She knew which won out.

"Fine, but don't think I'm wrong about that man." Mom inhaled and Addey imagined Mom sitting at her one hundred and fifty year old oak desk in her home office, the carpet cream colored and thick. An original painting of the sun rising over a river by an artist Addey could not recall the name of, hung above the desk. The transom window let the light in and overlooked the deck, where the river drifted past. Everything in that scene was perfect.

Except Mom's life was discordant, and Addey was part of that.

"As per our contract, you're required to provide us with a replacement." She was all business.

Addey rubbed her forehead. "I know and I can do that. I'll fulfil my obligations."

Mom was silent. Addey gripped her phone, her stomach tense as she waited out the silence.

Finally, Mom spoke. "There is no one to take your place."

"That wasn't the song you were singing on Sunday," Addey said.

"I want you to run this event." Mom's voice hardened.

"I don't want you to interfere in my life," Addey countered.

Mom didn't immediately reply. Addey could feel the tension ratcheting up. She kneaded her head and loosened her grip on the phone.

Mom spoke. "Then we're at an impasse. As your mother, I have a right to want to see you settle down with a good man."

Addey squeezed her eyes shut. "Then I'm not doing the party. I'll send through the names you need who can take my place."

"Adelaide." Mom's voice could cut steel. "Don't do this."

Addey gritted her teeth. "What? Are you going to take legal action?" A sliver of dread crept up her spine. Would her mother actually sue her for breach of contract? Would she stoop that low?

"I'll do what's needed. We'll talk about this later." Mom hung up.

Addey stood on shaky legs and made her way back to Holly.

"Well?" Holly had finished her bagel and had made in road into the second cup of coffee.

Addey took shaky breaths. "I think Mom might pursue legal avenues if I don't come back on board."

Holly's mouth dropped open.

"And she thinks Declan is targeting my family."

Holly raised her eyebrows and cracked up. "That's nuts." Then she sobered up. "But, for real about the legal implications? Are we in breach of contract?"

Addey stared at Holly, unblinking. "Yes."

Holly gasped.

Addey continued. "But it was something that was a formality and I never once thought she would act like this." All because Addey refused to date the men Mom paraded in front of her. "I've never had an issue with any other party she threw before."

Holly dipped her chin. "This isn't just any party."

"I know." Addey sighed, the weight of her life pressing down on her.

Should she tell Declan what her mother was possibly going to do? The other question lingered. How much could she truly trust Declan?

The pain that started in her eye slowly spread. Her life was too complicated, but deep in her gut, she knew the truth. She was starting to really care for this passionate man who loved his family with such fierceness it made her heart ache.

Because the only person who had ever loved her like that was dead.

***

Three hours of sleep wasn't enough, and six a.m. was far too early to be outside the Community Center doing the bakery run. But it was important—to him, to Eli, and to countless people he didn't know. Declan waited for Eli outside, a steaming take-out coffee in one hand. He'd need another one—no, make that five or six—to stay awake today. The sign out front was still an affront, but he worked to think about Addey every time he saw it in his peripheral vision. Lovely Addey. She was worth fighting for. But as soon as that thought dropped, a penny of doubt followed. Could he put aside his anger for her? For her family? He ran his hand over his face, as if it would work out the knot the confusion in himself, he couldn't untangle. The sun had yet to rise over the buildings and Declan hoped Eli was coping better than he was. The two of them and Nicky had all stayed well past midnight, getting Mom settled and calm.

Addey's help with the cards had only been a reprieve, but one Declan was grateful for. Her willingness to try touched his heart. There was no pity in her questions and offers of help, only genuine concern and it made him like her more. *Like her?* The words settled in and made themselves comfy. Yes, he did like Addey. He cast a glance at the offending sign and breathed out a long sigh. The complicated situation made his head hurt, but so far, Addey was nothing like her parents. And he was finding it harder and harder to stay away from her.

"I hope you have one for me." Eli's voice carried across the cold wind. "You look about as good as I feel." The shadows under his eyes told the same story that was no doubt reflected on Declan's face.

Declan opened the car door and pulled out another coffee and handed it to Eli. "Lucky you arrived when you did, I was about to drink it."

"Did Heritage Oaks call?" Eli shrugged out of his heavy black parka and tossed it into his beat-up cherry red SUV.

"No, I called them before I got here, and she's still asleep." Declan shed his own thick jacket and put it in the car. They'd nearly had to resort to sedating her, but thankfully hadn't had to go there—yet. He wasn't looking forward to it when the time came.

"I'll go over once we've picked up the baked goods." Eli sipped his cup before putting it in the cup holder.

"Get some sleep first," Declan said.

Eli nodded and steered the car into the busy morning traffic.

"Did you call the bakery?"

Eli drove with one hand on the wheel. His eyes trained ahead of him, watching the traffic. "Yep, they don't have much today though."

Declan ground his teeth. "It's okay. We'll take what they've got."

His phone beeped and he glanced at it. Addey's name appeared on the screen, sending a jolt of anticipation surging through him.

How's your mom? Did you get much sleep?

He typed back.

She's settled, took a while. Thanks for your help. It meant a lot. Didn't get much sleep.

He tossed the phone back onto the console and tried to hide the smile, but it wouldn't stay suppressed.

"You went out with Addey last night?" Eli asked, glancing at him as he drove.

Declan schooled his features into a blank canvas. "It wasn't a date."

His phone beeped again. He picked it up and saw Addey's message.

Glad to help. Hope the cookies were okay.

Declan grinned and tapped back his reply.

They were great. Broken cookies are still good, and bonus, they helped calm Mom down. See you Thursday, for a date with Frank Sinatra?

The three little dots said Addey was replying.

Yes, the residents are looking forward to it...and so am I.

I'm looking forward to it as well. The thought landed with a thud, and he found himself excited. Mom would love it and he'd get to see Addey again.

"Then what was it?" Eli's question intruded into his thoughts.

"What was what?" Declan said.

"Your 'not date'," Eli replied, giving his head a little shake.

Declan tipped his head against the headrest. "It was a cooking class. I was filling in for a friend, that's all."

"Sounds like a date to me," Eli's lips quirked. "Addey seems nice. She does great work at Heritage Oaks."

"I'll second that." Declan kept sipping his drink. He didn't know what to say about himself and Addey—there wasn't a "them". Did he want there to be? He thought about her parents and it left a hollow in his chest. "It's complicated. I have baggage and she does as well."

"Everyone has baggage," Eli said.

Declan snorted. "Not everyone has my baggage."

Eli tapped the steering wheel. "You're going to have to deal with it one of these days. It's not going to go away."

"Trust me, Eli, I'm not going to tell Addey about my felon of a father."

"So, you're going to date this woman and not share anything of your life with her?" Eli stopped at a red light and faced him, his eyebrows raised.

"We're not dating," Declan ground out.

Eli pressed the car forward when the light turned green. "When you go out with a woman and start texting regularly, I'm pretty sure it's called dating."

Declan groaned. "Thanks for the advice, but I know what I'm doing."

They lapsed into silence, the heater hummed, warming the car. Maybe Eli was right. Should he let Addey know about his past? She'd shared hers and that couldn't have been easy, except, the circumstances warranted it. And her secret, although not great, was only a personal one. His was a national humiliation and one he didn't talk about—*ever*. He'd worked so hard to change her perception of him, and as soon as she found out, would she wonder if he could do something like that? That if those genes that ran in his dad, they might run in him too?

In his deepest, darkest moments, he wondered this about himself.

The bakery came into sight, relieving Declan of his dark thoughts.

Eli pulled into the parking lot out in front of a small, square, red brick structure, set deep in a commercial warehouse. A white sign with block writing "Baking For Life" hung large across the entrance door. They got out and the smell of freshly-baked bread hit them before they even opened the door. They went inside and Declan immediately wanted to eat a bread roll smothered in butter.

A thick, black granite counter blocked them from entering the kitchen and served as a reception area. The counter was wide enough to put crates of baked bread, rolls, muffins, and other various baked goods on one end, and at the other end sat a cash register, which butted against the wall. A noticeboard hung on the wall with flyers advertising different places that bought the products from the bakery, community events, and a petition to save the Community Center. Declan walked over and pulled that one down, crumpled it up and jammed it into his pocket.

"Hey boys, cold this morning, isn't it?" Leonie, the manager, walked over while wiping her hands on her black apron. She was in her mid-twenties and short, with wild curly black hair that was pulled into a messy bun high on her head.

Eli stepped forward shivering. "Yes, Miss Leonie, it is. What have you got for us today?"

Declan stood next to him, eyeing the food in the kitchen, his stomach rumbling. He needed more than a cup of coffee for breakfast.

Leonie consulted a clipboard sitting next to the register. "Well, you're in luck today. A second order just got canceled. I'm sure glad we get people to pay in full when they place the orders. We'd go broke otherwise. Give me a sec and I'll get the boys to bring it out."

They waited in the warmth of the building. Moments later Leonie appeared with two young teens lugging four large crates filled with loaves of bread, bread rolls, muffins, and scones. Declan's mouth watered, but he wouldn't touch any of this.

Eli led the boys out to the car while he stayed with Leonie to sign the paperwork.

"How's your week been?" Declan leaned on the counter.

"Tiring. Family stuff is draining." Her tired voice and fatigue lined eyes was enough to tell Declan all he needed to know.

"It sure is. Anything we can do?"

Leonie looked after her two younger siblings, both in their teens. Their mother had left them to chase a new man six months ago.

"How about a miracle, in the form of moving this place closer to the city's center? That way, we could open a café and bakery. Get the benefit of the foot traffic and be a bit closer to everything, you know?"

"I'm fresh out of miracles." Declan touched the crumpled paper in his pocket. Since he'd failed at that, there was no way he could help others. Besides, when had he ever experienced a miracle?

"Who's got the boys today?" Declan grabbed the pen and signed on the bottom line of the form.

She nodded out back to the buzzing kitchen. "I've put them to work today. They're getting paid for this, so there's no complaining."

Declan handed the paperwork back when Eli returned, the teens in tow. "Ready?"

Eli nodded. "Let us know if we can help in any way, okay?"

"I will," Leonie replied. "When's the last day for the Center?"

"New Year's Eve." Eli stepped in, no emotion with the words. Just facts.

"That'll be a sad day." She tilted her head and exhaled softly.

Declan's chest tightened. Places like this were a lifeline for the Center. Getting this food meant the Community Center could distribute it to the families in the area who didn't have enough. As Christmas drew closer, the pressure on low-income families, single-parent homes, and homeless people would only increase. Once it was gone, those people would suffer. He hated it with every fiber of his being, but the woman who had owned the building had died and now the building was sold. A sale he'd spent a year fighting and one he'd lost.

They turned to leave, but Leonie called them back. "Oh, I forgot, are either of you able to pick up a load on Saturday morning?"

They stopped and turned back. Declan spoke first. "What's on this Saturday?"

"It's assessment day and there'll be loads more food being made. We'll definitely need an extra pair of hands."

Ah, assessment time. Baking for Life was a teaching bakery as well as being the top supplier to many businesses in the area.

Eli looked at Declan and shook his head. "I can't. I've got an appointment in D.C. at eight o'clock."

"I can do it," Declan said. "What time do you want me here?"

"Six a.m. work for you?"

"I can do that, it's no different from this morning." He waved. "I'll be here with some others to help!" he called over his shoulder. He didn't know who was going to help him.

Inside the car, which smelled heavenly, they headed back to the Community Center in comfortable silence.

"Will you see your mom today?" Eli asked.

"Yeah, after work." Declan rubbed his gritty eyes. He really needed more sleep, but as soon as he finished unloading the crates, he was headed straight to the office.

"I'll sit with her at lunch," Eli said.

Eli visited her every day. He'd been a constant friend since they'd arrived in Virginia. Declan took the moment to ask the question he probably should have asked years ago. "Eli, how come you never married Mom?"

The silence extended. Declan waited. Patience wasn't his strongest attribute, but he could manage it when really needed. They pulled up in front of the Community Center.

Eli unbuckled his belt and looked at Declan. "Two reasons: You can't marry someone who still loves someone else, and you can't marry someone who doesn't know how you feel."

"Why didn't you ever tell her?"

Eli watched him intently. "There's nothing to say, Declan."

Eli got out of the car and slammed the door. Declan tensed, and climbed out. Eli popped the trunk open, and they started moving the crates out. For once, Eli was much faster. Declan grabbed a crate, his mind whirling, and hurried to catch up. He put the crate on the kitchen bench where May and Georgia were bagging the food ready to be delivered. He nodded at them, then cast a glance at Eli. Nothing much had changed except an air of darkness now hung over his friend and mentor. Declan followed Eli out to the car.

They were about to grab the last two crates when Declan laid a hand on Eli's arm.

"I'm sorry I pried into something that's none of my business." He kept his gaze fixed on his friend. "No matter what I think, it's between you and Mom."

Eli sat on the open tailgate, frowning. "Your mother is the finest lady I know. She doesn't need any more complications in her life."

"I don't think Mom has ever thought of you as a complication."

Eli heaved himself up and tried to smile. It didn't work. "Thanks."

Truth be told, Declan didn't know how his mother felt about Eli. He understood their friendship was deep and strong, but did she love him? Declan had wanted a happily ever after for them for a few years, but seeing Mom's diagnosis now, he saw the wisdom in Eli's hesitation. Maybe it was enough for Eli to be there every day and not confuse things any further. But imagine loving someone but never telling them.

His phone buzzed. It was Addey. He scanned the text and almost dropped the phone.

I think my mom might sue me for breach of contract if I don't return to planning the party.

Without thinking, he called her.

She answered immediately. "It's been a fun morning."

"That's not funny. Is she serious?" Declan paced out front of his vehicle.

Addey's voice was tired. "She didn't say it outright, but the hint was there." Then she laughed, a hollow, exhausted sound that ripped at Declan's heart. "She also thinks you're targeting my family."

"What?" This was madness. "What does that even mean?"

Addey's sigh fell long and hard down the line. "The Emily Gilmore article, the positive spin on the Children's Benefit, all those earlier articles about Dad's business..."

"Did she expect me to say something negative about an organization that helps sick children just because rich people are there?"

"You don't like the world I come from," Addey said it so softly, he might have missed it, if the phone hadn't been glued hard to his ear.

"I don't." Declan kept pacing. "But this is nuts. You know that, right?"

"I know." The unspoken "but" hung in the air. "Mom is just being over-dramatic, which she's prone to." She was clearly trying to lighten the mood, but all Declan saw was giant red stop signs, telling him to back away from Addey. Their situation, whatever it was, was becoming untenable.

He needed to get through the Christmas party and get his column back. Dating anyone, let alone Addey—he glanced at the sign and flexed his fingers—was too complicated.

"Don't worry, Declan," Addey said. "Mom will settle down."

He didn't miss the doubt that hung on her every word. "I'm sure she will." Declan might as well play along, because what kind of parent would do something like that to their own daughter?

"You still coming on Thursday for the Frank Sinatra dance?" Addey asked quietly. As if he might not want to be near her.

"Yes." He glanced at Eli, who was watching Declan with quiet interest.

"Great...See you then."

"See you." Declan didn't know what to think. His chest heaved from the adrenaline coursing through him.

"Was that Addey? Everything okay? Maybe you could ask Addey to help you on Saturday."

Declan pressed his lips together, put the phone in his pocket and reached for a crate. "Oh, so you're allowed to interfere in my life, but I can't return the favor?"

Eli took the last crate and smiled. This time it was real. "Who else is going to?"

Declan mock-frowned. "You're hilarious."

"You going to ask her?" Eli prompted.

"I don't think that's a great idea." Not from the conversation they'd just had.

They dropped off the last two crates, waved to May and Georgia, and headed back to the car.

"Why is it not a great idea?" Eli closed the tailgate, resting his foot on the curb.

Declan shrugged. "It's just not." He would not break her confidence. Addey deserved his respect, and he would honor her in this.

"It's because she's the planner for the Hamilton party."

"Among other things," he replied, shifting his feet.

"Declan, don't miss out on something that could be amazing just because you're consumed with anger. It's not her fault the Hamiltons hired her. A girl needs to eat, too."

Eli had no idea what he was saying. And it wasn't Declan's place to fill him in. "It's more than that," Declan said. "There're things that could go very wrong." Like a lawsuit.

Eli half laughed. "Since when have you let anything like that ever stop you?"

"I don't want to make her life any harder than it needs to be." Declan shoved his hands in his pockets. And he truly didn't. Just knowing the way her parents would treat her if they even saw her standing with Declan, let alone anything else, made him feel ill. He didn't want to cause her added pain to what she was already experiencing.

And on top of that, he needed his column back.

Eli watched him before nodding. "You don't have to tell me what's going on, but I can see something is."

"Can you just trust me?" Declan eyed Eli.

"I do trust you," Eli said. "But do me a favor, don't let your anger and fear stop you from finding happiness."

Declan nodded, unable to speak past the ball of emotion that stuck in his chest. What would he do without Eli? Their lives would have been much harder if they'd never met him.

Later, as Declan drove to the newspaper office, Eli's words and images of Addey swirled through his mind. Was he afraid of finding happiness? Was he really letting his anger keep him away from people? If he was honest with himself, he would have said yes, he was doing all those things. But then the image of his father being led in handcuffs to jail, the sounds of Mom crying herself to sleep every night echoed through his mind, overtaking Eli's words. He wasn't ready to forgive, but maybe he could let go of *some* of the anger.

When he arrived at the office, he noticed a tiny ember of hope flicker deep inside him. Maybe if he gave hope a chance, it would be enough for him. However, he still needed to keep his distance from Addey, as much as that was possible, for both their sakes.

Chapter Nineteen

Addey sat in her office trying to work up the courage to call Mark from the Baker/Gibson Group. The clock on her wall ticked past ten-thirty. Yesterday's phone call with Mom had been the last she'd heard from her—no follow-up call, no message. It felt like watching a storm gather on the horizon, knowing it was only a matter of time before it broke loose. If Mom followed through on her implied threat, the sale of Addey's business would fall through. It would be one more thing for her parents to be disappointed in—another failure, especially in her father's world where success was measured in business deals and bottom lines.

Adding to the stress was Declan. Hearing his incredulous response to her mother's actions lifted her spirits. What would it be like to have someone as passionate as that in her corner? To have someone fight for her like he did for his causes? But she didn't have that and never could. Declan would run, like the rest of them, because her parents were too much. She'd heard it in his voice.

Addey wiped her hands on her pants, pushing away images of Declan. It was time to focus on her business. Taking a deep breath of courage, she began scrolling through her phone for Mark's number when Holly stuck her head in the office door.

"You're not going to like this." Holly's face was pale.

Addey put the phone down. "What am I not going to like?"

Holly's hands gripped the door frame. "Your Dad just walked in. Nina is holding him off. Do you want to see him?"

Addey closed her eyes. What now? Was he coming with more threats? He wasn't satisfied with how things had been left on Sunday and he needed to fix it—his way. Or Mom's way? Addey had no idea what lay ahead. She opened her eyes, pressed her hand to her chest. She could do this. She nodded. "Send him in." Or he'll just barge in.

"Good luck," Holly whispered.

Addey sat up straight and breathed in and out, preparing herself.

"Your receptionist is rather pushy." Dad stood in the doorway.

"Nina is very good at her job." Addey stood. "Come in and sit down."

Dad made a noise in his throat as he walked closer, but he didn't sit. Addey remained standing and waited him out.

"You've been ignoring our texts and calls." He narrowed his eyes.

Addey leaned her hands on the desk. "I didn't ignore Mom's text yesterday. We had an interesting phone call. Did she tell you?" She sucked in a heavy breath and remained focused on Dad. "She implied by her tone that she might be willing to pursue legal action for my defection from the party."

Dad blinked and licked his lips. It was his nervous tell. He always did that when he was trying to get what he wanted but knew that he was in the wrong.

Addey stayed standing.

"I did hear her version of the conversation—" Dad hesitated. He was still standing but was backed against the wall. "Things have gotten out of hand."

Addey raised her eyebrows. "So you're not planning on suing me?"

Dad stepped forward. "Absolutely not. I would never do that. I'm here to work out an agreement...it's just your mother can be difficult. She loves you, you know?"

Addey pressed her palms flat against the table as the stab of a headache started. *Would you stop defending her?* she shouted inwardly. If she wasn't careful, she was going to lose it—throw a tantrum worthy of her childhood worst. She tried Declan's trick: count to twenty.

By the time she reached twenty and had wrestled back control, she finally spoke.

"She had a funny way of showing it."

Dad licked his lips again. "Your mother's actions can be upsetting sometimes."

Addey crossed her arms and kept waiting.

"The events of the past two days have been out of line." He settled his stern gaze on her. "For both you and your mother." He paused. "Bringing up the Christmas party the way you did was out of line." His frown stretched across his face.

"Oh, so I'm in the wrong, but what Mom did was only upsetting?" Addey couldn't keep the cutting edge from her voice.

Dad sighed, loud and long. He finally sat.

Addey remained standing.

"Alright, she shouldn't have invited Justin over."

"And?" Addey tapped the desk with her fingers.

Dad's shoulders sagged. "She was out of line with the contracts."

Addey nodded as she slowly lowered herself into her chair. She kept her back straight and her elbows perched on the desk, hands clasped in front of her.

"So, what do you want to discuss with me?" Addey kept her gaze trained on him.

"Despite what happened on Sunday and yesterday" —he narrowed his eyes— "and the careless way both of you behaved, you made a good point."

Addey kept her face neutral, even as surprise washed over her. *Dad was admitting a fault?* She couldn't recall the last time that happened. That tiny light of hope inside her, the one that belonged to five year old Addey, the one that never went out, flickered.

"And what good point is that?" Her voice soft.

"That you have a stake in this party going well." Dad dipped his chin.

Addey sat back a little. "I'm still confused as to why you're here."

Dad started to lean forward, but stopped himself, as if that was going to lose him more ground in their power battle. There was a long pause. Dad's gaze flicked to Addey and to the floor and back again.

Addey leaned forward, heart beating fast.

Dad exhaled loudly and focused back on Addey. "I'm willing to remove the apartment building launch from the party agenda. If you come back on board to run it."

Addey sat all the way back and blinked several times. She was getting her wish! She tamped down the smile that threatened to bloom. Now was not the time to let him know how his words affected her.

"Despite what you think..." Dad cleared his throat. "We do care what happens to you. The sale of your business is a major milestone, and you deserve the best chance at making that happen."

The flicker of hope grew bigger. They—well, Dad, but Mom would fall lock step in with Dad—were giving up something...for her. For no other reason than it would benefit her. Her chest tightened with happiness. But she mentally squashed the feeling and kept her composure. One concession, although a big one, didn't mean everything was fine between them, but there *was* hope.

And she could live with hope.

"Thank you, Dad. I really appreciate that."

He cleared his throat. "Can you please tell your mother that you're back on board? She's been calling other event planners, but she says none of them have your vision. She's been at me day and night." The last word ended in a strangled cry, his face beseeching. "And she was wrong about her treatment of you with Justin and about yesterday."

The ice around Addey's thawed further. And she smiled big this time.

Dad, the man who faced business tycoons like himself on a regular basis, the man who was known for winning every battle he ever took on, was like a helpless little boy when it came to Vivien Hamilton.

"I'll call her today. We'll straighten things out." Addey jangled her leg under the desk. Would Mom be willing to compromise? To heal the breach?

Dad bowed his head, then looked up, his eyes bright. "Thank you."

An awkward silence hung between them. Addey didn't know what to say, and she was sure Dad didn't either.

"How're things at the nursing home?" Dad asked, his shoulders straight, that steely look back in his eyes.

Addey hid a smile. Dad must really want to get back in her good graces if he was bringing it up.

"Heritage Oaks is great. We're having a crooners' morning tomorrow. You know, Frank, Bing. The residents asked for it and I'm happy to oblige." She rarely talked about what she did there with her parents. Mom's constant dismissal of it hurt, and Dad was too busy to really care.

"I'm sure the residents appreciate your hard work." He nodded.

Addey kept the ever-growing ember of hope at bay because Declan's face popped up in her mind. She would see him tomorrow and he promised his mother a dance. Thinking about him brought a whole different kind of flicker to her heart. Worry battled with anticipation. Would he be happy to see her? Was her family too much, even for someone like him? Despite her fears, the image of him, sleeves rolled up, black apron on, laughing at her misshapen cookies tugged at her lips. She felt the smile bloom in spite of herself.

"So, there *is* someone," Dad chuckled.

Addey jerked, her cheeks flushing. "What on earth are you talking about?"

He leaned back in his chair, one leg casually resting on his opposite knee. His eyes were bright. "I don't know who the mystery man is, but this is the second time you've blushed when anyone mentions you dating."

Addey covered her cheeks with her hands. "No one mentioned dating in this room."

Dad actually chuckled. "You're right Adelaide, but that doesn't mean there isn't someone."

"If I recall correctly, Dad, it was Mom who jumped to those conclusions."

"You know your mother's conclusions are almost always right."

She stood, eager to get this conversation moved on.

Dad took the hint and stood as well. "Eager to get rid of me, I see." Dad's deep voice and frown were tempered by the twinkle she saw in his eyes.

He was enjoying this and, on some level, the level where Declan didn't exist, she was too. Bantering with her father was foreign, but...lovely. The flame of hope grew a tiny bit brighter.

"See you for brunch on Sunday as usual?"

Addey rounded the desk and stood nearby, the door frame between them. "Sure, Dad, I'll be there." Her heart was lighter, hope buoyed in her chest.

Dad stepped forward and placed a stiff hand on her shoulder, patted it awkwardly. Addey stilled. She couldn't remember the last time her father had been affectionate with her. Her breath stilled. A longing, deep and powerful, filled her. Experience reminded her that only bitter disappointment lay on this road. Still, she stayed and accepted this offer of affection because she couldn't not. One drop of water from a granite stone was better than nothing. Thirsty people could not be choosy about where their water came from.

Addey watched her father walk out. Little girl Addey wanted nothing more than her parents' love and acceptance. Adult Addey, well, she knew life was complicated. Like the dawn of a new day though, something had to change. To keep her sanity, to find what she longed for, she needed to stay away from Declan. Everything good that had just happened this morning would evaporate if anything ever happened between them. Addey rolled her shoulders to release the tension.

She would be professional with every encounter she had with Declan. No more flirting. No more wanting to know the man behind the façade.

It was the only way forward.

Chapter Twenty

Declan walked down the familiar hallway armed with another bouquet, this time poinsettias, the smooth sounds of Frank Sinatra tinkling away from the rec room. The barely-noticeable scratch on the wall near the floor was the halfway mark to Mom's room. He could hear one of the patients singing a mournful tune off-key and he glanced in as he walked past. Alone. His heart cramped for her. This is why he hated this place, parents or grandparents left to find a life in this abyss of purgatory.

And he'd put his own mother here.

He knocked lightly on the door. "Mom, I'm here." Would she be okay today? He walked in and found the room empty. The place was tidy, Mom's crocheting sitting in a little basket by her chair and the doors open to the courtyard garden, the music louder from here. He smiled, hoping she was enjoying herself.

Addey. His thoughts had been on her for days, if he admitted it to himself. Since Monday night and his conversation with Eli, he knew he needed to back off. But she was here every Thursday—there was no escaping her. But he had to try. He couldn't be falling for the daughter of the man tearing down his beloved Community Center, or be involved with people who would sue their own daughter. It reeked of betrayal and he'd had enough of that with his own family. Taking a deep breath, he vowed to himself that he would ease up.

He entered the rec room, where Frank Sinatra's familiar songs played loud enough to hear but not so loud as to drown everything else out. Small groups of residents sat in circles, tapping away to the music. Others, the more able-bodied, danced in the space cleared. He found Mom sitting with Maude and Vera—the three women deep in conversation. His heart lifted. Right now, he didn't totally hate himself for putting her here.

"She's doing really well today." Addey came up beside him. Declan zeroed in on her, unable to look away. His heart beat quickened. He was going to have trouble staying true to his vow. The green wrap dress floated around her knees, making her look like a mermaid on land. Her red hair cascading down her back only enhanced her beauty. For a moment they just stood there, not saying anything.

"Nice." He let his gaze linger a touch longer than he really should. "Do you normally dress up for this gig?"

Addey ducked her head and he saw a blush creep up her cheeks. "I'm dressing up for Frank," she said as she looked up, her lips twitching.

"Hm, thought it might be for another reason," Declan said, a teasing lilt in his voice. His pulse kicked up. Bantering with her was dangerous—too easy to enjoy.

Addey tilted her head, eyes steady. "Can't imagine what you mean," she said, all innocence, but the corner of her mouth betrayed her.

Declan shook himself. He took a small step away. He needed distance between them. Addey did the same thing. Seemed it was mutual.

"Are those for your mom?" Addey nodded at the flowers as she smoothed some of her flyaway hair.

Declan couldn't look away. Her question forced him to get a grip on himself.

"Yes." He nodded at where Mom was sitting. "She looks like she's having fun."

Addey stepped forward. "Come on, she's been talking about you all morning."

Declan followed.

"Look who I found." Addey approached the little group.

"Oh Dec, you made it!" Mom's eyes were bright and her smile big. She looked at the watch Declan and Nicky had bought her for her birthday five years ago—a gold, large face with tiny diamonds circling it. It had been expensive for them. They'd both saved for six months to afford it for her. Everyone deserved something nice, and it replaced the one given to her by Dad. She sold that one off after the divorce. She only had a few pieces of jewelry left. Her wedding and engagement rings, a necklace belonging to her late mother, and a bracelet. All the other fine jewelry was long gone, sold to repay Dad's victims.

"I told you I'd be here." He knelt and handed her the bouquet. "I brought you some new flowers." Plucking two of the flowers free, he handed one each to Maude and Vera. Vera smiled so big, it was like the sun shining. Maude gave him a long stare, which Declan met and held until Maude cracked her lips upwards. Not the smile he got last week, but he'd take it.

"You all look like you're having fun." He took Mom's hand and squeezed.

"Your son is not only handsome," Vera's eyes twinkled. "But he's well-mannered, too."

"I'm on my best behavior today, but some people" —he glanced at Addey— "think I'm stubborn and opinionated."

Addey didn't say anything, but he caught the barest of twitches on her mouth.

Mom laughed. "Declan is stubborn and dogged, sometimes to a fault. And yes, he's putting on his best behavior because he hates that I'm here."

The instant hush that came over the group railed at Declan. He smiled while he counted to twenty. Mom might have a good memory today, but that didn't mean she was better. Some days she was so blunt it was hurtful, frustrating, and another reminder that she was sick.

"I think you need to have a dance, Miss Susannah. You've been waiting for one all morning." Addey took the bouquet and saved the moment from disaster. "I'll put these in water."

"Come on, Mom." Declan offered his hand and Mom took it, a little unsteady on her feet. He caught Addey's eye while she held Mom's flowers and mouthed "thank you" to her as he slowly whirled Mom around the floor.

***

Not even the gentle tones of Frank could settle Addey's heart. Declan, walking in with flowers, looking so handsome as he searched for his mother, had stopped her short. Their banter and flirting heated her cheeks. This was not how today was meant to go. She arranged the flowers in the vase she got from Fiona and put them on the table next to the speaker. But the man was inescapable. He smelled manly, like the cool ice found at a rink, the same thing she'd thought when she met him after his ice hockey game. Trouble was knocking at her door, and she kept opening it to let him in.

But not today. She kept remembering Dad in her office yesterday.

Addey walked around the perimeter of the dance floor, trying not to watch as Declan easily steered his mother around the floor. Some residents who couldn't dance watched from their chairs tapping their feet while others simply stared off into the distance. She moved around the dancing couples and smiled as Saul led Maude around. Maude wasn't frowning, and that was always a good thing. Addey's heart was full as she watched everyone enjoying the event in whatever capacity they could.

Vera beckoned Addey over to where she sat tapping away to the music. "I'm so glad you put this on, Addey. It does the heart good."

Addey rested her hand on Vera's arm. "You guys requested it. I want you all to be happy."

Vera grinned. "You know my Earl used to dance me around the kitchen to Frank."

"Did he?" Addey knelt beside the older woman.

Vera tapped away to the music. "No TV back then, just the radio. Earl saved for months to buy that for us."

"That must have been special."

"Oh yes. Our home was nothing flashy, but it didn't matter. Life was hard then. The war was finished, but jobs were scarce. People were still finding their feet in a world gone mad."

Addey nodded and love swelled inside for this dear lady. She couldn't imagine a life apart from her own pampered upbringing, save for Granny, who'd told her stories of her life before she married wealthy Grandad. Addey and Vera lapsed into comfortable silence, watching the others. From where she stood, Declan's face remained unreadable, his posture tall as he led his mother around the room, slowly but assuredly.

"That boy knows how to dance," Vera said.

"He sure does," Addey murmured.

Susannah said something that brought a quick smile to Declan's face, and it transformed him. Like night and day. It reminded her of the way he teased her at cooking class.

"I take it you know Declan?"

Addey ignored the amused tone in Vera's voice. She didn't need to look at the woman to know she was grinning that "knowing" grin.

"We haven't known each other long." She moved to the chair beside Vera and sat with legs crossed and arms wrapped around her chest. She couldn't stop staring at him as he danced. Vera was right, he knew how to dance. She huffed. Baking, dancing, what couldn't he do?

A deep unsettling thought occurred. *Who was Declan Collins?* How hard it must be for him to deal with his mother's slowly worsening condition. It didn't take a genius to figure out how much he hated the situation. He wore that discomfort like a sign hanging from his neck.

So lost in her thoughts, she hadn't noticed that the song had ended and another had begun.

Then Declan was right there. Tall and impossibly handsome. Addey wiped her palms on her dress, then offered her seat to Susannah. Standing shoulder to shoulder with Declan, she was lost for words. By the way he was rubbing the back of his neck, he must not have any idea either.

"You haven't had a dance yet, Addey," Vera stated. Addey closed her eyes and imagined running from the room. "Susannah has been telling us all how proud she is of you, Declan. But she didn't tell me you are such a good dancer." Vera's eyes were dreamy as she bobbed her head to the music.

Addey cast a glance at Declan's mother, hoping rationale would prevail there. No such luck. The smile was demure but lingered.

"I don't need to dance—I'm just here for you lovely folks," Addey said, her smile stretched a little too wide, the brightness in her voice ringing just a note too high. She took a step back, already halfway to her escape. "I just need to check on something."

She was nearly gone when Declan's voice cut through.

"I'd be happy to dance with you."

The words were bold—but there, at the end, a slight catch, like he hadn't meant to say them out loud. It rooted her to the spot. She hadn't even looked at him yet, but something in his tone pulled her back.

Slowly, she turned. His gaze met hers—steady, clear, almost daring.

Did she want to dance? Absolutely not. That would close the space she'd been trying so hard to keep between them.

Her stomach clenched, but he was so handsome standing there, dress shirt open at the neck, black slacks. Frank's *The Way You Look Tonight* serenaded on the stereo. He held out his hand, a glint of dare sparked in his eyes—the man didn't know how to back off from a challenge.

"I should say no," she whispered.

He held her gaze. "And I shouldn't be asking you." He offered his hand.

Addey took it and he led them to the dance floor. Her hand felt small tucked inside his, his warm fingers brushing her palm. Addey shivered. "This is a very bad idea," she murmured.

Declan chuckled, his hand going to her waist like a proper gentleman. "Bad idea or bad timing?"

Addey looked up at him, which meant she had to just tilt her head, since in her heels she wasn't much shorter than him. She placed her hand on his very broad shoulder, and they began the waltz in time to the music. Her heart thudded in her chest as he took the first tentative steps and then she needed no other coaching. As if they'd always danced together, he whirled her around the floor and she followed easily, the steps coming back to her much quicker than she thought possible.

"Both," she offered.

His hand tightened on her waist. Addey stepped a millimeter closer to him.

Addey resisted the impulse to lean her head on his chest. "I know why I know how to dance, but what about you?"

He stiffened, and instinctively she squeezed his shoulder.

"My mom loved to dance, so I obliged her and let her teach me." She could tell his jaw was clenched. What was he not telling her? What was in his past that he wanted to keep hidden?

"That all?" The question slipped out, but even when his eyes widened, she didn't regret it. "You know my biggest secret." She eased a smile, trying to temper his wound-up emotions.

"I won't tell anyone." He gazed at her.

"I know," she replied as they spun around the room, the world a blur now, just the two of them. His frown and rigid back told her he was wrestling with something.

Finally, his shoulders edged downwards. "My mom did teach me how to dance and—" he halted, "—I had dance classes. Mom insisted. I used to dance her around our living room." He swallowed, as if whatever he was remembering was too painful. "Life wasn't easy when we got here. The Community Center was a lifeline." His face closed over. Addey's heart ached for him. She wanted to reach out and smooth the frown lines on his forehead, to ease the load from his shoulders. But that wasn't her place. They barely knew each other.

Yet here they were dancing like they'd been doing it for a lifetime.

Addey stepped closer. "That's why this is so personal to you?" she whispered. Whatever had happened scarred him deeply, that much she knew.

He squeezed her waist. "Yes, which is why, this—us, whatever this is, is—"

"Bad timing." They spoke at the same time. "A bad idea."

Falling silent, they continued to dance.

Addey's heart thudded. They were both right. Bad timing and a bad idea.

"I'm back in charge of the Christmas party." She looked at him, waiting for his reply, wondering how he would respond to the news.

His hand squeezed hers, and he cocked his head to one side. "How did that happen?"

Addey let a tiny sigh slip out. "My dad came and pleaded his case. Mom and I made peace about everything when I spoke to her this morning. She was never going to sue—"

"Just let you think she was?" Declan's sarcasm was unmissable. He frowned. "Family should never hurt each other like that."

"I hear you." She chewed her bottom lip. "Dad made an important concession—"

"And he normally wouldn't do that...for you?" Declan filled in, the last word spoken with reverence.

Addey nodded, her heart full. Declan got it.

"If that's the case, then I'm happy for you." Declan kept her moving even as the song changed. He cleared his throat, his gaze capturing hers, holding her to him. "I think it might be safer for both of us if we keep some distance between us." His voice floated, but the words dropped onto her heart like a weight.

"You're right," she replied, looking at the buttons on his shirt. "I think that's the best option we have. It's too complicated."

Declan tugged her a mite closer, his thumb now caressing her waist. Addey trembled and moved nearer. Could Declan hear the thumping of her heart?

She met his gaze, saw his eyes drop to her lips. This, them, was such a bad idea.

Suddenly Addey was bumped forward, her head butting against Declan's chest. He tightened his grip, a solid force keeping her upright.

Saul was dancing with Vera. "I'm sorry, Miss Addey," Saul exclaimed. "These feet aren't what they used to be."

"He's doing fine," Vera said softly, giving Addey a thumbs up as they swayed beside her and Declan. "But you two are showing us how it's done." The older woman winked.

Addey ducked her head.

Declan laughed. The sound set off a longing in Addey that she had to tamp down.

Declan leaned across to Saul and Vera. "If we didn't have you two to show us how it's done—we'd be lost."

"You're too much, Declan." Vera swatted his arm, her laugh high and joyous.

Addey peeked at him, she caught the glimmer in his eyes as he shot a look her way, his grin cheeky.

The song ended and Declan led her back to the group of ladies, his silence, and hers, only confirming what she already knew. They could not explore this—whatever it was.

That didn't stop her heart from aching.

Chapter Twenty-One

Declan sat on the hard plastic chair next to Mom while she slept in her recliner. It seemed that the excitement of yesterday had tired her out. He was working on an article about the history of Mount Vernon. He glanced at Mom, the frown lines relaxed in sleep, her breathing deep, her lips soft. An unexpected peace had settled on him. Mom was safe and well cared for here. She was happy here. Watching her yesterday had been a pleasure. Her smile, the easy way she'd talked with the other residents, the care from the nurses and Addey. Addey's sweet nature brought joy and hope, he could see it in how they all responded to her.

In truth, Addey had the same effect on him. He wanted to spend more time with her, no matter what he'd told himself, no matter what they'd agreed to yesterday. And that dance had lingered in his mind all day, from talking with Nicky at breakfast this morning, as he worked throughout the day, until now. Holding Addey close, just the two of them in a swirl of people, but the maddening knowledge of who her parents were, and what they were capable of, hung over them. It kept them apart. It made him uneasy and her, too, he suspected.

He shoved thoughts of Addey out of his head and kept reading about the Mount Vernon Ladies' Association. He added notes to his story, but it would be better if he interviewed one of the members. It would round the article out and, frankly, Julie would be impressed. And he wanted Julie to be impressed since he wanted his op-ed back.

He looked up a contact number from the website and glanced at Mom—still sleeping. He quietly closed the laptop and eased himself up and out into the hallway. Once tucked away in an alcove off the hall, he called the number. He was transferred to a lady who was more than happy to arrange an interview with one of the senior members. Declan gave her his number, told her he was available from tomorrow, and went back to Mom's room.

He was lowering himself onto the hard seat when she woke up. Declan tensed, bracing himself for her confusion. It was becoming more and more normal for her to wake up disoriented, which then led to longer bouts of memory loss. Mom tried to sit up, but the chair was reclined too far back. Declan jumped up and pressed the button to move it into a sitting position.

Mom looked around her, her brow wrinkled. "Declan, what are you doing here? Shouldn't you be at work?"

His tight chest eased and his shoulders relaxed. He was so used to getting stressed about her that sometimes he didn't even realize how tense he was around her anymore.

He pointed to his laptop. "I am working, but I thought I'd spend my lunch with you."

Mom's smile melted his heart. "That's very sweet of you. But I was asleep."

Declan shrugged. "I didn't mind. Besides, it was so peaceful here."

"I never thought I'd hear you say that about this place."

Mom's sideways glance made him chuckle. "Me too."

Mom adjusted her position and Declan helped get her lunch settled on the table. She opened it and frowned. "What is this?"

Declan peered over. "It looks like roast beef, beans, and mashed potato."

Mom looked up at him, eyes wide. "Do I like this?" The tremble in her voice reached in and tore at his heart.

Declan gently patted her hand. "You love it. You used to make us roast beef in winter back home in L.A. and we'd pretend that it was snowing, instead of sunny, bright, beach weather."

"We would pretend it was snowing," she repeated faintly. "We'd have the fire on, turn the air conditioning up and have roast beef."

"That's right," Declan encouraged, relieved she was remembering, and they could share this memory together.

"Your father would come too," Mom added.

Declan's face hardened. "Yes, sometimes," he said through a tight jaw.

Mom placed her hand on his arm and squeezed. "I see forgiving your father is going well."

Declan hung his head and gritted his teeth. "We've been over this. I'm not going to forgive him. He doesn't deserve it."

"Do any of us?" Mom said.

Declan raised his head, wanting to shake something. "Don't start, Mom."

"No one deserves forgiveness, it's something we gift to the offender and to ourselves."

Declan took a long breath and counted to twenty. "So, Dad gets a free pass?"

Mom shook her head. "He's paying for his crimes, and he needs to. But you need to let him know that you don't hold it against him anymore." She leaned forward and tapped his arm firmly. "You're letting him stop you from having a life. Forgiving him will release you from the prison you're in."

Declan flinched at her words. "I'm not the one in prison."

Mom held his gaze until Declan looked away. He stood, needing to get away from the words that pierced his well-formed armor. Words that made him ask himself questions he didn't want to answer. Frustrated, he sat back on the uncomfortable chair. He opened the laptop and brought up the Mount Vernon article.

"You can't run from this forever." Mom's pointed stare was like a laser.

Declan harrumphed, "I've got this."

"I'm always praying for you." Mom took a bite of her roast beef.

"Thanks," Declan muttered.

"What are you working on?" Mom asked.

Declan breathed easier. "A history of the Mount Vernon Ladies' Association and how they preserved the house and land of George Washington. Did you know in the five years, from 1853 to 1858, the Association raised two hundred thousand dollars to purchase the mansion and two hundred acres of surrounding land?"

Mom nodded. "I watched the movies they play at the educational center."

Declan sat back. "I thought you just toured the grounds."

"Well, when you've been there as often as I have, you find other things to do. Truthfully, if I'd had the time, I would have volunteered there."

Declan frowned. "I'm sorry about that."

Mom waved his comment away with her hand. "Don't be. Life is hard. We have to accept what we are dealt with. Now tell me, what do you have planned this weekend?"

Declan closed his laptop. "I'm picking a big load of goods from Baking for Life tomorrow."

Mom nodded. "Is Eli going with you?"

"No, he can't."

Mom put her spoon down. "Then who is going with you?"

Declan immediately thought of Addey and dismissed the idea. Asking her to help him was the opposite of keeping distance between them. "I don't know yet."

"What about Addey?" Mom tipped her head to the side, her eyes bright with mischief.

"Very funny." Declan swiped the fork off her tray and speared a few beans and popped them in his mouth.

"Well, you danced with her, why not ask her to help? I think she would love to." She got that dreamy look on her face, her eyes growing misty. "You danced so well together. That's very rare to find, you know."

Declan stuffed down his frustration and hope. The two emotions were at war within him. If Addey had been anyone else's daughter, he would have asked her out...but she wasn't anyone else's daughter.

"Do you think we can visit Mount Vernon?" Mom's abrupt topic change didn't faze him anymore. It had taken time to get used to.

Declan speared another bean. "I think we can organize that. I've got to go there for work again next week, so I can take you with me."

Mom folded her hands in her lap. "Good, I think it might make a good trip for the residents here as well. Why don't you mention it to Addey when you get her to help you with the bakery tomorrow?"

Why didn't he indeed? Because he wasn't supposed to be spending time with her. But that pull, their attraction, the goodness of her heart, compelled him to walk away from his vow to walk away from her.

Chapter Twenty-Two

Addey sat on the front steps of her townhouse, sipping a cup of steaming hot coffee, hoping it would wake her up and keep the cold at bay. The sun wasn't even peeking over the buildings as the time drew closer to six o'clock. The chill in the air stole her breath. Declan's text yesterday afternoon asking her to help him had come as a surprise, considering they were trying to keep distance between them. But she was too curious with what he needed her help with to say no. And a part of her wanted to see him again, wanted to make him smile, wanted to be near him.

"Argh," Addey groaned, putting down her coffee and burying her flushing face onto her knees. Of all the people for her to be attracted to, it had to be him.

Declan was arriving any minute, and since she had no idea what errand he had to run, she opted for black, flat boots with room to wiggle her toes, jeans, a thick, black sweater, her fuchsia parka, matching beanie, a black scarf and black woolen gloves.

The darkness of the morning didn't bother her. It was peaceful. She could hear in the distance the hum of traffic that would be crawling along Jefferson Davis Highway as people headed into D.C. for work. She was so grateful her office was less than a five-minute drive from her townhouse. King Street offered her everything she needed for her business, including the ability to walk to work if she wanted to.

Her thoughts turned back to Dad and the concession he made for her with the party. It still warmed her heart, further making this outing with Declan feel like a betrayal. It put a dampener on the memory with her dad. Doubts invaded. She really shouldn't have said yes, but it was too late now. Addey rested her head on her knees and let the darkness of the early morning settle around her. It didn't demand anything of her, it simply let her be.

Headlights turned onto her street and broke through her haven. Her heart rate picked up. Standing, she shoved her hands in her pockets and walked towards the SUV as Declan got out. His large frame was mammoth in his thick, black coat. "Morning. It's freezing, why'd you wait outside?" His breaths came out in cold puffs as he rubbed his bare hands together.

"Morning." She shed her parka. "I happen to find being outside in the morning peaceful." She climbed in the warm, toasty car. Declan shut the door after her before he climbed back in his side. His presence filled the space and Addey tried not to stare at him, but she couldn't help it.

"I'm glad you could make it." He smiled, his eyes crinkling at the edges. He had faint lines of fatigue around his eyes and the beginning of a five o'clock shadow. The car had that faint ice and manly scent she associated with him. She wanted to inhale it and let it sink into her body and soul. Addey sank lower into the seat as her cheeks went red again, wondering what Declan would think if he knew how embarrassing her thoughts were.

Mustering herself into something resembling normal, she faced him. "You had me curious," Addey croaked, hoping Declan would think her pink cheeks were from the cold and nothing else. He reached down, his shoulder brushing hers and Addey stilled, resisting the pull to lean into him.

He presented her with a large disposable coffee cup. "This is the first thank you for coming out with me this morning."

She took the cup, her fingers brushing his. A thrill ran up her hand at the touch and she was reminded of their dance and that unspoken link of attraction that kept drawing them together.

"What's the next thank you?" She sipped the hot liquid, letting the warmth spread through her and trying to settle her jumbled emotions.

He gave her a sideways glance as he pulled back onto the road. The headlights cut through the darkness ahead. "Demanding much?"

"You promised breakfast and while I'm grateful for this" —she held up the cup— "it's not breakfast."

"I thought coffee was the breakfast of all busy people such as ourselves." He glanced at her, a grin nudging the corners of his mouth.

"Ha," she shot back. "Just drive, would you?"

His lips twitched. "I am."

Addey loved the laughter in his voice. The more she got to know him, the more she was impressed. There really were layers underneath the exterior he presented to the world.

"Thanks for coming with me, by the way." He kept his attention on the road. "I know it was last minute and I've asked a lot of you."

Addey settled back, content to sip her drink and be in his presence. "I'll admit you have me very curious. Oh, on a different note, I read your article on Aladdin the Christmas Camel."

"Did I disgrace myself?" He glanced at Addey, but she caught the pause in his voice. He was asking her opinion on his work and considering their last conversation about one of his articles had led to a heated discussion, Addey sensed this mattered to him.

This time was different. They were different.

"I liked it. You reminded me of when Granny would take me there every year. I liked how you included the history of the animals at the property. It was a nice touch." She sipped her drink, watching him.

He slowed for a red light, then looked across at her. "Thanks." The warmth in his eyes and the way his lips curved gently sent her stomach into little dips, like the ones you might get on a kids' rollercoaster. "I'm glad this article met your approval."

Heat rushed to Addey's cheeks, and she looked out the window.

The light turned green and they moved forward.

Declan cleared his throat. Maybe he needed to find some levity too. "Speaking of Mount Vernon, Mom mentioned yesterday that she would like to visit there again."

Addey sat up straighter in her seat. "That's a great idea. We could only take residents who can physically manage it, but I think that it can work. When did you have in mind?"

"I have to go there next week to write an article on chocolate making—"

"That's perfect!" Addey jumped in, her brain ticking faster. "I can call them up and get a special section set up for a group of our residents. The Association would be happy to accommodate us. And if the weather is nice, we can have a picnic overlooking the river." She was suddenly aware of how loud she sounded. "Sorry, I got a little excited."

Declan laughed. "You're good at your job, you know that, right? The residents really love what you do for them."

"Thanks." Addey ducked her head. This was the third time someone said she was good with the residents. Her mood dipped, because someone would end up doing her job soon and she wouldn't be needed anymore.

"What's with the frown?" Declan asked as they turned into a parking lot.

Addey shook her head, clearing her thoughts. "I'm just worrying about things I don't need to bother you about."

Declan rested his hands on the steering wheel, the heater still humming. "I'm all ears if you want to share."

Addey smiled and drained the rest of her drink. "I'll keep that in mind." She unbuckled her belt. "Where are we?" They'd pulled up at a bakery, in an industrial area twenty minutes from Old Town. They got out and approached the store.

Declan held the door open "Come and find out."

Addey followed him, her curiosity piqued now. She passed under the sign "Baking for Life." She'd never heard of it. What a strange name and place for a bakery to be. Inside, the smell of freshly-baked bread set her stomach into overdrive. Coffee was not enough, not against this mouthwatering assault. She was aware her eyes must have looked like saucers but she didn't care. People scurried around the large kitchen, cooking, cleaning, sweeping, packing.

Declan approached the long counter that was holding big rectangular crates of baked goods. She peered inside. Bread rolls, loaves, sticky sweets, and buns were all lined up, one crate on top of another. It was pure bliss.

Addey looked up as a woman approached the counter. She gave Declan a big smile and gave Addey an uncertain one. Addey stood up straight, jammed her hands in her pockets and stepped up closer to the counter...and to Declan.

"I'm here as promised." His voice was relaxed and easy.

"Morning, Declan." The woman smiled again, then looked at Addey. "Who's your friend?"

The term *friend* sat uncomfortably. Declan turned and gave Addey an encouraging smile. "Leonie, meet Addey. Addey was gracious enough to hang out with me this morning and give me a hand."

Addey smiled her best Hamilton smile. It never failed to work in any situation. "Nice to meet you." She nodded to the building. "This place is great. And warm."

Leonie laughed. "That it is."

"Leonie runs this place," Declan said as he filled out some paperwork. He looked at the petite dark-haired woman. "How did the assessments go?" He handed over the completed documents.

Leonie looked back at the kitchen. "I think it went well, but we won't know the results until next week. They want it all sorted before Christmas."

Declan leaned on the counter. "Of course they do. I'll keep you guys all in mind. We're all rooting for you at the Community Center."

Addey stood there, confused and curious. She felt like a stranger in a foreign land. Who was this woman? What was this place? What did it have to do with the Community Center?

"I will and thanks for picking this up today. I know it's not your usual day and it's extra work."

"Don't say another word. I'm happy to do it." He sounded so relaxed, not a snarky comment in sight. Oh, he definitely had layers.

"Can you please grab one of the crates, Addey?" Declan directed as he hauled two crates balanced on top of each other and headed for the door. Addey rushed to open it for him and the cold air streamed in. She shut it behind him and went for a crate herself.

"Are you a new volunteer with the Center?" Leonie asked.

Addey shook her head. "No, I met Declan two weeks ago and..." She had no idea what to say next. So far, they had exchanged text messages, gone to cooking class, traded barbs, and shared one incredible, confusing dance in front of a group of nursing home residents. What exactly did you call that?

"...we're friends and he asked me to help, so here I am." She finished lamely.

Declan came back and Addey rushed outside and put the crate on top of the others in the back of the SUV. Then went back inside where four more crates were stacked up. She grabbed another two and put it in the back of the SUV. Declan came out with the last two.

"Can we stack these better?" He put the crates on the pile and they leaned a little. "Leonie says there's one more."

"Will we fit them all in?" Addey eyed the back of the SUV, all the seats were lowered to accommodate the crates, which were in two piles, the first four crates jammed up hard against the back of the front seats. There was just enough room behind them for four more. Where was the last crate going to go?

"We'll make it work." Declan grinned, as he dashed back inside.

Addey set about stabilizing the piles, making sure they were securely on top of each other.

"Room for one more?" Declan arrived.

Addey stepped back. "Maybe, if we can squeeze the last crate on top?"

Declan grinned, winking at her. "I think I can." He shuffled the final crate on top of the pile, pressing hard as it eked slowly inside the car, the top of the crate wedged tight, the edges of the crate pressing hard against the windows.

"Right."

They stepped back, surveying their work.

"Will they come out?" Addey asked.

"They'd better." Declan nudged her shoulder. "I don't want my car smelling of old bakery products forever."

Addey laughed as Declan closed the trunk.

"Right." Declan blew on his hands. "The Community Center next and then, as promised, breakfast."

***

Addey was quiet as they drove back to Old Town. Declan didn't know why.

He was about to ask when Addey piped up. "So, what is that place? It doesn't look like a standard bakery."

Declan turned up the heat. "No, it's not. It's a training place for people who need a second chance in life, people who need skills to help them get jobs."

Addey burrowed deeper into her seat. "Does Leonie own it or something? And the smell is amazing. I want to eat everything."

Declan chuckled. "I'm always starving, even if I've eaten before I pick up the crates." He'd spent the better half of the car ride catching glances of her. She did mornings well. She looked fresh and pretty, the cold turning her cheeks pink. "As for Leonie, she's the manager. A woman named Alice Lodge started it with her husband Frank. They used to take in boarders, people who needed emergency accommodation and the like. After a while they realized they could help in other ways, as they both worked in the hospitality and food industry, and they came up with this idea. The bakery sells their products to other stores and usually we—the Community Center—get the orders that were canceled, or like today, where we get the food that was made for assessment day."

"Assessment day?" Addey looked over at him.

"The people working there are apprentices. They work under a baker and pastry chef. They are graded on their work before they can move up levels until they graduate from their apprenticeship."

"Then they can move on and get positions elsewhere, is that right?"

He nodded. "That's the idea."

Addey played with the hem of her sweater. "I've heard of places like that. I'm always amazed at what people do to help others. It makes me believe in humanity."

They lapsed into silence. The traffic was piling up now and the sun was more than peeking over the buildings, chasing the last of the darkness away. They arrived at the Community Center and got out of the car. Declan was about to retrieve the crates when he stopped. Addey was standing stock still staring at the Hamilton Group sign outside the building. He'd forgotten for several hours that Addey was a Hamilton. He sighed, jammed his hands in his pockets and came up beside her. Her mouth was set in a straight line and her shoulders taut.

"It's just so..." Her quiet words trailed off and she looked across at him, her shoulders sagging. "It's right there, in your face. I feel like the sign is shouting at me." She stepped back as if needing space from it. Declan knew how she felt.

"I'm sorry this is happening," she said softly.

"It's not okay, but what can I do? According to Eli, I need to get better at accepting what I can't change." He shrugged, surprised that the anger that always reared up when he saw the sign didn't grab him by the throat like it always did. It was there, but more like a simmering sensation...and it was unsettling. What was more unsettling was the glimmer of peace that peeked in over the pot of simmering anger. Declan shut the thoughts down. He was *not* going to examine them and if he did, it definitely wasn't going to be right now.

"You're right, but it's hard to move on when something means so much to you." Addey was talking about the sign, the building, but her gaze caught his and it held there for several long beats. Declan stepped closer, pulled in by the force of attraction that couldn't keep them away from each other. Addey stepped toward him. His eyes roved her face, taking in her smooth forehead, the tiny mole above her right eye, the way her nose sloped down towards those lips he really wanted to kiss. But then his eye caught the sign that was standing between them, literally and metaphorically, and it was a stark reminder why this, the idea of them, was a bad idea.

Seeming to sense the change, Addey stepped away, her face masked by her hair falling across her cheek as she turned away.

"Shall we take this stuff inside?" she said, the words tight. Just like that, the air between them snapped back to normal, or as normal as it could ever be with them.

Taking her cue, he tugged hard on the first crate, successfully easing it out of its clamped in spot. "Can you put two more crates on top of mine?"

Addey did and then grabbed two crates of her own, following him inside.

In the kitchen they found May and Georgia waiting for them.

Declan put the crates on the counter. "Morning ladies, how's it going today?"

Georgia, the older of the two smiled, always pleasant, always finding joy in the rain. "It's a bright day, Declan, and thanks to you and Leonie's team, we have some lovely gifts for our families. We got a couple more requests last night for some food." She patted a crate.

May, who was younger, in her early fifties, with a severe blunt bob, frowned. "What'll they do once this place closes? I suppose they'll starve." Her frown deepened. "They call it progress, tearing this place down. I'd like to see one of those fancy Hamiltons step foot in here."

Addey stumbled as she put the crate down with others, her face white.

Declan stepped in front of her, shielding her. This wasn't her fault, none of this was. Maybe he shouldn't have brought her here.

Georgia was talking now. "Shush now, May, you're getting yourself all in a bother. Everything will work out. There are other places who can help people in need as well. We're not the only one."

May grunted in reply and began unpacking the crates and bagging the food. Addey stood in the corner of the kitchen, pale and out of her depth. He needed to get her out of here.

May stepped up to Declan. "Have you forgotten your manners, young man?" she chided gently as she gave his hand a quick squeeze.

"I'm sorry. Ladies, come and meet Addey Bennet." Declan walked over to Addey, who was leaning against the bench in the far corner, her gaze taking in the room as she worried at her bottom lip. "Addey, this is May and Georgia, two very dedicated volunteers and equally lovely women."

"Hi, it's lovely to meet you." Addey stepped forward, her voice only slightly unsteady but the fixed smile on her face was one Declan had seen before. It was the one he'd seen twice now when he'd made her uncomfortable. Like any girl with "good" breeding, she had smiled what he now knew was her fake, stiff smile to cover her discomfort. He hated that he'd made her feel that way.

"There's four more crates to grab." Addey glanced at Declan.

Declan went back outside, Addey on his heels. They didn't say anything until the last crate was placed on the bench.

"We'd love to stay and chat, but we both have busy mornings," Declan said, hyper aware of the need to get Addey somewhere else.

"Of course you do," Georgia smiled. "I'm just glad to see you spending time with new people, Declan. Lovely to meet you, Addey." Both women waved as Declan left, eager to escape for Addey's sake. Addey followed right behind him. Declan was climbing into the SUV when his phone rang.

He looked at the number, an unfamiliar one, and answered. "Declan Collins."

It was the lady he'd spoken to yesterday from the Mount Vernon Ladies' Association. They had someone happy to conduct an interview this morning for his article.

He looked at Addey, sitting in the passenger seat staring at the sign out front, like it might leap down and capture her. He was going to make sure her day got better.

He assured the lady he could do the interview and hung up.

He pulled the door shut and turned the car on, letting the heat warm the space.

"Work call?" Addey looked across at him, her hands fidgeting with the zipper on her parka.

"Yeah, I have an interview at Mount Vernon with one of the members of the Association. They just called to ask if I could do it this morning."

He wasn't going to ask her to come with him. Not after bringing her here. He really should have thought it through more. "I'm sorry I brought you here. I didn't think about the sign." Or what the sign represented, or even how she might feel about her parents tearing down this place.

Addey turned to face him and tucked one leg under her. "Don't be sorry. I'm glad you asked me. I liked coming with you."

The air between them charged. The air inside the car seemed to evaporate. He couldn't take his eyes off her. "So, you like my company?" He breathed out. "Because I like yours." He held his breath as he waited for her reply. He was putting himself out there, reaching for some happiness, and it was long overdue.

Her soft smile was all he needed to let out the air of his lungs.

"I do like your company, even with that" —Addey jerked her thumb to the sign behind them— "in the way."

There was the Addey he was coming to know well. A girl with enough backbone to change her last name and risk the ire of her family might just be brave enough to see what could happen between them.

Declan reached for her hand and held it. It was smooth and small, but her grip was as sure as his.

"Still want breakfast?" He kept staring, not wanting to break the moment.

She nodded, not letting go of his hand. "I'll even walk around Mount Vernon while you conduct your interview." She squeezed his hand. "Plus, it'll give me a chance to check out things for the party anyway."

She wanted to spend even more time with him. He grinned at her and loved the way she smiled back.

"Deal."

As they drove off, hope burned bright in his chest for the first time in years.

Chapter Twenty-Three

Did she know how cute she looked? Declan's grin wouldn't slide off his face. And he didn't want it to.

"I'll wander around. Just text when you're finished." Addey lingered by Declan's car, snuggled into her parka. They'd grabbed a quick breakfast at a hole-in-the-wall café they'd found on the way to Mount Vernon. Their conversation had been easy...well, easy for him. They'd stayed away from the topic of the Community Center and her parents, which he was more than happy about. It was nice to not think about them, and if he was honest, he was starting to realize they took up more space in his head than needed.

Maybe Eli's words over the years were finally sinking in.

"The interview is in the theater. It shouldn't take me too long." He stood next to her, his shoulder leaning against hers. "Besides, there's someone else I'd rather spend my time with."

Addey looked around as if searching for someone, her eyes wide. "Who?"

He nudged her with his shoulder and laughed. "Go for a walk, would you?"

"Alright, I'm going." She started walking off.

"You free tonight?" He called after her.

Addey turned. "I'm free after seven. I've got an afternoon Christmas party I'm organizing."

"Come ice skating with me?" The hope in his chest continued to burn strong.

She cocked her head, one finger pressed against her lips. Declan's pulse kicked up a notch. She was stunning.

"I don't think I want to show you my subpar ice skating skills. They're worse than my cooking skills."

He laughed. "You have been ice skating before, haven't you? If this California boy has, I'm sure you have."

Addey grinned. "I'll happily accept your offer, but don't expect anything brilliant. I'll be doing my best to stay upright."

"Remember, I'm a boy scout, I can help you."

Addey rolled her eyes. "I'm going for a walk now." She fluttered her fingers and disappeared into the building crowd.

Declan walked into the education center, his smile growing with each step. Just before he got to the theater, where he was to meet the former Vice Regent for the Virginia Chapter, he stopped to compose himself.

Debbie, the lady he'd spoken to on the phone met him by the theater doors. They shook hands. "Charlotte's inside."

Declan nodded. He followed her into the lit theater where an older woman, maybe in her late sixties or early seventies, and dressed in a pressed pantsuit, sat on the chair at the end of the aisle. She stood to face him, and something about her seemed familiar.

"Thanks Debbie," Charlotte said. "I'll take it from here."

Debbie left, and Declan was alone with Charlotte. Her regal air would normally have irritated him, but he was trying change. He didn't want Julie to have any doubts about giving him his column back. Besides, he wanted to see Addey again. Just knowing she was walking around the place gave him a reason to keep this interview short.

"Come and sit down, Mr. Collins." She indicated the chair opposite her, across the aisle.

"You know my name, but I don't know yours."

The woman looked at him with penetrating blue eyes. Firm was the word that came to mind when he looked at her. Firm nose, firm mouth, and firm posture.

She blinked twice. "I'm surprised you don't know who I am."

Declan slowly lowered himself and the cushion felt squishy under his weight. "I don't know much about Mount Vernon, ma'am. But I would dearly like to know with whom I'm speaking with?" He sat back, resting his arm on the armrest, but keeping his gaze fixed on her.

"Charlotte Hamilton." Each word was short and crisp. There was no triumph in her voice, but no pity either.

Declan looked at the ceiling and immediately started counting to twenty while he tried to process his thoughts.

Charlotte Hamilton had ambushed him. It was typical of this family, but as the negative thoughts started to gather, he pictured Addey, sweet and lovely Addey, walking around the grounds completely unaware of what was happening. He needed to handle this situation better. For himself, his career, and for Addey. He swallowed down the lump growing in his chest.

She appeared to be waiting patiently for him to gather himself. Again, he found no censure in her unflinching expression.

"Pleasure to meet you, Mrs. Hamilton. Thanks for making time to talk with me. I'm sure you'll be the perfect person to help with my interview." He offered his hand.

It was her turn to pause. They sat, facing off silently. Finally, she took his hand and gave it a confident shake, her palm soft and wrinkled. Declan made sure he didn't crush her hand with his firm grip.

She pressed her lips together. "Alright then, let's get this interview under way, shall we?"

Declan pulled out his phone and held it up. "Do you mind if I record this?"

Charlotte paused, then gave a sharp nod.

Declan leaned forward. "I think you're a woman who appreciates an honest conversation."

Her gaze captured his. "I do."

"Then let's be clear. We're not going to talk about the Community Center, your son, or the Hamilton Group."

"That's acceptable." Her voice was firm.

Declan put his phone on the arm rest. "Good. Let's begin."

"Lead the way." She pressed her fingers into the thick fabric of the chair.

Had he unsettled her? He had no idea, but the brick on his chest that had landed the moment she mentioned her name was easing off.

"Tell me about the Mount Vernon Ladies' Association and how it came to own this property?"

"I'm sure you've done your research." She raised one eyebrow.

Declan sat back in the chair trying to settle into the unusual dynamic between them. "I have, but I want to hear it from you."

Charlotte began outlining the history of how Ann Pamela Cunningham, after receiving a letter from her mother about the poor state of the house, had been inspired to gather strong, like-minded women who could use their influence to raise the money needed to buy the house and surrounding land.

"What made you get involved with the association?" Declan asked, genuinely curious.

Charlotte rested her hands on her lap. "I've been involved with the Ladies' Association for forty years. I believe in preserving history, both the good and the bad, for people to learn from. History teaches us many things, but being able to show it in such an interesting and hands-on way, like we do here, is a gift to future generations." She looked around the small theater, as if the walls could soak up her words. "Besides, we cannot teach others if we do not keep learning ourselves."

"I think you and I are in agreement." It was strange knowing that he and this woman thought similarly on a topic He turned off the recorder.

"Do you want me to quote you in this article?"

Charlotte let out a small huff, not an unkind one, more like an undecided one. "Yes." The word was as firm as the hard dip of her chin.

"No one will mind?" He carefully tossed out the question.

"Are we now talking about topics that are off limits?" Her direct gaze and forthright words were welcome to him.

He appreciated people who could be fair and honest. "We're both professionals. I think we can keep it civil." He shifted in his seat. "You know I'm reviewing the party?" How close was Addey to Charlotte? Addey hadn't mentioned her.

Charlotte raised her eyebrows. "I'm aware of that."

"And you don't want me taken off the story?" Declan was confused by this woman. Charlotte looked and sounded as formidable as her son, yet from everything he'd seen so far, she wasn't interested in taking him down. He had no idea why.

"I won't tell my son, if that's what you're thinking." She steepled her fingers on her lap. "I'd like to see this situation play out. So yes, you can quote me for your article. It will be good to show that a Hamilton can get along with you, Declan Collins."

"Alright," he said slowly. He felt like he was walking into a trap, but so far, their chat held no hidden landmines. His thoughts went straight to Addey. He was the one with a landmine this time. What on earth would this woman say if she saw Addey with him? His stomach dipped. He was definitely stumbling into dangerous territory, but just thinking about Addey, in his car, hand in his, he couldn't bring himself to walk away from her.

"That's the smile of a man smitten with someone."

Declan jerked his attention back to Charlotte, who had an eyebrow raised ever so slightly, and an impish smile that looked just like Addey's.

"Thanks for your time, Mrs. Hamilton." He stood. "I think I have enough for my article." He didn't, but he would get by with what he had. It was more about making Julie happy than anything else.

Charlotte stood. "Your Gilmore Girls article was interesting."

Declan looked at her. "In what way?"

"My daughter-in-law seems to think it's nothing but a personal attack on her."

Declan tipped his head. "And you don't, do you?"

"Of course not." She huffed and Declan could have sworn that the woman wanted to roll her eyes, but she was far too refined to do that. "It's just telling, that's all. It explains a lot about you."

Then she walked past, leaving Declan frowning, her words piercing his well-padded armor. What did it reveal about him? What did she know? No one here knew about his family. They no longer traveled in wealthy circles, they had no money, their last name was different. Charlotte Hamilton could *not* know about them. He followed after her. His steps faltered. Addey was standing outside the theater—waiting for him.

***

This couldn't be happening. Addey tried to duck out of sight but it was too late. Grandmother had already seen her. Declan followed Grandmother out and by his panic-filled eyes, he was as shocked as she was.

Grandmother stopped walking. "Adelaide, what on earth are you doing here?"

Addey opened her mouth to say something, but nothing came out. She glanced at Declan who still stood behind Grandmother. What was she going to do? What were *they* going to do?

"Adelaide, you didn't answer me."

Suddenly Declan was beside her. "Mrs. Hamilton, Addey and I arranged to meet to go over plans for the party next week, since, as you know, I'm writing the review."

His words, his very presence, the way he jumped in and faced the situation head on was Declan through and through. He didn't back away from the things that scared him. So this is what it was like to have him in her corner.

Grandmother looked between the two of them and exhaled softly.

Declan stood steady beside Addey and it boosted her unsteady resolve.

Grandmother settled her iron gaze on Addey. "I'll see you at brunch tomorrow." There was no room for discussion on the issue.

Addey nodded. "I'll be there." And she would. Dad had smoothed things over and the hope she carried for a better relationship with them still sputtered, barely. Addey only hoped that Grandmother wouldn't say anything, because at this point, there was nothing to say anything about. Technically, Addey and Declan hadn't even gone out on a date. Except Addey knew that wasn't completely true.

And Grandmother's sharp eyes missed absolutely nothing.

Grandmother turned to Declan. "It was interesting meeting you."

Addey wanted to faint. How on earth had these two sat in a room together for twenty minutes and not killed each other? Her estimation of Declan rose.

"Thank you for your time." Declan's smooth voice and twinkle in his eye caught Addey's attention—something he'd been doing since the moment they met.

Grandmother watched the two of them, pausing to meet Addey's gaze and then Declan's. Addey tried to fight off the tremble that started in her hands and spread up her body. She had nothing to be afraid of—they'd done nothing wrong. But no one would see it that way. And all three of them knew that.

Grandmother finally spoke, her voice heavy. "This isn't going to end well." She stepped up to Addey and yanked her into a hard hug. "I'll see you tomorrow." She squeezed her arm tight and Addey winced.

"Have a good day, you two." With that parting line, Grandmother walked out, leaving them standing there in her wake.

They turned to each other and exhaled at the same time. Declan's shoulders dropped. Addey could feel the pressure releasing off them like a vice being loosened.

"Come on, let's get out of here." Declan grabbed her hand and tugged Addey away from the building. Once inside his car, they headed away from Mount Vernon. Addey gripped the seat as Declan drove just above the speed limit as he weaved his way through the suburbs.

"Declan..."

"I don't want to talk right now, Addey. I just want to get us far away from there." His clipped words set off a string of doubts in Addey's mind. He was changing his mind about them. Grandmother had said something to make him hate her family even more. What if he wanted to walk away from her?

But Declan's hand on hers, his gentle squeeze brought her racing thoughts to a halt. "Come, we can talk inside."

It was then that she realized he'd stopped his car outside a small, red brick complex. It was old but well-maintained and had several large oak trees out front. It overlooked a serene park. Addey loved it. "It's pretty here."

He held the main door open for her and followed her inside, shutting the cold wind behind them. She followed him up three flights of stairs, winded and out of breath trying to keep up with his long stride.

"Sorry, we don't have an elevator in this old place," he called over his shoulder.

He unlocked the door and Addey followed him inside. She was immediately drawn to the picture window that overlooked the park. Sunshine spilled in through the window, giving the room a warm feel and making it look much bigger than it really was. There was a small table sitting in front of the window and between her and the table was a set of steel blue sofas that looked squashy and comfortable—something she could snuggle into. No bouncing.

"Come on in," he said, taking off his jacket and hanging it on the coat rack by the door. "Your coat?" She handed it over while stepping deeper into the room. The place wasn't adorned with much, just a handful of framed photos of Declan and his family on the wall opposite the kitchen. She didn't see a father in any of the pictures. She looked over at him but he wasn't looking at her, he was pulling his wallet from his pocket and putting it on the end of the kitchen bench. The clink of his keys followed. She didn't know why, but there was something so masculine about what he just did. It was really intimate being here in his place, watching him do something so mundane, yet so manly.

"Do you want something to drink?" Declan looked around the space, looking lost, and Addey tried to smile.

"I'm fine, thanks." But she wasn't. Were they over before they could get the chance to begin? She should be happy, but she wasn't.

"I didn't know who I would be interviewing until I got there." Declan settled against the kitchen bench, facing her, his hands resting on the countertop behind him.

"How did you two not kill each other?" Addey asked, still shaky from the encounter.

Declan ran a hand down the back of his neck. "Do you really think I could be that unprofessional?" He sagged against the counter, his expression pained. "Am I the same guy who baited you at the cupcake shop?"

Yes... "No, you're not that guy..."

***

Declan stood still, waiting for Addey to elaborate. Her brow was furrowed, confusion haunting her. It haunted him too. He wanted more with her, but every time they took a step forward, another obstacle would spring up. "I said yes in my head because my grandmother is scary. The woman is like a general ordering an army around." Addey tugged at the hem of her sweater. "My family is tough. People run from them."

Would he run from her? That's what she was asking. "Did you think she would be unprofessional? That she might cause a scene?"

Addey gave a little laugh. "My grandmother can cause a scene with the quirk of one eyebrow. I was more worried she would say something to get a rise out of you."

He thought she might too. Declan's gaze went to the ceiling, but he didn't start counting. Instead, he looked back at Addey, who was watching him with wide eyes.

"Did you count to twenty?" she whispered.

He chuckled. "No, but I counted to twenty twice after she told me her name."

Addey laughed. The confusion and tension that stretched between them eased.

"What do you think your grandmother thinks of you hanging out with me?" Declan edged closer.

Addey blew out a hard breath. "She won't say anything to my parents if that's what you're asking. Grandmother doesn't like to interfere in our lives. She prefers to sit back and watch and let the chips fall where they land."

Declan stepped closer. "We had a pleasant conversation. I kind of like her." Addey was within reach.

"I don't know what she'd think of that." Addey's gaze dragged him closer.

"I think maybe we should do the same thing..."

"What's that?" Addey whispered.

"See where the chips fall with us..."

They were standing so close Addey had to tilt her head, but she never broke eye contact. Declan's eyes roved her face, settling on her lips. This was wrong, but as he lay a hand on her soft cheek, watched as her lips formed a perfect O, and with his pulse thundering, he didn't care anymore. He leaned down and claimed her lips with his.

***

Addey couldn't do anything but kiss Declan back. His kiss was tentative at first but as she pulled him closer, rising on tiptoe to do so, his kiss grew surer, more confident, and very thorough. His hand pressed the small of her back, pulling her closer. Her arms wrapped around his neck and she ran a hand along the back of his neck. The kisses slowed and they broke apart, foreheads touching. Both breathing hard. He was still holding her. And Addey leaned into his strong embrace. Feeling safe, felt and seen for the first time in years.

"We're in deep now," Addey breathed, loving the feel of him so close.

"Yep." His five o'clock shadow tickled her cheek.

"I'm sorry if I made you think at any point you would be unprofessional." Addey drew herself closer, letting her head rest on his chest.

Declan stroked her cheek and moved his hand to her hair. She shivered but stayed right where she was.

"It's okay." He breathed out. "I would have been a few weeks ago." He ran his hand down her jawline. Addey shivered. "But I met someone who is intent on believing I can be a better man."

She looked at him, the vulnerability in his voice tugging at her. Those walls Eli had mentioned were coming down. Was she ready for it? Was Declan? She touched his cheek, loving how the stubble felt under her thumb. It soothed her.

He watched her watch him. Then he slowly tugged her in for a second kiss and the doubts Addey had got lost in this moment.

Their moment.

Chapter Twenty-Four

Holding only one coffee cup—hers—Addey was about to walk inside her parents' house when Grandmother Hamilton walked out of the front door.

Addey stilled, adjusted her purse strap with her free hand, and waited, trying to get her heart rate to settle down. What was Grandmother going to say?

Grandmother walked up close. "When I said to tell the man who you were, I didn't mean date him."

Addey lifted her chin. "I'm not dating him."

Grandmother almost smiled, but it faded before it materialized. "Don't give me that. I am in full possession of all my faculties, and I know what I saw."

Addey took a sip of her coffee. "I don't know what you want me to say."

Grandmother's stare was iron. "Are you dating him?"

Addey held her cup near her lips. "If you already know, why do you need to ask?"

Addey wanted to tell her no, but she couldn't. Their kisses last night were the final step over a line she had been trying not to cross ever since she met Declan. And they were going ice skating tonight, as their plans for last night had been scuttled because her clients' party had lasted far longer than expected.

"I want to hear it from you." Grandmother crossed one arm at her chest, the other held tight to her purse strap.

"Grandmother," Addey lowered her voice and leaned forward. "Are you interfering?" She grinned, needing to lighten the mood. It was going to be grim when she went inside.

Grandmother huffed quietly, but a smile ghosted her lips. "I'm looking out for your interests."

Addey raised one eyebrow, still smiling. "If you won't give me a straight answer, neither will I."

"You're impossible." Grandmother lifted her chin, her eyes bright. Then they dimmed. Worry lined her forehead. "Adelaide, you're playing with fire."

"I know," she whispered.

"I won't say anything," Grandmother sighed. "But everyone is going to get hurt when this gets out."

Addey's shoulders tensed. "I'm not ready to walk away from him," she whispered.

A gentle smile touched Grandmother's lips.

Addey raised her eyebrows. "What's that smile for?"

"You're happy. And of all the people to make you happy, it's Declan Collins. Sometimes I think I've seen it all in this world, but then I get surprised."

"Is this a good surprise?"

Grandmother laughed. "That depends on who is asking."

Addey sipped her drink. She shivered in the cold morning air. "Why did you interview Declan?"

Grandmother eyed her. "When I heard that he wanted to do an interview with a member of the Association, I volunteered. I wanted to see him up close." She looked up at the big house, towering behind them. "I wanted to see for myself what he was like."

"And?" Addey held her breath. Was it crazy to hope that one member of her family could like him? Maybe even accept him?

"He was very professional and pleasant enough," she said slowly, seeming to choose her words carefully. "What do you know of his past?"

Addey was surprised at the question. "His parents are divorced and he's from California. He doesn't talk about it much. Why do you ask?" She wanted to know more about him, but she wouldn't push him until he was ready to talk. If she pushed too hard, too fast, he would shut down.

"Don't look so suspicious." Grandmother placed her hands in the pockets of her long black cardigan, which matched her black pants. The sky-blue top underneath made her pale blue eyes brighter.

Addey tilted her head to one side. "Why do you want to know?"

"That Gilmore Girls article."

What did his spoof piece have to do with it? "What about it?"

Grandmother frowned. "I think he's from our world."

"Really?" Addey watched her grandmother closely, her mind racing.

"Only someone from our world would be able to say the things he does," Grandmother said.

"He could have done research," Addey interjected, but she kept thinking back, his dancing ability, the way he could charm the folks at Heritage Oaks. The way his mother gave off the same regal air Granny, Grandmother, and Mom had. Except Granny and Susannah Collins were the friendlier versions. All these things didn't add up to someone who was brought up wealthy, but it did raise questions.

Grandmother waved the idea away. "Don't be silly. There's research and there's living it. There's a difference and I can see it."

"Do you think everyone can see it?" Addey leaned forward.

"Did you see it?" Grandmother said.

"Not at first, but now that you point it out…" It was strange having this conversation with Grandmother of all people.

Grandmother nodded. "I thought so, but I don't think everyone will know the way we do."

"If he is from our world, why doesn't he talk about it? He knows who I am." *But he hates the world I'm from.* Addey adjusted her purse strap. She was getting tired standing outside. For a second, she longed for her mother's bouncy sofa. But that longing disappeared as quickly as it came.

"I think he has his reasons," Grandmother murmured.

Eli had said the same thing. "What do you know?" Addey narrowed her eyes.

"I don't know anything. I have my own ideas, that's all." Grandmother touched Addey's arm, the older woman's skin still relatively smooth for her age. But her grip was strong. "Adelaide, trouble always brings more trouble. And this has trouble all over it."

"I know," Addey said. "Thanks for taking the time to care about me."

Grandmother leaned in and pressed a kiss to Addey's cheek. Two of her family members showing affection in the same week? One might think the world had turned upside down.

"You know, regardless of what you think about your parents, you were loved and wanted, Adelaide. You still are." The note of sadness in Grandmother's voice tugged at Addey, she leaned and rested her head on Grandmother's shoulder. Grandmother stroked her hair. The familiar scent of peppermint tea enveloped Addey and, for a few glorious minutes, she felt safe and loved.

"Go on in and make peace with them." Grandmother stepped back, giving Addey a little push.

Addey's heart grew heavy. "That's never going to happen."

"Since I'm still being surprised by this world, I won't take that bet." Grandmother got in her car and drove off.

Addey held her half-empty cup and took a deep breath. The hope she carried from her meeting with Dad days ago still flickered and the feel of Grandmother's fingers in her hair lingered. Maybe there *was* a chance it would all work out.

Addey found the sitting room empty. For a wonderful moment, she hoped they forgot about brunch. But years of experience told her that was statistically impossible. Walking to the large windows overlooking the deck and the river further down, she caught a glimpse of movement outside. She turned around just as the maid walked in.

"Your parents are on the deck."

"Thanks."

Addey paused at the door, steeling herself for whatever was to come. As always, the deck was splendid and the view stunning. It was her favorite spot in the whole house. The river was washed bright from the sparkling sun. Winter was cold, but at least the sunshine made today bearable. It was like a little present given to Addey to help survive another visit.

She found Mom seated in one of the chairs, a white, thick woolen shawl draped across her shoulders, and wide sunglasses covering her eyes. A pot of tea, a book, and an assortment of tiny pastries sat in the middle of the table. Dad was wearing his power suit and his phone was glued to his ear. Addey swallowed down any lingering frustrations and took a seat.

"Venue change today?" she offered, dropping her purse beside the chair. She pulled her thick red coat tighter around her.

Mom nodded.

Dad looked at her and winked. "No coffee and newspaper for me today?"

"Nope." She crossed her legs. At least out here she could enjoy the sunshine.

"Now, about the party," Mom said, launching into the topic with more gusto than Addey could ever muster. "The flowers are all arranged? I want people to feel like we're in a winter spectacular. And the lobster is still on the menu? I want it to be perfect."

Addey could feel a headache coming on so she focused on the water and concentrated on its soothing rhythms. Maybe the sun would warm her mood as much as her body. "It's all in order, Mom. Since I've been back on the job, everything is going smoothly." There was no point in telling her that the two whole days of being away from the job had changed nothing about the schedule or the party itself.

Mom smoothed her shawl. "There was no reason to quit in the first place."

Addey flicked a glance to Dad, who approached the table. "Whatever the case Vivien, it's all sorted now. We're all on the same page." He shot Addey a pleading look.

Mom remained silent.

Addey swiped a piece of pastry from the plate. It was the size of her thumb. Thankfully she wasn't hungry. She imagined Declan eating one of these and it getting lost in his big hand. She almost smiled, but held it in check. There would be no discussing her love life today.

"We're okay." Addey sent Dad a small smile. He returned with a sharp dip of his chin, like he approved of their conversation. It was so weird being on friendly terms with him. It was almost like they were in a secret club or something.

"There's nothing wrong with being interested in your life," Mom pouted.

Addey looked over at her mother. Mom just couldn't let this go. "Thanks for your concern, but we've been over this." She was tired of having to always find the middle ground. "My love life is my own." So much for not talking about it.

Internally she shivered and hoped they would drop the topic.

"Adelaide is being perfectly reasonable, darling." Dad's defense of Addey was welcome if not for the irony in his words. He wouldn't be so supportive if he knew the truth. The hope that burned inside her warred with the fear of them finding out. She didn't need another excuse for them to reject her.

"Fine," Mom said between sips of tea.

Silence reigned and the moment between them was almost peaceful. The well-established trees that dotted the backyard swayed in the gentle breeze that came off the water. It was a perfect winter morning for a boat ride on the river.

Addey stood and wandered to the railing. This house was stunning and, she had to admit, being out here on the deck overlooking the water had soothed any frayed nerves she had. Maybe it had the same effect on her parents.

She leaned back against the railing, watching them. They were sitting beside each other, a solid two chair spaces between them. Mom was elegantly sipping tea, while Dad was reading a book, his phone close by at his elbow. She squinted so she could better see the title. *Death Train by Alistair McNeal*. She held back a smile. Dad had always loved his action books. He'd been reading them for as long as she could remember.

Her thoughts skittered back to the conversation with Grandmother in the driveway. Had her parents really wanted her? Could she ever ask them why they'd let Granny take care of her? Was it the right time now? A small surge of adrenaline raced through her.

She summoned her courage and prayed a prayer for herself—the first in a long, long time—that the peaceful setting and the sunshine would work their magic.

"Can I ask you guys a question?"

Their heads snapped up and, instantly, Addey regretted her words. Too late now.

"Of course," Mom said stiffly, her body rigid like she was ready to pounce.

"Don't panic, it's about Granny."

Dad's shoulders relaxed. "What about her?"

"Um..." Addey's stomach clenched as she looked for the words. It should be a simple question, but there was nothing simple about this. How did you ask someone why they didn't love you? "How come you let me live with her?"

"You were here every other weekend and you had dinner here twice a week." Mom's voice was thick and defensive.

"I know and I'm not mad, I guess I just want to know..." The words limped out as they left her lips. Mom was back to sipping her tea but she'd wrapped her shawl tighter around her like armor.

Dad sat forward, his eyebrows knitted together. "We both were brought up with nannies, and I think your Granny regretted that, given how her life turned out." He tipped his head towards Mom, who sat stiff and silent, sunglasses still firmly on her face. She looked like a movie star from the golden age of Hollywood. "You already spent so much time with her that when she made the suggestion, and knowing you'd be only a fifteen-minute drive from here, well—we just figured it was the best thing."

"We still had total say in your life back then," Mom added, her tone less hostile, but full of authority. "We're not allowed to have a say in your life anymore."

Addey bristled. Anger and frustration, her old friends, made her head and heart ache. "Mom, please." Maybe she should just give up on them altogether.

But no. As soon as she'd thought it, guilt followed. Sadness seeped deep into her bones. She could no more disown them than she could stop breathing, but there were days the weight of this unhappy dance they did truly felt too heavy.

Mom sniffed in reply and Dad shot her a warning look, which Mom ignored.

Addey walked towards her purse, more than ready to leave. "I'm heading home now. The party I did last night ran later than I expected it to." Surprised when no one objected, she gathered her purse and the half full, but now cold, coffee. "I'll call if I need to discuss anything with the party."

"Yes." Mom stood, the shawl draped regally across her body. Her sunglasses perched on her face. "We should go shopping one afternoon when you finish work."

"Maybe," Addey hedged.

"Fine. See you later." Mom walked back inside.

Dad rose slowly, his gaze trained on her. He looked behind him as if to make sure her mother was gone. Addey tensed.

He closed the distance between them, and when he was standing near enough to talk quietly, his voice halted. "Your mother's father...he wasn't the best person and, well, he treated your grandmother very badly and almost turned your mother against her." He rubbed a hand across his face. "When he divorced her, as you know, he didn't leave her with much and she was here a lot because of that. She saw you with your first nanny. Do you remember Felicia?"

Addey shook her head. Dad gave a wistful smile. "That's a good thing then. Deborah saw your attachment to her growing and she didn't want you to be attached to someone who would just leave. So, she suggested living with her during the week and honestly, I was the one who persuaded your mother to do it."

"Why?"

"Adelaide, you know your mother." He looked behind him, as if reassuring himself that Mom was out of earshot before he continued. "She's not the most maternal woman. She struggled to relate to you when you were little, and still now. I think your grandmother wanted to avoid what she had with your mom—a stilted and distant relationship. By doing this, she encouraged you to spend time with us while being with her most of the time."

"Our relationship" —she nodded at him, and jerked her chin in Mom's departing direction— "isn't, well, shall we say very..." She searched for the right words.

"Close?" Dad finished for her. Addey swallowed the rising hurt that was gathering. *But why can't we be closer?* It was the question she'd been echoing for years.

"I'll tell you something, it could be so much worse. How many of your school friends see their parents weekly? How many still talk to their parents?"

She looked away. "Not that many."

He pointed in a random direction. "They take their trust fund money, show up for events that require them to be there, and sponge off the family when the money runs out."

He leaned across so that she had no choice but to look at him. "You don't do that and we all have your grandmother to thank for that."

"But we fight so much..." Addey whispered.

"We do. It's not perfect and it never will be."

"I'm not looking for perfection, Dad, I'm looking for acceptance." She wrapped her arms around herself.

Dad raised his eyebrows. "Which you don't think you get?"

Addey gave a watery laugh. "Do I even need to answer that?"

"Fair enough, you have a point. But maybe your idea of acceptance looks different to ours." He took a step towards her and dropped a kiss on her forehead. Addey settled in, took a big breath, and let herself savor this moment. She let his affection and words soak in. Maybe there was hope after all. Confusion swirled inside her.

"See you next week." He squeezed her arm and walked inside.

Addey stood there, defeated. As far as she knew, acceptance was acceptance. It was being loved for who you were, not being criticized for all your failings—real or imagined. A shiver rippled over her. Not even the sunshine could dispel the dark mood that had descended. Whatever it looked like to them, Addey knew that she would never find a home here. She should stop trying, but as she walked to her car, she realized the unfortunate truth.

The little girl inside her would always fight for their love.

Chapter Twenty-Five

Addey was staring at the growing pile of clothes on her bed when the doorbell rang. She looked at the clock on her bedside table. Declan was forty minutes early for their date. That couldn't be right.

Just thinking about their date brought a smile to Addey's lips and the smile stayed in place as she padded downstairs and opened the door to find Carmel.

"Carmel! When did you get back? How's your dad?" Addey yanked her friend inside, closing the winter wind out, and pulled Carmel into a long hug.

Carmel squeezed back. They stood there for long seconds. Finally, they pulled away.

"Come sit, you look tired." Addey grabbed her friend's hand and pulled her toward the sofa.

Carmel let out a fractious laugh. "I am so tired. But Dad is on the mend, Mom is fretting like a mother hen, my sisters are arguing with each other about the best way forward, and Mom keeps looking to me to make all the decisions."

"Wow, that's a lot."

"It is." Carmel fingered her messy top knot, a hairstyle Addey never saw on her fashionable friend. "I just wanted to come over and hang for a bit and see how you are doing, but I should've called first."

"It's fine and I'm fine." Addey didn't want to look at the clock on her wall or hurry her friend along, but she did need to get ready for her date.

Carmel eyed her. "What's going on? You have that uncertain look on your face."

Addey fidgeted with the ruffled edge of a cushion. "I have plans tonight, that's all."

Carmel sat up straighter, a gleam in her eyes. "Please tell me you are going on a date with a man?"

Addey rolled her eyes. "You act like I never go on dates."

Carmel poked her in the side.

"Hey!" Addey swatted her hand away.

"You haven't been on a date that wasn't orchestrated by your mother in, like, two years."

Addey's eyes widened. "Really? Am I that sad? And they weren't even dates."

"No, but I'm glad you're doing this. So, tell me, who is the guy?" Carmel leaned forward, her eyes bright and her lips curved into a mischievous smile. "Please tell me it's Declan?"

Addey ducked her head and let the flush take full control.

Carmel clapped her hands. "Yay! I'm so excited for you! Tell me everything that's been going on. I need a break from my life."

Addey couldn't keep the grin from her face. It was wonderful to have someone excited about this. So far everyone, including herself, was so busy stressing about the implications of her and Declan, that she hadn't stopped to enjoy it.

Addey filled Carmel in on the last week and a half.

Carmel was beaming by the time Addey finished her story. "I'm so proud of you for standing up to them and going after your man."

"He's not my man." Addey tossed the cushion at her friend.

Carmel caught it. "Whatever, honey. Now what are you going to wear?"

"I was deciding that when you came over."

"Come on, we've got work to do." Carmel stood, grabbed her hand, and dragged her upstairs.

***

By the time Addey finished trying on clothes her face hurt from laughing and smiling. It was so good to have her friend back and to have her acceptance. Addey really needed more people like Carmel in her life. They'd settled on a sea-green, fitted, turtleneck sweater, jeans, and tall black boots. Comfy but chic.

"It's almost time." Carmel tapped her wristwatch.

Addey stopped at her doorway, suddenly overwhelmed. "What if it goes badly?"

Carmel cocked her head. "Honey, the man has cooked with you, fought with you, knows who your family is, and he's still interested. It's going to be fine."

"Don't forget the kiss," Addey whispered, her insides going giddy at the memory.

Carmel laughed. "Would you stop overthinking this and just enjoy yourself?"

The doorbell rang.

Addey's eyes widened and she froze.

"I'll open the door if you don't." Carmel stood, eyeballing Addey.

"No, no, I'll do it."

Addey's boots made no sound as she bounced down the carpeted stairs, her heart tripping with every step.

She opened the door and exhaled. Declan stood there looking far too handsome in jeans, and a white button-up, with the collar showing over a black sweater. He was clean shaven tonight

"Hey," she said breathlessly.

"Hey yourself," he replied, his voice low and sexy. Addey wanted to hang onto the door frame for support, but Declan stepped in and wrapped his arm around her waist, saving her the trouble. He leaned down and dropped a soft, lingering kiss on her lips. Addey wrapped one arm around his neck and kissed him back, never wanting the moment to end.

Slowly he pulled back, his nose touching hers. "I was going to wait to kiss you at the end of the night but, as you know, I'm not the most patient guy around."

Addey shivered. "And here I thought you were a boy scout." She loved the feel of him being so close.

Her phone buzzed in her pocket. She pulled it out and laughed. Carmel.

Go on your date already. I'll lock up when you leave. Don't forget to have fun!

"Carmel is back," Addey filled him in.

"And she's upstairs?" Declan asked, his sly grin made her heart thump harder.

"How'd you know?"

He used his thumb to point behind him. "Her car is parked outside."

Addey laughed, her face heating. "She helped me find an outfit." She still hadn't moved away from him and Declan didn't seem to be in a hurry either.

His gaze traveled down her body and back up. "I approve." He lingered far longer on her face, his hand caressing the inside of her wrist.

Addey ducked her head, her hand holding his jacket. "Are we really going on a date?" She spoke into his jacket.

Declan's gentle chuckle rumbled through his chest, making Addey want to lean in further, drink him in, memorize how he smelled, how he felt in her arms. "Not if we stand in this doorway all night."

With great reluctance, Addey stepped away. "I'll grab my purse."

***

Declan pulled into the parking lot of Pentagon Row. As expected, it was crowded tonight with people strolling the shops and grabbing food at the local eateries. He watched Addey exit the car and join him as they walked in the direction of Westpost Outdoor Ice Skating. Without taking another second, he snagged her hand, sending her a smile. Addey grinned back. The night was cold, but clear and calm. The perfect night for skating with a pretty woman.

"When was the last time you ice skated?" Declan tugged her closer to avoid the passing foot traffic.

"Um, it's been a while. I'm not the most coordinated person." She looked sheepish.

"I don't know about that. Those boots look like they take some coordination." He glanced down at the shoes. Four inches at least with a skinny heel.

She laughed. "They're surprisingly comfortable."

"I'll take your word for it." He loved the sound of her laughter and the smile that came with it. It was like sipping a hot chocolate on a cold snowy morning.

"You're going to have to go easy on me, you know. I'm not a pro like you are."

He snorted. "Hardly a pro."

They joined the line to pay for their tickets and skates. They got their skates and found a spare seat by the rink. "It's busy tonight," Addey commented as she wrestled with her boots before finally yanking them off with a huff.

"Comfy, huh?" He cocked an eyebrow.

Addey swatted his arm. "You have a sister...beauty is pain. You should know that."

Declan laughed. "I'm not going to touch that one."

They stowed their gear in the storage section under the seats. Declan clipped his skates on. He watched, amused, as Addey struggled to get hers on.

"Need some help?" he offered.

"Yes, please, they're always awful to get on." She dropped her half-covered foot with a thud onto the ground.

He knelt down and picked the left skate, adjusted the straps to make more room. "Here, slide your foot in."

She stood up to get more leverage and her foot slid right into the skate.

He strapped it up and looked up. "Too tight?"

She rotated her ankle and shook her head.

"Next one." He pulled the right skate up and did the same thing with the straps, creating more room.

"Ready to do this?" he asked.

"I sure am." Her voice was steady as she squeezed his hand.

The rink was busy, but it wasn't so crowded that they couldn't move. Young kids using animal-shaped frames to help them move skated by, parents pushing strollers on the ice and chasing after their other kids. Christmas music piped through the speakers. Couples skated past holding hands. Christmas lights were strung up in the trees that surrounded the rink and the lights from the surrounding plaza created the perfect atmosphere.

He followed Addey and watched her step onto the ice and cling to the rail, her legs wobbly. He grinned before taking pity on her. He stepped onto the ice and felt the sureness of his legs, then his feet propelled him forward. He used his torso to anchor himself and directed his legs towards Addey.

"Do you want a frame?" he teased as he skated beside her—just as a kid whizzed past on a penguin frame. She was still holding onto the rail, her face full of concentration.

"I'm fine," she said through clenched teeth. He watched her move her feet, slide them across the ice. "Those kids are doing better than me," she muttered.

"Come on." He held his hand out. "We'll go slow, I promise."

"Okay," she said slowly, eyeing his hand. "Don't even think about trying anything fancy with me."

He chuckled. "I wouldn't dream of it."

She stepped forward, grasped his hand firmly and, just like that, he was taken back to their kiss. She must have been thinking the same thing, because a pretty stain of pink showed on her cheeks and she tucked a smile away before meeting his eyes and glancing away. Carefully, he pulled her away from the rail and led them forward at a snail's pace. But he'd crawl along the ice if it meant getting to spend more evenings like this with her.

"You should be in the Olympics," she said, her voice tense. He could feel her trying to smooth out her jerky motions as she moved forward. She kept watching her feet, but she moved along slowly.

"It's like riding a bike, right?" he prompted.

She looked up quickly and wobbled. "I haven't done that in a long time either!" she puffed out.

He squeezed her hand a little tighter. It fit so nicely in his. "Just relax and let your feet glide you forward."

After two trips around the rink, Addey began to relax. She wasn't looking at her feet as much and was less wobbly. In fact, she'd even picked up some speed, but on the curves, she became unsteady and clutched him for dear life. She hadn't let go of his hand yet either. Not that he minded that a bit.

"You make this look so natural. Are you sure you're not a professional ice skater?" She zig-zagged through the curve.

"Trust me, I'm nothing compared to those guys. They'd pound me into the ground."

Addey's shoulder bumped his. "Besides ice hockey, what do you do for fun?"

"I run sometimes." He shrugged. "I'd say visiting Mom, but we both know that's not fun."

Addey's smile dimmed. "But it's gotten better, hasn't it? I don't mean her condition, but your feelings toward the situation?"

Declan loved how honest and direct she was, loved how she didn't pretend it wasn't happening. It was refreshing and something he sorely needed in his life. "It has gotten a little easier, I'll admit. Seeing her so happy on Thursday made me realize that it was a good decision to place her there."

Even still, though, the familiar guilt washed over him. Guilt for putting her there because he was unable to care for her properly himself. Guilt because his life had routine again because she was being cared for by others. The seesaw of emotions was maddening.

Addey squeezed his hand. "Don't feel bad because you have eased the load on yourself because she's now at Heritage Oaks. I know it's hard, but you're all doing great."

"How'd you know that's what I was thinking?"

Addey leaned closer, wobbling on her legs. He was glad they were skating so slowly.

"It's really common for people to think that. To feel guilt for everything they do or don't do. Just know, you did the best thing you could with the options in front of you."

Declan's chest tightened and for the first time in years, it wasn't anger related. Addey cared about how he felt. He was tempted to kiss her right there on the ice.

"You're right. I'll try and remember that." He gazed at her. "You're getting so much better. Think you can pick up the pace?" The challenge was issued and she took the bait with a gleam in her eyes and a hesitant smile.

Even when scared, she was brave.

He moved faster. The ice was still fairly smooth considering all the people on the rink. He felt her hand grip his tighter as he led them both through the curve.

"Don't go too fast!" She squealed as he pulled them into the straight.

"Lean into the curve on the next one, it'll be easier. Like riding a motorbike, lean with the bends."

"I'm going to take it that you know that from experience?" she yelled as the wind rushed over them.

"I might have ridden a time or two, but I don't own a bike, if that's what you're thinking."

"I've never even sat on one." Her words came out breathless as they picked up more speed.

"Here's the next curve, lean!" He hollered behind him as he sped them through the turn. He felt her turn and the movement was much more fluid this time.

Suddenly she was right beside him, a determined gleam in her eye as she raised an eyebrow. "I think I can keep up with you a bit now." The challenge in her voice lit a fire inside him. It was more than competition...something he couldn't identify, but he liked it. He let go of her hand, and he immediately wanted it back.

Addey propelled herself forward, using her arms and leaning forward to maximize her speed. Declan chuckled. She was so cute, and she didn't even know it. He did the same thing, only his legs didn't wobble. He used his core to keep himself steady as he let loose and sailed forward, enjoying the feeling of freedom that skating gave him. He easily dodged people and soon Addey was far behind. He overtook her twice before he slowed down.

She stopped near the rail, resting her hands on her knees, breathing hard. "Baking, dancing, now ice skating. Show off," she puffed.

"What can I say? I'm a talented man." He raised his eyebrows and loved it when Addey mock glared at him.

"Did you know you have an ego problem?"

Declan laughed, delighted by her. "It has come up once or twice in my life." He reached for her hand, not liking being away from her for too long. "I promise I'll go slow."

Addey willingly came and they skated around until she looked done in.

Red cheeked and out of breath, she slowed down when they neared the gate.

"Come on, let's get the skates off and find something to eat." He aimed them toward the exit gate when Addey let go of his hand and darted ahead of him. He threw his head back, letting a long laugh take over. "Cheater," he called.

She turned her head and stuck her tongue out.

He saw the collision coming before she did.

"Addey, move!" he yelled, waving his arms to get her to change directions.

The smile vanished as she saw the look on his face. She swiveled her head back and he watched as she tried to move herself sideways to avoid a group of teenagers who weren't paying attention. It was too late. Shrieks filled the air as Addey collided with the group. Three of them went down as Declan skated up to the tangle of arms and legs. A chorus of voices erupted at the same time.

"Get off me!"

"Ow! My arm hurts!"

"I'm putting this on Snapchat!"

"Addey?" Declan hunched down. He found her tangled up with two girls, all three of them looking highly embarrassed and sore.

"Can you help me up please?" Her voice was muffled. Two of the other teens still standing near Declan helped everyone untangle themselves.

"Sorry," Addey said. "Are you all okay?"

The two girls brushed off the ice and rolled their eyes. "We're fine."

Declan guided her slowly off the rink.

"You are *not* putting that on social media!" One of the teen's shrill voices followed them off.

Someone else snorted. "Oh yes he is!"

They sat down on the seats where they'd stowed their things. "You okay?" Declan asked, giving her the once over.

Addey was massaging her hip and frowning. "My hip hurts, but besides my broken ego, I'm fine."

"It wasn't that bad," he soothed.

"You can barely keep the smile off your face," she puffed.

His grin grew bigger. "If it makes you feel better, I've had much worse spills. I broke my nose once after a collision with another player."

She struggled with her skates but managed to get them off. She winced with the movement. "You don't even look like this was an effort."

"You should see me on hockey night. It's a different picture."

"Can I see you play one night?" The tentative question tugged at him, pulling at his heart.

He leaned over and swept his finger along her cheek. "I'd like that," he whispered and was surprised when Addey closed the gap and pressed her lips to his. It was chaste and sweet—and he never wanted it to end. Was this what it felt like to fall in love? He didn't know, but now wasn't the time to figure it out. Now was the time to savor the moment.

Chapter Twenty-Six

Declan grabbed their takeout bags and followed Addey up the path to her townhouse.

"Sorry about this," she called as she unlocked the door. Her limp had become more pronounced after they left the rink.

Declan shut the door behind them, put the bags on the coffee table, and reached for Addey, steering her gently to the sofa. "Sit down and I'll get the food sorted. Do you need a painkiller?"

"I can walk." Addey stood, touched her hip and frowned before she followed him to the kitchen. "I can be stubborn when I want to be."

"Alright." He stepped aside, leaning on the peninsula bench while she limped around the kitchen, pulling out plates and glasses. "I can help, you know."

"I know, but I don't want you doing everything in my house, okay?" The soft way she ended the sentence told Declan more about her than she knew. Addey wanted to be in control in her house, probably due to her parents' rejection. He could understand that need to feel in control when the world around you was turned upside down, but she wasn't so stubborn as to be mean about it. One thing Addey definitely wasn't, was mean. The woman was kind and gentle with a heart for others.

Declan walked back to the coffee table, admiring the way the townhouse was decorated. If he had to call it something, he would have said casual beach meets elegance. Beach blues of the rug met the soft white of the cozy looking sofa. The light wooden coffee table complemented the other colors. As he walked back to the kitchen with the takeout containers, he stopped to admire the pictures hanging on the walls, and noted a metal cross hung above the pictures.

One of the photos was of Addey sitting atop Aladdin the Christmas Camel at Mount Vernon, looking about eight years old. Her red hair catching the sun and her smile big. Another showed her sitting next to her Granny—he knew, because he recognized her in the pictures at Heritage Oaks—at a restaurant, their arms wrapped around each other, heads together, smiling at the camera. He moved along the wall, captivated by the images. Addey and Granny at Heritage Oaks, Addey at her graduation with Granny's arm around her beaming with pride.

The last photo was of Addey and her parents. The only one with her parents at all. Everything about it was forced, from the clearly posed position to the uncomfortable faces each of them wore. Jonathan stood behind a hard, square sofa with Vivien sitting at one end and Addey, an adult, at the other end. They were all smiling, but none of the smiles reached their eyes. It was strange, the contrast between this photo and the rest.

"Why do you have this one up?" Declan asked.

Addey limped over. "Would you believe that's one of the only ones I have of the three of us?" The sadness in her voice made him wrap his arm around her. He wanted to take away her pain, make her not hurt like that ever again.

"I'm sorry," he murmured into her hair, which smelled like flowers.

"The other ones of us—before I lived with Granny—are at Mom and Dad's house." She leaned in closer, and Declan just held her.

Slowly, with a sigh, she pulled away. "Let's eat."

Without letting go of his hand, she walked them to the kitchen. They unloaded the food, her kung pao chicken and his beef chow mein. Addey offered a simple prayer and Declan found he didn't mind it. Addey's faith wasn't front and center like some people's, but he knew it was what kept her talking to her parents, what drove her love for the residents at Heritage Oaks.

"What?" she asked when she caught him watching her.

Declan forked a piece of beef. "I like that you haven't stopped believing even after all that's happened."

"God didn't make my parents reject me," she replied. "I asked them about that, you know, yesterday at their house."

He paused, fork half to his mouth. "Asked them what, exactly?"

"Why they let me live with Granny." Addey was staring at her plate.

Declan put his fork down. "What did they say?" He kept his tone even. He really hoped they'd been decent and gave her a good reason. Not that there would be a good enough reason, but maybe he could borrow some of Addey's hope.

Her shrug told him plenty.

"Dad said it kind of just happened." She pushed her food around her plate. "He cast it in a positive light."

That's not good enough. Declan pressed his lips together, willing himself to keep his mouth shut. Addey didn't need his anger on top of her hurt and disappointment. He reached for his can of soda and took a long drink. It was cold going down, giving him time to pull himself together. He set the can down and reached for her hand.

"That's a lousy reason. I'm sorry, Addey. I wish it was different for you."

"Thanks for not ripping into them, I appreciate it." A flicker of a smile hinted at her lips. "Did you need to count to twenty?"

Sassy girl. "Not this time. I must be growing as a person. Eli would be proud."

When they'd finished the food and cleaned up, Addey limped to the fridge and pulled out a tub of ice cream from the freezer. She held it up. "Ice cream? Cookie dough flavor?" She waved the tub around.

"As long as you let me serve it and you sit down."

Declan took the tub from her, put it on the bench, and walked her to the sofa. "Need any painkillers yet?"

Addey eased herself down and pressed her lips together. "I'm okay."

"Liar," he chuckled. "Where are the painkillers?"

Addey leaned back and tilted her head up so she could see him. "I'm fine."

"I'm going to search your house—"

"The cupboard on top of the fridge."

Declan found the pills and handed them to her with a glass of water. She didn't say anything as she took them.

Declan filled two bowls with ice cream and joined her on the sofa. He sat close enough to make sure she knew he wanted to be there—with her.

"What's your favorite ice cream flavor?" Addey asked between bites.

Declan swirled the ice cream around in his bowl, like he'd always done when he was a kid. "This is good, but I like—"

"Vanilla?" she filled in for him.

He cocked an eyebrow. "How'd you know?"

She shrugged, her lips turning up in that adorable way. "I guessed. Vanilla cupcakes, vanilla ice cream."

"I'm not a flavor adventurist."

Addey smiled around a spoonful of ice cream and Declan wanted to stay here with her forever. Here with Addey the world was simple, easy, calm, fun.

"We've talked at length about my parents, what about yours? When did your mom get diagnosed?"

Easy suddenly became hard. How much did he want to share? He looked at Addey sitting there with an open expression, and noted the way she moved closer, how she waited for him. No pressure or judgment.

"Mom got diagnosed two years ago. It was little things at first, like forgetting her keys, or mistaking a date, or getting appointments mixed up, you know, normal stuff with aging."

"Except your mom is only in her early sixties," Addey supplied.

"Right." Declan kept stirring his ice cream. "Nicky decided to take her to the doctors first and it took a few months to get the official diagnosis. But it changed everything."

"I'll bet it did." Addey put her bowl down and reached for his hand. "You guys are doing a great job. Did you know that? Does anyone ever tell you that?" Her gentle voice and the way her thumb stroked the inside of his wrist held him still, unwilling—no—unable to move.

The lump in his throat was there before he could stop it. When had anyone ever told him that? When had anyone believed in him besides Eli, his mom, or his sister? He had always been a failure in the eyes of so many—the angry kid, the outspoken journalist, the guy who failed to save the Community Center.

"Thanks, I needed to hear that," he breathed through the lump in his throat.

"Can I ask you something else?"

His stomach clenched at her serious tone.

Addey continued running her thumb in gentle circles on his wrist, watching him. He leaned against the sofa and watched her in return. Warm eyes and a kind heart. How had he ended up with her, and how on earth was she related to the Hamiltons?

"I know your parents are divorced, but what happened to your dad? What does he think about your mom's situation?"

Declan couldn't move. This was the moment he'd dreaded. No one knew except Eli, and it'd taken him two years to tell him. Could he dare tell another person? His palms grew sweaty, his instinct to pull away assailed him. Indecision battled with fear. What would she think of him when she found out? Would she tell the world? Would she run? He'd run when she'd told him who she was. He'd reacted badly, but look where they were now. No matter the proof in front of him, letting someone in so deeply was terrifying. The fear of rejection, of not being worthy was crippling.

"Dec…" She leaned in, her face inches from his. "You don't have to talk about this if you don't want to."

Her using his shortened name was a surprise and it felt wonderful. No one really used it. He was simply Declan to everyone.

He looked around at the photos of Addey's happy childhood. She wouldn't have had that if she'd never lived with her granny. Granny's love is what made Addey the kind, selfless woman Declan was falling for.

Eli's words from the other day came to mind: *Are you going to date this girl and not share anything about your life?* Maybe it was time to grab some more of that hope.

Declan swallowed back the building stress that threatened to claw out from his chest. He wrapped his fingers around Addey's. She squeezed them, giving him an encouraging smile.

"Does the name Edward Sheridan mean anything to you?"

She frowned, thinking, before nodding slowly. "Yes, he was the man behind the big Ponzi scheme in California years ago." She pressed her hand to her mouth, her eyes growing wide. "Oh Dec, was your family one of his victims?"

Declan took his hand from hers. *Please God, don't let her hate me.* His first prayer in years.

"I wish," he rasped out. "Addey, Edward Sheridan is my father."

***

Addey blinked, unable to process what Declan had said. Declan was from one of the wealthiest families in California, the son of the man convicted of stealing millions from people across the state.

The son of a man serving life in prison.

"Oh Dec, I'm so sorry." It all made sense now. The anger at the rich, the Gilmore Girls article, the way he could dance, his mother's understated refinement.

"You don't have to say anything. I know what you're thinking." Declan tried to move but Addey reached out, snagged his wrist, and held him in place.

"Nope, you have no idea what I'm thinking and I'm not letting you go—not that easily, Declan Collins." Her voice was fierce and she meant every word.

He stared at her, his beautiful eyes stormy, like the man she'd met at Mount Vernon. Inside those stormy eyes, in the way he didn't pull away, in the tautness of the muscles in his arm, she could feel it radiating up and taking his whole body, he was asking her a question—would she run from him, like everyone had? He and his mom and sister had been abandoned and left to fend for themselves in a cruel world, through no fault of their own. Addey's heart broke at the thought of fifteen year old Declan cooking meals while waiting for his mother to come home, taking care of his little sister, watching his father being put in prison.

"Tell me," she whispered. "I'm not going anywhere. There is nothing but right now, right here. You and me." She touched his cheek, felt the muscles tense under her touch, and she could almost feel the burn from the intensity of his gaze.

After several seconds, Declan reached up and touched her hand on his cheek and exhaled. She could feel his muscles start to relax, sense the tension begin to drain from him.

"I was twelve when our world fell apart." His quiet voice vibrated through the house—like it, too, was holding its breath—waiting to hear the story. "Dad was arrested at home, on an ordinary Tuesday night." He stopped and took Addey's hand and just held it in his lap. Addey moved closer, holding back a grimace from the pain in her hip.

"The feds had been building a case for months. They took Dad away. Mom had been completely innocent. She had no idea." He looked at her and his eyes were bright with unshed tears. "She didn't believe it at first, but when they showed her everything they had on him, I think she knew, deep down, something wasn't right. But it's your husband, you're supposed to trust him, right?"

Addey nodded and squeezed his hand.

He kept talking. "It took two years to go to trial. The world hated Dad and rightly so, he'd stolen millions from ordinary families, from our friends." A spark of anger lit his face. "By the time the trial came around, everything we owned had been sold, except for the property and possessions Mom had brought into the marriage. My grandmother, Mom's mom, had been a savvy woman. She was big on women's rights and believed that Mom should always have access to her own money. It wasn't much, as Mom kept only enough to get a divorce, move us far away, and put a deposit on our condo. The rest of the money, her own money, she gave back to the victims."

His shoulders heaved and Addey pressed her head against his chest. "Oh Dec, I love your mother even more now. The strength it took to deal with all that, to start life all over again, was huge."

His arm came around her and he pulled her close. Addey sat in his embrace, just feeling him breathe. "She changed our last name to keep us away from the relentless press. We moved here just a few weeks before my fifteenth birthday. The Community Center..." His words faltered and Addey hugged him tighter, "...became our second home. Eli became the family we needed. Nicky and I would go to the Community Center after school. Eli would give me chores." He chuckled. "He saw it as a way to channel my anger, and he just stayed nearby until one day, I finally talked. I was seventeen when I told him the truth."

His voice was croaky. Addey pulled away enough to see him and the unshed tears started to fall. Addey wiped them away. "I didn't know that Eli already knew our story. Mom had told him and he just patiently waited me out." This time a smile ghosted his face. "Eli has been the real father to me, when my dad" —the ire his voice made Addey shiver— "was rotting in jail for ripping people off and plunging our lives into disarray. He's selfish and deserves what he got."

Addey let him talk, let his anger leech out. She understood it now. Where it came from, why he carried it like a compass, firmly guiding his every step.

"This is why I fought so hard and why I'll always fight when people like your dad take away from the ones who need it the most." The flint in his voice was back and she could feel his chest tighten.

"I understand, Dec, I get it." And she did. Everything about him she now understood and, instead of wanting to run away from him, it only made her want to stay. "I'm so sorry for all of it."

He gave a short nod but averted his eyes.

Addey sensed he would pull away, that baring his soul like that might be too much and he'd run. She touched his chin and made him look at her. "Declan, I don't hate you. I'm glad I know you and I'm surprised..." She smiled as he drank her in, making her shiver. "Given what you've told me, I'm surprised you wanted to even talk to me, after I told you who I was."

This time his smile, thought tentative, met his eyes and the storm in there subsided. "Well, you said you saw something in me that might be different from what I project to the world. That stayed with me and it gave me hope that I wasn't a total lost cause."

"Dec, you're not a lost cause, far from it. And I'll prove it to you," Addey whispered. She kissed him, softly, letting her hands explore his face. Letting him know that she was in this all the way. It was freeing knowing they both knew the worst thing about each other and she tried to show it in her kiss. Declan's kiss was restrained at first, but soon deepened in reply to her enthusiasm. Then the man she was falling in love with took over and pulled her closer. He was fighting for her as much as she was for him.

Finally, he pulled away, his lips grazing hers, their noses touching, breaths mingling. "We're going to have to slow down," he whispered. "I may not have much faith left, but I know you do. And that matters to me."

Addey's heart soared. "Thank you for telling me, Declan. I'll keep your secret."

"I trust you, Addey, and for the record, you're nothing like your parents. Don't believe it when they tell you you're not good enough. You're more than enough, for God and for me." The soft way he ended the sentence burned hope so brightly in Addey.

When Declan tucked her into his chest, Addey could hear his heart thumping as fast as hers.

"We're in really deep now, Dec," she said into his chest.

His arms tightened around her. "I know, but I don't want to be anywhere else."

"Me neither."

Chapter Twenty-Seven

"I'm impressed, Declan!" Julie called as Declan walked past her office. The days ticking to Christmas edged closer. The ladies who manned the front desk were also in charge of decorating. Tinsel hung around door frames, a Christmas tree had been put in the corner next to the front desk, and a wreath hung on Julie's door. But it was the ever present click-clack of the keyboards, the hum of voices, and the sense of anticipation that hung in the air—everyone was waiting for their next story, their next interview—that Declan loved. It was in his veins.

He stopped, ducking his head inside. "And what have I done to deserve your praise?" Declan hoped it was the article he'd turned in about the Mount Vernon Ladies' Association. Between seeing Addey most of the weekend, he'd worked hard on it. He wanted Julie to like it.

"The fact that you interviewed Charlotte Hamilton and didn't eviscerate her is a miracle." Julie turned the laptop to face him, revealing the mock-up of the article.

"Eviscerate is a strong word, Julie. I never went that far." He stood center in the doorframe.

"Yes, but you came close—too close." She stared at him.

Decland nodded. "I agree, I was closing in on a dangerous line."

Julie blinked a few times, clearly struck by his admission. "It's good to hear you say that."

The too-long pause brought an inward sigh. Didn't people know he could sense their pity long before they said anything?

Julie cleared her throat. "How are things with your mom?"

"As well as can be expected. She has good days and bad ones. I think having her at Heritage Oaks, though hard, is best for her and us. We have a routine now."

"I'm glad to know that there is some good in what's an awful situation." Julie's smile flickered. "I can tell you are more focused now and, dare I say it" —she raised one eyebrow— "less angry?"

Declan thought back to last night. Telling Addey had been hard, but letting her in was worth it. She hadn't run from him—in fact—it only brought them closer. They'd been exchanging texts on and off all morning. As for his anger, it was still there, but not as overwhelming as before. Maybe he was finally beginning to let go, heal, even.

"If you're asking me if I'm okay with the Community Center closing, the answer is no. But I'm handling it better." His phone beeped. He pulled it out and saw a text from Addey.

"I'll let you take that," Julie said, looking back at the screen. "Keep up the good work, Declan."

Declan nodded and walked back to his desk as he read Addey's text.

Mount Vernon trip confirmed for this Thursday with the residents.

He quickly texted back.

Great. Mom will love it.

He paused before typing the question he wanted to ask. But he remembered last night and how they'd only grown closer because of his confession. He pushed back the doubts in his mind and typed.

Feel up for helping me tomorrow morning with another bakery run?

Her reply was instant.

I'd love to.

Declan grinned as he opened his latest article. Life was improving beyond his expectations.

***

"You're going with him on *what*?" Carmel asked as she pulled the first batch of angel-shaped cookies from the oven.

"We take canceled bakery orders to the Community Center so they can be distributed to the people who need it." Addey decorated Carmel's batch of now-cooled brownies. After last week, she was sticking to her strengths.

"At six in the morning?" Carmel scrunched her nose. "That's way too early."

"Yep." Addey nodded, unable to take off the stupid, happy grin that bloomed across her cheeks.

"Based on that dopey expression on your face, I take it the date was good?" Carmel mixed the next batch of brownies.

"We went ice skating, and I fell and hurt my hip." Addey used an icing pen to trace a gold star in the middle of a brownie. "But yes, it was a good date." She shifted in her seat, trying to get the throbbing pain in her hip to ease. The pain medication had taken the edge off but not enough, it seemed. When she showered this morning, she found a purple and black bruise the size of a closed fist.

Carmel sat and started decorating a brownie. "What on earth are you going to tell your parents?"

Addey put the icing pen down and frowned. Declan's raw confession the other night had kept her awake for a long time. Instead of anger, all she felt was compassion for him and his family. It wasn't his fault what his father had done. He'd been a victim as much as everyone else, but the anger he carried, while understandable, would eat away at him if he didn't resolve it. Addey hoped that this might be the beginning of a new road for Declan. "Honestly, I have no idea. He's not at all like what I first thought he was. He's got this big caring heart and he's someone who I think, when he commits to something, he's all in, you know?"

"And that's scary?"

Addey played with the edge of the baking paper. "Yes and no. This whole thing is scary, but Carmel" —she looked across at her friend, who was watching her with concern— "I don't want to be anywhere else."

"You're falling for him, aren't you?"

"So hard," Addey whispered.

Carmel gave her arm a quick squeeze. "Then just go with this. Declan might be complicated, but one thing we both know, he's not afraid of your parents. And he's not afraid to fight for what he wants." She bumped Addey's shoulder with hers. "And sweetie, you're what he wants."

***

This time Addey didn't ask herself what she was doing at six in the morning, waiting for Declan to show up. This time her heart beat fast with excited anticipation. This time, instead of enjoying the darkness, she longed for the sun to peek over the buildings and shine over her happy heart. Had she ever been this happy?

She thought across her life, all the safe, wonderful years with Granny, and knew she had felt such happiness. But since Granny's death? That was an easy answer. No. Not until Declan. It was wonderful to feel happy again, to look forward to a new day, and to not be alone.

Declan's familiar SUV arrived out front and Addey jumped up, unable to wait any longer to see him. Before she got to the car, Declan had already met her at the curb and was kissing her. Addey flung her arms around his neck and kissed him right back.

"Morning," he murmured, finally pulling away, his voice rough.

Addey leaned against him, shivering but not from the cold. "Morning yourself."

"Come on, let's get this bread order done so we can have breakfast." He opened the door for her and Addey climbed in, grinning and she didn't even to try and make it go away. When Declan shut the door behind him, he produced, like last time, a large disposable cup for her.

"Mmm, thanks." She inhaled the aroma of coffee and of Declan. Being in his car was like being wrapped in his hug. Addey settled against the seat, relishing being here with him.

"So, what's the plan for Thursday at Mount Vernon?" Declan asked.

"We'll go first thing in the morning, watch the chocolate making, have a picnic near the piazza, and then take a short tour of the house. We'll be back home for a late lunch," Addey replied.

Declan nodded as he weaved through traffic. "Okay. I'll drop in on Mom for lunch today and tell her."

The smile that tugged on the corners of his lips warmed Addey's heart. He may not have liked that his mom was at Heritage Oaks, but he was getting used to it.

"After I left your place last night, I was thinking how before she moved there, our life was totally consumed with making sure someone was with her twenty-four seven. Between Nicky, Eli and me, it took all our effort and it was exhausting. My exhaustion and my growing issue with the Hamilton Group" —he glanced at her, a quick *I'm sorry* turn of his lips— "was what got me kicked off my weekly column."

"Ah." Addey nodded. "I wondered why you stopped doing that and started reviewing museum openings and the like." A laugh escaped and she tried to stuff it back down but couldn't.

"What's so funny?" Declan asked.

"I'm just picturing you standing at a museum opening and trying to act like you care. It must have driven you nuts!"

Declan chuckled. "I won't deny that I wasn't impressed with the last year, but if all goes well, after the Christmas party, I'll have my weekly column back."

Addey sat forward, understanding dawning. "That's why your boss wants you to review the party? She wants to see how professional you can be..."

"I get my column back if I'm a good boy scout." The way he said *boy scout*, using a higher voice accompanied by a twinkle in his eye, made Addey laugh.

"So, this party is as important to you as it is to me."

Declan looked across at her, frowning. "I know any event you do is important to you, but I'm a bit lost as to why it's *so* important to you." They'd left the main road and were now snaking their way through back streets to get to Baking for Life.

Addey looked out the window and debated telling him about the Baker/Gibson Group. She might as well. Declan would keep his mouth shut. "It's pretty hush-hush, but my business is going to be bought out by the Baker/Gibson Group and then expanded. How much they offer for the business depends on how well the Christmas party goes."

Declan pulled into the parking lot of the bakery, turned the car off, and reached across and gave Addey a hug. "That's amazing, congratulations!"

The warmth in his voice, in his hug, warmed Addey all the way down to her toes.

"Thanks," she replied softly.

"Will you go with the company?" He asked, his hand now holding hers.

Addey looked up at him, and worried her bottom lip with her top one. "That's the plan."

"But you don't look happy about that?"

Addey shrugged, thinking of Heritage Oaks. "If I go with them, I'll have to leave my job at Heritage Oaks. I suppose it won't matter in the end anyway..."

Declan squeezed her hand tighter. "What won't matter?"

"Carmel told me the company that owns Heritage Oaks is thinking of employing someone to be a full-time event coordinator across their three facilities." Maybe it was time to move on. The direction for the business was a positive thing and it would put her on a level she hadn't been in before. But the hollow in her chest lingered. "I don't want to leave Heritage Oaks."

"It's a part of you and Granny, I get that. But nothing is for sure right now. The guys who own it may do nothing. And you never know what this Baker/Gibson Group will end up doing."

"When did you become such an optimist?"

Declan's smile spread across his face. He had no idea how much it changed his face—he needed to smile more and Addey was more than up to the task of making that happen. "Maybe I'm finally seeing the world through a better lens." Declan climbed out of the car. "Come on."

She wondered what her parents would say when she told them she was dating Declan. She shuddered just thinking about it.

In no time they'd taken the crates and driven back to the Community Center. The sign out front seemed to loom larger today, but Addey did her best to ignore it. They couldn't change what was going to happen, but it didn't stop her gut from twisting. They delivered the baked goods quickly and headed back to the car.

As they climbed back in the car, Addey's phone rang. She reached for it and froze when she saw who the caller was.

"What's wrong?" Declan asked.

"It's my mom." Addey stared wide eyed at Declan.

"Are you going to answer it?"

Addey shook her head—hard. "No, I'll call her back later."

Declan drove away from the curb.

A message beeped on Addey's phone. Addey glanced at it—Mom again.

The silence in the car was stuffy and Addey wanted to escape. Not from Declan but from the internal conflict that plagued her.

"Are you worried about your parents?" Declan asked, keeping one hand on the wheel, the other lying casually on his lap.

"Yep. Seeing that sign is a neon reminder that our situation is—"

"Problematic?"

"That's one word for it."

Declan's free hand rested on hers. "Let's just wait until after the party to tell them, okay?"

Addey nodded, but the knowledge that no matter what she did she would lose someone kept her from being settled. Peace was not coming, even though the hope she carried burned deeper inside and brighter. Could her worry coexist with her hope?

Looking at Declan, knowing what he'd gone through and how he'd found the courage to tell her, bolstered her resolve. If he could be brave enough to share his secret with her, she could be brave enough to face her parents with this. Addey squeezed his hand. She'd been brave with her parents lately, and back when she'd turned eighteen and changed her last name. But she'd paid a price each time. Dad relenting on the building unveiling was different. Addey had stepped up, been brave and told them her feelings and, in the end, Dad had come through for her. But that wasn't always going to happen.

In truth, Addey was tired of being brave to get her parents' love and respect. When was she going to get to be just Addey?

When was *she* going to be enough?

Chapter Twenty-Eight

The Mount Vernon trip was here and the excitement on the minibus was palpable. The eight residents, four caretakers, plus Addey and Declan made up the party. Declan had to admit he was excited too, not just to see Addey again, but because Mom was delighted with the trip. She'd talked about it nonstop when Declan had dropped by to tell her the news.

Mom's face was bright as the bus pulled into the parking lot. Two seats ahead, Maude and Vera sat together. Saul sat next to someone Declan didn't know. The three other residents sat with nurses and Addey sat by the driver.

"Oh Declan, I've wanted to come back here for years." Mom turned to him, her smile the biggest he'd seen in a long while.

"I know, Mom." He gave her hand a gentle squeeze. While it made him happy to see her so happy, it also hurt. How many more good days would she have? A nagging thought planted in the back of his brain. Should he tell his father about her condition? His immediate reaction was a firm *no*, but since he was beginning to find some peace with their situation, and Mom's question from weeks ago settled like an unwanted pebble in his shoe. Did the man deserve to know about her? No, he didn't think so, but he'd not broached the topic with Nicky. If Mom insisted, could he do it? For her? The questions continued to roll through his brain and the weight of it settled on his shoulders.

He rolled his shoulders and helped Mom off the bus and put his unsettling thoughts away. He was here to enjoy the morning with Mom and to get information on his latest article.

"Your mom looks so excited." Addey sidled up beside them.

Declan brushed his shoulder with hers. They'd both agreed to keep it professional between them today, but he couldn't help but take a second to be close to her.

Addey nudged him back. "Be good, boy scout," she murmured.

Declan chuckled. "Always."

The bus driver unloaded the wheelchairs. The weather was still fine, the bright sunshine taking the chill from the air. As they approached the entrance, jaunty music from a fife player filled the air.

"It's magical, isn't it?" Mom chirped. Declan looked down at her, her smile was huge and eyes big as she drank it all in. The entrance was decorated with wreaths and holly, the musicians wearing the traditional dress of the period. A red rope separated them from the visitors streaming past as they played. Declan searched for Addey and found her at the head of the group, walking and gesturing to one of the nurses next to her.

He followed the small line of the group through the grounds. They walked slowly to ensure everyone stayed together. Addey led them to the chocolate making area. The tent was set up so that groups of people could watch while the presenters explained the process.

"Ladies and gentlemen," Addey called to the group. "We are a priority group, so we'll get a front row look at the fine art of traditional chocolate making. We'll even get to taste some!" The eager expression and musical tone in her voice drew everyone in the group towards her. She would be great at this job full-time, Declan mused, realizing that Addey may not even think she was worthy of applying for the full-time job with the Heritage Oaks should it actually happen. Instead, her first thought was to stay with her business. Addey's future was bright, and he sometimes wondered if she saw it that way. Addey might be too busy focusing on what she didn't have, to really see all that she had before her. Truthfully, Declan could only watch and be there on her journey—for however long that might be. Once she told her parents about them, they wouldn't talk to her—he knew that. It was their way. Then how long could she stand that?

"It had better taste good," Maude commented loudly, jolting him from his melancholy thoughts.

"Shush Maude! If you don't like yours, I'll happily take your share," Vera called out.

"I'm sure it'll be delicious, Maude," Addey laid a hand on Maude's shoulder.

As the chocolate makers assembled ready to start, the group moved forward. It was a bit awkward but they got the wheelchairs lined up, right at the front, so they could see and hear everything going on.

Declan took out his phone and started filming. It was a fascinating process. The shelled, roasted cocoa beans were ground into tiny nibs using a mortar and pestle. After this, the ground nibs were placed onto a special wooden board and rolled over and over with a wooden block. The constant motion, combined with the building heat, slowly melted the nibs into runny chocolate. The chocolate was then put into molds and left to harden. The presenters had fast-forwarded the process by having the chocolate already cut and ready to serve, but as they explained the method, they kept everyone involved and happily answered questions that popped up.

"It's so complicated," Mom tugged on his arm. "They are very clever and patient to do all this."

Declan squatted down next to her. "It's fascinating." And it was. But what was more enchanting was seeing Mom so alive. This place really was a haven for her. He vowed to bring her back here more often.

A sudden movement caught his eye. Addey swiftly moved out of sight. Declan stood, looking to see what was wrong. Nothing appeared to be amiss. The residents were all still watching the display. Where was Addey? It was then his gaze connected with Charlotte Hamilton, who was frowning. Why was she here?

A vice grip on his arm made him startle. It was Addey. "We have a problem."

***

"My mother is here!" Addey's hoarse whisper sounded as awful to herself as it must have to Declan.

The immediate taut lines at the corners of his mouth, the slight narrowing of his eyes, his arm muscles quivering under her stranglehold of a grip told her everything.

"Is she here right now?" He leaned in, his words just for her. His sturdy presence helped settle Addey but only for a moment. This was a disaster. What on earth was her mother doing here?

"No. Grandmother just told me she's on her way to this spot." The panic continued to claw at her.

Declan gently moved her hand from his arm. He squatted down and spoke to his mom. "Mom, I've got to help Addey with something for a minute. I'll be right back."

"I'll be right here." Susannah's open expression made Addey's heart melt. What she wouldn't give for her own mother to look at her with such love.

Without another word, Addey steered Declan to a cluster of trees in a bricked-off garden, a perfect hiding spot. This was going to be their life. Was dating Declan worth this stress?

Addey turned to Declan. "You have to hide."

"What?"

Addey grabbed the front of his shirt, curling her fingers into the fabric. "You need to hide. She can't see you anywhere near me!"

Declan's hand found hers and he gently unfurled her fingers. "You're panicking."

"Of course I am! My. Mother. Is. Here." Addey's heart raced in time with her tumbling thoughts. "And why on earth are you so calm? Aren't you supposed to be the hot-headed one of the two of us?"

His frown and cocked head signaled his irritation was climbing. "I don't want to hide." The clipped tone tore at Addey. "My mother is out there. I'm not going to leave and hide. I told her I would be right back."

Addey smoothed the wrinkled fabric of his shirt over and over.

Declan's hand found hers again. The tenderness there, the gentle caress of his hand, was why she hadn't walked away from him.

"What are we going to do?" she whispered.

Declan's sigh didn't give her any hope.

His fingers tightened around hers. "I'll take Mom for a walk, and I'll text you when I'm out of sight. You get your mom to leave and, when it's safe, text me and we'll meet at the animal shelter. It's closed to visitors this time of year."

"But we can't get in there because it's closed—"

"Addey, that's not the issue right now."

"You're right." Addey stepped away, her fingers trembling only enough that she would notice it.

Before Declan walked away, he pulled her in and wrapped his arms around her. Addey let herself lean into his strength, breathed him in. "We'll figure this out. Remember we just have to make it to next week. Nine days. We can do that."

Addey nodded, not wanting to move. Reluctantly, she stepped away. "Okay. Let's do this."

Declan gave her hand one last squeeze before he ducked out.

Addey paced the short pathway that wound around the garden, waiting for Declan's text to come in.

After what seemed like an eternity, it came in and Addey breathed out a long, shaky breath. Okay, it was time to face her mother. Addey squared her shoulders, shooting up a quick prayer. So maybe, every now and then, she could pray for herself.

Addey found her mother walking up to Grandmother Charlotte at the same time she was, from the opposite direction. Addey's gut twisted. Had she walked past Declan?

"Mom, what a surprise! What brings you here?" Addey knew she sounded too forced and cheerful. Unable to help herself, she glanced around and, sure enough, Declan and his mom were not there. The relief that should have come, didn't. Addey's stomach was as tight as a lead ball. Guilt did that to a person. She'd made Declan hide, along with his mother. The woman was sick and she'd been the one to force her to leave. It only strengthened Addey's resolve to get her mother away from this place—now.

"Adelaide, you're here." Mom's cool nod made Addey feel as welcome as a skunk at a lawn party.

"Yes. I'm giving the residents a morning out. As you know, this is my other job." Addey continued talking and tried to settle herself. Counting to twenty worked last time, so she tried it again. It worked.

Addey smiled to herself. She'd have to let Declan know how good his influence was on her.

"If you had answered my call on Tuesday morning, I would have known you were going to be here."

"You did call really early, Mom," Addey said.

"I know you get up early. I didn't think it would be an issue."

Mom had a point. "You're right. The last couple of days have just gotten away from me."

"You've been like that for a couple of weeks now." Mom eyed Addey.

Grandmother stood silently between them, not interfering, just listening, and watching. Addey didn't feel particularly reassured by her presence.

Addey tensed at Mom's laser accuracy observation. "You know I kind of lose touch with the world the closer an event gets, especially one as important as this one." Addey scanned the area and let out another breath when she still couldn't see Declan. Mom was right, Declan had completely interfered in her orderly life, upending everything.

"Looking for someone?" Mom asked.

Addey felt the weight of the question rest of her shoulders. "I'm just checking to see if everyone is doing alright. The residents are the focus of my attention."

"I can see that," Mom huffed, but only loud enough that Addey and Grandmother would hear it.

Addey wanted to massage her temples, but she stopped herself. "Did you come together?"

"No, but we met up and thought you might like to join us. But I can see you're busy." Mom's voice was stiff and her face unreadable.

"Sorry, I wish we'd been able to catch up before now." And not just because of Declan. How often did Mom call to simply spend time with her? Was she trying to connect, like Dad was? Mom was always so much harder to read than Dad. Was Mom angry that Addey had lived with her mother? That familiar confusion settled on Addey like itchy blanket. If Mom hadn't liked the idea, why had she let her go? Dad's explanation the other day hadn't really given Addey anything concrete to go on.

Addey looked at the residents, now holding boxes of freshly-made chocolate, wrapped in white linen, and held together by red ribbons. Even Maude was smiling. The group was preparing to assemble under the trees for a picnic morning tea.

"Mom, I'm sorry, but I'm needed now."

"Of course."

Mom's stilted tone gnawed at Addey. How could she make things better between them? She already saw them weekly, worked with Mom on occasion, and tried to be an involved daughter, yet she always came up short.

"Have a good rest of the day," Grandmother said.

There was nothing for Addey to sag against, yet her shaky knees demanded she sit down. But first she needed to text Declan.

***

Declan paced the lawn near the animal enclosure. After getting Addey's text, he'd made sure Mom was settled with the group, then gone straight there.

No one had wandered down this quiet path.

"I just slipped under a fence that said *Closed to Visitors.*" Addey called as she walked down the path towards him.

Declan stopped pacing. "But you're here."

Addey raised an eyebrow. "Yep, every time I think I shouldn't be with you, I am."

The brittle tone in her voice drew him closer to her.

"Are you mad at me?" Her tone was hollow, lost, and it took the edge of his anger off.

He sighed. "I don't know what I am right now." His emotions warred with each other, torn between frustration, and understanding. "I get why you asked me to hide, but Mom was confused, and I can't be the one making things harder for her."

"I know, and I'm so sorry. I panicked. What would we have done if my mother had seen you and recognized you? She would have put two and two together. Mom has an eagle eye, you know."

Declan ran a hand down his face and kicked at the sturdy fence post but not hard enough to do any damage. The sheep just ambled around the enclosure, eating, and huddled together in one group. The scent of animals and hay tickled his nose, heightening his irritation. Addey joined him.

"I'm stuck between being annoyed at this and knowing why this happened."

"What are we going to do?" Addey asked into the silence.

"What do you think we should do?" Declan leaned against the fence.

Addey stared at the sheep, as if they'd give her the answers. A cool breeze picked up. She shivered and huddled closer to him. "No matter what I do, they're going to hate me. You're like a pariah to my family. Dad hates that you delayed the project. He hates that you were relentless in your pursuit to rally the community against the development."

Declan looked across at her. "I don't regret any of that."

Addey gave a broken laugh. "I know, and if you did, you wouldn't be you—the man I'm falling for more every day."

Her words were like a light in the darkness. His chest tightened and any anger he felt just drained away. He reached out and tugged Addey into his arms, and she buried her head in his chest. She smelled sweet, a simple delicate smell that embodied everything about her—delightful, and brave.

"I'm falling for you, too." He sounded husky to his ears.

Her arms gripped tighter around his waist in response.

"I don't want to walk away from us," he continued, loving what they'd found in the most unlikely place.

Addey stepped back enough to meet his gaze. "Me either. But I'm scared."

"Okay." He took a deep breath. "Then let's keep things simple until the Christmas party is over. After today, we'll text and call each other only, no more dates." Just saying it hurt. "You'll be crazy busy with the party preparation next week anyway and your parents will be around a lot more."

"I don't like it," she said slowly.

Declan's pulse picked up a notch at the tightening of her hands on his coat. She really didn't like his idea. He could relate.

"But...you're right."

The long exhale and tiny wrinkles on her forehead only made her cuter.

"But what about after the party?"

Declan touched her cheek, letting his thumb move to her lips. "We tell them. I'll go with you if that's what it takes. I'll look your father in the eye and tell him we're dating."

Addey croaked out a laugh. "I think I'd better tell them first on my own."

"Just know that I'm not going to back down. I'm not going to let your family scare me away from you, believe me."

Declan drew her closer and kissed her, softly at first but then he deepened the kiss, knowing this would be their last until the Christmas party. Reluctantly, he pulled away.

"I believe you," she whispered back.

"We'd better get back. Mom will be worried."

His phone rang, and he frowned at the unknown number. "Hello?"

"Declan? This is Betty, I'm one of the nurses."

Declan tensed, his heart pounding. That couldn't be good. "Yes, is everything okay?"

"I'm afraid not."

He closed his eyes as Betty continued, then opened them to meet Addey's worried gaze. "What's wrong?" She mouthed.

He swallowed hard. "Mom's missing."

Chapter Twenty-Nine

This was all his fault. Declan's thoughts churned in time with his stomach. Mom went missing on his watch. He knew better but he was too focused on Addey to remember Mom was his first responsibility.

His legs ate up the distance with Addey keeping pace beside him. All thoughts of their predicament disappeared as his worry for Mom took over. *Where was she?* His mind tripped over the thoughts as his legs steadily brought them to the group he'd left a few minutes ago.

Betty's white face jerked him to a stop. Addey stopped beside him, breathing heavy.

"What happened? How long has she been missing?" He fired the questions at Betty who flinched.

Addey stepped between them. She gave Betty a hug and said, "We need to make sure our other residents are accounted for and get them to the bus. You do that. Declan and I will stay here to begin searching. I'll call to get help from the staff here." She stepped away to make the call.

Declan whirled in a circle, scanning the grounds, looking for any sign of Mom.

"First, tell me everything before you leave." He asked the nurse brusquely.

"Susannah needed to go to the bathroom, so I took her. On the way back, we stopped at the gift shop because she wanted to look around. After we left the shop, we headed back here to meet the others when she saw something that caught her attention. She headed off in that direction before I could stop her." Betty pointed to the large group of tourists who had just come from Mansion Circle. "We got separated by that throng of tourists and then I couldn't see her anymore." Her voice faltered on the last word.

Addey appeared beside them. "Alright, we've got staff members arriving any minute to help with the search. Tell me where Mrs. Collins was last seen?"

Betty repeated the information.

Declan stopped listening. "I know where to start." He ran off before he'd even finished his sentence.

"Declan, I know you're worried, but we need to make a coordinated search!" Addey called after him.

He stopped long enough to wave his phone in the air. "I'm going to the upper gardens. She loves flowers. Call me on my phone."

He ran, his heart pounding like it had when he'd come home from work to find the condo on fire. Was she injured?

He hurried into the garden. "Mom? Mom?" He followed every path, checked every seat in the garden. He searched the green house. Nothing. People looked at him, curious, but he didn't care. He thought back to all the times she'd come here, seeking the solace this place offered her. She loved the gardens, the quiet, sheltered walks. It was her refuge from a life that had spun spectacularly out of control.

He sunk on an empty bench, racking his brain. Where would she go next? Was she okay? Was she scared?

Footsteps crunched on the gravel. His head shot up. Addey appeared, looking both frazzled but determined. She sat down beside him.

"We've got staff members doing a coordinated search. She's been missing for thirty minutes now."

"That's too long," Declan stood up, his legs thrumming with the need to move, to find her. "She's been here hundreds of times. She knows this place like it's her own. She's scared, Addey."

Pain seared across Addey's face as she stood to meet him. "I know. With Alzheimer's, even familiar places can be strange, especially if she's lost."

"We have to find her!" He paced back and forth. Tried counting to twenty. It didn't work.

Addey stopped him and placed her hands on either side of his face. "Shh. We will. We'll do it together." She held him steady. "I need you to breathe, okay?"

Declan drank in her steadiness, leaned into it. He needed it like he needed air. "Okay."

"Good." She removed her hands from his face and clasped one hand to his wrist. With the other hand she pulled out her phone and dialed, telling whoever answered that they'd searched the gardens with no sign of Mom.

"Tell me where else she would go." Addey lead him to a chair and pulled him down beside her. "You are our best chance of finding her." Addey touched his arm, grounding him to the present reality.

"The other gardens...um..."

"We've got a team heading there now. Every area will be searched, but help us help your mom."

"The wharf." Panic crept inside his chest. Images of the river and how deep it was tumbled through his mind, and his breath tightened. "She liked to go to the wharf, it was quiet there as well."

"Then let's go." She pulled him with her as she made another call.

"Addey, there's five hundred acres to this whole place, she could be anywhere."

Addey picked up her pace. "Don't think like that, Declan, just move."

Together they jogged the long winding pathways, passing through the livestock enclosures, past the Washington Tomb, and down towards the wharf. It was quiet, too quiet. Declan skidded to a stop, Addey right behind him. She slammed into his back and he reached to steady her, both of them breathing hard. They scanned the open space, all the way down to the sandy shore where the wharf started. Empty. Declan ran across to the covered pavilion. There was no sign of Mom.

With trembling hands, he walked to the end of the dock and peered into the water, praying he wouldn't find anything there. His eyes found nothing but the muddy waters and swift current of the Potomac. He didn't feel comforted by what he saw.

Addey's phone rung.

Declan whirled around, heart thumping.

"Yes?" Addey answered, not taking her eyes off him.

Declan couldn't breathe. He leaned forward, straining to hear. Addey's face, taut with tension, softened and a smile lit up her face.

Hope bloomed in his chest.

"They've found her!" Addey hung up the phone.

Declan seized her up in a hug and swung her around. "Where is she?"

"Watching the George Washington movie in the orientation center."

"Let's go."

Time slowed to a crawl as they alternated between jogging and walking to the other side of the property. Though they didn't talk, Declan felt the mood shift. But he wouldn't feel settled until he'd seen Mom himself and made sure she was okay.

They rushed into the orientation center with Addey leading the way through the maze of rooms.

"I don't know what all the fuss is about!"

Declan heard her before he saw her. Crisp, clear and cranky. Relief rushed over him. His legs shook, his pulse raced, but a part of him curled up inside. His mother was here, she'd been found, but this woman wasn't really Mom. He walked into the room and immediately slowed his pace and pretended everything was normal.

"Mom, how was the movie?" He sat down beside her, resisting the urge wrap her in a bear hug and never let her go. She looked fine, fiery but fine.

"Well, I would have enjoyed it more if these people hadn't interrupted me and insisted I leave with them." Her arms were crossed over her chest. "I flatly refused. I told them my husband would be meeting me here."

Declan nodded, while inside a part of him shriveled up, like an autumn leaf. "These lovely people are just worried about you, that's all."

Mom sniffed, looking slightly mollified. "My husband isn't here yet. When is he coming?"

"Not for a while, Mom," Declan said, trying to find the words to make the situation right, but there never were those words, no matter how hard he tried. Mom looked around at the small crowd of people gathered outside the door to the theater room. She turned to him with surprise in her eyes. "Declan, what are you doing here? You should be working."

Was she back? "I am, Mom, I'm doing an assignment for the paper."

She patted his arm. "Oh, that's good then. Now Declan, your father will be here soon, so I don't need you worrying about me."

She wasn't back. His shoulders sagged. "I wasn't worrying Mom. I just thought I'd drop by to see you, that's all."

"You're such a good son." She brushed his cheek. Declan stood slowly. "Why don't we wait outside for Dad?"

She shook her head. "No, I told him I'd be here."

Declan held out his phone. "I'll message him and let him know where we are, how does that sound?" He kept his voice light and easy. Startling her always made it worse and it was better to play along until she came back to the present.

Declan was aware of Addey beside him and someone else dispersing the crowd from the doorway of the theater. He was thankful to whoever it was. Mom reluctantly stood leaning on his arm as she did. He led her outside, asking her questions about the movie. The crowd was gone by the time they emerged from the orientation center. The sunlight too bright. The sky too blue. Life wasn't fair. He shielded Mom from the sun and looked around for a quiet place to sit, away from the crowds.

The sudden change of her grip on his arm told him she'd come back to the present. He stroked her hand, needing a way out before she got really distressed. "Declan, where am I?" The fear in her voice sliced him to the core.

"We're at George and Martha's, Mom, having a visit," he replied, using his easy-going voice. "Let's find somewhere nice out of the sun."

One of the nurses piped up. "She needs to get back to the nursing home."

Mom heard it too. She grabbed his sleeves, tugging them. "No! I don't want to go anywhere, Declan. Please, don't make me."

Before he could say anything, Charlotte Hamilton walked up.

"Come this way, I know a nice spot."

He followed her and realized that Addey was no longer there. He didn't stop to think why, he just kept moving, wanting to get Mom to a safe spot. The upper garden, where he'd started his search, was where Charlotte was leading them. She led them to the bench under a large beech tree and produced a bottle of water from her purse. She gave it to Mom, who looked warily at her before accepting.

"Do you know her?" Mom asked, her hands trembling. He hated this disease that was stealing pieces of his mother.

"Yes, this is Mrs. Hamilton, Mom." Declan eyed Charlotte, who only nodded . "She's in charge around here. She's safe."

Charlotte held his gaze and an understanding passed between them—a truce. Declan could no longer claim that all the Hamiltons were terrible people. He had proof that at least two of them were kind souls.

"We met many years ago, Susannah." Charlotte sat beside Mom on the other side of Declan.

Declan glanced sharply at Charlotte. "Here at Mount Vernon?"

Charlotte ignored Declan and reached for Mom's hand, giving it a light squeeze. "I'll leave you to it. Stay here as long as you need."

As she walked past, she laid a hand on Declan's shoulder. It was so brief he almost missed it. Then Mom's grip on Declan's arm tightened. He placed his hand over hers and ran a thumb over her pale skin, only just starting to wrinkle. It struck him again at how young she was to have this disease.

"We'll sit here as long as you want, okay?" He started humming a Frank Sinatra song, hoping it would help settle her sooner.

Addey entered the garden. The worry lines around her eyes were clear, but the tentative smile she gave him buoyed his spirits. With his other hand, he flicked a thumbs up. Addey nodded and disappeared.

Time slowed down in the garden. Here under the shade of the trees, even in the cold, the world was muted. It was as if the trees could block out the sound around them, leaving them with nothing but serenity. The earthy scent of the gardens encased them in privacy, an extra layer of protection.

"I'm sorry, Declan, I forgot where I was for a while." Mom's hand shook but at least her eyes were clear. This was the mother he'd known his whole life—assured, patient, gentle, and dignified in everything she did. Even drinking from the water bottle was done with class and poise.

"I'm just glad you're alright." He squeezed her fingers gently.

"One day, I'll be gone."

"Don't, Mom." His voice thick.

She leaned her head on his arm. "I will, Declan. My mind will go first, and it will be what kills me."

"Please," Declan whispered. "Not today."

She closed her eyes and swallowed. "Alright, but you will have to face this at some point, my son."

"I'm facing it every day," he replied softly. "You think I like you living at Heritage Oaks? You think I don't worry about you every day?"

It was her turn to shush him. "It's for the best. I have so many good days still, but the bad ones, oh" —her voice quivered and he saw tears forming at the corners of her eyes— "they scare me. I know I can't be left alone anymore. It's right that I'm there, Declan," She lifted her head and raised her chin. "Now, I think it's time we left this hiding place and went back to our normal life."

"What's normal these days?" Declan muttered.

"You've never been one to look on the bright side. You might want to try it some time." Mom's impish smile touched the corners of her lips.

"I'm fine, Mom." He stood and helped her up. He tucked her arm into the crook of his elbow and led her out of the gardens and down the path towards the entrance.

"Addey and the others must be beside themselves," she said quietly.

"Everyone is just happy you're safe and well."

"Addey's lovely."

She sure is.

But Mom didn't drop the topic. "Is there something going on between you?"

"There might be," Declan said.

Mom nudged him. "When you want to tell me more, I'll be happy to listen."

He was aware of Mom watching him as they walked through the food court, and then felt the shift in her attention from him to their surroundings when she tightened his grip on her arm. People milled everywhere, lights blazed, and the din from the cafeteria and souvenir store was like a bucket of cold water after the peace and quiet of the garden.

He pulled Mom closer, trying to shield her from the noise and lights. He knew it would take her days, maybe even a few weeks, to recover from this morning. He wasn't sure how long it would take him to recover either. He needed to call Nicky and let her know what happened, but he'd do it away from Mom. She didn't need to know how badly he'd been scared by today's events.

The bus came into sight and he saw Addey waiting, watching for him.

He wondered if Mom missed the life she'd left behind in L.A. to come here and give them a new start? It was another question he filed away, waiting for a better time. There were so many things he needed to ask her before he ran out of time.

Addey's strained expression and serious eyes met his. He gave her shoulder a quick squeeze. He must look as disheveled as she did. Her shirt was wrinkly, askew, and half untucked. Her appearance wasn't surprising since she'd run the length of this place beside him.

Addey stepped up to Mom and drew her into a long hug.

Mom returned the hug, seeming to melt into Addey's embrace.

"Susannah, I'm very sorry this happened." Her voice caught on the words, low and uneven, as if she were carrying the weight of them in her chest.

Declan wanted to hug her too, to get lost in the hope that Addey naturally brought with her into every situation.

But the hope he'd carried around last week was slipping away.

Chapter Thirty

"You don't need to see Mom twice a day," Declan said at breakfast Saturday morning, two days after Mom went missing. Nicky was inhaling her cereal and Declan was worried she'd get indigestion.

She stopped for a moment to spare him an impatient grunt before continuing to empty her bowl. Then he watched as she power-walked around the apartment, moving from one thing to the next. Every movement hurried, her face taut. The furrow between her eyebrows would be permanent soon.

"I'll probably be back late for dinner," she said.

"If you wait a few minutes, we can head out to see Mom together?" he offered, trying to slowly eat the breakfast he didn't even want.

"No, it's fine." She tossed a smile over her shoulder. "I'll just drop in on Mom on my way to my hair appointment."

Declan set down his bowl, a dull thunk on the table. Nicky paused. "Mom's safe there, Nic."

"I know, I know…" She grabbed her coat and bag. "I just want her to know I'm there for her."

Her tone might have been light, even airy, but he didn't miss the implication of her words. He sat back, tired, and frustrated. "Are you saying I wasn't there for Mom?"

She stopped this time, only steps from the door. She turned, an awkward look on her face. "No, no, no…" She kept her eyes averted and was looking out the window. "It's just this last episode would have really scared her—"

"Scared me, too."

A flicker of annoyance flashed across her face, but she hid it quickly. "I know, so I just want to make sure she knows we'll always be there."

"But we can't always be there, not every day, and not alone. Let me come with you."

She twisted away, heading for the door. "It's easier if we do this separately, okay? I'll see you later." She opened the door.

"Just one more question, little sister?"

"What?" The impatience was clear, even though she didn't turn around.

"It's been two days. When are you going to stop blaming me for what happened?"

She turned to face him, her frown more pronounced and the workings of a glare coming. "I don't know. Maybe when you take responsibility for what happened."

With that, she turned and fled the apartment, the door slamming shut behind her. Declan flinched at the harsh sound, leaving him alone in the too-quiet house. He stood, taking the breakfast dishes and dumping them with a clatter in the sink.

He leaned against the counter, the anger building. He could feel it pressing against his chest. Why couldn't she understand that he fully accepted the blame? Just because he didn't visit Mom every day didn't mean he didn't feel responsible. He'd never forget the hour it took to find her, the wondering if she would be okay, where she was. Hoping she hadn't fallen and hurt herself. The what-ifs followed him everywhere.

He needed to get out.

The ice rink was busy, but the training area was empty at this early hour. Skating several quick laps warmed him up. He took the bucket of pucks and aimed one at the goal. It raced across the ice and hit the net. *Slam.* He repeated the action several times until the net had more pucks than the bucket. He still didn't feel any better. Guilt chased him. It was his fault he'd lost her. If he hadn't have gone to see Addey, Mom wouldn't have gotten lost. He'd put his feelings for Addey before his mom's safety.

That was unacceptable.

Maybe it was a good thing he and Addey were scaling things back for now. He needed to spend more time with Mom. Nicky needed him to step up. But that didn't stop him from missing Addey and wishing the Christmas party was over so they could go public with their relationship. The hiding was getting to them both.

He drove home and showered, his thoughts still churning. The only solution was to visit Mom.

Armed with cupcakes and bright bouquet of sunny flowers, Declan wandered down the hall to Mom's room. Soft voices met him at the doorway. He paused. Was Nicky still there? But they were talking too quietly for him to be sure.

He knocked softly before opening the door. To say he was surprised was an understatement.

Charlotte Hamilton sat across from Mom.

"Declan, this is Charlotte. She's been so lovely, coming to visit me." Mom sounded clear and lucid today. Her crocheting sat in her lap, the blanket growing steadily bigger with progress. Her face was open, and dare he say it—even content? An invisible weight lifted from him, at least for now. Would he and Nicky ever feel confident taking her on more outings?

"Charlotte and I were talking all about Mount Vernon and our favorite places." Mom's chatter warmed Declan's heart.

He put the cupcakes down and found the vase, completing his weekly ritual.

"We knew each other in L.A., did you know that? We shared a similar circle of friends once upon a time."

Declan jerked before stilling, but his pulse rate kicked hard into high gear. "What do you mean, Mom?" Was she lucid? Was she really referring to their life pre-Alexandria?

Charlotte stood. "I'd better be off now. I'll come again soon, Susannah."

"I would love that."

The two women hugged and Declan felt like his world had tipped upside down. Charlotte Hamilton was hugging his mother. Did Mom know who she was? Which Hamilton family she belonged to?

"Walk me out, Declan?" Charlotte's tone brooked no opposition.

"Of course." Declan held the door open. "I'll be back soon."

Mom waved and picked up her crocheting, smiling.

He fell into step beside Charlotte. She was short, barely reaching his shoulder. They walked in silence. When they reached the steps outside, the older woman stopped. Three steps separated them, but because she stayed on the top stair, they were eye level. No doubt, something she planned. He hid a smile, shoving his hands in his jacket pockets.

"Thanks for visiting Mom. I can tell it made her day." He hated saying it, but the truth was right there when he'd walked into the room. Mom looked relaxed, calm, and happy. And as much as he didn't like who had been the cause, he would not begrudge his mom that precious time.

"It was the least I could do," she said stiffly, her shoulders rigid, back ramrod straight.

She opened her mouth to continue.

"Hang on, I'm not finished yet."

She raised an eyebrow and cocked her head to one side.

"Thank you for taking care of Mom on Thursday."

Her face relaxed. "I didn't do anything."

"Yes, you did. You got the crowds away and found Mom a quiet place to recoup—that's big."

"I like Susannah." Her smile was soft. "I've always liked your mother."

Declan looked her directly in the eyes. "So, you did know her back in L.A.?"

Her pause was answer enough.

But he still needed to hear the words. "Did you?"

"Yes, I knew her. And your father."

Declan closed his eyes. He stepped back, unwilling to see the judgment in her eyes. What would she say to Addey now? She would tell her to walk away from him because his family was a disgrace. That's what they'd all done. Anyone who'd dared to remain their friends hadn't done so for long, as they too were dragged into the social pariah that was the Sheridan family.

Charlotte stepped off the step and stood beside him, looking up at him with eyes that reminded him of Addey's, not for the color, but the determination in them.

"Your mother can't hide who she is, because it is who she is. I met her a long time ago, at an event in Los Angeles. I don't even remember what it was for anymore." The words rasped out and she swallowed. "My husband had made a few financial missteps. Nothing illegal, you understand. An investment project had failed and our friends who joined the investment lost millions."

Declan listened with interest.

Charlotte continued. "Things were difficult at home. I'd gone to L.A. for a fundraiser and to get away from things here for a week or so, but bad news travels fast—as you well know." She shot him a look. "Certain people in my social group weren't letting me forget my husband's blunder. I didn't want to be here or there. No matter where I was, I was snubbed by people who I had called friends." Her gaze searched his face. "I remember your mother like it was yesterday. Kindness for kindness's sake is a rare quality in our world."

Declan's cheek muscle twitched at her use of the word *our*. That wasn't his world anymore and one he never wanted to go back to.

"Susannah took me around with her and let everyone know that she didn't care what they thought." She laid her hand on his arm. "When everything went bad for all of you, I tried getting in contact with her, but she never replied. I didn't hold it against her, but I did wonder where she'd gotten to. I always hoped she was okay."

Declan was stunned by her words. He took another step back. He looked at her and her light blue eyes bore into his, her mouth a sad line across her wrinkled face. "You never came across her during any of the visits she made to Mount Vernon over the years?"

"No."

Declan didn't know what to say, but one question kept buzzing around his mind. "So, in light of everything, will you keep my family's secret?"

"I will."

He shifted. "Just like that?"

"I don't like to interfere in people's lives."

"Addey mentioned that."

"I'm sure she did."

"Then, I'll let you get on with your life."

Declan moved to go back inside, but Charlotte stopped him. "Don't let the Community Center come between you and Addey."

"That's not going to be an issue. And I thought you didn't meddle?" His smile quirked halfway.

"I don't."

Chapter Thirty-One

"Seems you made quite an impression on Charlotte Hamilton," Mom said when Declan re-entered her room. A cupcake sat on a plate, cut into quarters.

Declan took a seat across from her. "I make impressions on people all the time." He smirked as he used the fork to snare a piece of cupcake. The tangy lemon flavor exploded in his mouth. Declan coughed and forced himself to swallow it down. He reached for the water jug and poured himself a glass. He guzzled the water and poured himself another.

Mom was grinning. "Did you forget that you hate lemon-flavored anything?"

"They weren't meant for me," he said after he'd drained the second glass. "I bought them for you."

Mom took a dainty bite of her piece, closed her eyes, and sighed. "Thank you for bringing them."

Declan pushed the last two pieces over to her.

"Did you have a nice chat with Charlotte?"

"It was nice enough."

"You know you would catch more flies with honey than vinegar."

"Who said I'm looking to catch anything?" He took another drink, even swished the water around in his mouth, but the lemon taste lingered.

"I would have thought that Addey might be worth catching," she said it so mildly he almost missed it.

He put the glass down. "My private life is just that, Mom," he said it gently, since he didn't want to offend her, but he didn't want to talk about Addey either. "Speaking of, Mrs. Hamilton informed me she knows who we are."

"Yes, she does and don't look like that, Declan."

"She's not as bad as she makes herself out to be," he conceded.

Mom pinned him with a fierce look. "Yes, and neither are you. You might try to remember that."

He chuckled.

"One day, someone is going to tear down your grumpy exterior and force you to publicly admit that you have a heart of gold buried deep down."

"I'm not publicly admitting to anything." He grinned at her, not wanting this moment to descend into anything deep and dark.

"Are you seeing Addey any time soon?" Mom popped the question in between bites and Declan groaned.

"Why is it important?"

"The people in your life are important to me." Mom took a drink of her water. "Addey is lovely, and I can see she's become important to you."

He thought the same thing, but he didn't want to say it out loud. "She comes from money."

"Being wealthy isn't a crime, you know." Mom speared him with a firm look, reminding him of when he was younger. He wasn't so scared of it anymore, but it still had the power to keep him in check.

"No, it's not, but the rich use their wealth to hurt others." *Even sue their daughter.*

She reached over and laid her hand on his arm. Her grip was strong. "One day, you're going to have to let go of this chip on your shoulder. You'll be walking lopsided from the weight of it—"

"Someone needs to hold them accountable for their actions."

"While you do that, don't break your jaw from the clenching it so hard," Mom continued.

Declan shifted in his chair.

"You've been skating very close to the line between reporting the facts and letting your prejudices get in the way."

He ground his teeth. She was starting to sound like Julie.

"Don't worry, Mom, I'm paying my penance for my sins." He couldn't keep the sarcasm from his voice.

Mom sat back, her nostrils flaring.

He'd gone too far. "Sorry, that was out of line."

"You can't even see it, can you? How angry you are? Declan, it was fifteen years ago. You need to let it go."

"Have you?" he countered, not able to face the questions she was aiming at him.

She stared at him. "When we moved here with our new last name, I was angry at how my life had turned out. At how your father had lied to me, to you, to Nicky, and to his clients. I was angry that I was left to deal with the fallout for his crimes." She'd half-risen in her chair, hands gripping the armrests.

"That's quite a list."

Mom sat back down. "Yes, it is. But I realized years ago that I could either stay angry forever or I could forgive him and make a life for us. I chose the latter. There will be a time when you have to make that same choice."

They sat in silence. Memories flooded. Their long trek across the country in the old car Mom bought with the only money she'd kept for herself after repaying Dad's victims. Moving into the apartment that was tiny compared to what they'd lived in back in L.A. Baked beans on toast for dinner, cheap hot dogs or mac and cheese the other nights. Mom working all day as a medical receptionist to pay the bills and the mortgage on the apartment. She'd come home tired, but with a ready smile for her sullen son and overly perky daughter. She'd managed to keep them from falling off the edge that felt so near for so many years.

Other questions bubbled in his mind. Could he ever ask her about Eli?

"When the Community Center closes, what will happen to Eli?" He used the topic to hopefully ease in.

She rested back into the chair. "He's talked about spending more time with his sister and finding work closer to her family."

"You guys have always talked a lot," Declan said gingerly.

She gave him a sideways glance. "We've always been good friends. He's been very good to you."

Declan looked at his hands. "I know, Mom, he's like a dad to me."

"As much as you'd let anyone be to you," she said dryly.

He hesitated before asking the question. "Is that all you two have ever been? Just friends?"

She looked away from him, focusing on something outside the sliding doors. She was quiet for so long he thought she might not answer. He heard her take in a shaky breath, before she turned to face him.

His heart lurched at the pain he saw in her eyes.

"I'm surprised you waited so long to ask the question." She touched her chest, her eyes bright with unshed tears. "Eli would have married me in a heart beat, but no matter what your father has done, I married Edward Sheridan for better or for worse."

"But you're divorced..."

She nodded, tears pooling in the corners of her eyes. "Yes, but I married for life, and I couldn't marry again. I didn't want to bring any more instability to you and Nicky."

Declan couldn't find any words. "But Eli loves you. He was there for everything and still is."

"I know." This time the tears started to fall freely. Declan stood up, rounded the table, and wrapped her in a hug.

"You know I can't cope when you cry." He rubbed her back. She sniffled before pulling back and wiping her tears.

"Eli understood and never pushed the topic. He's remained my best and most faithful friend these fifteen years. It's enough."

Declan had trouble believing this. How could two people who loved each other just walk away from each other? How could they be content to stay friends when so much beckoned between them?

"But, Mom—"

"Please, leave it now." Her face clouded over before it went clear. She'd tucked the emotions away where only she could access them. "Thank you for visiting. It's always lovely to see you."

He understood. He took the empty plate and dropped it off at the kitchen. By the time he came back, Mom was sitting back in the recliner, eyes closed. Today had been a good day and he breathed out the rising emotions. Considering Thursday's events, she could have still been in a state. Maybe Nicky was onto something. He'd come back tomorrow and hope Nicky would forgive him.

Until then he'd treasure every day they had. He swallowed the lump forming in his throat, but it only made the pain in his chest hurt more. He walked over and kissed her forehead gently. "I'll be back tomorrow."

She opened her eyes and smiled, placing a hand on his cheek. "You're a good man."

Chapter Thirty-Two

Declan followed the twinkling pathway, feeling like he was going down a rabbit hole. The long awaited Christmas party was finally here. All he has to do was survive tonight. Survive with a smile on his face, pretend he didn't know Addey, and make Julie happy with his ability to be professional. He shoved his hands deep inside his coat pockets. All of that was easier said than done, but no one had ever said Declan wasn't committed to something when it mattered.

And tonight mattered—professionally and personally.

Ushers dressed in tuxedos stood at various intervals, smiling and indicating to continue along the path. He smiled at them and hoped they were being paid well to stand outside in the cold. Snow was forecast for tomorrow. Tonight, the stars winked down at him, but they didn't chase the cold away. He kept walking, trying to dispel the trepidation brewing inside him.

The events Julie had lumped him with all year had featured heavily on the wealthier set from Alexandria and its surrounds. He'd coped fine, though bored and frustrated, able to escape as more of an observer. Tonight, there was no observing. He was expected to mingle, to talk, and be present for everything. He frowned, knowing he would be surrounded by people like his father. Deep down, he knew they all weren't like Edward Sheridan. But he still didn't like being here.

Charlotte Hamilton seemed to have some moral compass, but time would tell there.

And Addey. Of course, Addey. The one bright light in the darkness that was tonight. Addey was nothing like her parents. She was light and joy. Addey saw something in him and once he'd let her in, there was no going back. Addey had captured his heart and held it.

And he didn't want it back.

Addey would be run off her feet tonight and they wouldn't get a chance to talk, which was a good thing. Not seeing her for the last week had been torture. Their texts and phone calls weren't enough. He longed to tuck her against him, kiss her, and laugh with her.

Gentle strains of classical music beckoned him up the path. It was like a scent in the air, pulling everyone closer. He nodded and smiled at the other guests he passed. Everyone was decked out in black tie and fancy dresses hidden by coats. He passed the upper garden where he'd sat with Mom the previous week. Images of him and Addey tearing from one end of the grounds to the other desperately looking for her flickered across his mind.

Tonight, he would not think about Mom. Instead, he would play nice, hopefully see Addey, maybe steal a kiss if he was exceptionally lucky, and go home. He could almost taste the liberty he would have once he finished the review. Julie would give him back his freedom to shine the light on the unheard voices in the community. It was a good feeling.

And he and Addey could go public. That was the scary part, but he would tackle it head on. Addey wouldn't be in this alone.

Rounding the bend from Mansion Circle, the world dropped away and he stopped to simply admire what was before him. A twinkling pathway led down to the lawn where two large marquees were set up on the east lawn overlooking the Potomac River. Tiny lights were strung along the lines of the marquee, making them look like the stars had come down from the sky and rested on them. His eyes traveled down to the river. Two moored river boats were elegantly decked out in twinkle lights so guests could enjoy their view of the river. It was a perfect fit to a perfect picture.

He treaded the grassy path down to the marquees. He could see guests mingling inside as large heaters fought to keep the cold away. He approached the entrance where another usher took his invitation. Stepping inside, the cold disappeared and the din of guests chattering and laughing drowned out the outside noise. The music flowed from the string quartet, washing over the crowd like a gentle lullaby. More lights, this time in soft hues of pink, silver, and gold hung like chandeliers around the tent. At the far end, a small stage had been erected with a lectern, microphone, and a screen. Tables were covered with heavy white linen. Gold rimmed plates, champagne flutes, and wine glasses were laid out to precision.

Pride burst in his chest. Addey had truly outdone herself.

A waiter approached him with a tray of drinks. Declan selected a white wine and took a sip.

Declan was searching the seating chart for his name when he was tapped on the shoulder.

"Declan, you scrub up very well," Julie said.

"I could say the same thing about you, Julie." He nodded to his boss. "Not checking up on me, are you?"

"You'd think so," she replied dryly, a smile teasing her lips, "but I'm a stand in for a friend who couldn't make it."

"Ah, I see. So, fraternizing with the wealthy and powerful tonight, then?"

Her eyes narrowed slightly.

"Relax, Julie," he chuckled, enjoying watching her blood pressure rise. "I'm being good. I've even made some friends."

"Who?" She sounded suspicious as she took a sip of her champagne.

He pointed to Charlotte Hamilton who was holding court not too far away. "None other than Mrs. Charlotte Hamilton herself. I did interview her, if you remember."

"Stop being so cheeky. She's not threatening to kick you off the grounds, is she?"

"Not that I know of, but you never know. The night is still young," Declan teased.

"Whatever has happened to you these last few weeks, I like it. You're the reporter I hired three years ago."

"I've decided it's time to let things go that I can't control." He offered Julie his arm. She took it but kept glancing at him like he was an alien.

He glanced at Charlotte and waved when she caught his eye. Charlotte excused herself and weaved her way through the crowd toward them. For a moment, doubts about Charlotte assailed him. Would she expose his family to this group of vultures? But then he recalled her help at Mount Vernon when Mom had been found. Her steady, steel voice when she said she would keep their secret.

"Declan, so glad you could make it." She offered her hand. He took it and kissed it. She nodded approvingly.

Declan's shoulders relaxed. "Mrs. Hamilton, I'd like you to meet Julie Carter, my editor."

The women shook hands.

"You must have your hands full keeping this man in line." Charlotte sipped her champagne, eyes twinkling.

"It's not easy some days." Julie smiled back. "This is so wonderful. The decorations and everything." She wisely changed the topic.

Charlotte glanced around at the room. "Yes, I'm very proud that the estate can host the party tonight."

Charlotte snagged Declan's arm as she said, "It was a pleasure to meet you, Julie. Now, if you'll excuse me, I need to borrow Declan. There is someone I'd like him to meet." What was Charlotte up to?

"See you later," Julie replied, just as someone walking past grabbed her attention.

"This will be an interesting night, I think." Charlotte turned her head to the right a little and nodded to a small cluster of men—one of whom was the CEO of a pharmaceuticals company, another was the head of a hedge fund—standing in a far corner, deep in discussion. Holding court in the circle was Jonathan Hamilton. "My son has promised to be a gentleman tonight—to everyone. He doesn't know you're here." She cast him a sideways glance.

Declan got the message loud and clear. Don't make a scene.

He nodded.

"Good," she said. "Now, I know someone you might like to see."

Charlotte held his arm with a firm grip as she led them to the back of the marquee to a metal door attached to an annex. It led to the second smaller marquee. Clattering dishes and loud voices sounded from the other tent.

"She'll be glad to see a friendly face." She reached for his wine glass. "I'll look after that for you."

"Is this your idea of not interfering?" Declan cocked one eyebrow.

"I'm just showing the local reporter a behind-the-scenes glimpse of the party." Her innocent tone made him laugh.

He leaned closer. "Or you want me out of the way for a bit longer." He indicated his head in the direction of her son.

Charlotte raised his glass. "I want Adelaide happy."

"Then we both want the same thing."

"And no one is interfering."

"Of course not."

Declan chuckled as Charlotte disappeared into the crowd. He didn't even mind one bit that Charlotte was doing triple duty tonight. Working the room to smooth the edges of the guests was clearly a skill she had. Then keeping him away from Jonathan Hamilton for as long as possible was an admirable goal and he couldn't fault her for it. And bringing him to Addey was even better.

Yep, Declan liked Charlotte Hamilton. And he couldn't even make himself take the thought back.

Still smiling, he pushed the door and entered into the highly-controlled fray of the kitchen. Hot, humid air rushed over him. It felt like a stinking hot summer day compared to the other marquee where the temperature was regulated. Declan stepped through the annex and deeper into the kitchen, where the clattering of dishes and voices from the chefs grew louder. Waiters hovered over trays of appetizers, waiting to take them to the guests. Declan weaved his way through the maze of people, searching for Addey. The scent of garlic and other spices wrapped around him, injecting deep into his pores, making his stomach rumble and his tongue dance with anticipation.

Then he saw her.

Addey was standing by a table in the far corner, her head dipped close to a woman he guessed was her assistant. They were consulting a tablet. Addey was gesturing with great animation and pointing to something on the screen. He moved closer, simply enjoying watching her. The other woman looked up at his approach and startled a bit before whispering to Addey.

Addey turned, her gaze colliding with his.

The world stopped. His breath caught.

Addey put the tablet down and walked over to him, her eyes never leaving his. Declan couldn't keep his eyes off her. The black one-shouldered cocktail dress ended just above her knees, and her gorgeous red hair was styled in loose curls that fell down her back. Declan couldn't have moved if he'd tried.

Addey stood close enough for them to talk, but not close enough for him to easily reach her. "You're here."

"You're stunning."

A blush crept up her cheeks. Declan wanted to tug her into his arms and kiss her, but he didn't dare. Not tonight.

"Stressed out?" he offered.

Addey exhaled and her shoulders slumped. "You have no idea."

"Your grandmother took the liberty of walking me here. She seemed to think you needed to see a friendly face."

"I'm surprised. Grandmother doesn't usually meddle." Addey glanced around the room, her fingers playing with the edge of her curls.

"Maybe she's finally found the right reason to meddle." Declan resisted the urge to lean closer.

"Come with me." Addey tugged his arm and led him to the back of the kitchen, through another door. She led him outside, into the cold and away from the noise. He followed her to the back of several food vans. He stopped to look at them. They looked like buildings from the time of George and Martha themselves.

"Wow, that's amazing, they're like smaller versions of the buildings here. They blend in."

"That's the point. Come on."

He didn't resist.

Addey led him to a spot behind the trees and vans.

Then she kissed him.

Declan was surprised, but not for long. He wrapped his arms around her waist and kissed her right back, letting his fingers run down her back, enjoying the way he made her shiver. Her hands roamed his face, as if she was taking him in, her lips exploring his with a passion she hadn't shown since the night he'd told her about his family.

Easing away, Addey stroked his cheek, her breathing fast, matching his.

"I thought we were going to keep things professional tonight," he murmured against her lips. "Not that I'm complaining or anything."

Addey gave a soft laugh. "I was trying to, but then you walked in..."

Declan kissed her again, letting himself enjoy the feel of her in his arms, the taste of her on his lips.

When they came up for air, the tremble on her lips stilled him.

"What's going on?" He swept loose curls away from her face.

Addey rested her head on his chest, the rise and fall of her chest deep. "Addey? What's wrong?"

She closed her fist around his jacket lapel. "Nothing and...everything."

He ran his hands down her arms. "You're going to have to help me out here."

Addey looked up at him, her mouth twisted into a frown. "I can't help but think that it can't be this easy. Tonight, I mean. I have this sense of dread that won't leave me alone. I thought I'd be fine, but seeing them out there, then seeing you...what if it all comes crashing down?" The last word came out in a strangled cry.

Declan stroked her shoulders. "If it helps, I'm on my best behavior tonight. I have no plans to make this night harder for you. If we're lucky, your dad won't even know I'm here."

Addey gave a hoarse laugh. "That's not possible."

"I know, but we can be positive."

Addey's laugh this time was clear and genuine. "What happened to my cynical journalist?"

Declan leaned in, whispered in her ear. "He met you."

Addey closed her eyes and buried her head in his chest again. Goose bumps dotted her arms. Was she cold or scared? Or both? She looked up, her gaze holding his. "Promise me that no matter what happens tonight, we'll be okay?" The edge in her voice surprised him, like she really was expecting the night to fall apart.

"Addey, it's going to be okay. You've put something together tonight that's amazing. You should be proud of yourself." Declan ran his hands up and down her arms, trying to warm her up and calm her down.

"Promise me, Declan," she whispered.

"I promise, Addey."

Addey dropped a kiss on lips, letting it linger. Like it was going to be their last.

"I need to get back." She stepped away. "I'll go first and you follow me in a few minutes."

Declan watched Addey dash away. Was she right? Would tonight be as bad as she feared? He didn't want to believe her, but as he made his way back to the party, doubts crept in and settled in the far recesses of his mind.

Chapter Thirty-Three

"What are you doing in here?" Dad's irritated voice wasn't hard to miss, even in all the noise of the kitchen.

Addey counted to twenty while she consulted her screen—fifteen minutes until the main meal was served. She glanced at Holly, who was busy organizing the wait staff.

An usher came up, looking green. "Miss Bennet, someone is stuck in one of the portable toilets."

Addey put down her run sheet. She could feel Dad's impatience like a dentist drill boring into her. "Glen, you'll find maintenance staff out by the vans. Tell him what's happening and I'll be out in just a moment."

Addey needed a Advil and this night to end.

"Mark from the Gibson/Baker group is here." Dad pounced the second Glen was out of ear shot. "Why haven't you been to see him? You are supposed to be out there, not in here."

"Dad," Addey breathed through clenched teeth. "I am not a hostess. I am an event planner. This is where I should be."

Dad's rigid jaw added to Addey's headache. Had he seen Declan yet? He must not have, otherwise he would have led with that. That was a blessing, at least.

"Excuse me while I check on the person stuck in the toilet." Addey snagged her coat from the back of her chair and escaped outside.

Squaring her shoulders, she found Glen, still looking terrified, and the maintenance guy, who was calmly talking to the stranded woman.

"I've seen this a few times. Sometimes the door just catches shut and it can be a real bear to undo it, but don't worry, I've almost got it undone."

"Ma'am," Addey addressed the door. "I'm Addey Bennet, I'm the manager here tonight. Once the door is unlatched, I'll tell these gentlemen to leave, and I'll help you out."

"Thank you." The relief was fierce even through the door. "I didn't bring my jacket, I'm so cold."

"I got it," the man grunted.

Addey turned to Glen. "Please make sure when she arrives back at the tent that an extra glass of wine and a plate of our best dessert is ready for her."

Glen nodded and took off.

"Alright ma'am, I've got my coat ready."

"Just tug the door off and I'll put it back on once you're gone." The maintenance man stepped away.

"Thank you."

Addey gently knocked twice. "I'm going to pull the door open. Are you decent?"

"Yes." The woman's strained voice came through the door.

Addey tugged the door off, placed it against the other doors, and helped the woman out. She was about Addey's age and dressed in a sky-blue halter neck dress.

"Here." Addey helped her into her coat. "I'm very sorry this happened. Let me walk you back to the tent."

"That was so embarrassing." The woman cheeks were red as she tugged the jacket tighter. "Has this type of thing really happened before?"

Addey chuckled. "Yes. I know of one event where two of the toilets backed up."

The woman's eyes widened.

Addey chuckled. "It comes with the territory with this job." They arrived at the entrance. "Glen is going to take care of you now."

"What about your coat?" She shrugged it off.

Addey waved away the comment. "You give it to Glen once you're settled, okay?"

Addey marched back to the kitchen and found Dad standing right where she'd left him. Pausing, she unclenched her fists and let out a huff. This was one very long night.

"I take it you got the situation sorted?" Dad said stiffly.

Addey went back to her run sheet. "Yes, all is right with the world."

Dad stepped closer so that only Addey could hear him. "I can tell you that all is not right out there."

Addey wanted to step away but there was nowhere to move. "I believe it's going perfectly fine." And it was, other than the toilet door issue. The food service was running on time, the music was flowing, and guests were enjoying themselves. All that was left was dessert to be served, speeches to be tolerated, and dancing to close out the night.

Dad didn't budge. Addey looked up from her screen and met Dad's steely glare with a quiet sigh. "What's bothering you, Dad? So far, I've put on the elegant event you guys wanted and everybody is happy. I'm not seeing a problem."

"You might be right on that score, but there is still a big problem with tonight. That journalist, Declan Collins, is sitting out there like he owns the place." Dad's lips flattened.

Every word was a knife slicing through her.

Addey stilled and fought for breath. It was okay. So far, Dad had only seen Declan. This was nothing to panic about. Her fingers grew sweaty and her headache ramped up. She forced herself to meet his gaze and saw understanding dawn in his eyes.

"You knew he would be here and you didn't tell us?" Dad's steely gaze bored into Addey.

"Yes." Her pulse kicked up. "I didn't think it was something to bother you about. He's been sent here by the newspaper to do a write-up of this event." She spoke each word evenly, never taking her eyes off her father.

But inside, her gut was turning circles, as was her heart. This was it. She and Declan were done. Dad couldn't even be in the same room as Declan with two hundred people between them. He would never be okay with Addey dating Declan.

Never.

Her knees shook, but she kept it together.

"I knew there was a reason you pushed so hard to take the building announcement out tonight. You knew he'd be here." His accusation stung. "Why would you keep something like this from us?"

"I did it for both of us," she said. "We both need tonight to be a hit." Addey found her voice, and a little bit of courage. "If you go up there and announce this building with Dec in the room, it's going to give him ammo for a bad write-up. Do you want that? Do you want my business to suffer along with yours?" Her knees were shaking but Addey was proud of herself for not cowing to him.

"Dec?" he arched his eyebrow.

Addey gasped. *Oops.* Mom wasn't the only sharp one.

But it was too late. His nickname slipped out. How could she have been so careless?

He put his one hand on his waist, and she saw the answers clicking in his eyes. "He's the man you've been dating, isn't he? The one you won't tell us about?"

Each word was like a bullet and Addey absorbed the hits. She couldn't look at him, lest he see the truth in her eyes. She almost laughed with the absurdity of her thoughts.

"Well, I know how to act." Dad sent one final glare before sweeping out of the room, leaving people staring in his wake.

Addey sunk into the chair and tried to get her breathing under control. She'd failed Dad tonight. No matter what else happened, she'd lost his respect. The thawing of their relationship these past few weeks was undone—all because she fell in love with a man he couldn't stand.

Wait. *Love?* The word reverberated through Addey's mind. Did she love Declan? She loved his caring heart, his passion to give a voice to the voiceless, the way he loved his mother. She'd tried not to love him but, really, she hadn't stood a chance.

Her parents would reject her again. How could there be a future for her and Declan now?

Addey's chest tightened as her fingers grew stiff.

"What's going on?" Holly ran up.

Addey forced herself to breathe, but every time she calmed, another wave of panic hit.

Holly patted her back. "Breathe in and out. It's okay, Addey."

Addey looked at Holly and forced the words out. "I've been secretly dating Declan Collins and my dad just found out."

Holly patted Addey faster. "We can fix this."

Addey shook her head. "No. No, I don't think we can."

***

Declan checked his watch. Jonathan Hamilton had been in the kitchen for too long. Was the man picking a fight with Addey? Declan wanted this night to go perfectly for her, which is why he'd been politely engaging and interested in the people at his table. He'd made sure to keep a low profile, too. It was his gift to Addey, and himself. Not to mention Julie was seated at his table and he didn't want to blow this night for her either.

Jonathan emerged from the kitchen and joined his wife at their table by the front of the stage. He leaned over and said something to man beside him. The man nodded, stood and left. Jonathan's jovial smile said nothing was wrong, but Declan sensed otherwise. For a second their eyes met and Declan nodded in acknowledgment. Jonathan turned away. Declan let the snub slide, he expected nothing less from him. The man returned, sat next to Jonathan and spoke in his ear. Jonathan shook his head vigorously. The man nodded again and sat back, frowning.

Something was up.

His worry for Addey increased.

"You're different tonight," Julie commented beside him.

"So are you." Declan pointed to her table name which said *Arthur Bridges*.

Julie turned the card face down. "They didn't even get a chance to change the names," she laughed.

"I might just call you Arthur all night now."

"Only if you don't want your job," she quipped back.

They both laughed. It felt good to relax. But it didn't last long. The sense of doom snaked around his chest. He couldn't name it, but it was the same feeling he'd experienced before Dad had been arrested. Declan remembered waking up and just thinking something was off, but he'd swept it aside and, later that day, their world fell apart. He'd learned since then to pay attention to his gut.

"You look like you belong here," Julie said as their dinner arrived.

Declan raised his eyebrows.

Julie leaned over so her voice wouldn't carry to the others. "Seriously, not only do you look the part, but I've listened to you tonight. You talk to these people like you know their world."

Declan shrugged. "Maybe I'm a good actor." Declan had spent ten minutes with the man across from him, discussing the pros and cons of the current economic environment.

"Not that good," she said, before tucking into her lobster. "I had no idea you knew so much about the economy."

Declan glanced at Julie. "It's my job to be able to talk with anyone I come to meet."

Julie pointed her fork at him. "Yes, but you do it with this air of confidence—"

Declan took a sip of his sparkling water. "Can we drop it, please?" He shifted in his seat, his own plate of braised beef no longer holding any appeal. Julie had seen what others hadn't, but tonight, amongst these people, would others guess at his upbringing? Would others know who he was?

Holly's arrival on stage pulled him from his thoughts.

"Ladies and gentlemen, may I please have your attention?" Holly had been the main face of the party all evening. "First of all, we want to extend a wonderful thank you to the Mount Vernon Ladies' Association for allowing our event to be hosted in such a spectacular setting. I'm sure George and Martha would be proud." Applause went through the room. When it died down, Holly continued. "We also wish to extend a thank you to our official hosts for the evening—Jonathan and Vivien Hamilton." The applause kicked in again. Declan clapped his hands. But it was all for Addey.

The Hamiltons waved and smiled from their table. Joathan held Declan's gaze for a long second, before he broke away and continued smiling to the crowd. An unexpected wave of disquiet washed over him. In two weeks, demolition would start on the Community Center. No, he needed to chill. He was over this...he'd made peace with the outcome. He ground his teeth and thought of Addey.

"Stop looking like you want to murder them," Julie hissed into his ear. He sent her a scowl before finding his neutral face, and concentrated on what Holly was saying.

"They've graciously put this lovely event on to celebrate the festive season. We'll be hearing more from them later in the evening." She smiled at Jonathan and Vivien. "Our fearless organizer is swamped at the moment, but I'm sure I can wrangle her on stage later tonight so we can give her the proper attention due for such a spectacular night."

Declan ate his food and made small talk with the man on his other side.

The night was beautiful, but inside, a storm was brewing.

Chapter Thirty-Four

essert was finished, and there'd still been no sign of Addey. Declan shifted, his unease growing by the minute. He needed to see her.

Holly took the stage again. "Ladies and gentlemen, may I please have your attention?" The din of conversation died down as people shifted in their chairs. "I'd like to call our hosts, Jonathan and Vivien Hamilton, to the stage." Holly stepped back and began to clap. Applause resounded through the marquee.

Vivien was smooth looking. From her red hair, a shade lighter than Addey's, to her black sleek ball gown, to the way she stood. Even her smile was smooth, practiced. She looked like an unfamiliar version of Addey, except Addey's genuine nature shone like a beacon. Vivien posed beside Jonathan, clearly enjoying her role in this world. Jonathan was another matter entirely. They'd never personally crossed paths, as the man would never take an interview with him, but the impression Declan got was that Jonathan was a man of strong opinions, clever and bulldog tough. It wasn't just his clothes, but the way he carried himself. A confident stride, an easy manner, articulate clear voice, and a set of sharp eyes.

"Friends, friends!" he boomed. "Thank you for coming tonight." He clasped Vivien's hand. "We're glad you can all be here to ring in the holiday season." He paused and glanced at Declan.

Declan sat forward, his eyes riveted on the stage.

The room erupted into more applause.

"Now," he spoke again, waiting for the noise to settle. "We're here to celebrate more than the festive season tonight."

Declan sat up straighter, his journalist antennae on high alert. Beside him, Julie looked as focused.

The screen behind them came alive.

An image of the Community Center filled the screen, large enough that every person in the room could clearly see it.

Declan couldn't move. He couldn't look away. His chest and throat tightened but he stayed perfectly still.

"Oh no," Julie murmured.

"As many of you know, I have spent the last two years getting my company's new apartment building ready for development."

Everything around him stilled and slowed. Declan's pulse pumped quickly as he sat there. His thoughts ran around his mind, chasing themselves. Why was there a picture of the Community Center? This was meant to be a Christmas party that raised money for people in need—an idea that repulsed him considering that Jonathan was shutting down the Community Center.

Where was Addey? What was going on?

"As we all know," he paused for dramatic affect.

Declan wanted to be sick.

"The community wasn't immediately happy that a new apartment building would replace a beloved existing structure. But after almost two years of hard work and working with the community, I might add." He glanced at Declan again. "We are pleased to announce that the construction of the Garden Grove Apartment Building will commence in the new year. The Hamilton Group is looking forward to creating more opportunities for the people of this great city."

Images sliced across the screen of the mock-ups of the apartments.

The applause in the room had dimmed to nothing but a faint buzz. Declan couldn't move for the rage building inside. Jonathan looked across the room at Declan, his smile big, his face hard. It was a moment of pure hate.

Julie's hand on his arm startled him. He glared at her and shook her hand off.

She shook her head at him and drew a line across her mouth.

"Now, we have one last person to thank, before we end this evening's festivities. As you know Holly has been our most gracious host tonight. However, none of this grandeur before you tonight would have been possible without one other person." He smiled wide and cast another glance at Declan before he continued, "Put your hands together for the event coordinator, the woman who made this whole night possible, our daughter, Adelaide Hamilton."

Declan tried to avert his eyes, but he couldn't. Surely Addey would put things right. But when he saw her pale face as she emerged from the kitchen, his hopes died as she walked—to them. It was like leaving L.A. all over again and watching the life his family had built fall with every mile Mom put on the car.

Addey reached the microphone, held it, and met his gaze. The pain in her eyes reached him from across the room and across the miles of his life. Declan looked away. "Thank you all for coming tonight." Her unsteady voice pulled at his heart, but Declan hardened it. Why had she kept this from him? Did she want to watch him make a fool of himself over her? Was she so desperate for her parents' love that she'd resort to something so low? "It's been a pleasure to put this event on tonight. As with most events, there's always something that's unplanned."

She gave her father a long stare.

"But, seeing you all here brings me such joy." The room broke into clapping again. "One last thing." She spoke louder, her clear words ringing across the room. "Being the daughter of such accomplished parents has always been an exciting way to live."

People chuckled in the audience.

"However, I was blessed to spend many years with my maternal grandmother, Deborah Bennet, who taught me grace under pressure and that love will always win the day. Even when the darkness over-whelms." Her voice wobbled as her gaze sought Declan's again.

He stared back.

She looked away, signaling a waiter, who came over with a tray of drinks, and selected one. "Please raise your glasses to the ones we've lost these past years, when Christmas can be very hard without them...and cheers to happier memories to come."

Everyone raised their glasses, but the mood was somber. People glanced around at each other as they drank. Addey left the stage, a fast yet measured gait.

"Well, on that note." Jonathan was back at the microphone, panic tinging his voice. "Let's call this evening to an end, shall we? Merry Christmas, everyone!" He gestured for the musicians to play as he took Vivien's hand, left the stage and disappeared through the kitchen doors.

Declan stood. He wouldn't make a scene, but that didn't mean he had to stay a minute longer.

He moved away, weaving through the tables, ignoring Julie's hissed pleas to come back and behave. He needed air. How could Addey have kept this from him? He was such a fool to fall in love with a woman whose family thought nothing of others. They were just like his father. He made it to the door and glanced over his shoulder, his gaze colliding with Charlotte's. The profound sadness etched across her face riveted him to the spot. She gave him a sad smile. Declan turned away.

He'd had enough of these people.

***

Addey had to find Declan.

Oh, he was angry. She could still see his livid expression. But what stayed with her the most was the look of hurt that followed the anger. Her heart ached knowing that she'd put it there via her father's betrayal. Addey choked on a sob. How could Dad have done this to her? Did she mean so little to him?

She picked up the pace and dashed outside the marquee tent. Christmas lights twinkled, strung across the ancient trees. Mount Vernon had never looked better. With no jacket on, the cold rushed over her, but she didn't care. She kicked off her heels and carried them in one hand. She jogged along the path, rounding the piazza and headed past the Mount Vernon servant quarters.

Her heart hammered, not just from running but from the knowledge that Declan would never forgive her.

"I take it Declan Collins had no idea who you are."

She stopped. *Dad.* He was the reason she was running barefoot in the dead of winter chasing down a man who would surely reject her.

She turned to see Dad standing near where she'd rushed past, his expression bleak.

"Don't you ever talk to me again." Addey's fists clenched. "You are so selfish. All you care about is your work, what your friends think of you, and how you can control people."

"You made this problem, Adelaide. This is on you," Dad said. "How could you date a man intent on ruining my business? The man called our family a bunch of selfish, soul-sucking vultures."

"No, he called *you* that. And he was right." Tears streaked down her face.

"You betrayed me." Dad pointed at her. "You put your business and mine in jeopardy for a man who will never care about you."

"I did that?" The shoes twitched in her hand. "I'm not the one who did the presentation. I'm not the one who changed the plan for tonight. You put my business and yours in jeopardy because you wanted revenge on me." Addey was shaking. "Declan is nothing like you. Even if he never speaks to me again, he is ten times the man you are."

Dad smirked. He actually smirked. "He won't love you, Adelaide. He's the type of man who can't love, he's so consumed by whatever his latest crusade is."

Dad's words were a knife and the pain sliced deep.

"I'm used to people not loving me. I'm just glad Granny raised me. I'm glad you didn't care enough about me to do it yourself. Do you know why?"

"Please, enlighten me." Dad's lip curled. His disdain made her sick.

"Because she made sure I wouldn't turn out to be like either of you."

Dad's silence filled the air.

Addey could see the party marquee lights still visible in the distance, still faintly heard the hum of the crowd. It looked like a fairy haven, a place for someone to hide from a storm.

There was no hiding from this one.

"You don't care that the new apartments are taking away vital services for the area. You could have made money elsewhere. But, no, you had to make the most money you possibly could. Now people in the community that you claim to love and support are worse off."

Dad slashed his hand across the air. "The building was for sale. There is no crime in buying a building and repurposing it." Dad's expression was like a stone, his voice icy.

Addey wanted to scream at him. She inhaled a ragged breath. "You could have rebuilt it and kept the services."

Dad shook his head. "That makes no business sense."

"Not everything is about making money." She wrapped her arms around her waist and took a step away.

He rested on hand on his hip, his frown deep. "You really think I don't care?"

Addey laughed, long and bitter. "This was fought in the public sphere for two years, Dad. Even if Declan wasn't the one writing the articles, the community didn't want to get rid of the Center. So, yes, I think you don't care." She backed away. Declan could be gone right now. Panic raced up her spine. It was time to go. She glanced behind her, praying he was still on the grounds.

"That's it, then? You're just going to give up on us?"

She turned back. Dad's posture was rigid, his face taut.

"You gave up on me a long time ago." Her raspy, uneven voice carried across the cold air. Her heart pounded as the hurt of a lifetime of rejection threatened to erupt. It was time her parents got a dose of how she'd felt for all her life. Unloved, unaccepted, and never measuring up.

She turned away.

"Adelaide, we're not finished."

Addey didn't turn back. "Well, I am. And it's Addey." She headed up the path to the parking lot. It was too late. There was no way he'd still be here. Still, she pressed on. It was the only place he could be.

Cold puffs of air lifted into the night with every breath. Addey reached the parking area. She glanced around the semi-empty lot. He was gone. The shoes dropped from her hand and clattered to the ground. Big, fat snowflakes began to fall—the weather prediction early.

Then she saw him. A lone figure at the far end of the lot, almost lost in the dim light and the gently swirling snow. Her heart surged as she ran down the pathway. Her feet hurt on the freezing gravel, but any pain was worth trying to win back the man she loved.

"Declan!" she called.

He was standing there, leaning unmoving against the hood of his car, his face a picture of pain. Her steps faltered as she drew near him. *Oh, what had Dad done?* This was all her fault. She should have known he would do this, go back on his word. She's been so gullable and hopeful.

"What was that tonight, Addey? Oh, I'm sorry, Adelaide." The scorn in his voice hit her. "You lied to me for weeks. In fact" —he gestured to their surroundings and then pointed to a spot not far from where they stood— "this is where it all started. You lied from right over there." He jabbed his finger in that direction, his eyes blazing, his voice unforgiving. "You knew what he was going to do, and you let it happen."

"He promised me the announcement was scrubbed. He finally listened to me and decided it wouldn't be a good idea to run it." Addey reached out to him, but he backed away.

"Before or after you knew I was reviewing the party?"

"After," she whispered, hating the anger and the hurt on his face. Hating what he thought of her.

"We talked about this. It was a Christmas party." Declan ground out. "Julie didn't even know about the announcement, otherwise she would never have given me the job."

"As soon as I found out you were reviewing the party, I convinced Dad to drop it from the schedule. I knew it would have been a horrible idea. There was no need to tell you because it wasn't an issue anymore."

"Don't tell me you didn't think he'd do this! Are you that naïve about your family?" He spat the words out, his body rigid, the emotion coming off him in waves.

Addey wanted to reach out, but she didn't dare.

"Dad found out about us tonight and did this. He wanted to hurt me...and you. I'm so sorry, Dec. It wasn't part of the plan." She clawed at the panic and despair slamming like pounding waves, relentless, cold, and savage.

"The plan?" Declan raised his eyebrows. "Can you hear yourself? You're chasing their approval and they're never going to give it. You changed your last name. You might not be in a Hamilton in name, but you want to be one, just without the trappings that come with it." Declan ran a hand down his face. "Tonight, that stunt your dad pulled, that's what comes with being a Hamilton."

"You don't know what you're talking about." Addey shivered, numb from the biting air, and her broken heart.

Declan breathed ragged, cold breaths. "I do. I know him—"

"My father is not yours. My dad wouldn't steal from people." Her fingers curled around the shoes in her hand.

Declan stopped. Silence. Nothing except the snowflakes falling. "And there it is." He looked at the snow-dusted ground then up at her, eyes bleak. "There's no future here. If you can't see your parents for who they are, you can't see me either." He laughed, a wounded, strangled laugh. "And I'm not going to spend my life convincing your parents that I'm worthy of a daughter they don't love." He turned.

Addey stepped forward, her shoes clattering on the ground. "You're running." She grabbed his arm and pulled him around to face her. "You said we'd be okay no matter what happened tonight."

He pulled away but she continued.

"You said you wouldn't let my family scare you away and that's exactly what you're doing." Addey kept following him. "If I'm in denial about my family, then you're in denial too. You can't accept that you come from my world." She shook. "You can't forgive your dad, me, even my father, because of your pride. You are so angry that you can't see reason, Declan. You can't let go of the past and see that not everyone is like your father."

Declan pointed. "Everyone in that room tonight is some version of my father."

"Don't you lump me into that group, or your boss, Julie. I'm sure she'd really love to know that's what you think of her." Addey stepped up to him, trembling. "Not everyone who is wealthy is like that. You can't be that blind." She stepped back. "But maybe you are. This isn't about my family or yours." She hugged herself. "This is about you being too afraid to let someone in. Until you do, you'll always be alone."

Declan's silence ignited a flicker of hope.

Addey dropped her voice. "I kept one thing from you, Declan, and you act like I'm the biggest sinner the world has ever seen. I fell in love with you, don't you know that?"

He became very still as he watched her, his frown deep, his hands hanging limp by his side.

"Clearly, I don't know about love. Or forgiveness. But know this, the article that I write will finish the lot of you." He got in his car and drove off, leaving her alone in the cold and darkness, with her world torn apart, and no shelter from the storm.

Chapter Thirty-Five

Everyone needed a haven. And tonight, Declan needed the haven only Eli's house could provide. Addey's words hounded him, only outstripped by the anger that roared back to life this evening. He pulled up to the single-story, gray clapboard house. He banged on the door, not caring if he woke his friend.

A light switched on and he heard shuffling behind the door. The door swung open, spilling light onto the porch. Eli, wearing his reading glasses and blue-checked flannel pajamas and holding a book in one hand, gave him the once over.

"Declan, what on earth..." Eli's voice held a quiet note of worry. "Is your mother okay?"

"She's fine."

"You're not." He opened the door further and Declan pushed past him. The house was in its usual cluttered state. Bookshelves piled with books, with more books spilling onto the floor beside the squashy beige sofa. Frames covered most of the walls. They held pictures from far-off places that Declan was never sure whether Eli had been to or not.

"You had that fancy party tonight, didn't you?" Eli perched on the edge of the sofa and dropped the book to his feet.

Declan paced the room. Five steps to the window. Five steps back. The clock ticked.

"It was everything a lavish Christmas party should be." Sarcasm dripped off every word.

"That bad, huh?" Eli spoke slowly, as if trying to settle him with his measured words. "Did you at least see Addey?"

He made a guttural sound. "Of course. She was stunning."

"What exactly is going on?" Eli continued talking in his reasonable tone.

He stopped. "Addey isn't who you think she is."

"What do you mean?"

"She's the daughter of Jonathan and Vivien Hamilton."

A beat of silence followed.

Eli whistled. "I didn't see that coming."

Declan ran a hand through his hair and resumed his prowling. "She told me who she was not long after we met."

Eli rested his hand on his leg. "That's why you wouldn't pursue anything with her?'

Declan didn't reply. He kept pacing.

"But that wasn't what happened was it?"

Five steps to the window. Five steps back.

"You fell in love with her, didn't you?"

"I did not." He growled out the words. He could still hear their angry exchange, hear her words aimed straight over the walls he'd put up his whole life. He kept moving, unable to find peace.

"What happened tonight?"

He looked at Eli, his anger ratcheting up a notch. "Jonathan crowed over his buying of the Community Center. He had pictures of the new apartment building." Declan wanted to hit something. "He even had the gall to boast about how much he cared for the local community."

"What does this have to do with Addey?" Eli asked.

"She knew this was going to happen and didn't say anything."

Eli waited while Declan paced. Eli's silence sent Declan's anger deeper inside him.

"The party was always going to be a launch for the new building, but when she found out I was doing the review, she got her dad to change the plans. All for the sake of a good review for her precious business. She's just like him." He nearly spat out the last words.

Eli was far too calm for Declan's liking. "Sounds like Addey took steps to take care of everybody."

Declan glared. "Whose side are you on?"

Eli pinned Declan with paternal stare. "I'm on the side that gets you to look past your anger. Are you sure about her relationship with her family?"

Declan stood there, grinding his teeth, remembering Addey's confession about her family weeks ago.

"Granny was always there. She taught me how to drive, helped me fill out my college applications, she tried to teach me how to cook, and mostly she tried to keep my relationship with my parents going."

"How'd that work out?"

"I changed my last name to hers when I was eighteen."

A slight crack appeared in the shell of his anger. It allowed for a speck of compassion to seep into his hard heart. A heart he'd guarded for years—until he'd met her.

Declan stalked to the window and peered outside. A thin layer of snow covered the ground and was still falling softly now. Perfect Christmas weather.

Christmas. The word left a bitter taste in his mouth. It was bad enough they'd be spending Christmas at Heritage Oaks. And now Christmas without Addey...

"What does Addey have to say about tonight's events? Do you *really* think she'd let you be blindsided like that?" Eli readjusted his glasses.

Declan wanted to shout yes, but he couldn't. "We talked about the Community Center closing. She *said* she was against it." Bitterness bled through every word. "She said Jonathan found out about us tonight and backtracked on their agreement."

"So, he used Addey as his missile to wound you?" Eli sighed. "He betrayed his own daughter."

"Stop defending her," Declan snapped. "She's not who she said she is. How can I trust her?"

"From what I can understand, Addey left something out, but she never hid who she was to you. What about the secrets you've kept?"

Declan stood still. "I told her everything, Eli." His heart thudded at the confession, how exposed he'd felt in that moment when he'd shared his deepest secret with her.

"That took a lot of courage. I'm proud of you." Eli remained perched on the edge of the couch as if he understood that Declan needed space. "Did she reject you like you expected?" Eli's piercing question found its mark. Addey had held him and encouraged him. For a few moments, she'd been his safe place. But no matter how good the intentions were, the damage was done.

"She still should have warned me. Someone like Jonathan Hamilton can't be trusted."

"You would have Addey believe the worst about her own father?" Eli asked.

"Her parents couldn't be bothered to raise her, why should she think anything good of them?" Declan resumed his pacing, wishing Eli would quit defending her.

"Seems to me you and Addey have a lot in common," Eli said.

"Don't go there, Eli."

"You've both changed your last name—"

"That's not the point."

"—don't get along with at least one parent—" Eli kept talking.

"It's not unusual for parents and adult children to not talk—"

"—and you both come from wealthy families." Eli sat back. "Seems similar to me."

Declan folded his arms across his chest. "My father is a criminal who is spending the rest of his life in jail."

"Yes, he is," Eli said. "But Addey has the right to give her family the benefit of the doubt. You need to do the same for her."

Declan worked his jaw, arms crossed over his chest. Eli's logic was maddening.

"Addey hurt you tonight, but this isn't about that. It's about your father and the unforgiveness you have in your heart." Eli ran a hand down his face, impatience edging his words.

Declan jaw ached. "We lost everything and everyone hated us. Mom had to move us to the other side of the country, Eli."

"You know why she did that?" Eli frowned.

"Because everyone abandoned us." He stubbornly clung to the hurt from all those years ago.

"No, it wasn't just that." Eli paused, as if searching for the right words. "She was getting death threats."

He dropped his arms to his side. "What?"

Eli rubbed his face. "People were threatening to kidnap you and Nicky and hold you for ransom."

Declan's heart thumped as Eli's words sunk in. He sunk into the armchair. "Kidnap us?" He couldn't wrap his mind around it.

"We talked often, your mother and I." Eli's voice was soft as he leaned back in his chair, and he suddenly looked so much older. "She had no choice but to get the three of you as far away as she could."

Oh, how much Mom had endured thanks to his father's crimes. His thoughts were as tumultuous as a ship caught in a storm.

"You know your mother. She could have handled being snubbed, if that's all it had been."

"Why didn't she ever tell me?" Declan leaned forward, his head in his hands.

"You were fifteen and Nicky was twelve," Eli said. "She didn't want to frighten you."

Declan stared at the carpet. "I had no idea."

"You know how much she worried when you or Nicky were late home from school, or anywhere really..."

Declan looked up at Eli. "That explains why the neighbor always checked in on us, and why we had to go to the Community Center after school. Why we were never allowed to walk alone."

Eli nodded, his eyes dim with sadness and a frown etched on his face.

Declan hurt, just watching Eli. The man loved his mom—that was clear in everything he did for her. Eli kept her secrets and visited her every day. Loved Declan like a father would. A longing so deep welled up inside and nearly overcame him.

"Why didn't you marry her? You could have been my father." He choked on the last word. Eli would never be his father, but, oh, how he wished things might have been different.

Silence filled the room. The clock ticked louder.

"Declan." Eli finally spoke, his voice strong and clear. "We've been over this. Your mother didn't want to remarry. For all the love she is capable of and even the forgiveness she has extended to your father—"

Declan rolled his eyes.

"I don't think she wanted to take that risk again. And given what happened to you all, I don't blame her." He sat forward. "Look at me, Declan."

Declan met Eli's unwavering gaze.

"I might not have had the chance to marry your mother, but I did get the chance to be a father."

Declan ducked his head and stared at his shoes, unable to look up.

Eli continued speaking, his voice now thick and unsteady. "I'm proud of you, Declan. I'm proud of the man you've become, but I don't like what I've seen lately. The Community Center closing has sparked your rage in ways I haven't seen for a long time."

"It shouldn't be closing." Declan bit out the words. He saw again Jonathan's grin as he announced the new project.

"But it is." Eli spoke with such firmness that it jolted Declan. "Don't let your father's crimes taint every rich man who crosses your path, even on something like this. You'll end up pushing away the people you love."

He jerked at the word *love*. "I don't love her."

Because loving someone meant getting hurt.

The ache in his heart betrayed him.

"I'm not saying you do, but you could. And you'll never know if you keep her and everyone else at arm's length because you're afraid they'll hurt you like your father did."

The words pierced him, right down to the places in his heart that he kept locked away. Addey had his measure just like Eli did.

"She should have told me what was going on." His argument sounded weak, even to his own ears.

Eli raised one eyebrow and gave Declan such a fatherly look of disapproval, it would have been funny if this wasn't so serious. "You're angry that it's her father tearing down the Community Center. And he was gleeful about it. That says more about him than you."

"That's reason enough." He folded his arms across his chest, trying to protect himself from the truth in Eli's words.

"It's never reason enough, Declan. You need to forgive Addey...and your father."

"It's not that simple." His jaw hurt from clenching it so tight.

"I never said it would be, but it's a road you need to start walking."

"You pick now to act like a dad," Declan complained, a wry smile flickering across his face.

Eli shrugged. "Well, no one else is going to tell you what you don't want to hear."

Declan stood up slowly, measuring his words. He wanted to make sure Eli knew. "You're right, I don't want to hear what you have to say." He walked to the front door before turning around. "But you're the only one allowed to say it to me."

Eli stepped up to Declan and pulled him into a firm hug. For several long precious seconds, Declan allowed this man, who was his father in every way that mattered, to love him.

"I have a review to write," he said, his voice thick, his hands trembling as he stepped away from Eli.

"Don't write anything that you'll regret."

Eli's warning followed him outside as he stepped out into the gently falling snow. His heart was heavy, and his mind raced.

There was nothing he could write that could fix this mess.

Chapter Thirty-Six

Declan had kissed her here on this sofa. On the same spot, where he'd told her his biggest secret and then, somewhere along the way, Addey fell in love.

She sat in the darkness of her townhouse, letting her tears fall unchecked. Grabbing the quilt that lived on the sofa, she draped it over her shoulders so that it covered her completely. She shivered and pulled it tighter.

But no matter how much she hid, there was no escaping the truth: She was a disappointment to everyone.

A sob tore through her and it echoed around the empty room, reminding her that without Granny, there was no one to love her.

Her father's betrayal hurt more than she ever thought it could. Was Declan, right? Was she really that naïve to think her father would just let the Community Center business drop?

But it was Declan's anger and hurt that tore her to pieces. Addey wanted to hide from his words, from the unforgiveness she found there. But there was no escaping it when she couldn't stop replaying it over and over.

A sharp knock on her door made her jerk.

"Adelaide, let me in please," Grandmother called through the door.

Addey burrowed deeper into the quilt.

"I want to make sure you're okay," Grandmother said. "I'll wait outside all night."

An image of Grandmother in her fine clothes sitting outside all night would have been funny on any other day.

"I mean it, Adelaide."

Throwing off the quilt, Addey shivered in the cold, but being cold was better than anything else. She yanked open the door and returned to her cocoon under the quilt, this time lying down so she was covered from head to toe.

The closed door told her that Grandmother was inside.

"It's freezing in here. Did you turn the thermostat up?" Grandmother's efficient footsteps sounded through the house.

Under the quilt, Addey could see dim lights.

"I'm making myself some tea, and you a hot chocolate." Banging of crockery sounded from the kitchen. "When I come back to the room, I would like to talk to you, not a lump of blankets."

Addey stayed where she was. What was the point when no one cared anyway? The tears still slid down her cheeks, and she sniffed. Everything she loved had been ripped away from her. Wasn't that the way with her life though?

The scent of chocolate and creamy milk tickled her nose and without warning her stomach grumbled. That's right, she hadn't eaten dinner, because everything had fallen apart.

"I might suggest you go shopping. There's not much in the kitchen, but I did find some cookies."

Addey lifted the blanket until her head was visible. Grandmother sat perched on the edge of the sofa where Addey's feet were. She'd changed from her formal wear and was now dressed in a warm, fitted sweater and her tailored pants. Even at midnight, Grandmother was always ready for anything.

Grandmother moved to the coffee table, so she was near Addey's face. Without a word, she reached across and stroked Addey's cheek.

Then Addey saw it.

Tears rolling down Grandmother's cheeks.

"I'm sorry about tonight." Grandmother blinked and the tears stopped, but her voice remained thick. "I'm so ashamed of my son."

Addey sat up. "Grandmother, what he did wasn't your fault."

Grandmother's laugh was short and brittle. "Wasn't it? He's my son, I raised him."

Grandmother moved beside Addey and pulled her close. Addey's shoulders shook as she leaned into the embrace, tears falling harder and faster. Grandmother stroked her back, her own quiet sobs mixing with Addey's.

"Why don't they love me?"

Grandmother hugged her tighter. "They do, it's just hard for them to show it."

Addey continued to sob, letting all her tears out from years of rejection. "Why can't I be good enough for them? What did I ever do to them?"

"You did nothing," Grandmother said. "You were just a little girl."

"Declan said I'm just like them," she shuddered through tears. Saying the words was like stabbing herself in the heart. Every time she relived their fight, it was like someone was plunging the knife deeper until she might die of this pain.

Dad's rejection was a second knife.

"No darling. He's wrong," Grandmother soothed. "Declan is angry and hurt. And that hurt is not something you caused." She used her bony finger to tilt Addey's chin up so that their eyes met. "Declan's hurt is from his father. His betrayal of their family left that young boy shattered. He's been making others pay for his father's mistakes ever since."

"You know about his family? Who he really is?" Addey wiped her eyes and grabbed a tissue from the coffee table. "How did you find out?"

"That Declan is Edward Sheridan's son?"

Addey's mouth dropped open. "I never told anyone."

Grandmother patted her leg. "I didn't know at first, but I realized the truth when Susannah went missing at Mount Vernon." She reached for a cookie and handed it to Addey. "I knew Susannah a little, from before. We were different ages, on opposite sides of the country, but we'd come into contact with each other through charities and functions." Grandmother paused, her shoulders sagging a touch. "She was kind to me many years ago and I've always been very grateful. When everything with Edward came out, I reached out but never heard back. I never knew what happened to her and the kids."

"Until you saw her at Mount Vernon?"

Grandmother nodded. "Yes, then everything about Declan made sense." She squeezed Addey's hand. "Including his being in love with you."

Addey stared at her uneaten cookie, the knife digging deeper as she recalled their few short weeks together. "Declan doesn't love me."

"If he didn't love you, why would he be so hurt? We only get hurt when we truly love. He wouldn't have told you about his family if he didn't love you, Adelaide."

"It doesn't matter anymore. It's over." A fresh wave of tears fell down her cheeks.

"I can't fix any of this, but please know you are loved. By me, by your granny." A tender smile touched Grandmother's lips. "Deborah saw the writing on the wall, knew how much your grandfather, through cruel words, had hurt your mother. She knew you'd be more settled with her. Yet she tried to make sure you had a relationship with them. It was far from perfect, but Adelaide, you are loved."

She sunk into Grandmother's embrace, her words seeping into Addey's broken heart. Memories rushed over her of the years with Granny. No matter how little attention her parents paid to her, Granny would always tell her that her parents loved her, they just showed it in ways that were hard to understand. Granny would always tell Addey to love with strength. As Addey grew older, Granny let her take the lead in whether she visited them.

After she passed away, Addey had wanted to spend more time with her parents. They were her only link to the grandmother she grieved. And deep down, she hoped that by sharing in their common loss, it might draw them closer. In a strange way it had, but more time with someone didn't mean you were closer to them. It simply meant they took up more space in your life.

"You know, I don't care about the review he writes anymore," Addey said.

"What do you mean?"

Addey gave a humorless laugh. "There's nothing more he can do to make things worse. Dad's stunt at the party will be more than enough for the Baker/Gibson Group to pull out from the deal."

She expected to feel worse about it, but she didn't. She'd been scrambling to make sure everything went to plan so her business would thrive, her parents would be proud of her, and she'd finally make it in their eyes. But none of that happened. Instead, she was left with a business no one wanted. Would anyone want to work with her after tonight? Right now, Addey didn't care.

"I think Declan might surprise you." Grandmother reached for her tea. "It's probably cold now."

Addey picked up her hot chocolate. Grandmother had prepared it in Granny's mermaid-handled mug. She gripped the mug tighter as the sadness cut deeper. "He called Dad a selfish, soul-sucking vulture with no moral compass. I don't think he's going to hold back this time."

Grandmother raised an eyebrow. The tears were gone, but her mouth remained set in its grim line. "I still think he'll come through."

Addey sipped her drink. It, too, was cold now, but she kept drinking. "When did you get so optimistic?"

"Since I saw you so happy. He makes you happy and that's a rare thing."

Addey choked back another set of tears. "He's not the person people think he is." A sob escaped. "He's so much more giving and kinder than you would ever know."

The tears continued to fall. Grandmother let Addey cry while they drank.

"I've told Carmel to come by when I leave." Grandmother put her empty cup down. She took a deep breath, apparently thinking before she spoke. Addey watched her closely.

"Adelaide," Grandmother looked at her. "What your parents did tonight was wrong. What they've done for years is wrong. I'm sorry I didn't help more. Can you forgive an old woman stuck in her ways?"

Each word was like a small stitch in repairing her bleeding heart. Addey nodded and clasped Grandmother's hand as she swallowed back another round of tears.

"Can you do something else for me?" Grandmother asked.

"I'll try."

"Be happy without them."

"But—"

Grandmother held up her hand, cutting Addey off. "I'm not saying cut them out of your life. After tonight, I think time away—lots of it—from your parents is more than healthy."

"I told Dad I never want to see him again. Mom's included in that." It should hurt to say it, let alone think it, but the thought of not seeing them gave her peace. Peace was something Addey hadn't found in years.

"I don't blame you," Grandmother replied. "What I'm trying to say is, with or without them, you need to be happy, Adelaide."

"I've tried."

"Have you really?" Grandmother looked around the room, her expression softening when she caught the photos on the wall. "You have a home here. A house with real love and real memories. But as much as you love Granny and this house, you are still chasing acceptance from your parents and it's stopping you from being happy."

Addey leaned back against the sofa, Grandmother's words needling her, making her damaged heart hurt more. They echoed Declan's words, too. She closed her eyes and tried to block out the advice, but it was impossible. Could she really be happy without their love? Their approval?

Did she want to be?

She opened her eyes. "Granny always wanted me to keep trying with them."

Grandmother shook her head. "I'm sure she did, but I don't think she wanted you to be miserable. I knew Deborah, too. She wanted you to keep the door open, not let them slam you with it. There is a difference." Grandmother stood. "Now, it's late. Give me a hug."

Addey stood and pulled her into a long hug. "Thanks for coming and interfering."

Grandmother chuckled. "I seem to have broken my 'no interfering' rule several times these last few weeks."

"I'm grateful for it." Addey gave her a final squeeze, her heart still bleeding, broken, but Grandmother's presence had taken her off life support. Maybe tomorrow would be better than she hoped, but as she closed the door behind, the silence of the house reigned. Addey pressed her back against the door, letting her gaze sweep the room. The small cross hanging above the photos caught her eye. Slowly she slid down the door until she found the floor, breathed out long, and her chest tightened as the tears fell. Would they ever stop? Granny would tell her to pray, so for the second time in four weeks, Addey closed her eyes and let her tears flow.

And prayed.

Chapter Thirty-Seven

Declan's empty screen stared back at him, taunting him to find the words that wouldn't come. The official party review was expected to go online tomorrow—Monday.

He had twenty hours to come up with something.

He blew out a breath and tapped the keyboard, letting random characters fill the white space. It was better than a blank screen. The review he wanted to write, the ireful one that would ruin Addey, and the words he needed for it, wouldn't come. No matter how angry he was, he couldn't do that to her. And more than anything else, he wanted to look Eli in the eye and tell him he'd done the right thing.

He still didn't know what that was, but ruining Addey wasn't it.

Nicky banged around the kitchen.

"Can you keep it down?"

"I will, if you write something," she called back. Declan smiled at the sass in her tone. She'd forgiven him days ago and conceded that she might have overreacted.

Declan dutifully typed some words on the screen. "How's this? *Can you please stop banging around in there?*"

She laughed and then walked up beside him, pulled one of the dining table chairs up closer. "Why can't you write the review?"

He shrugged. "Eli's in my head."

"That means he's stopped you from doing something dumb."

Nicky was right. And no matter which way he looked at the situation, his anger towards Addey was fading. Since he'd met her, he wanted to be different—to be better and not the bitter man she'd met at Mount Vernon. But the rub was her father. What he'd done was inexcusable. His chest tightened at the memory of Jonathan Hamilton's smug face.

Nicky poked him.

Declan scowled at her.

Nicky ignored it. "What did Eli say?"

"Eli said that I was angry that Addey was a Hamilton and it's her father who's tearing down the Community Center." He didn't look at her as he said it, he couldn't, he was afraid of what he'd see there.

Nicky tapped her fingers on the table. The sound was the only noise in the house. Declan wanted to tell her to quit it, but that was only his irritation talking.

"Well, he has a point," Nicky said. "What I don't get is that you knew Addey was their daughter for ages and you still went out with her. Why does it bother you now that she's a Hamilton?"

Declan made a noise in his throat. "Her father deliberately ruined the night to hurt her and spite me."

"Yeah, but he's one man."

"He's her father, Nicky."

"I know, but can I ask you something?" Nicky lowered her voice.

"What is it?" he asked slowly.

She started tracing the grain lines on the table. "What if Addey wasn't a Hamilton, and it wasn't her dad tearing down the Community Center? What if she was just rich...would it matter then?"

Her question was as pointed as Eli's and pained him because its aim was true. He leaned back and stared at the ceiling. "How do I get around the fact that she's a Hamilton and it's her father tearing the place down?"

She stopped tracing the table. "You accept it and then tell Addey you're sorry for overreacting and being a jerk."

Declan looked back at her, squirming under her steady gaze. "You make it sound so easy."

She shrugged. "It's as easy as you want it to be. Maybe you have to decide what you want the most."

"What do you mean?"

She sighed. "For a bright guy, sometimes you are so dumb." She smiled as she spoke. "You can't stop the Community Center from being torn down, so find a way to accept that. And then you can find out if you and Addey have something special."

"Have you forgiven Dad?" he asked, holding his breath.

She looked at him, her mouth drawing into a half smile, but sadness curled around the edges. "More than you have. Have you told her about him?"

He paused. "Yes." Even saying it made his breath hitch and his heart rate pick up. "It was scary but…"

"Good?" Nicky supplied.

"Yeah."

"The first time I told my friend Bethany about Dad, I wanted to die. I thought she'd hate me, but she didn't." Nicky watched him.

Declan's eyes widened. "You told people about us?"

"Cool your jets, big brother." She rolled her eyes. "I didn't put it all over social media. Just Beth and her husband. Also my pastor and his wife know. That's it." She gave him a hard look, as if daring him to fight her on her decision.

Declan wasn't going to argue with her. Again, deep down, telling Addey had been freeing, and now that his anger had subsided enough to think clearly, he was glad she knew.

"Why did you tell them?"

Nicky bumped his arm with hers like they'd done when they were kids. "Because, you need people to share life with, to let them help you carry the burdens that are too heavy." She grew serious. "And telling them helped me start to forgive Dad. It was like the more I held everything inside, it made what Dad did worse and then the burden got heavier."

"So that's it, you've just forgiven him?" He couldn't keep the edge from dripping out.

Nicky sighed. "It's a day by day thing. Some days I ask for help to forgive him a hundred times a day, others it's just once. And then there are the days where I don't need to ask for help because I have forgiven him. My point is by asking for help, I'm saying that I'm willing to forgive."

Nicky's words settled on Declan like a wooly sweater. The things about wooly sweaters were that you had to get used to them, and once that happened, they didn't itch so much. "By asking for help, you mean praying?"

"Yes." She tapped his arm. "And by being open with the people who care about me."

"When did you get so smart?" he teased, wanting to break the somber mood that hung in the air.

Nicky laughed. "I've always been a fast learner. You, my stubborn brother, have always been a dog with a bone about things, but when you decide to do something, you commit one hundred percent. You're all in." She stood. "Write the review and don't let Addey get away."

Nicky's bedroom door closed, and Declan was left with swirling thoughts. He closed his laptop and let the silence fall around him. Mom, Nicky, and Eli had been hammering him about the need to forgive, to stop running, and to find a way forward. Meeting Addey had upended his world—in the best way. Addey, with her brave heart, had coaxed him to find the ember of hope and build it into something warm and inviting. He wanted that more than he wanted to be the old Declan.

Even if Addey never forgave him, he wanted to step into a brighter future, one where he wasn't held back by bitterness and anger.

For the second time in as many weeks, Declan prayed.

Chapter Thirty-Eight

"I don't want to know what it says," Addey told Carmel as they sat on her sofa on her townhouse. It had been three days since her world upended.

Grandmother had called again today to check on her and Addey was still ignoring her parents' texts and calls. She was tired, having trouble sleeping, and waiting for the Baker/Gibson Group to drop their deal. And her heart was still broken over Declan.

Carmel eyed her. "I really think you should read whatever it says. You know, rip the band-aid off."

Addey smiled in spite of everything. "I tried ripping the band-aid off. It didn't go well."

Carmel scanned her tablet, refreshing it every few minutes to check if the review had gone up, while her other hand held a nail polish brush. They'd been painting their toenails, eating ice cream, and watching sad romance movies. Leo DiCaprio's *Romeo and Juliet* played on the TV.

"You didn't have to take the day off, I know you can't afford it." On the screen, Leo's Romeo fell to his knees in agony overhearing the news of Juliet's death.

Carmel looked up, nail polish brush poised in midair. "That's what best friends do." She grinned. "Besides, playing hooky once in a while is good for the soul."

A wave of tears threatened to fall. Though Addey had gotten the bad end in the parental draw, she'd been given some fantastic people to fill the gap they'd left.

"I'm not going to let my parents stop me from doing what I want to do anymore." The words came out shaky. She still felt like they could hear her and they'd come and stomp all over her. Carmel had suggested she see a counselor about her abandonment issues, and she was going to do it.

"Good for you!" Carmel beamed.

"It's time to take back my life." Now Romeo was begging Friar Laurence to free him of his agony. "Although, I have no idea what my future looks like." It was scary, losing so much in such a short time, and if she thought too much about it, Addey would hyperventilate. So instead, she watched Romeo take his poison and profess his undying love for Juliet.

"I think that's when you're free. When you don't know the future, but step into it anyway." Carmel gasped. "His review is up."

Addey stilled, her mouth going dry.

"Do you want me to read it?" Carmel asked.

Addey sat frozen to the spot, her eyes fixed on Claire Danes's Juliet as she cried over the loss of Romeo and then took her own life. That was it. Broken hearts and death—all because two families couldn't get along.

"I'm not ready," she whispered, her hands shaking.

"Okay." Carmel squeezed her hand. "You don't have to do anything right now."

The credits rolled on the screen.

***

Addey walked past her tablet for the umpteenth time. After Carmel left, Addey went grocery shopping, watched two episodes of *Virgin River*, cleaned her kitchen, mopped the floor, and reorganized her small book collection. When she was on the verge of calling her parents, she finally gave in.

She sat on the sofa, took a deep breath, sent out a silent prayer for strength, and clicked on the website link.

Her heart thumped loudly in her chest as she began to read, knowing that her fate was about to be sealed.

Christmas Isn't What You Think It Is

Christmas should be a time of joy when families gather to celebrate. It's a time filled with laughter and happy memories. Over the weekend I attended a Christmas dinner at George and Martha's Mount Vernon Estate. It was delightful, filled with scrumptious food, lovely music, and rousing company. However, the event was tainted and fell flat at the end, but that was my fault, not anyone else's.

Addey stopped reading, confused. Where was the evisceration she'd been expecting? She kept reading.

My expectations of this dinner were met, but I was still let down by certain events that transpired that night, and upon reflection, it was my own shortcomings that allowed the night to be ruined. The guests enjoyed themselves thoroughly and Addey Bennet—

Her heart thumped harder at the use of her name—

of Elegant Events *presented a classy evening, in a setting that couldn't get any further from my Californian upbringing. Christmas on the grounds of our first president was an inspired idea. It was a magical night and one that will linger long in the memory of those who attended.*

Christmas is a time people often reflect on what their life has been, and what it might be in the future. This season I found myself coming up short in many areas of my life. The last two years, and the last six weeks in particular, have been a heavy learning curve for me. I let my personal prejudices get in the way of my ability to report things from an unbiased place. Those prejudices affected how I viewed people and circumstances.

Where was Declan going with this? Addey continued reading, greedy for more of his words.

The truth is, I don't enjoy Christmas, and I don't like dwelling on the past. Being the son of financial disgrace Edward Sheridan is something I don't like thinking about, let alone talking about.

Addey almost dropped the tablet. She blinked several times and reread his words. Tears sprang in her eyes. What was he doing? With tears falling freely and a hand over her mouth, she kept reading, unable to stop.

We moved here not long after my father's fall from grace, changed our last name, and tried to get on with living a quiet, normal life. Our mother did everything she could to shield my sister and I from the understandable backlash. This moment in our family history has shaped how I view the world. How could it not? I'm not proud to admit that I have lumped all wealthy people in the same category as my father since then. I was more than unbiased. I allowed my personal history to inflame my views. It has hurt more people than I know and one person in particular has borne the brunt of my prejudice and rejection. To her and all the others I've hurt, I say a heartfelt apology.

May the new year bring all of us the time to reflect and grant forgiveness, even to the ones who don't deserve it.

Addey put the tablet down, unable to believe what she'd read. He'd done it—told the world who he was. All his hard work in keeping his family secret was gone. Why had he done it? The question kept battering her and Addey knew she couldn't rest until she'd talked to Declan and seen him with her own eyes. As she scrambled around for an outfit that wasn't sweats, she knew one thing. He hadn't trashed her or her dad. He'd been so giving, considering what Dad had done. Hope burned in her chest. A flame she'd believed had burned away grew with each moment. Boots in hand, she opened the door, intent on finding Declan but stopped at the sight of Dad standing there, hand poised to knock.

"Dad!" She stepped back. "I said I didn't want to see you right now."

"Actually, you said never again. Did you see the review?" He shouldered past her, not bothering to ask if he was welcome. He stopped by the couch, cold air rushing in along with fluttering flakes. She shut the door.

"Did you know about this?" Dad asked, his voice taut.

"I just finished reading it and, no, I didn't know anything about it," she replied coldly. "But I knew who he was. He told me himself."

Dad looked away, unable to hold her gaze.

Addey itched to see Declan. There was so much to say. But first she needed to know something else. "Did you know Edward Sheridan? Grandmother says she knew Susannah a little."

Dad ran a hand through his hair and sighed so deeply it was unnerving. "Not well. I'd met him a few times, but it was more about being in the same space as each other rather than being friends. They were West Coast people."

"So, you never did business with him?" She watched him as his eyes hardened at her question.

"Adelaide, no. I've done business with people who push the limits, but they don't break the law, and they don't ruin people's lives. The man is where he deserves to be." Anger lined every word he spoke.

A wave of relief washed over her and she breathed deeply, not even realizing she'd been shallow breathing since she found him on her doorstep. Maybe even since she'd read the article.

She really needed to see Declan.

"It explains a lot of things," he said.

"He told me when they got here, they relied on the help of the Community Center for several years."

She let her words sink in and watched Dad absorb them. He nodded his head slowly. He looked so defeated, with worry lines marking his forehead, tired eyes, and a grim line to his mouth that looked like it might become permanent.

"I think I need to have talk with him," Dad said quietly.

Addey stepped forward and shook her head. "Not before I do."

"He's that important to you, is he?" Dad ventured.

Addey crossed her arms across her chest. "I don't know if that's any of your business."

He sighed again and a sadness came over him that permeated the room. Addey hugged her herself to ward it off. "I'm sorry, Adelaide. I've been wrong about everything."

His face was so open, so honest, something she rarely saw on him. She looked at the floor. The same thing always happened, anger warring with the need to be loved by her parents. It was like a rollercoaster she could never get off.

She looked up at him, her voice unsteady. "You've said things like that before. What makes this time any different?"

"Nothing except time to show you that it will be different."

She raised an eyebrow.

He cracked a smile, but it disappeared. "Our family has such a complicated history. Your grandmother raised you and, in the end, you took her last name." His voice dropped, his shoulders dropped.

"After you didn't talk to me for a year, you said you didn't mind." She kept her tone steely, while inside she was falling apart. She wanted to make things right with Declan, but maybe facing Dad right now was the best thing.

"What was I supposed to say? You were eighteen. We figured as long as you kept coming around, it didn't matter what your last name was." He sounded tired.

Addey was so sick of having this conversation with him.

"Are you saying, you cared that I changed my last name, but not that you let her raise me? I don't see much care in that."

"It didn't happen overnight." He sat down on the edge of the couch and looked up at her. "It was little things. She'd babysit you when we were away, come over for dinners to see you You always adored her, and it slowly became natural that you spent more time with her. We didn't need a nanny because we had her. When she'd leave for the night, you'd cry and call out for her."

Addey kept herself tucked away by the door, remembering some of what he was saying. "Your mother was joining me on a big trip to Dubai, so we asked if you could stay with Deborah while we were away, rather than disrupt your life. You were about to start Kindergarten." He shrugged. "When we got back, you didn't want to leave. She didn't want you to leave, and work was snowballing for me and your mom..." He didn't finish the sentence. Addey didn't need to finish it for him. Mom wasn't a warm person, and she'd always left the mothering to someone else. Addey tried not to think about it most days. If she ever became a mother, she hoped—no, she *knew*—she'd do it differently.

"Mom loves you in the best way she can," Dad said, pain in his voice. "Her parents' divorce was hard on her, and she learned to keep things inside, to not care about the important things because she'd lose them."

Addey stepped away from the door and walked towards Dad. She bent down to pick up her tablet. If Declan could forgive a man who stole millions from people and ruined their lives, maybe she could forgive her parents, and even herself. It was a heavy weight to bear and maybe it was time to let it go.

"Forgiveness doesn't happen overnight. I need you to prove you're going to change. Show me, Dad. Don't just tell me." She clenched her jaw as she spoke. "I don't trust either of you."

He hung his head. "I know. We need time to prove it. Please don't write us off yet, Addey." He looked up at her, his eyes beseeching her.

She gave him a curt nod, still breathing hard. "I need to go."

But would Declan want to see her?

Chapter Thirty-Nine

T he puck slammed into the net.

"Good shot," Camden called.

Declan grabbed another puck and sent it home.

Camden intercepted and shot it back. Declan covered it, maneuvered around Camden, and sent the puck flying.

"Thanks for meeting me last night." Declan breathed hard as they joined each other by the net.

"You called and said you had something important to tell me," Camden paused. "I'm glad you told me about your dad" —there was a waver in his voice— "but you could have told me years ago."

Declan scraped his stick along the ice, his fingers gripping the handle hard. He breathed out the emotions stirring up in him. "I know. I'm sorry." He looked at Camden. "I didn't want anyone to think worse of me than I already did."

Camden gave a hard nod. "I get it. Thanks for telling me before you went public with it. Are you all going to be okay when it reaches critical mass?"

Declan breathed out a shuddering breath. "I don't know, but Mom and Nicky were on board with the idea. We agreed to no interviews and to keep off social media for the time being."

"Sounds like a good plan."

"I hope so," Declan muttered. He'd never felt so ill in his life as when he sent the review to Julie. He wanted her to see it before he let it out onto the internet where he could never get it back. Julie had been stunned and asked him four times if he was sure about this. Nicky was right, telling Camden had been hard, but freeing.

Now all he had to do was see Addey, but he wanted to give her a chance to read it for herself first.

Declan checked his watch. It was nearly three in the afternoon. The review had been up for almost three hours.

It was time to see if Addey could forgive him.

As they packed up, the lightness Declan carried with him was due to letting go of the anger and starting on a new path. With or without Addey, he wanted to stay the course.

But he really wanted Addey with him on this new journey.

***

Declan leaned against his SUV outside Addey's townhouse in the soft falling snow. He didn't dare knock, not now. Declan had been turning onto Addey's street when Jonathan Hamilton had powered up the steps to Addey's front door.

One battle at a time.

His pulse thrummed, his neck was sore from stress and lack of sleep, but as he waited, that tiny flicker of hope still burned. There was hope for him yet.

Finally, the front door opened and Addey burst out.

Declan's heart raced at the sight of her. He stood straight, drinking her in.

Addey skidded to a stop when she saw him, her feet bare, boots in one hand. She was like an angel standing there, eyes wide, mouth slightly open, the snow falling around her.

Declan moved forward, his gaze fixed on her. He stopped three feet away. His mouth was dry, and his palms were sweaty, but it was now or never.

"I was just coming to find you." Her voice hitched.

"And I came to beg your forgiveness." The words rushed out. "I said things that I wish I could take back, but I can't. Addey, I was wrong and I'm so sorry. I abandoned you, like others have, and what's worse, I did if after I told you I wouldn't. That makes me the worst of the worst." He ran a hand over his face. "Even if you can't love me, I'm hoping you can forgive me."

Addey's eyes grew bright with unshed tears. "Are you so unlovable?"

He rushed on. "That's not it at all. I understand how much I hurt you. Loving me after what I did, I get it if it's too much." Declan wanted to kick himself. "This is coming out all wrong." He took a breath and tried again. "Addey, you're brave even when you're scared, and you see the best in people, and you have hope for them. It was your hope that spoke to me that night at the café when you called me out for being a jerk."

Addey closed her eyes, tears running down her cheeks.

"The truth is, Addey, it shouldn't be you." He took a step closer. Addey opened her eyes, pulling him in with that sea-green gaze that captivated him from day one. "But no matter what family situation we're in—I don't want it to be anyone else but you."

Declan's voice trembled and he breathed out a shaky breath. "The truth is Addey, I love you, and I want to find a future with you...if you want that...with me."

A slow smile bloomed across her face.

Addey dropped her boots and stepped up to him. Declan stepped closer but he didn't reach out. Fear still held him back, even though the flame of hope burned brighter.

He licked his lips, needing to explain more. "Eli, Mom, and Nicky continuously pointed out that I can't keep harboring unforgiveness. I never listened. I didn't want to listen." He reached out and touched her cheek. "I was angry and happy to stay that way until I met you." He shrugged. "So, can you forgive me?"

"I forgave you the moment I read your review," she said through her tears. "And I love you, too."

Declan cradled her cheeks in his hands and gently kissed her.

He pulled back, resting his head on her forehead.

"My dad is inside," Addey whispered.

"I know."

Declan pulled Addey into his arms, her face burrowing in his chest.

Jonathan stood in the doorway.

Addey moved so she could see her father but kept her head leaning against Declan. He hugged her tighter, feeling their combined strength.

For a moment, Declan held Jonathan's gaze, his heart thumping right in time with Addey's.

The man appeared to release a long sigh.

Then he nodded at Declan. "I think we should chat when you have time."

Addey squeezed Declan's waist. Her muffled sob made him hold her tighter.

"I think that's a good place to start." Declan nodded back.

Jonathan walked past them and patted Addey on the shoulder. Declan saw a blink-and-you'll-miss-it smile on his face as he walked past, climbed in his car, and drove off.

Addey wound her arms around Declan's neck, tears falling, her smile as bright as the sun. "I think Dad just gave you the seal of approval."

Declan chuckled. "Let's hope so."

He leaned down and kissed her.

Addey returned it with passion and the promise of hope.

Epilogue

Declan Collins and Jonathan Hamilton stood side by side outside the Community Center. They jointly held a giant pair of scissors for cutting the bright red ribbon that was across the doors of the new complex. Life had changed and Declan was still getting used to it.

Jonathan let go of the scissors and stepped up to the microphone. The crowd gathered in front of the complex spilled out onto the sidewalk. Reporters crowded around, and Declan spied Julie off to the side near the front. She gave him a big thumbs up. This story was becoming a big human interest piece for the area and even the national stage. Declan had kept himself out of it as much as he could. Interest in his family had exploded when the public got wind of the story, but by keeping their heads down, things had died down quicker than they'd expected.

"As many of you know, Mr. Collins and I got off to a very rocky start." Jonathan held the microphone.

The crowd laughed and cheered. "But, as things often go, there are misunderstandings and wrongs that need to be made right. We both stand here—" He turned and gestured Declan to come and stand beside him. He moved next to him, albeit reluctantly.

Jonathan continued, "—admitting we made mistakes. Instead of working against each other, we chose to work together." The crowd applauded his words.

Declan listened with pride and smiled at Addey, who was waving madly at them both from the front of the crowd. Mom sat in a chair in front of Addey. Every few minutes Addey ducked down to say something and the two of them kept smiling and laughing. Beside them was Addey's mother, looking uncomfortable, but he knew how much her being here meant to Addey. Nicky was on Addey's other side, grinning, the two of them having become very close these last few months. Carmel stood behind Maude, Saul, and Vera. Vera was beaming, Saul was chatting to someone beside him, and Maude was frowning. Declan caught Maude's eye and winked at her. She frowned deeper, but Declan caught the flash of a smile before it disappeared.

And Charlotte. She stood beside Susannah, her smile wide as she chatted to those around her. Declan would be forever grateful to her.

The sight of Eli sitting proudly next to Mom, with his hand on her shoulder and her hand resting on his, filled Declan with so much hope it was hard to contain. Maybe, just maybe, there might be another miracle in the near future.

Declan tuned back into what Jonathan was saying. "Declan and I are proud to open the Heights Community Center featuring the Baking for Life Bakery and Café along with the community service offices. We have chosen to refurbish the building and expand it to make it an even better community center than it was before. We are committed to bringing the best we can offer to those in the community who need it."

The crowd cheered as the two men stepped back to cut the ribbon.

They shook hands and left the stage for the mayor to speak. They headed into the crowd. Addey threw her arms around Declan. "I'm so proud of you!" she squealed. The clouds rolled by lazily and the summer sun made everything brighter.

"Are we all going to lunch?" Jonathan said to the group gathered. Declan had to laugh. If someone had told him six months ago that he'd be having regular lunches with the Hamiltons, he would have called them crazy.

"What's so funny?" Addey whispered, looking up at him.

"Life is, that's all," he said. "Are you able to have lunch with us? Or are you needed at work?"

"No, I'm finished for the day at Heritage Oaks after we get everyone back there." She turned and waved to Vera, Maude, Saul and the others.

"I'm glad you took the job. You've been much more settled there," Declan commented.

She nodded, leaning into him. "It's crazy that the Baker/Gibson Group still wanted the company, even if I wasn't on board." She waved at Carmel. "The job offer as full-time events coordinator at Heritage Oaks and their two other facilities was such a surprise, but it was one I needed. I love it there."

"And I love you, Addey." He never got sick of saying it.

She met his gaze, grinning. "Right back at you."

He leaned down and dropped a kiss on her forehead. He reached into his pocket and felt for the diamond ring he'd spent the last three months saving for.

He had a question to ask her tonight.

A Note to the Reader

In March 2014, I got to experience a literal dream come true. I flew to the USA for the first time. It was number one on my life bucket list to go there. So, I ventured onto my experience first solo international flight—with my three-year-old daughter in tow. Because, for my first solo flight, I thought it would be good to take a three-year-old on two flights, totaling nineteen hours to the other side of the world. My girl (who is now fifteen) was fantastic on the flights. So many prayers went into that trip—for me and for her. I'm forever glad I took her with me.

We stayed with my good friends, the Kubacz family. Josh, his wife Michaele and their daughter Anabel moved to Australia in 2011 she and I became friends. Our girls, little though they were, loved spending time together. When they moved back to the USA in 2013, Michaele told me to visit and bring Eleyna. So, I did. We got to see falling snow—for these two Aussie girls it was incredible.

And *It Shouldn't Be You* was born as I walked through Alexandria's Old Town, toured Mount Vernon, and hung out with Michaele, her family, and their friends. When I got home from our trip, during my girl's preschool days and daytime naps, I wrote Dec and Addey's story across twelve months. And then rewrote it the following year.

As the story is set in a real place with snippets of history mentioned, I want you to know that the character of Charlotte Hamilton is entirely fictional, as is every character in the book. She was never a former Vice Regent of the Virginia Chapter of the Mount Vernon Ladies' Association. The snippets of history about Mount Vernon can be found on the Mount Vernon website. I spent hours poring over the website, using all the video links, to make Mount Vernon come alive for you all. Any mistakes about the house and grounds are my own.

Thanks for reading *It Shouldn't Be You*. Did you know that reviews help other readers find new authors? Did you also know that a review doesn't need to be very long? A simple, "I loved it" works great. If you want to, you can review *It Shouldn't Be You* on Amazon and Goodreads.

Acknowledgements

A book is never done alone, despite how many hours I'm alone writing. It's always a collaborative thing and for my third book, yes, that's right, it was no different.

There are many people to thank.

To Candace Calvert, you walked through so much of this story with me. Endless Facetime chats talking about ways to improve Addey and Dec, ways to make the conflict stronger, and all the encouragement. You still encourage me today and I'm so grateful.

A huge thanks to my editor Betsy St. Amant Haddox. You get me and my writing. You push me to write better and dig deeper—even when I really don't want to.

To my proofreader, Elizabeth Bird, thanks for your gift of attention to detail and your friendship. I need both in my life—but I'll always need your friendship more.

To Liwen Y.Ho, thanks for the amazing book cover. So glad we crossed paths on this writing journey.

Thanks to Di Ponsen for always being ready to read my manuscript, give feedback, and give me a hug.

To Laurinda, for laughing our way through life together.

To my local Newcastle Romance Writers Group, thank you for all the laughs and support. I love our group.

To my beta readers and ARC team—you guys are great! You catch things I miss, and you are so enthusiastic about my books.

To Mindy and Jen, you girls are such a blessing to me. So glad we got to hang out together last year. We need more of that.

And to the writers on the Discord group, I feel like I've found a home amongst you girls.I love the laughs we share, the memes—so many memes —the sprints, advice, and prayers.

To my Mum, thanks for all the prayers over all the years.

To my sister Helen. I literally don't know what I'd do without you. No one makes me laugh like you do and no one knows me like you do. Thanks for encouraging me and believing in me.

To my husband, Ben. You are the calm in my storm and you carved out time in our life for me to pursue this dream.

To my girls, I love you both so much.

To my readers, I hope you enjoyed this book as much as I enjoyed writing it.

Thank you, Jesus, for the blessings and for sustaining me through the good and the bad times.

Coming September 29th 2025

A New Novella.

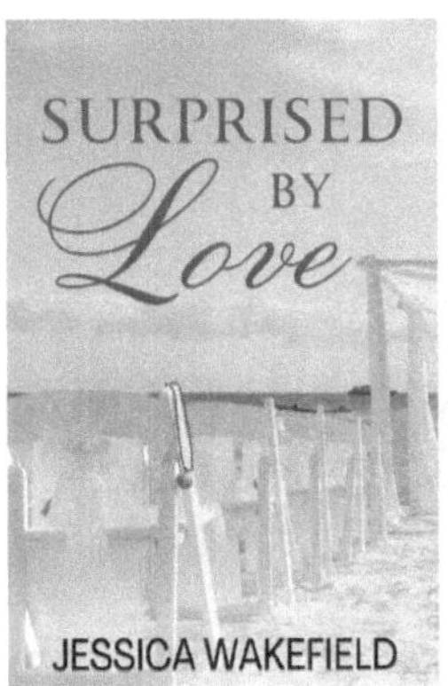

Remember Camden, Declan's best friend?

Follow Camden to Summer Shore on the Gulf Coast of Florida, where he's a security guard for an influencer couple's wedding. He did not expect to run into Viana Lawson, the wedding coordinator and his ex-girlfriend—the one he never got over.

Now he has to work with her, save her career and his and try not to fall in love all over again.

Pre-order your E-book today. Find out more at: jessicawakefield.com

Can she keep her heart safe from the pain love always causes?

When sports nutritionist Rachel Marshall tracks down ex-NFL bad boy Hayden Donovan in Trinity Lakes, she's desperate to strike a deal that could save her mother's life.

Hayden agrees to help—but only if Rachel helps him prove to the world he's not the man the headlines make him out to be. As sparks fly and secrets surface, they must decide if redemption—and love—are worth the risk.

Find out more at: jessicawakefield.com

Can Christmas be saved by a mysterious box?

Across three decades, three couples discover love where they least expect it—on a snowy tree farm, in a blizzard-bound cabin, and at a holiday engagement party with a fake boyfriend.

Warm, witty, and filled with festive charm, this trio of holiday romances celebrates courage, hope and the magic of the season.

Find out more at: jessicawakefield.com

About the author

 As a kid, Australian author Jessica Wakefield penned really bad *Anne of Green Gables* fan fiction. Nowadays she lives in Newcastle with her husband, two daughters and a fluffy mini-groodle. Jessica has a lifelong love of *Sweet Valley High* books and is a recovering *Gilmore Girls* addict. When she's not fawning over her cuddly dog Ginny, you can find her reading, going for walks or baking. Find out more at: www.jessicawakefield.com